THE TORTURE TRIAL OF GEORGE W. BUSH

JOSEPH SUSTE

• Chicago •

THE TORTURE TRIAL OF GEORGE W. BUSH
JOSEPH SUSTE

Published by

JoshuaTreePublishing.com
• Chicago •

13-Digit ISBN: 978-1-941049-82-2 (Second Edition)
978-1-941049-46-4 (First Edition)

Book Cover Design: Paige C. Suste

Printed in the United States of America

To all victims of cruel, inhumane,

or degrading treatment,

anywhere in the world.

May we embrace our humanity and

demand an end to cruelty.

AUTHOR'S NOTE

During a dark period in the history of the United States, a few powerful government officials twisted the meaning of our laws and trivialized universal human rights principles. This novel peels back a deceitful veneer of legal gamesmanship to reveal flagrant violations of international law and the U.S. Constitution.

The narrative exposes the criminal actions of individuals who continue to make bold assertions that torture is not torture, that what they did was necessary, and that torturers are above the law. It does not redeem us, the American people, of our culpability. Crimes against humanity have been committed, and we have yet to meet our responsibility to confront the perpetrators.

The story unfolds within the framework of existing statutes and develops a practical approach for bringing the guilty to justice—the first step in any attempt at reconciliation. There is realism in the premise which relies heavily on information gathered by professional journalists and investigators around the world. The legal basis draws on U.S. Code and the published opinions of qualified legal experts.

Here is a work of fiction, with fictional paladins reacting to the actions of non-fictional characters and historical events. We can envision real people following in the footsteps of the story's protagonists. It is only necessary to find the courage to act.

Torture should never happen again—but if left unchallenged and unpunished, it will.

"President Obama signed Executive Order 13491 in January 2009 to prohibit the CIA from holding detainees other than on a "short-term, transitory basis" and to limit interrogation techniques to those included in the Army Field Manual. However, these limitations are not part of U.S. law and could be overturned by a future president with the stroke of a pen."[1]

It is critical to our democracy that we re-establish our nation under the principle touted by John Adams who championed a government of laws—not of men.

---

[1] Diane Feinstein, Chairman of Senate Select Committee on Intelligence, Forward to Senate Select Committee on Intelligence, Committee Study of the Central Intelligence Agency's Detention and Interrogation Program, December 3, 2014. Page 4. http://fas.org/irp/congress/2014_rpt/ssci-rdi.pdf

Author's 2018 Update

As this edition goes to print, President Donald J. Trump has nominated Mike Pompeo for the position of U.S. Secretary of State and Gina Haspel to become the Director of the CIA. These three people have a common moral flaw: they support the use of the torture known as waterboarding.

Donald Trump campaigned on his love of waterboarding and promised to authorize even worse tortures. Mike Pompeo is on-record stating his opinion that waterboarding is not torture.

Gina Haspel is known to have operated a secret CIA site in Thailand, where she directed the waterboarding of detainee Abd al-Rahim al-Nashiri. She later oversaw the destruction of video tapes of the torture of Abu Zubayda and al-Nashiri. Her excuse for violating U.S. law against torture and destruction of evidence is that she was directed to do it. Under the Trump administration, it is conceivable that she could be directed to do it again.

The United States will never be free from the potential to torture until U.S. law makes it explicitly illegal. No person in the custody of the United States Government should ever be subjected to torture. It is in the power of congress to amend the United States Code of Laws by adding subparagraph (2)(E) under *Title 18—Crimes and Criminal Procedure, Chapter 113C—Torture, §2340. Definitions.*

Below is a proposal for the new paragraph.

(2)(E) The following acts are always torture: waterboarding or other means of preventing a person from normal breathing, forced nudity, shackling a person's hands above their heads, sleep deprivation, subjecting a person to extreme temperatures, confinement in a box, slamming a person into a wall, sexual humiliation, threatening a person with animals or insects, stress positions (pain positions), withholding food, medical attention or toilet and washing facilities, solitary confinement, subjecting a person to loud noises or loud music, sensory deprivation, slapping, water-dousing, standing for long periods, electric shock, and rape.

As citizens, we are each responsible for the actions of our government. It is up to us to tell our representatives that we want to put an end to torture and show the world that the United States is serious when we call for all nations to respect human rights.

Joseph Suste, March 2018

CHAPTER 1

Nothing strengthens authority so much as silence.
—Leonardo da Vinci

A larger-than-life video image of President George W. Bush spoke from a drop-down projection screen in a dimly-lit conference room. Reflected light flashed over an assembly of federal attorneys sitting at a twenty-foot-long table, staffers behind them against the walls on folding chairs. The Assistant Attorney General, Criminal Division, Andy Ricker, presided over his monthly staff meeting on a Monday morning in July.

In the video, Bush sat in an upholstered burgundy armchair, one leg crossed over the other, holding a wireless microphone. He was relaxed and confident, speaking to an attentive audience about his tenure as president—promoting his book Decision Points.[2]

"I approved techniques, including waterboarding, on three people. In my book, I make two points clear. One,…"[3]

"Kill the damn video and turn on the lights—now!" Ricker stepped in front of the screen where the video image painted his face and torso as Bush droned on. The room lights came up. The video faded and was gone.

"Madegen! I want you out in the hall. The rest of you ignore what you just saw. Haney, pick it up at the next agenda item and proceed until I get back."

"Does everyone realize what you just witnessed?" Assistant Prosecutor Timothy Madegen said to the room. He stood next to his laptop and clicked the lid shut.

---

2   Bush, George W., *Decision Points*. Crown Publishing Group, Random House. New York. 2010.

3   Video record of the 27th Annual Miami Book Fair International, at Miami Dade College, November 14, 2010. The C-SPAN recording can be viewed at: http://www.c-span.org/video/?296496-1/book-discussion-decision-points Accessed 8 March 2018. Approximately thirty minutes into video. Words of President George W. Bush.

"Shut up, Madegen," the chief said.

Madegen kept on, "President George W. Bush, freely and without coercion of any kind, confessed on a video recording—"

"Dammit, Madegen—"

"—to the crime of torture which is forbidden under USC Title 18, Chapter 113C."[4]

"That's enough Madegen, get out!" Ricker took him by the arm and pushed him toward the door. He followed Madegen into the hall and slammed the door behind them. A muted buzz of voices could still be heard, along with the shouts of Deputy Assistant Attorney Haney demanding control of the meeting.

"What the hell was that, Madegen? Where did this crap come from?" Madegen's red-faced boss spat the words through clenched jaws. "You are way out of line."

"I'm only doing my job, sir," Madegen's honest, determined eyes stared back at his boss. "I took an oath to uphold the Constitution and all the laws derived from it." Timothy Madegen stood ramrod straight, his chin high, shoulders back as if called to attention by a merciless drill sergeant. His calm declaration contrasted with the angry words of his excited boss. "We have a confessed criminal, the worst kind, a torturer, and nobody is doing anything about it."

"That's right! Nobody—including you—is going to prosecute a former President of the United States. We have our orders from the top; we're going to look forward, not backward, and you will follow them."[5]

"Barack also said nobody is above the law."[6]

"This is not a debate, Madegen. We're through here."

"So we have a confessed criminal and—"

Ricker leaned in so close Madegen could feel the man's breath on his face. "One more word on this, and you're fired. Do you understand me?" One of his hands made a stiff fist, while the other extended an index finger that stopped short of poking Madegen in the chest.

"I get it," Madegen said with stoic acquiescence.

---

4 United States Code (USC) Title 18- Crimes and Criminal Procedure, Part 1, Chapter 113c-Torture.
 http://www.gpo.gov/fdsys/pkg/USCODE-2011-title18/pdf/USCODE-2011-title18-partI-chap113C.pdf

5 President Barak Obama interviewed on This Week. ABC. January 11, 2009.
 http://www.youtube.com/watch?feature=player_detailpage&v=0K27oIJlAlA

6 Ibid.

"And if this bullshit leaks to the press, I assure you that you will never practice law in any state in this country ever again. Got it?"

Madegen turned to walk away.

Ricker grabbed his shoulder and spun him back around, "Are you hearing me, Madegen?"

"Yes sir. I heard every word you said."

Ricker gave him a scowl and reached for the knob on the conference room door. "Not one more word," he said and went back in.

Timothy Madegen tucked his laptop under his arm and headed back to his office. The confrontation with his boss had him re-evaluating his future, but his discomfort did not weaken his resolve. It was exactly ten o'clock when he set his case down and hooked his jacket on the tree behind the glass door. The intercom buzzed before he could settle at his desk.

"Mr. Madegen?"

"Yes, Annie?"

"How did the staff meeting go? Do you need anything from me?"

"It was fine, Annie, just fine."

"Good. I want to remind you about the two officers on the Verner case. They'll be here at one o'clock for their interviews. I reserved the small conference room for you."

"Please get one of the paralegals to interview them. Charley knows the file; he'll be able to handle it. Then get me John Mayfield on the phone. He's legal counsel to Senator Brandt. Don't let them put you off. Make sure they know it's me calling for John."

Timothy waited. The scene in the conference room ended more abruptly than he'd expected, but it had to be done. He'd made a serious attempt to work through channels, and a room full of witnesses could vouch for the fact he'd tried. He knew he was going to be fighting the most powerful forces in the country, but he was convinced of the necessity, and that outweighed the many downsides.

He stood looking out his seventh-floor window at miniature cars and people on the street. Washington, D.C. was a long way from home, a city not known for easy friendships. He longed for the camaraderie of his college days and thought about the events that brought him to the Capitol.

He pictured that day, enjoying a Saturday afternoon over beers with Clarissa and John in one of the tall black-lacquer booths at the back of Blackie's Bar. The bar was a noisy mix of students and professors.

"We're one year away from graduation, you guys; it's time to start working on law school applications," John said.

"Won't need that with my engineering degree. I've already applied for the graduate program right here," Timothy replied.

"You are so boring," Clarissa said. "You need to go into the law with John and me. It's way more exciting than engineering. It's about real life."

Timothy sat across from John and Clarissa in the booth. He tilted a heavy glass pitcher and refilled three mugs, dribbling the beer down the inside wall of each glass.

"Lawyers run the world, Tim," John said. "Sixty percent of U.S. Senators are attorneys, and a third of U.S. Congressmen have law degrees. These guys are running our country. It makes sense; we're a nation of laws. We need people who know and understand the law in all three branches of government. Your country needs you. You're a critical thinker. You're a natural to be a leader. Why do you want to go tinkering around with electrons and all that? Let the geeks do it. You're too valuable for that stuff."

"And the judges," said Clarissa, "who do you think the judges are? They're lawyers. And what do the judges do? They're the last word in the law: constitutional or unconstitutional. The judges are more powerful than the president of the United States. They have all the power. They made George W. Bush president for Chrissake." Clarissa's expressive blue eyes didn't waver when she challenged him. "I can't see you sitting at a desk in a cubicle drawing diagrams and coding software for the rest of your life. Why would you want to do that?"

"Ask yourself," John pressed, "are you OK with the two stupid wars we're fighting? And don't think marching with a bunch of undergrads waving signs and pounding bongos on the quad is going to change anything. If you want to do something worthwhile—have any influence on the direction of this country and the world—you need to be in government and politics. You need a law degree for that."

Timothy smiled at their insistence. "You guys need to think about the contribution we geeks are making in the world too: communications, power systems, medical equipment, transportation; without us, you'd still be living in caves and clubbing wild animals. Come-on, we make the world better for everybody in our own way. Want to give up that cell phone you've got in your pocket?"

"We get that, Tim. It's not unimportant, but there are lots of creative people who are committed to that stuff. We're talking about being a leader, being part of the decision-making process that determines where the human race is going. You can have all the hardware in the world, but if you don't make laws that take care of the environment, or keep our food supply safe, or provide infrastructure systems, the hardware won't make any difference. And if you care about those things and want to lead in the right direction, the best way to do it is by getting a law degree."

"Look, you guys are going to Harvard, and that's great, but I can't afford that," Timothy said. "This state school is the best I can do. I'm not going to argue against what you say. Both of you are incredibly talented, and I expect great things of you. I hope you take Washington by storm and stir up all those old fuddy-duddies. And I'm going to miss you guys when you go, but it's not in the cards for me. I'm not the Harvard type. I'd never fit in."

"That, Tim, is a load of crap," John said. "Tell him, Clarissa. He's got to get it out of his head that the amount of money he has, or his parents have, has nothing to do with who he is. We're not gonna leave you here, Tim. You're going."

"That's right, Tim. We are all three going to Harvard, so stop being so small-minded and face your destiny, kiddo. We're going, and we're going together," Clarissa said.

Timothy hated the idea of watching his two best friends go off without him, and he understood the confidence they had in him. He had never considered the law before these two started working on him, but the money was a real obstacle, or so he thought.

"We can get you a full-ride scholarship, Tim, and it's not charity. You deserve it, and Harvard will be lucky to have you. My uncle can make it happen. You need to go with us," John said.

"I've made it this far on my own, and I can make it through grad school right here. My physics professor already offered me a research lab position. I don't want anybody pulling strings for me, John."

"You know, Tim, sometimes I think you are totally naïve about life. How do you think half the Harvard law school candidates get accepted? It's not academic excellence and good looks, that's for sure. They have sponsors: senators, congressmen, governors, millionaires, billionaires—people with connections working it for them. Me and Clarissa wouldn't have a chance at Harvard if it wasn't for my dad and her grandfather. We're getting you in, Tim. If you don't go, it will be the biggest mistake of your life."

"Let's have another pitcher and let this go, OK?" Timothy said. "We have another year to go before any of us are going anywhere, so give me a break right now."

"Have it your way, for now, old buddy," John said, "but this is not the last time we're going to have this conversation." His voice grew thick and ominous as he looked down into his glass, his fingertips on his forehead. "As I peer into this crystal beer mug, I see in the golden liquid, a middle-aged Timothy Madegen dressed in Florsheim wingtips and an expensive gray flannel suit." He looked up at Timothy and smiled, then picked up the empty pitcher and carried it over to the bar.

"Yeah, and we're going to use the next year to work you over, Tim," Clarissa said.

* * *

It was that evening that Timothy Madegen watched Dan Rather on 60 Minutes II give the world the first glimpse of photographs of the torture taking place at the United States controlled Abu Ghraib prison in Iraq. He didn't want to believe what he was seeing.

The disgusting images merged with his graphic memory of his father lying dead on the basement floor. The terror of that discovery flooded back to Timothy in a smothering visceral wave. Revelations at his father's funeral came back to him in full force. He felt shock and sorrow for what his country had done and relief that his father would never know about it. The pictures haunted Timothy, and he followed the story as facts continued to come to light about U.S. torture. He mused over the injustice of it and the betrayal of his father's sacrifice.

When he became a federal prosecutor, he'd rationalized inaction. He worried about his inexperience and thought his feelings might be a manifestation of naïveté. But time was now up. Harvard Law School had prepared him for the District of Columbia bar which he sailed through like a racing yacht on a following wind. Timothy had been an A student. A year had gone by since he started his career, and he'd grown confident in his abilities and understanding of the law. He was convinced that this was the cause he had trained for.

He paced his office, called Annie for some coffee, sat in his desk chair, wiggled his mouse, and watched the CNN headlines brighten on his screen as the backlight warmed up.

The intercom buzzed. "Mr. Mayfield is on two for you," Annie said.

"Thank you." He cleared his throat as if preparing to deliver a speech, then picked up the handpiece. He punched in the line.

"Hey, John."

"Timothy R. Madegen. How the hell are you, old man? Nobody's heard from you since graduation."

"Good to hear your voice, John. I hear you finagled a cushy job advising Brandt over at the Capitol."

"Oh yeah! It didn't hurt to know a few people through my dad. I'm not at the Capitol though. Brandt's office is in the Hart Building, but it's still like standing at the center of the universe. When you gonna come see me, Ol'Buddy? Where'd you land?"

"I'm at Justice, in the Federal Prosecutors Office. Started here one year ago, right after we graduated. I'm an Assistant Prosecutor, so you better watch your step. I already have more dirt on you than anybody in my position should know," Timothy teased.

"OK, I've been wondering when the blackmail was gonna start."

"You're safe for now. I'm in the Justice Building over on 4th St. Not too far away. It's been an eye-opener."

"Hey, this is great. We need to connect. Meet me tonight for drinks at the Point of View Lounge around nine."

"Why don't we have lunch tomorrow, and we can talk."

"Same ol' stick in the mud. Come'on, Tim, drinks tonight. Hey—Clarissa's in town from New York. It'll be a reunion."

Timothy paused.

"You still there, Tim?"

"OK, where is this place?"

"I'll send you driving directions. The parking's tricky."

"Don't have a car."

"What? Look, I'll pick you up. Where do you live?"

"Up in Kalorama, it's OK. I'll take the Metro."

"Great. I'm glad you called Tim. See you tonight."

"Later, John."

Timothy hung up the phone, sat back in his chair, and closed his eyes. He frowned. He shivered. He opened his desk drawer and pulled out a worn, white envelope.

CHAPTER 2

What sets us apart from our enemies in this fight…is how we behave. In everything we do, we must observe the standards and values that dictate that we treat noncombatants and detainees with dignity and respect. While we are warriors, we are also all human beings.
— General David Petraeus, May 10, 2007

Timothy's father, Brian R. Madegen, was nineteen years old in 1969 when Representative Alexander Pirnie of the U.S. House of Representatives reached into a glass jar and pulled out the first plastic capsule that determined the two-year future of thousands of American boys. The capsule contained a slip of paper marked 258, code for the 258th day of the year, September 14th, Brian's birthday. A letter from the Selective Service System arrived within weeks. It ordered him to report to his local draft board for transportation to the Armed Forces Examining and Entrance Station at 615 West Van Buren Street, Chicago, Illinois.

Brian spent eight weeks in basic training and four months in helicopter gunner training before flying to South Vietnam on a military transport with forty other conscripts holding orders from President Richard M. Nixon. The mind-bending disorientation he experienced when he transitioned from clicking the nozzle on a gas pump at the Standard station on U.S. Route 52 in downtown Kankakee, Illinois—to pulling the trigger on a .50 caliber machine gun shooting tracer rounds out the door-less cabin of a Huey helicopter hovering over a North Vietnam jungle was exhilarating. Corporal Brian Madegen was "gung-ho" for the war, a dedicated and trusted member of his flight crew. The crew flew fifty sorties before crashing in a rice paddy behind enemy lines where they were captured immediately by a regular platoon of the North Vietnamese Army.

The Hanoi Hilton was anything but a luxury hotel. Brian was incarcerated with hundreds of other airmen and infantrymen captured by General Tran Van Quang's forces. He spent three years in the prison the North Vietnamese named Hoa Lo, in their language—Hell Hole, in ours. Brian was released in 1973 after Henry Kissinger negotiated the Paris Peace Accords. He came home to Kankakee a different person.

Brian bounced from job to job in the railroad and steel mill industries as a laborer, until he met Lee Ann and went to work for her father as a mechanic at her dad's Ford dealership. He was thirty-four when Lee Ann gave birth to what everybody claimed was the most beautiful, red-headed baby boy they had ever seen. Timothy R. Madegen was named after Brian's father.

Timothy was fifteen years old when Brian spent a sunny Saturday afternoon on his 49th birthday cleaning his service revolver in the basement of their suburban home and put a bullet in his own right ear just as Lee Ann was lighting the candles on a cake she'd baked for the occasion. She sent Timothy down to investigate the noise. When he didn't come back up, she went down and found him lying on top of his father's body, holding the gun and sobbing. The sheriff said there was only one bullet in the Colt, and it was spent.

* * *

The oaks and maples were brilliant with fall color at the cemetery where Timothy walked with his mother on his arm behind six casket bearers down a gravel path to his father's gravesite. The teenage Timothy was slight in appearance, an impression compounded by his pale freckled skin, red hair, and tall, skinny frame. That day at the cemetery he was a rock, fully aware of who his mother needed him to be. A U.S. Army sergeant made a brief speech about Brian's service to his country and removed a regulation-size U.S. flag that had draped the coffin. The sergeant and a uniformed private held the flag between them and folded it in a routine ceremony. The sergeant presented a red, white, and blue triangle to Lee Ann. Timothy caught her when she fainted. After a few minutes of upset and supporting a revived but pale Lee Ann, he asked the preacher to make it short.

Timothy was walking his mother back to their car when a black man dressed in faded blue jeans and military fatigue jacket approached Timothy. He was over six feet tall and broad as a bull. His long hair was pulled back into a loose ponytail. He introduced himself as a friend of his father and pulled Timothy off to the side.

"I knew this would happen," he said.

"What? What are you talking about?" Timothy asked.

"I have something to tell you about your father you should know."

"Who are you?"

"I was the intel officer on his Huey. Didn't he tell you about it?"

"No, he never said anything about the war. I know he was in it, but he didn't say much," Timothy said. "My dad wasn't very talkative. How good did you know him?"

Timothy looked the man over. He didn't look like someone you would want to trust. His dress was shabby, and he had an untrimmed chin beard, not quite a goatee. He was a little older than his father. He smelled of alcohol.

"I was in the hell hole with him."

"Go away," Timothy said. "I just buried my dad. I don't know who you are, but I don't want to talk to you. Go away." Timothy started to turn and leave, but the man came around him and blocked his way.

"He was a prisoner of war—I was with him," the man said.

Timothy stopped. "What?"

"You need to know about your dad. Come on, have a beer with me," the man said.

"I'm fifteen. Who are you anyway?"

"Meet me at Misty's Bar over on Water Street in an hour, and I'll tell you about your dad, and what we went through together in the war. You owe it to your father to listen to me, kid. He was the toughest son-of-a-bitch in the Hanoi Hilton, and there are guys from all over this country who would be here to honor Brian, if they knew he was being buried today."

Timothy looked toward the car where his mother waited.

"I have to go, maybe I'll come. I have to go," Timothy said.

"I'll wait for you," the man said.

* * *

Misty's is a neighborhood bar in a converted house on the corner of Water and Third Street in the oldest residential section of Kankakee. The pride of the place is a mahogany bar with a brass foot rail. They claim the mirrored wall behind the bar was rescued from the Chicago fire. There are five booths and a worn pool table, which everyone knows has unpredictable rails and a slight run favoring the pocket nearest the cue rack.

Two regulars sat at the bar talking. Behind the bar, Sally, a pretty, middle-aged, bottle-blonde, washed glasses and dusted whiskey bottles.

The man who'd met Timothy at the funeral sat alone on a stool nearest the door. It was a typical weekday afternoon; the bar stools and tables didn't fill up until six or so, except on Fridays when Sally fried fish and her husband, Tommy, sponsored a double elimination nine-ball tournament that filled the place with noisy talk and laughter until midnight.

Timothy leaned his bicycle on the wrought iron railing at the front steps and walked up to the entrance. The grainy odor of stale beer rushed out at him when he opened the door and entered the bar. His first instinct was to turn and run, to leave the unfamiliar place, but he froze just inside the door when he realized all eyes were on him. The man from the funeral jumped off his stool and took him by the arm.

"It's OK, Sally. He's here to see me," the man said.

"I don't know, Axel. He shouldn't be in here."

"Just bring him a Coke, and I'll have another beer." He took Timothy to a table at the back of the room.

Timothy looked over the man's appearance. His clothes were worn but clean. It had been some time since he'd sat in a barber's chair; his chin-beard grew untrimmed and blended with long gray sideburns to make a continuous fuzzy frame for his broad face. On a younger man, his untamed head hair would have been a statement of rebellion. On this old guy, it carried a message of dissipation. Yet, there was a quality in his expression and bearing, that made Timothy feel respectful. He decided the man deserved a hearing.

"My name is Alexander Johnson, but they call me, Axel," the man started. "I served as an intelligence officer during the Vietnam War in '69. I rode a Huey recon gunship with your dad."

The bartender brought the Coke and the beer. She looked hard at Timothy, then gave Johnson a wary look, but she didn't say anything and left the two alone. Axel picked up the beer and took a sip, a spot of white foam caught in his mustache, and he wiped it with the back of his hand.

It was after five, and a stream of tired factory workers began coming in. The volume of conversation rose and fell with each new face as bar stools filled up.

"He called me. Your dad called me last Saturday. I hadn't heard from him for a long time. We used to get together once in a while, but he stopped answering my calls five years ago. Then, last week, he called me and said he wanted to see me. I met him in Chicago, and he gave me this." Axel pulled a white envelope from his jacket pocket and laid it on the table. "It's addressed to you."

Timothy recognized his father's script on the envelope and looked up into the man's sad, brown eyes. Axel took a long pull on the beer, slammed down the empty glass, and called for Sally to bring another.

"You don't know about your dad's time in Vietnam, do you?"

"He didn't tell me about it," Timothy replied. "I don't think he even talked to my mom about it; he had a lot of medals, that's all I know. My dad didn't talk much about that."

"I don't know what's in this envelope, kid. He only asked me to give it to you, but there's some things, I think you should know about Brian, that he could never tell you. Terrible things."

He shot a worried look at Timothy, trying to decide if this boy was ready to hear what he was about to tell him. Axel looked into a face that mirrored nineteen-year-old Corporal Brian Madegen, assigned to the 227th Assault Helicopter Battalion, 1st Cavalry Division, whom he'd met at Da Nang air base so many years ago. He looked hard into the boy's eyes for a sign that he was doing the right thing.

"We were brothers in arms. I was his senior officer, but we were a team. We flew over fifty missions. Your dad and me and the other men on that chopper were a force to be reckoned with. Every man knew his job, and we depended on each other to survive. Our luck ran out when an enemy rocket wiped our tail rotor. We went spinning down into the North Vietnamese jungle somewhere between Tay Ninh and Xuan Loc."

Axel's voice grew louder as he recalled the details of that day.

"We hit the ground hard. The pilot, co-pilot, and the other gunner died in the crash. We only had seconds to get out of the ship. Your dad pulled the M60 from its mount and sprayed the jungle with tracers in all directions for cover while we jumped from the burning wreck and ran into the jungle. The ship exploded, which must have drawn the attention of every NV fighter within miles. We held off twenty-five or thirty gooks for two hours with his machine gun and my .38 revolver until we ran out of ammunition and had to give it up.

"When they realized we had no ammo, they rushed us. Your dad pulled out a knife, but I stopped him because I knew it was useless. There must have been twenty AK-47 muzzles pointed in our faces when the

North Vietnamese lieutenant told his men to back off and spoke to us in East Coast English. 'You guys are war criminals, and I'm taking you to prison. Get down on your knees, put your hands on your head, and maybe I can keep these men from killing you right here, right now.'"

Sally brought another beer, and Axel swilled down half of it. By this time, everybody in the bar was quiet—listening to Axel's story.

"We were transferred from NV unit to NV unit until we arrived at the prison. It was not a pleasant trip. On the trail, they fed us scraps, and by the time we got to Hoa Lo, we were weak from dysentery."

"Why didn't the army rescue you?" Timothy asked.

"We were behind enemy lines, Timothy. There was no way they could even find us in that jungle, let alone rescue us. Oh no, we were on our own.

"The first thing the prison guards did was hand us a confession to sign. They wanted us to confess to all kinds of war crimes. They put us in separate cells and started working us over to get a confession. The beatings were bad, but the worst was the water torture. They put a rag over your nose and mouth, and poured water on it until you couldn't get any air."

Timothy's eyes began to widen, and Axel wasn't sure if he should go on. It was tough enough for an adult to hear what he was saying, but this was a fifteen-year-old kid.

"You OK, Tim?"

Timothy gave a slight nod.

"They tied you down so you couldn't move, and they did the water torture on you. I remember the whole thing like it was yesterday. The water pours through the rag on your face and into your sinuses and throat. You try to force the water out with pressure from your lungs, but then you can't take in anymore air. Your body gets weaker, and you pull in less and less air through the wet rag. It felt like I was drowning, and I was sure I was going to die and never see my family again. I saw my wife and kids mourning me. My autonomic nervous system went into panic mode, and I tried to break free from the bonds that tied me, but it was no use. My body had the instinct I was dying. I would convulse, trying to get air, sucking in water instead, then they poured more water, and I was sure I was dead. But I must have passed out because I woke up without the rag on my face and saw them smiling down at me; then here comes the rag and the water, again. After going through that for what seemed like forever, I couldn't take any more of it, and I signed their goddamn confession. And there's a shame with that, Tim. It's not the shame that I gave up. It's the shame that they could do that to me. But you know the worst part? Almost every night I dream I'm still there—or even walking down the street, all of a sudden, I'm getting the water torture, and I can't breathe. It happens a lot."

"Why are you telling me this?" Timothy asked.

Sally came over to the table with two glasses of whiskey and set them down in front of Axel.

"On the house," she said. She put her hand on Axel's shoulder, then went back to the bar.

Axel took one of the glasses and downed it. Timothy watched him closely and didn't move.

"Now I'm going to tell you the tough part, Timothy," he said, then took a deep breath and leaned forward with his arms on the table. "Your father went through the same thing, but he didn't give up like I did. We had a communication system in that prison. They kept us in isolated cells, but the guys figured out a code, and we could tap out messages. That's how I knew what was happening to your dad. Every day, the message went around, "BWT." Everybody knew it was Brian getting the water torture again. He wouldn't give up. It went on for days. They beat him and tortured him, but he wouldn't sign. They couldn't break him, no matter what they did to him. Then one day, it all stopped. They seemed to have let it go. We thought he'd won. There were over four hundred U.S. soldiers in that prison, and every one of them knew Brian had won—or so we thought.

"The prison commander had Brian brought out to the yard. Two guards damn near carried him out there. He could barely walk. When the commander told him to sign the confession, Brian answered 'fuck you!'

"The commander had a U.S. soldier with him, the youngest soldier in the prison. The commandant pulled a pistol from his holster and pointed it at the boy's temple, then said to Brian, 'You will sign the confession, or I will kill this boy.'

"Your father had resisted all attempts to force him to give up, but this he couldn't fight. The kid was shaking and looking back and forth between the commandant and Brian, who took the confession and told the commandant, 'put the gun down.' The commandant holstered the pistol. Brian looked at the kid, signed the paper, and handed it back to the commander. The commander looked at it for a long time before he said, 'Brian Madegen, you and all the men in this prison are war criminals. Your confession proves it, but I don't like the way you signed this document.

You're making me do this.' He turned to the young soldier, pulled out his revolver, and shot him in the temple.

"We heard Brian's screams all over that prison.

"They left him alone after that. He was beaten, and we all knew it.

"We survived three more years in that hell hole. After the Paris Peace Accords, we were released with the rest of the POWs. I met your dad back in the states. He wasn't the same Brian I knew when we first met. I wasn't the same either. We talked about it many times. He couldn't stop thinking about what they'd done to him in that prison and blamed himself for that boy's death. In a way, I did too.

"When I saw him last week, he told me he was sorry. He was sorry that boy was killed because of him. He cried and said we should have fought them in the jungle and never let them take us to that prison. He gave me this envelope, and I asked him what was going on. He made me promise to see you got it if anything happened to him."

Axel looked at Timothy and saw the tears in his eyes. He pushed the second glass of whiskey across the table.

"Drink it, Timothy."

Timothy looked down at the glass, then slid it back to Axel. "She brought it for you, mister." He stared at Axel trying to decide whether to fear him, hate him, or thank him.

Axel picked up the letter. "I'm sorry, Timothy. I loved him too."

Timothy grabbed the envelope and walked toward the door with his eyes on the floor; he didn't want them to see him crying.

Axel watched him leave, then picked up the whiskey glass, and emptied it.

* * *

When Timothy left Misty's, he rode to Jellers Park and dropped his bike next to a bench facing the river. It was getting dark, and the low sun was little help in holding off the chill from the damp air that drifted off the water. Timothy shivered and zipped up his jacket. He sat on the bench, pulled the envelope from his pocket, and held it in front of him, his hands shaking. Here was a message from his dad. The funeral had given him a sense of finality. He had accepted that his father was gone from his life, but now, here was a chance to hear from him one more time. It unsettled him.

He thought about the times he'd spent with his father. Ball games, the tree house they built in the backyard, how his dad let him drive sometimes even when he wasn't old enough. The way he smiled when he was happy with a broad grin that seemed to fill his whole face. He remembered a day when he was little, sitting on his dad's shoulders for a good view of the 4th of July parade. He looked around to see if anyone was watching him cry. Tears dripped on the envelope in his hands.

Timothy felt in his jeans for his pocket knife and opened the blade. He slipped the knife under the sealed flap and slit the envelope open. There was only one handwritten page in the envelope.

Timothy read the letter several times and cried until he could cry no more. He put it back in the envelope with care and tucked it back in his pocket. The words in the letter repeated in his mind as he rode home.

Dear Timothy,

I am so sorry to have to leave you like this. I know you will never understand why, but I'll make this feeble try to explain. When I was a young man, a few years older than you are now, I put my life on the line for my country. I believed we were doing the right thing in Vietnam. I was all in. After three years, I came home, but my experiences followed me back. I was proud to serve my country but I gave more than I could afford to give and I can no longer carry the burden of memories from those days. God knows I tried to forget, but I can't. I hope when you are faced with important challenges, you will find the strength and courage to meet them. Go all in. You are my legacy.

I love you very much. Please remember me with kindness and always do your best to make me proud of you.

Forgive me,

Dad.

CHAPTER 3

*Piglet sidled up to Pooh from behind. "Pooh!" he whispered.
"Yes, Piglet?" "Nothing," said Piglet, taking Pooh's paw.
"I just wanted to be sure of you."*
—A.A. Milne

Three friends stepped out of the hotel elevator laughing at John's sarcastic remarks on the plight of the people waiting in a line that stretched from the street door to the elevators—waiting to advance to the bar they'd just left. Clarissa walked between them, holding tight to John's arm, and hand-in-hand with Timothy on her other side. John and Clarissa moved with the unsteady step of an over-served bar patron. Timothy held them back at the curb to avoid a speeding taxi that demanded right-of-way with a blasting horn.

"Hey, Clarissa, Assistant Prosecutor Timothy R. Madegen just saved our asses!" John said.

Clarissa laughed, "Good thing one of us is sober."

"Hey, Tim, where we goin' anyway?" John asked.

Timothy looked up and down the street for a taxi, "I'm going to hail a cab and get us all home safe and sound."

"Wait a minute, what about my car? I don't want to leave my Beemer here. You can drive it, Tim. It's right over there in the garage on the green level."

"I don't have a license, John."

"Oh come on, you don't need a license. Let's go get the car."

"I'm not going to lose my job over a stupid thing like that. Believe me, I have much better ways to get canned." Timothy knew his meaning was lost on John. "Nope, we're going to take a taxi tonight, and you can get the car in the morning."

"Tim's right, John, let's get a cab. We can drop Tim at his place, then take it over to yours," Clarissa said.

Timothy opened the door on a yellow taxi that swerved over to the curb in front of them. The three squeezed into the back with Clarissa in the middle. Timothy leaned up over the back of the front seat to instruct the driver.

"2700 block on Cathedral Northwest, please."

Without acknowledging the instruction, the driver pulled out into traffic.

"My ears are still numb from that disco," Clarissa said. "So what have you been doing with yourself for over a year of not talking to us, Tim?"

"Trying to keep my first job, mostly. But John, I do need to talk to you about something when we're all sober. Can we have lunch tomorrow? There's a café at the Botanic Garden, at your end of the Mall, say twelve-thirty?"

"Am I not invited?" Clarissa asked.

"Of course, you can come," John said, "if you can break away from the Governor's lunch."

"It's settled then. I'll have Annie call John to confirm. If anything changes for you, Clarissa, let John know," Timothy said. "And here's my place, see you guys tomorrow."

Timothy hopped out of the cab, tossed a twenty to John, gave Clarissa a peck on the cheek, and they drove away. He watched the car until it was out of sight, thinking about how he was going to approach this with John. He hoped Clarissa wouldn't be able to go; that would make it easier. She'd probably be busy with the Governor's entourage. He'd surely want his showpiece legal advisor with him, wherever he was going to be tomorrow.

Timothy had enjoyed the evening, in spite of his pre-occupation. The camaraderie with his old classmates was genuine. He hadn't counted on Clarissa coming into the picture, but he realized tonight, they were the only people on the planet he could trust completely. He could not do this alone. He needed help. They were smart, qualified, and loyal. And they had connections. He was going to need resources he could count on.

* * *

Timothy was finished with his lunch by the time Mayfield arrived twenty minutes late. He waved him over.

"Sorry, Tim, couldn't be helped. When the senator calls, I jump," John said.

"Understand. I ordered you a salad, hope that's OK."

"Yeah, that's good." John waved down a waiter. "Can I have a coffee? Black, please." Then he turned to Timothy, "Still recovering from last night. Clarissa called, she can't make it—the Governor—you know. So what is it you wanted to see me about?"

"I need a private meeting with the Chief U.S. District Court Judge for the District of Columbia."

John stopped his fork in midair and looked at Timothy.

"What?" His face wrinkled with the question. "You need a judge? What for? Why are you asking me, you're the Assistant Federal Prosecutor?"

"Not so loud, John. Not just a judge, I need the Chief Judge."

The waiter delivered the coffee to John with the cream and sugar he didn't want. They waited for him to leave the table.

"It can't be to fix a parking ticket; you don't even drive. What's up?"

"I can't tell you. I need a judge who's appointed for life, can't be fired, and believes in the law."[7]

"And you think I can hand over this judge out of my stockpile of judges and not ask you any questions because I'm your old school chum? Why do you even think I can do this?"

"Because I know your aunt is married to Judge Henry Jarvis. She's the one who helped me get into Harvard, and she likes you."

"You're giving me a headache, Tim."

"That's not my fault."

"Yeah," John said massaging his temple.

"Look, this is important," Timothy said. "I want you to be part of it, but I can't tell you or anyone else what it's about until after we hold a grand jury. I need to work with a judge who's not afraid of politics or losing his job; who will call a Special Grand Jury. You know as well as I, that means total secrecy for the prosecutor, the jurors, and the judge. I can't risk the whole thing by telling you. I need a judge who'll listen to my arguments for convening the jury and has the cojones to see it through."

"Why the hell don't you do this through channels? You're in the damn Justice Department; you can call for a grand jury. There's a protocol around here. You can't just go around everyone, just because you think it's a good idea. You're headed for the end of a very short career, pal. Get real."

---

7 United States Constitution Article III. Section 1. "The Judges, both of the supreme and inferior Courts, shall hold their Offices, during good Behavior, …"

"I can't, John. I tried that. I tried to get my boss to let me work it, and he shut me up. This is important. It has to be resolved, for the good of this country."

John looked around the room and lowered his voice to a whisper. "Who is it, Tim? Who you after?"

"I swear, John, I'll tell you everything as soon as I can, but you have to trust me on this. I need that judge. Don't tell anyone why. Just get me an in camera appointment with the guy, and I'll take it from there. Don't tell Clarissa or anyone. Just do this for me—please."

John's phone beeped with a text message, he looked at it, wiped his lips with his napkin, then dropped it on the table.

"You know, Tim, you have a lot of fuckin' nerve. I don't see or hear from you for over a year; then you pop up acting like best of buddy school pals, ask me to stick my neck out for some cause you won't even tell me about, and promise everything will be OK." He stood up and walked around the table to where Timothy sat, bent down, and whispered into his ear. "Fuck you."

John walked to the door.

"John," Timothy called after him. "You gotta do this for me."

Several heads in the restaurant turned.

John stopped and turned back to look at Timothy for a long second. When he couldn't decide how to answer Timothy's plea, he told him, "You get lunch. I gotta go."

CHAPTER 4

Torture and abuse cost American lives…Our policy of torture was directly and swiftly recruiting fighters for al-Qaeda in Iraq…How anyone can say that torture keeps Americans safe is beyond me— unless you don't count American soldiers as Americans.[8]
—Matthew Alexander, leader of an interrogations team assigned to a Special Operations task force in Iraq in 2006.

The chambers of Judge Henry A. Jarvis were on the ground floor of the U.S. District Courthouse on Constitution Avenue. Timothy Madegen entered the building through the marble-clad, three-story cupola at the front of the building, passed through the magnetometer, and showed his Federal I.D. to U.S. marshals guarding the entrance. He was twenty minutes early for his appointment with Chief Judge Jarvis. The information desk attendant directed him through a maze of hallways to double-cherrywood doors that opened to an office vestibule.

"Timothy Madegen to see Judge Jarvis," he said to the bespectacled receptionist, who sat behind a grand desk, elevated like a judge's bench, putting the occupant in position to look down on the supplicant.

"Good morning, Mr. Madegen," she said, "and what is it you're here to see the judge about?"

"I'm on his schedule. I have a nine o'clock appointment," he looked at the name plate on the desk. "I'm a little early, but please let him know I'm here, Ms. Branson."

The receptionist clicked her keyboard and examined a computer screen.

---

8   Alexander, Matthew. "I'm Still Tortured by What I Saw in Iraq." Opinion, Washington Post, November 30, 2008.
http://www.washingtonpost.com/wp-dyn/content/article/2008/11/28/AR2008112802242.html

"Yes, I see you on the calendar; the judge has a busy day today, so he might not be able to see you right on schedule. Please take a seat."

"OK, I'll be patient," he said and gave the woman a big smile, which she did not return.

For the first hour, Timothy busied himself reading case files from a backlog in his briefcase. His inquiries of the receptionist were returned with a request to be patient, "The judge is a very busy man."

A stream of men and women passed in and out of the judge's chambers, none of whom seemed to have to wait like Timothy. When the receptionist announced that the offices were closing for lunch, Timothy was ushered out and told to return in an hour, "or so." He returned in an hour to locked doors and waited in the hall for another half hour before the receptionist appeared and unlocked the doors to the antechamber. It was around 4:30 in the afternoon when both hall doors flew open and banged against the stops. A fashionably dressed woman in high heels burst into the room and walked directly up to the receptionist.

"Who's he got in there, Julie?" she asked. She didn't pause in front of the desk but walked around to the side and stepped up to be eye-to-eye with Julie Branson.

"Good afternoon, Mrs. Jarvis. I'll let him know you're here."

"Where's Madegen? Is this him?" She stepped down and walked over to where Timothy sat waiting.

"Come on, Madegen. I had a feeling you'd be cooling your heels out here. Let's go."

Timothy stood up and hurriedly grabbed for his briefcase. She put her arm through his and swept him along. Together they walked through the doors to the judge's inner chamber. They could hear a frantic receptionist on the intercom warning the judge that his wife was on her way in.

"Isabel, what a pleasant surprise," the judge said, as he got up from his chair and came around his desk.

"Henry, what's the idea of making Timothy wait all day to see you? You were going to leave without seeing him at all, weren't you? You promised me you would see him. Now here he is. You're going to hear him out."

"Oh, Isabel, I had a very busy day today, I was—"

"No you weren't. You were going to stiff him. You had no intention of seeing him. Sit down, we're going to hear what he's got to say."

The judge's face fell. He made no more attempt to argue with his wife.

"Timothy, let me introduce you to my husband, The Honorable Henry A. Jarvis."

Henry Jarvis presented an impressive figure. He had a youthful face, complemented by a thick shock of trim brown hair, parted in the middle, showing only a few gray strands in his sideburns. He wore a pinstriped business suit that was only a couple of years out of style. He had broad shoulders, but his overall physique was on the slender side, even athletic. The look on his clean-shaven face was stern, slightly softened by his intense blue eyes.

"I got you this appointment at the request of my favorite nephew, John Mayfield," Isabel said. "Johnny must think a lot of you to ask for this favor without even knowing what it's about."

Timothy wasn't sure if he should offer to shake hands, or what to do. The judge returned to his chair and motioned for Timothy to take a seat in front him, but Timothy remained standing. Isabel followed the judge around the desk and stood beside him waiting for Timothy, who was having a little trouble deciding exactly where to start.

"Well, young man, what is it?" the judge asked and looked up at Isabel.

"I came to ask you to appoint me as a special counsel for a criminal case that has been overlooked," Timothy said.

"Are you coming here in an official capacity, son? Who are you exactly?"

"I'm a federal prosecutor; I'm with the United States Attorney's Office. I'm an Assistant Attorney."

"This is extraordinary, sir. These things are done through channels. You can't walk in here and expect me to approve special cases for anyone who wants one. Does your boss know you're here? You need to follow protocol. Go on, get out of here. The Attorney General is going to hear about this."

"Wait a minute, Henry," Isabel said. "I want you to hear him out. Johnny trusts him. There must be something to this."

"I understand your surprise, sir, but this is a unique criminal case. It can't go through regular channels, or it would have been prosecuted long ago. There's plenty of evidence of criminal wrongdoing, but the perpetrator—the perpetrator and his accomplices—are highly controversial and powerfully connected."

"Oh God, not another Ponzi scheme," the judge gave his wife a look of disgust, then turned back to Timothy. "Look that's not my district.

Wall Street is in the second district; you have to see Judge Harrison for that."

"No sir, it's worse than that, and the crime is in your district. It was perpetrated under direct orders from Washington, D.C. We need to prosecute President George W. Bush for torture."

The judge jumped from his seat, threw his arm out with his index finger pointing to the door, and yelled down at Timothy. "Get out of here, right now! You're wasting my time!" He turned to his wife. "This is ridiculous, Isabel. You're way out of line on this. How many times have I told you to keep your nose out of my official business? There is no damn way I'm getting involved with this wacko. I don't want anyone to know I've even had this conversation. If you don't leave right now, I'll have Julie call security. If you tell anyone about this meeting, I'll have your license. I'll have you disbarred; you'll be—"

"Stop it, Henry!" Now Isabel was yelling. "Stop it right now." She softened her voice when she realized she was too loud. "If Johnny says Timothy's OK, we need to hear him out. Now sit back down and let him make his case." She pulled on his shoulder until he settled back into his chair.

Julie opened the door and looked in. "Is everything OK, Your Honor?"

The judge looked at Isabel, then at Julie. Timothy Madegen stood still, holding his breath.

The judge sat back in his padded chair, "Just a little domestic spat is all, Julie. You can lock up and take the rest of the day off. We'll leave by my private entrance when we're finished."

Julie scanned the three of them and backed out the door.

"And Julie," the judge called. Julie poked her head back in through the door opening. "You won't say anything about this to anyone, right?"

"No, sir," she said. The door closed, followed by the soft click of a lock being turned.

Jarvis glared at Isabel. "Dammit, Isabel," he said, then turned to Timothy. "Look Madegen, even though you managed to wheedle your way in here through unofficial channels," he looked at Isabel again, "and with unfair influence, I'm going to give you five minutes to state your case, before I tell you to go. At the end of the five minutes, I expect you to leave my office and follow security calmly out of the building. Got it?"

"Yes, sir."

"Go ahead," Isabel said. She rested a hand on the judge's shoulder with a nod that confirmed Timothy's privilege.

Timothy Madegen was prepared. He had a case laid out with a chronology, a list of possible co-conspirators, selected witnesses that would corroborate his evidence, and a grand jury plan, which he had been preparing and updating for months. He answered questions before they could be asked.

"Why hasn't this been done before? Because it has been considered too disruptive and would appear to be a political vendetta if taken up by a Democratic administration."

Timothy's confidence grew as he spoke. His delivery was efficient and forceful. The thick carpet and wall tapestries gave the judge's chamber an anechoic feel; he felt in control of the room.

"Why should Judge Henry A. Jarvis stick his neck out to enable this prosecution, when it will be enormously controversial, and there will be huge pressures brought to bear to stop it? Because Judge Henry A. Jarvis has sworn that he will administer justice without respect to persons."[9]

This drew an indignant glare from Jarvis, and he started to speak, but a nudge from Isabel kept him silent.

"Why not forget the ugly past and look forward instead of backward? Because by that standard, we should never prosecute anyone for anything they have already done. We would only prosecute future crimes. And if we don't do this, we are no longer a country of laws; we'll have become a nation of men, run freely by the wealthy and the powerful at their will."

Timothy consulted his notes for a half minute, then said, "Finally, if we don't prosecute these crimes, we establish a platform for more of them to be committed. Some national leaders feel free to make light of torture and describe it in doublethink terms, declaring waterboarding to be a form of baptism.[10] The longer this goes unpunished, the more likely it will become accepted and used again."

With his arguments exhausted, Timothy returned to his core request.

"I'm asking you to appoint me as a special prosecutor, with all the powers previously granted to special counsels. I'm asking you to call a special grand jury to determine if a crime has been committed."

---

9   The oath is from the Judiciary Act of 1789, that established an oath taken by federal judges.

10   Sarah Palin address to National Rifle Association Annual Meeting, 2014. http://www.cbsnews.com/videos/sarah-palin-waterboarding-is-how-we-baptize-terrorists/

He had kept the judge and his wife engaged for over an hour. It was late when Timothy rested his case. At the conclusion, he settled into a chair and succumbed to a release of tension that came with the completion of his appeal and said, "I guess you can call security now."

Isabel spoke first, "You know they'll come after you, don't you? They'll look for any reason to blacken your name, make you look foolish, lie about you, threaten you, even your family."

"I don't have any family. My father took his own life when I was fifteen, and my mother passed away a couple of years ago. It's just me."

"Do you think you can get anyone with the nerve to staff you on this?"

"I have two good friends I can count on. Your nephew is one of them," Timothy said.

The judge fidgeted in his chair. "You need to study the law, son. I don't have the authority to start an investigation like that, and judges don't assign special counsels. I couldn't do this even if I wanted to, which I don't."

"There is a way," said Timothy. "Use your authority and responsibility to call a special grand jury.[11] Order the special grand jury to subpoena the secret September 17, 2001, Presidential Memorandum of Notification granting the CIA authority to set up detention facilities outside the United States for the interrogation of detainees.[12] If they give it up, the grand jury will have the proof that President Bush authorized secret CIA prisons, that he is responsible for what happened in those prisons, and the Justice Department will be forced to assign a prosecutor to the grand jury. If they don't give it up, which is more likely, you find them in criminal contempt, and that gives you the right to assign a special counsel."[13]

Isabel looked at the judge and grinned with a smile that said, "I told you."

---

11   Title 18 U.S.C. § 3331 Chapter 216—SPECIAL GRAND JURY.
http://www.gpo.gov/fdsys/pkg/USCODE-2011-title18/pdf/USCODE-2011-title18-partII-chap216-sec3331.pdf

12   Sixth Declaration of Marilyn A. Dorn, Information Review Officer, Central Intelligence Agency, Item 61, page 34, January 5th, 2007.
https://www.aclu.org/files/pdfs/natsec/20070105_Dorn_Declaration_8.pdf

13   Federal Rules of Criminal Procedure, Rule 42. Criminal Contempt.
https://www.federalrulesofcriminalprocedure.org/title-viii/rule-42-criminal-contempt/

Jarvis sat silent until, "Damn! OK, Madegen, I've heard you out. Now you listen to me. Do you know why nobody has attempted to do what you are proposing? It's because it's a thankless, no-win undertaking."

The judge rose from his chair and began pacing. "They're brutal, these politicians, and they have power—power you can't even imagine. Your quixotic quest is naïve at best and stupid at worst. You were a boy when Archibald Cox took on Richard Nixon. You know who I'm talking about?" He stopped walking and looked to see if Madegen was following him.

"Yes, sir," Timothy said.

"You know why he got that job as special prosecutor?"

"No, sir."

"It was because every other qualified lawyer approached by Attorney General Elliott Richardson turned it down flat. They were all too smart to get involved. Now I'm not saying that Cox wasn't smart. He was eminently qualified, but he had no political ambitions and took the job as a patriot.[14] And the fact of the matter is, he did a helluva job, and they fired him for it. Fired him to get rid of him. When he got too close to the truth, Nixon ordered Richardson to fire Cox. Richardson refused and resigned. Then Nixon ordered the Deputy Attorney General, William Ruckelhaus, to do it, and Ruckelhaus resigned. That left Robert Bork in charge of the Justice Department, and he fired Cox.[15] Sooner or later, they'll get you. You can't fight these guys."

"But the truth did come out, sir, and they can't fire you. If you give me a shot at this, you are the only one who could fire me," Timothy said.

Jarvis' face took on a black look. He stood in front of the seated Madegen. "You know son, you have a lot of nerve coming in here and telling me what I can and can't do, and what my duty to my country is and how to go about doing it." His voice rose in volume. "In the forty years I've been on the bench, you are not the first overzealous young prosecutor I have had to deal with, but you are by far the boldest. You know that?"

"Yes, sir, but—"

"Henry, please think about this. We can talk about it after you've had some time," Isabel said.

"Madegen, you don't know what you're asking, but I do," Jarvis said. He took his wife's hand. "Let's get some dinner, Isabel."

---

14   Ken Gormley, Archibald Cox, Conscience of a Nation, Perseus Books, Reading Massachusetts, 1997, page 240.

15   Ibid. page 357

Chapter 5

*There is still much debate about whether torture has been effective in
eliciting information—the assumption being, apparently, that
if it is effective, then it may be justified.*
—Noam Chomsky

Isabel gave her husband the space of several days to deliberate Timothy Madegen's proposal. She knew Henry Jarvis could not be pushed. During that time, she reflected on her own reasons for supporting Madegen.

At the age of ten, her family had emigrated from Chile, fleeing Pinochet's campaign of killing, imprisonment, and torture of his opponents to consolidate and maintain his power. It was the nagging memory of those days that brought her to confront the judge after dinner one evening.

She rose from her chair opposite the judge and began stacking dishes. She looked at her husband and tried to sense his mood as she refilled his wine glass. "We need to talk about Timothy Madegen," she said and sat down in the chair next to him, leaning forward to engage her husband. "You can't ignore Timothy. I won't let you. It's not going to just go away."

The judge pushed back in his chair, elbows on the armrests, hands clasped over his satisfied belly, and returned Isabel's challenging gaze. "I never thought you'd let it go, Isabel," he said, "but I hoped for some other way to satisfy you on this."

"This isn't about me, Henry. It's about our country. We can't let this happen here. You've never felt the fear of torture. The terror that consumes you, when your cousin disappears. The awful image of my uncle's mutilated body on our door step never leaves me. I still have terrible dreams about those days. We ran from Pinochet, a cruel dictator. And now, I find my new country—the supposed beacon of human rights—is using torture."

"Obama put a stop to it as soon as he was sworn in—it's over."

"No, it isn't," Isabel said. "If one president can do it and get away with it, any future leader has a precedent to rely on, and he can do it too. Who knows what the next president might do? You can stop this, Henry. It falls on you. You're in a position to do it."

"But Isabel, you were right to tell Madegen how hard it would be for him. It would be the same for us, probably worse, because it would be my position and authority that holds them off. They'd try every way they could to make me stop him. I'd have to fight all of them legally and politically: the president, the justices, the attorney general, and even the Congress, who could impeach me. Are you ready for that?"

The question rested unanswered on the table while the judge picked up his wine glass and took a sip. Isabel waited for him to continue.

"And what do we know of this guy, Madegen, anyway? Why should we have confidence in him? How do I know he's competent? He could cause me a huge embarrassment. Isn't this the same kid for whom you and Johnny lobbied to get him a Harvard Law School scholarship? Here he comes again, asking for another favor. He seems awfully needy to me."

"He's not a kid, Henry. He's a smart attorney, and he isn't asking for a favor," she said. "He's asking for you to do your duty."

Jarvis winced at the last remark, stood up, and carried his glass with him across the room to stand at the window. The street below was quiet. He turned back to her in his defense. "Why do you think it's up to me? Why am I to decide this?"

"You don't have to decide anything," Isabel said. "Let a secret grand jury determine if there should be an indictment. It isn't really up to you, is it? All you have to do is unlock the door; Timothy is ready to take it from there."

"Secret grand jury?" He frowned. "We both know there are no secrets in Washington, D.C. As soon as two people know a thing, it's no longer a secret. Yes, a special grand jury is supposed to be secret, but something this controversial can't be contained. If I consent, it will be in the papers in hours. Yes, Isabel, *it is* up to me, and everyone will know it."

"You're sixty years old, Henry. You have had a good and comfortable life. If it's enough for you, you should not help Timothy. But if you want to be remembered as the proud and courageous man I married thirty years ago—"

"It scares me, Isabel."

Isabel came to him and took his hands in both of hers. "Me too, Henry. I know what powerful people can do. I've seen it. They have the press, and the money and the congressmen, but we can't let them have torture. That's too much power. They can terrorize an entire country like Pinochet and Saddam Hussein did. This has to be stopped now, before it gets worse. The Justice Department and the Congress are already terrorized, or they would have prosecuted Bush years ago. Nobody has the guts for it. Nobody but Timothy Madegen. And maybe he is naïve, but he knows what torture did to his dad, and I know what it did to my family, and we can't let this go on because we want to be comfortable for one more day. If we do, if we're too afraid to work for truth and justice, if we're too selfish to confront the bullies, then the torture worked, and the torturers win. And they'll do it again. We can't let them scare us into silence, and we can't let them kill the soul of our country without a fight. Please, Henry—"

"Dammit, Isabel! I'll talk to Madegen, but I'm not making any promises," he said.

* * *

Timothy walked from Dupont Circle Metro to the Jarvis home on R Street, Georgetown, in a state of mind that teetered between optimism and pessimism. When he rang the bell, Isabel opened the door to the brownstone.

"Hello, Timothy. Thank you for coming," she said inviting him into the entrance hall.

"Is the judge going to see me?" he asked.

"You have presented him with quite a challenge, Timothy. I've worked on him over the last few days, but I don't know what he's going to do. He's getting tired; he doesn't have the energy he used to have. I worry about his health. What you are asking will drain him. I don't know if he can help you. You might have picked the wrong man. I don't know."

"I understand, Mrs. Jarvis. You talked to Johnny about it, didn't you?"

"Yes," she said. "He came to the house to apologize for getting us involved with you. He's furious. He feels you used him unfairly to get to Henry. Johnny thinks you're crazy, naïve, and dangerous—and I'm borderline insane for supporting you. He's like so many people who've never been touched by the horror. You should talk to him."

"He's been calling me five times a day, but I haven't answered," Timothy said. "I don't want to talk to anyone on the phone about this yet."

"The judge is downstairs in the billiard room; I'll show you the way."

Isabel led Timothy to the stairwell and left him at the top of the stairs.

"Good luck," she said and squeezed his arm.

At the bottom of the flight, Timothy stepped into a short hall leading to a paneled room with a full-size pool table in the center. Henry Jarvis stood bent over the table looking down the length of a cue stick. He glanced up as Timothy entered, hit the cue ball a solid blow, and straightened up. The ivory ball struck a striped one that shot across the table and dropped into a corner pocket.

"You play nine ball?" Jarvis asked.

Timothy looked around the room. A well-stocked wet bar stood at the far end. The room had a rich smell of sweet pipe tobacco mixed with old whiskey. Framed photographs commemorating family events covered the paneled walls.

"Yes, sir," he said. "I played some in college." He paused at the near end of the table opposite the judge.

"Rack 'em up. I'll pour us a drink. What'll it be?"

"I'll have soda, sir," Timothy said.

"No fair, I'm havin' a whiskey rocks. I'll pour you one too." The judge handed Timothy the racking form, then went to the bar while Timothy set up the diamond shaped array and dropped the nine-ball in the center.

"Bourbon or scotch?" the judge asked from across the room.

"Bourbon, sir."

"Atta boy," the judge said. "Good Ol' American Kentucky whiskey."

Timothy chose one of the heaviest cue sticks from several on the wall rack, looked down the stick, and satisfied himself it was straight enough. He chalked the tip.

The judge came back with the drinks and handed one to Timothy.

"Cheers," he said, clinked with Timothy's and knocked back half the glass. "You break 'em."

Timothy stepped up to the end of the table, set his glass on the rail, and broke the game. The violet four-ball dropped into a side pocket; the others scattered the table.

"Nice tight rack," the judge said.

Timothy came around to the side of the table, made a gentle shot that sank the yellow one-ball and positioned his leave behind the blue two. The nine-ball sat next to a center side pocket. When he sank the two, the ivory cue ball came off the rail and tapped the nine, dropping it in the side. He looked up at the judge, a little embarrassed at his win.

"Well son, you might have warned me I was playin' a pro," Jarvis said, in a playful complaint.

"Lucky, sir. I was lucky."

The judge walked over to the cue rack and put up his stick. "OK, if you say so," he said and went back to the bar to touch up his glass. He returned to the table where Timothy stood.

"I'm crazy to even consider this, Madegen, and I wouldn't be doing it if it weren't for Isabel. I promised her I'd take you seriously, but that just means I'll talk to you about it. It's my decision, not hers. So let's start with your experience. You have one year of experience as a federal prosecutor; that doesn't qualify you to take on a former president of the United States now, does it? Do you know how this is going to look? I'm going to be the one accused of appointing an incompetent, whether you are or you aren't. If you screw up, I'll wear the blame like a scarlet letter."

Timothy stood erect, giving Jarvis his full attention. He considered his words carefully.

"I understand, sir, and I would be pleased to have someone else, anyone else, take the job, but no one is willing to do it. We learned our government was torturing people over ten years ago, and as of today, nobody has taken up the issue. It's been ignored by most and rationalized by some in the press, but no one has invoked our system of justice to investigate the case, even though many of the details are there for all to see."

The judge sensed the passion in Timothy's response and acknowledged the truth in what he said.

"If you don't appoint me to do it, appoint someone you think is more capable, but please don't be blind to the issue and ignore it. I understand your concern about my experience, and I propose to enlist the services of an experienced prosecutor to help me. I'm sure there are some who have the courage to do it if given the chance."

"Do you understand that this is not a stepping stone to a prestigious legal or political berth? It's not," Jarvis said. "If you do this, you'll be identified for the rest of your career with this one case, and it could be a very short career—depending on how it goes."

"I have no interest in politics, sir. I only want to see that justice is done, and the truth is exposed for our country now and for future generations. If a person's status can put them above the law, our system of justice is meaningless. If our Congress can vote to make torture legal, and immunize the torturers from prosecution, we will always live under the threat of torture.[16] We're living under the threat right now, if you believe what President Bush said. He calls torture a tool and claims he has made that tool available for use by future presidents.[17] We can't ignore this."

"How do I know I can trust you?"

"Well, I'll have to earn your trust, but I am aware that if you give me this authority, you will have the power to fire me. I do ask that you give me the same guarantee that Elliott Richardson gave Archibald Cox—that he would not be dismissed except for *gross misconduct or extraordinary improprieties.*"[18]

"Look, I understand the politics of this way more than you do," Jarvis said.

Timothy was not cowered. "And I know we will both be taking on a tough job. If the facts show President Bush has ordered criminal acts, his supporters will say he's being railroaded for partisan reasons. If the facts show otherwise, his opponents will say that we were bought off in some way. I get it, sir. I still want to do it."

"What information will you report to me?" Jarvis asked him. "How informed are you willing to keep me about your activities and progress?"

"Nothing until after the grand jury makes their decision. After that, only the information you receive in court. It has to be that way to keep you from being charged with influencing the case or making a biased judgment."

---

16 Reference Military Commissions Act of 2006 making Detainee Treatment Act of 2005 retroactive to September 11, 2001
https://www.icrc.org/ihl-nat/a24d1cf3344e99934125673e00508142/
b22319a0da00fa02c1257b8600397d29/$FILE/Detainee%20Treatment%20
Act%20of%202005%20.pdf

17 Supra 3. Approximately thirty minutes into video

18 Supra 14. page237

"You know that anything you do will reflect on me, don't you? I'll be taking the heat for you. I have to know you're going to do it right."

"I promise you. I will work within the law and the Constitution. That's all they can expect of any of us. I agree with Archibald Cox, this is not worth doing if it doesn't show that a fair inquiry can be conducted under our system of government.[19] It has to be done within the law; that's what this is all about."

The judge set his glass down on the rail and racked the balls. He nodded at Timothy to break the game. Nine balls scattered, but nothing dropped. Jarvis chalked his cue and circled the table as he planned his play. He sank the one and the two right away. His smile at sinking the three on a long shot turned to a frown when the cue ball rolled too far and he faced the four hidden behind the eight. He bent low to the table to set up a bank shot that sent the cue ball around the eight and tapped the four into the nine which dropped with a final thud into the far corner pocket.

"Nice shot," Timothy said and lifted his glass to toast the judge's win.

The judge laid his cue stick on the table and looked at Timothy. "Right now, Madegen, if I don't do anything stupid, I'm on a guaranteed track to spending my leisure years practicing my bank shots, drinking fine whiskey, reading good books, and traveling the world. I've got a year or two left in my career before that."

"Sounds nice, sir."

"I hope they'll say I did a good job when they hand me the gold watch, but I can't say there is anything I can really be proud of."

"You can be proud of being a federal judge, sir."

"I was appointed to the federal bench by President Lyndon Baines Johnson. He was a man's man. I always saw him as a role model. He met triumph and disaster head on. If he were here right now, he'd tell me to man-up."

Judge Henry Jarvis stepped in close to Madegen. "I can't find any flaws in the logic of your proposal or your motives. There's an imprudent boldness in it that might have appealed to me when I was younger—now it frightens me."

He downed his glass of whiskey. "But, I'll do it, and you better get ready for a wild ride because there is going to be hell to pay."

---

19   Supra 14. page240.

* * *

Jarvis and Isabel closed the door as Timothy left.

Henry Jarvis took his wife in his arms and held her close. She looked up at him with tears in her eyes, and she saw the tears welling up in his.

"Thank you," she whispered, and he kissed her gently.

CHAPTER 6

The purpose of torture is not getting information. It's spreading fear.
—Eduardo Galeano

Two weeks later, at 8:00 a.m. in the morning, the Honorable Henry A. Jarvis, Chief Judge of the United States for the District of Columbia, signed an order impaneling a special grand jury to determine if President George W. Bush committed a crime by ordering or enabling the torture of individuals incarcerated by the government of the United States. At 8:30 a.m., the Chief Justice of the United States Supreme Court phoned the Honorable Henry A. Jarvis and told him to rescind the order, which the judge adamantly refused to do. The Chief Justice then asked for Judge Jarvis' resignation which Jarvis refused to give. He then reminded the Chief Justice that, "with all due respect, according to Article III, Section 1, of the Constitution, I hold my office during good behavior." Jarvis stated that he intended to remain on the bench until the grand jury completed its assignment to his satisfaction. At 1:00 p.m. the same day, Judge Jarvis issued a subpoena demanding the current administration provide the special grand jury with a copy of Presidential Memorandum of Notification issued by the office of President George W. Bush on September 17, 2001.[20]

The phones in the judge's offices went dead at 2:00 p.m., and a telephone repairman arrived within minutes to install bugs on every phone in the office suite. A cable installer called unannounced at the

---

20   Supra 12. Item No. 61, pages 33-39.

Georgetown residence of Henry and Isabel Jarvis to upgrade the system "free of charge" and installed bugs throughout the house.

Ms. Julie Branson answered a continuous stream of phone calls from reporters of national and international news services and told callers that Judge Jarvis was sequestered in his chambers for the foreseeable future, and she would be happy to inform them when and if he had a comment of any kind to share with them.

The Republican National Committee chairman issued a statement saying it was all a partisan scheme to diminish the Bush Administration's record of being strong on defense and that President Bush should be lauded for making tough choices that the Democrats were too weak to consider.

Andy Ricker made an unannounced visit to Madegen's office and confronted Timothy at his desk.

"Madegen, did you have anything to do with this?" He leaned over and spit it out at the seated Madegen.

"If you're talking about the Special Grand Jury, it's a Judicial Branch action, not a Justice Department thing." Timothy later regretted his equivocation but rationalized it by his being caught off guard.

"I'm warning you, Madegen, you better stay away from this business. I've got the AG, White House people, half of the old Bush cabinet, and CIA people all over me on this. If anybody in this organization has anything to do with this, I swear they're going to pay." He slammed his fist down on the desk, turned, and stomped out.

Madegen's secretary Annie Young rushed in. "I'm so sorry, Mr. Madegen, he ran past me without a word. I couldn't warn you. Is there anything I can do?"

"It's OK, Annie. People are going to be a little excited around here for a while."

* * *

Timothy emerged from the Woodley Park Metro Station late that night and walked up Connecticut Avenue. He groped his way up the creaky outside stairs to his second-floor apartment in the dark, briefcase in hand, thinking he'd have to replace the bulb in the motion sensor right away. At the top landing, he felt the crunch of broken glass underfoot, found the screen door propped open and the security door off its hinges. He stepped into his one-room flat, stumbled over something on the floor, and groped for the light switch inside the door to no avail.

Using the dim light of his cell phone, he saw the floor covered in his personal belongings. Everything was on the carpet: books, clothes, the contents of his refrigerator, and pieces of his desktop computer. Every shelf and table top was cleared. He turned over his computer tower; the hard drive was gone. Timothy stood quietly in the middle of the turmoil, started to dial his cell phone, thought better of it, turned off the phone, took out the SIM card and battery, and dropped the three pieces into a pocket of his briefcase. He turned and went back down the stairs.

He walked directly back to the Metro, boarded the next train to Union Station, and got a table at the Thunder Grill. The waiter brought a menu, and Timothy asked for a phone. The waiter gave him his cell to use. He called John Mayfield.

"John, I know it's late," Timothy spoke softly into the phone.

"Madegen? You son-of-a-bitch. You used me to get to my uncle, and now he's in hot water. We're done, buddy. I'll never trust you again. Goodbye."

"Wait, John! Wait! Don't hang-up!"

Timothy hit redial. When John answered, he said. "It's already started; they've trashed my room."

"So what? Are you calling me for help after what you did? Are you nuts?"

"I'm going to need a place to stay for tonight."

"Fuck you. Goodbye."

Madegen called back. The phone rang many times before John picked up.

"This is not OK, Tim. Leave me out of this."

"Don't you want to support your uncle? We're in this together, the judge and me. We need you. I need help I can trust."

"Trust!" John gave a derisive laugh. "Oh, that's a good one. The asshole needs somebody he can trust. Where the fuck are you?"

"Thunder Grill, Union Station."

"Stay there."

"OK."

John picked up Timothy half an hour later.

"I've been calling you for days. Why didn't you answer?" John asked.

"I knew Isabel told you about my meetings with your uncle, and I didn't want to talk about it on the phone. You know why. It had to be kept quiet until the judge took action."

"Yeah, well, it's not a big secret anymore," John said and merged the BMW onto South Capitol Street. "It'll be the headline on the front page of the *Times* in the morning."

"It won't be the whole story, John."

"And…?"

"Didn't Isabel tell you about the rest of it?"

"There's more?"

"Judge Jarvis is going to appoint me Special Counsel."

The BMW swerved over to the side of the road, bumped the curb, and squealed to a stop.

"What! Are you crazy?" John turned in his seat to face Timothy. "Is *he* crazy? What gives you the idea an Assistant Federal Prosecutor with one-year experience is ready to take on a former president of the United States? How did you con the old boy into this? This is nuts. I never should have gotten you in to see him. I'm going to put a stop to this madness. You guys are out of your mind. Jesus, Tim, there's no way."

"Calm down, John." Timothy sat with stoic resolve in the passenger seat and looked his friend in the eye. "It has to be this way. Nobody else will do it. I know I'll need help. I'll need you and Clarissa and—"

"Oh great, three inexperienced lawyers are going to—"

"…and I was going to say, Beecker, Otto Beecker. And other qualified people will pitch in. Once the whole thing is out there, we're going to get support. I know it. It's just that somebody had to set the stage. With the amount of evidence accumulated over the last decade, this should be a slam-dunk once we put the ball in play."

"It's a career killer if you ask me—nobody will want to touch it," John said.

"Does that mean you're out?"

John turned away to watch the cars pass by in his side mirror, then jumped the BMW back into the traffic stream. He didn't speak until he made the right turn onto M Street.

"God dammit, Tim. I'm in, but it's only because I feel responsible to my uncle since he wouldn't be involved in this elmore, if I hadn't vouched for you. As far as Clarissa goes, you're on your own with her; I'm not going to influence her to risk her career on this madness."

"I knew I could count on you, John." Timothy gave John a smile and put his hand on his friend's shoulder. "We can do this; I know we can."

The BMW turned into an underground garage, and the two friends took the elevator up to John's eleventh-floor apartment. They stepped out onto the balcony and looked out over the city at the Capitol Dome and the monolith of the Washington Monument. They started making plans.

CHAPTER 7

One day I'll tell my daughter a story about a dark time, the dark days before she was born, and how her coming was a ray of light. We got lost for a while, the story will begin, but then we found our way.
—Nick Flynn, *The Ticking is the Bomb*,
The Best American Nonrequired Reading 2009

As he passed in front of her secretarial desk on the way to his office, Annie handed him the newspaper. "Here's the morning news, Mr. Madegen. The front page headline is about the special grand jury investigation of President Bush." She pointed at the front page.

"BUSH GRAND JURY ORDERED."

"What about the *Post*?" he asked and came back to stop in front of her.

"The same, boss."

"Please don't call me that," Madegen said. "Who's mentioned in the story?"

"Judge Henry A. Jarvis. It's all about him, and how the administration is caught totally by surprise," Annie said with a smile. "'Pants down,' is the way they put it."

"Are there any calls, miss?"

"Please don't call me that, sir."

Madegen lifted his gaze from the paper to look at her as if he were seeing her for the first time. She was dressed in a fitted flower print dress that showed off a young but mature figure. Her brown hair was pulled back and wrapped in a tight bun. The natural luster complemented her pale complexion. Her cheeks grew pink at the audacity of her declaration, but she didn't shrink from her request, and that assurance was not wasted on Timothy. When their eyes met, they confirmed a mutual understanding. The unexpected *tête-à-tête* blurred Timothy's narrow focus for a moment, and he rephrased the question. "Were there any calls for me this morning, Annie?"

"Your boss called a couple of times according to the answering machine, but he didn't leave a message. Do you want to call him back?"

"No."

"Yes, sir."

"Timothy," he told her.

"Yes, Timothy."

"That doesn't sound right either. Look, it's going to get tense around here. You might want to start looking for another spot," he said.

"Are you letting me go?"

"No—giving you a little heads up and a chance to bail, while you can."

"I don't want to bail."

"What does that mean?"

"Can I talk to you in your office?"

Timothy nodded and started for his office with Annie following.

Annie closed the door. Timothy walked around his desk and sat in his chair. Annie stood in front of the desk.

"Judge Jarvis' receptionist, Julie Branson, is talking about your meeting with Judge Jarvis and the subject of your meeting. It won't be long before somebody in the press reveals the plan to appoint you special counsel."

"How do you know about this, Annie?"

"The gossip machine in this town is way efficient. If Judge Jarvis doesn't get out in front of this, it's going to look awful for him, and you are going to lose any leverage you might have had with the AG."

"What?"

"It's about the spin and managing the news. I think I can help. You didn't read my resume when you hired me, did you? I graduated in political science. While you spent three years hanging around Harvard Square, I was here in D.C. learning how it works from behind a secretarial desk. Trust me on this, you better call your boss right now and get to Judge Jarvis right away."

Timothy looked his secretary up and down. He appreciated her bold appraisal of the situation and sensed her real concern. She felt right.

"OK, call him."

Annie grabbed his desk phone and dialed the assistant AG's extension. She handed the receiver to Timothy. "Here's the Assistant AG, I'll go back to my desk and call you a cab."

Timothy nodded and lifted the handset to his ear.

"Madegen here."

"I told you to stay out of this."

"It had to be done, sir."

"You're fired," Ricker said in a tired voice.

"I know—I have a new job at Judicial."

"Madegen—I'm no Elliot Richardson—I'm sorry."

"I understand."

"Timothy—I wish you luck—I mean it."

"Thank you, sir."

"Goodbye."

When Madegen emerged from his office, Annie handed him a slip of paper with a name and phone number on it. "That's a reporter I know at the *Times.* If you and the judge are ready to take the lead, call that number and give him an exclusive. He has a pipeline to the *CBS Evening News* team. It's not too late to control the press on this. I wrote a press release for the judge," she said and handed him a second page.

"*You* wrote it?" Timothy asked her.

"Am I overstepping?" she asked. "You need to get the papers on your side."

Timothy took the page, looked at it then back at Annie. "Thank you."

"There's a yellow cab waiting for you at the front door."

"Get some boxes and start packing my office while I'm gone."

"Oh!"

"It's OK, Annie, we'll be fine."

Madegen rode the cab to the U.S. District Courthouse. He walked into the judge's ante-chamber where he pushed through a crowd, ignored the objections of Julie Branson, and entered the judge's chambers.

The judge looked up from a meeting with two attorneys.

"I need to speak with you, Your Honor. This is an emergency," Madegen said without waiting for permission.

The judge stood up, annoyed. "Excuse me, gentlemen," he said, eyes on Timothy. "Please give me a minute." He signaled Madegen to follow him to a small side office.

"Your secretary is a mole, Judge, and she's going to sell the story about our strategy."

"Julie?"

"Yes, we need to get out in front of this. My secretary knew this morning about the plan to appoint me special counsel, and she didn't get it from me. We need to break it and set the frame, before the administration and the politicos do it," Timothy said.

"How do we do that, son? I've never needed a political expert before; I deal in law, not spin."

Timothy pulled out the page Annie had given him. "I have a press contact here," he said, "and this is a short press release Annie wrote for me." He read it to the judge:

JUDGE APPOINTS EXPERT TO SPECIAL COUNSEL POSITION

The Honorable Henry A. Jarvis, Chief Justice of the United States District Court for the District of Columbia, has announced the appointment of attorney Timothy R. Madegen as a Special Counsel to work with the recently established special grand jury evaluating the alleged crime of torture by the administration of President George W. Bush. Madegen worked for the Criminal Division of the Justice Department where he was well-known as an expert on U.S. and International law relating to the Geneva Conventions, the UN Convention Against Torture, and the War Crimes Act. Judge Jarvis has made the tentative appointment in anticipation of the expected administration response to his subpoena demanding the secret September 17, 2001, Presidential Memorandum of Notification granting the CIA the authority to set up detention facilities outside the United States and for interrogation of suspected terrorist detainees. Several commentators have speculated that the judge is announcing Madegen's selection as a means of putting the administration on notice that he will file a charge of criminal contempt if the subject memo is not released as ordered within fourteen days.

"This is what I was afraid of, Madegen. I never wanted to have my motives evaluated on the front page of the *Times*. Let me read that thing again."

Madegen handed him the paper. The judge pulled out some reading glasses and went over it once silently, then read it out loud. He looked at Timothy over the top of his glasses, "I'm not too sure about that last part, son. It makes me sound a little underhanded."

"It's hardball, sir, but I'm afraid that's the game we're playing. We need to get a hit before they do."

The judge handed the page back to Madegen. "OK, go with it—in for a penny, in for a pound," Jarvis said. "I should probably fire, Julie."

"Let's see if we can use her instead. With Julie, you know what you've got. If you replace her, you'll just add a new unknown. No, you should probably keep her for now."

"Good idea, give me that back." The judge crossed off the last sentence, wrote **FOR IMMEDIATE RELEASE** at the top, and signed and dated it. "Your media people can use the last line, but I don't want it coming from this office. Give it to Julie on your way out, I'm going to lock my chambers and slip out the back."

Madegen walked across the Mall to the public phone on Independence Avenue and called his office.

"Assistant Prosecutor Madegen's office," Annie said.

"Annie, it's Timothy. The judge agreed to the news release you wrote, and they're posting it from his office. You can send a copy to your contact, but let him know he can't attribute the last line to the judge."

"You should know I'm not the only one who got the gossip on your appointment. I've been getting calls from reporters since you left. They're fishing for information; you need to give them something."

"Get your reporter contact on the phone and give him my statement. Confirm my acceptance of the position of special counsel per the court order, and say I won't be able to discuss the investigation while it's ongoing. Give him an exclusive on this and stonewall the others," he said.

"Can I promise him an interview with you?"

"Do I have to?"

"Yes."

"OK, but let him know it will have to be about generalities."

"When will I hear from you again?"

"I don't know—and Annie—"

"Yes!"

"I want you on the team, Annie."

"I was hoping."

"Good, I'll be in touch, goodbye."

CHAPTER 8

Cowards make the best torturers.
Cowards understand fear and they can use it.
— Mark Lawrence, *Prince of Thorns*

Timothy, John, Clarissa, and Annie entered Austin Hall past stout, floral-topped columns and ornate arches that took Timothy's thoughts back to simpler times. He fought his nostalgia to focus on the imminent meeting with their difficult but brilliant constitutional law professor.

John walked with Annie. "You are about to meet a cranky old curmudgeon. He knows everything there is to know about constitutional law and thinks a lot of himself. None of us would be here, if we didn't need him. Don't let him scare you."

"Don't worry about me, John. I've been secretary to a lot of pompous asses in the last few years. Let me soften him up for you." She stopped in the hall, rolled three inches of skirt into her waistband and unbuttoned two top buttons of her blouse.

John stood back to look her over and gave an appreciative low whistle. "Oh yeah," he said nodding his head. "That ought to do it."

At the door to the professor's office, Timothy turned to John with a smile, shrugged, and raised his right eyebrow the way John had often seen him do before tackling a difficult challenge. He gave a hard knock, then without waiting for a reply, turned the brass knob and led the team in.

"Excuse the interruption, Professor. We would like to have a word with you," Timothy said.

Professor Otto Beecker looked up from the paper chaos on his desk and pulled off his reading glasses. "Madegen? Mayfield? And Morrison? I thought I was done with the three M's a year ago. Back then, I didn't realize I was releasing a plague of under-educated, self-deluded, legal misfits on the unsuspecting Capitol of my country. How did you people get in here? The security around here has broken down completely. Haven't you had enough abuse from me?"

"No sir, I mean, yes sir. I mean, we came to get your help, sir," John Mayfield said.

"And who are *you*, my dear?" Beecker said, looking Annie over.

"Professor Beecker, I want you to meet Annie Young," Madegen said. "She's our political advisor."

Annie feigned a loss of words, then managed, "Nice to meet you Professor Beecker," and offered him her pale, slim hand.

"Otto—please call me Otto," he said. He accepted the hand with a lingering touch, then turned back to the others.

"And here's Clarissa. I was sure you were on your way when I heard you landed on the Governor's staff. Why are you involved in this?"

"Please hear Timothy out, Professor. It's important and not as crazy as you think," she said.

"Timothy Madegen—I had some hope for you too and now this. What the hell are you thinking? I can't believe you're doing this to Henry Jarvis. I don't get how a man of conservative principles like Henry could have allowed you to con him into this. If it's some sort of blackmail, you should be ashamed of yourself."

"Judge Jarvis is going into this with his eyes wide open, sir. The whole country needs to take a serious look at what we're—"

"Can it, Madegen! Do you understand you people have created a constitutional crisis? This is the first time in history the Judicial Branch has instituted an investigation of the Executive Branch. It's unprecedented! The Congress killed the special prosecutor option back in 1999.[21] When it expired, everyone breathed a sigh of relief. Now you people are resurrecting the damnable thing, and you can be sure that nobody, and I mean nobody, is going to like it."

---

21   Ethics in Government Act, 1978. The special prosecutor provision was renewed several times but finally left to expire in 1999. http://www.senate.gov/ artandhistory/history/common/investigations/pdf/Watergate_EthicsGov.pdf

"It's in the U.S. Code, sir. The Chief Judge has the right in a criminal contempt case."[22]

"But a president! You're going after a former president?" Otto held the fingertips of both hands to his temples and squinted his eyes at them as if he was fighting a sudden migraine. "My God, man! Sit down all of you. Let's get this over with; I don't think the A/C can handle too much more of your hot air."

There was a chair for everyone but Timothy. Annie sat in front of the professor's desk and crossed her legs.

"Yes, sir. We're trying to look at the big picture here," Timothy said. "We know it's a constitutional challenge. We need your help with that, and with preparing a strategy to take to the Special Grand Jury."

"It's a quagmire, Madegen. If you investigate Bush for criminal malfeasance, you're going to have to include all the co-conspirators, and there are a lot of them. It'll include half his cabinet, the irresponsible attorneys that counseled him, the soldiers in the prisons that did it, the CIA operatives and contractors, and the heads of several European and North African countries that allowed it.[23] Maybe even members of Congress. Hell! If you are successful in getting a conviction, the current administration could get pulled into it for committing misprision and being an accessory after the fact."[24,25] It could go from the President on down. Where is it going to stop?"

"So you're saying it's too hard, and we should let it go?" John asked.

Beecker jumped out of his chair and turned on Mayfield. If there was one principal Professor Otto Beecker drilled into his students, it was John Adams' pride in "a nation of laws, not of men."[26]

"Dammit, John, you have to pick your battles. Have you even thought about the end game here? Madegen's going to be fired—if I had to bet—I'd say he'll be out of the Justice Department by noon tomorrow."

---

22   Supra 13.

23   DEP'T OF JUSTICE, OFFICE OF PROF'L RESPONSIBILITY REPORT, INVESTIGATION INTO THE OFFICE OF LEGAL COUNSEL'S MEMORANDA CONCERNING ISSUES RELATING TO THE CENTRAL INTELLIGENCE AGENCY'S USE OF "ENHANCED INTERROGATION TECHNIQUES" ON SUSPECTED TERRORISTS 160 (2009). http://www.fas.org/irp/agency/doj/opr-2nddraft.pdf

24   US Code Title 18 Crimes and Criminal Procedure, Chapter 1, paragraph 3, Accessory after the fact.

25   Ibid, paragraph 4, Misprision of a felony.

26   John Adams seventh Novanglus essay.

"Actually, that's already happened, sir."

Beecker smiled and nodded at Timothy. His aggressive tone turned more conciliatory. "So what are you going to do if the grand jury returns an indictment, and you've got nobody in the department to sign it? The Attorney General won't sign it.[27] You'll be dead in the water, and the cannons will be blasting away at you for being foolish enough to try it. And you'll have destroyed a very respectable judge."

"It's Washington, D.C., Professor. Nothing is inevitable in our town," Annie said. "There's a nation of people who don't believe what happened is right. When the time comes, we'll take it to the people. If they don't stand up and support us, you'll be right, but we have to take the chance."

"The news media is going to skewer the bunch of you. When they find out you're only one year out of law school, they're going to have a blast, painting you as the most ridiculous bunch of immature children to hit Washington, D.C."

"No, sir," Annie said. "Timothy, John, and Clarissa are going to be seen as a real-life embodiment of Mr. Smith, outsiders taking on Washington to bring courage and honesty back to the Capitol and re-establishing the moral high ground for our country. I can make that case. I know how."

"Wow, beautiful *and* smart," Beecker said with an appreciative smile. "You are courageous, but you're naïve too. I hope you're capable of bailing these people out, Annie."

Annie came around to Beecker's side and put her hand on his arm. "Are you going to help us, Otto?"

Beecker stared at Annie, then looked over the other three supplicants. When the Russian Bells broke the silence, everyone turned to the open window and listened to the soft peal from Lowell House tower. The last ring faded, and Beecker turned back to the four.

"What do you want from me?"

---

27   Supra 13. Rule 7.

CHAPTER 9

Justice for crimes against humanity must have no limitations.
—Simon Wiesenthal

They hunkered down with Beecker in one of the third-floor study rooms at the Harvard Law School Library. Timothy, John, and Clarissa worked on strategy while Annie took notes. Beecker popped in and out, between classes and consulting commitments, challenging every premise and proposal. He sat at the head of an oak library table.

"Here are the ground rules. I'll give you two days. Nobody comes to my office. I'll meet you here, when I can break away. You will not call me as a witness. I will not see my name mentioned in the press. When the two days are over, you will not contact me again until this whole sordid affair is over. I will give you my thoughts, advice, and counsel, but no one outside of this room can ever know I am associated in any way with this judicial Armageddon. Do you agree?"

"Yes, sir," Madegen said.

"Right. Then let me hear why you think you even have a case."

"We have a video confession," Timothy said. "This is the foundation of our case. There is a lot more back-up evidence, but the video is the primary evidentiary piece. Everything flows from that. You have to see this to understand where we're going with the whole thing."

Timothy turned on his laptop and brought up the Miami Book Fair video for Beecker to see. He showed him the opening, then jumped to the scene where George Bush announced, "I approved techniques, including waterboarding, on three people." Then he killed the video.

"Where did you get that?" Beecker asked. The look on his face was incredulous. "I can't recall when I've seen anyone volunteer a confession so clearly stated and absolute."

"It's a public video. Anyone can see it on C-SPAN.[28] It's there today. You can pull it up from archives. He made the confession in front of hundreds of people in an auditorium. Some of the witnesses' faces are recorded in the video. The crowd cheered him."

"What if it's a lie?" Beecker asked. "What if he's just bragging for his audience? Do you think Cheney would let him go on record for authorizing torture? His staff is trained to make sure that sort of thing doesn't happen. It seems like a gotcha to you people, but you better be careful if you think this is your whole case."

"There's more, there's a lot more," John said. "George Bush wrote a memoir called *Decision Points*.[29] In it, he tells of a request by CIA Director George Tenet for permission to waterboard Khalid Sheikh Mohammed, and Bush gives the go-ahead. Another confession, this time in writing. It's only the tip of the iceberg, Professor."

"You think it's that simple? It's not. They've thrown up a lot of roadblocks in case somebody like you came along and tried to prosecute them. Your first obstacle is going to be the MCA. You have studied the MCA, haven't you?"[30]

They knew to expect this challenge, and John was prepared. "It's an ex-post facto law, wouldn't stand up to casual scrutiny by a traffic court judge, let alone the Supreme Court."

"Article I, section 9—No Bill of Attainder or ex-post facto law shall be passed.[31] Don't these legislators read the basis for all of our laws before they vote on a new one?" Clarissa asked.

"Not everybody has a photographic memory like you, Clarissa."

"What are you talking about?" Annie asked. "What's an MCA, ex-post facto and article one all about? I need to be able to explain this stuff to the public in language we non-attorneys can understand."

"Sorry Annie," Clarissa said. "I know we get carried away with the jargon. MCA stands for the Military Commissions Act of 2006, which the Bush Administration pushed through Congress in an attempt to deprive

---

28   Supra 3. Approximately thirty minutes into video.
29   Supra 2. Page 170
30   Supra 16.
31   The Constitution of the United States of America, Article I, Section 9

prisoners of the right to challenge their detention, but it also included a section to protect Bush Administration officials and their agents from being prosecuted for the mistreatment or torture of prisoners. It was made retroactive to September 11, 2001. That's the ex-post facto part; they made a law that decriminalized actions committed before the law was passed. Ex-post facto laws are expressly prohibited by Article I, Section 9 of our Constitution. Alexander Hamilton called them contrary to the tenor of our Constitution.[32] Thomas Jefferson wrote, "The sentiment of ex-post facto laws is against natural right."[33]

"How can they do that?" Annie asked.

"They can do it until somebody takes it to the Supreme Court, and nobody has done that—yet," Timothy said.

"So now we're going to the Supreme Court, Madegen? Where does this stop?"

"I'm afraid it goes wherever it leads, sir," Timothy said.

It was difficult to discern from the professor's expression, whether he was exasperated by the naiveté of the young attorneys, or exhilarated by the courage they showed in their willingness to challenge a powerful establishment. He got out of his chair and paced the room, eyes on his shoes as he walked the floor. The others sat in silence, waiting like students for the professor to begin a lecture.

"Let's say, for the case of argument, that the MCA does not hold up. There's still the protections of executive privilege and presidential immunity to be considered. Because a President has enormous responsibilities, he's given special privileges that allow him to operate without constantly looking over his shoulder."

"Not in the Constitution, sir," Clarissa said.

"There are cases where the Supreme Court has granted the president executive privilege to hold back information, and immunity from prosecution in civil cases, but there is no precedent that immunizes a sitting president or an ex-president from criminal prosecution," John said.[34]

---

32   Federalist Papers number 78, Alexander Hamilton

33   Thomas Jefferson 1813 letter to Isaac McPherson.

34   U.S. Supreme Court, NIXON v. FITZGERALD, 457 U.S. 731 (1982). In a 5-4 decision, the Supreme Court ruled that the President is entitled to absolute immunity from liability for civil damages based on his official acts. The court emphasized that the President is not immune from criminal charges stemming from his official (or unofficial) acts while in office. See opinion by Justice White et al. http://caselaw.lp.findlaw.com/scripts/getcase.pl?court=us&vol=457&invol=731

"This discussion is moot anyway because every grant of presidential immunity has always been based on the office, the presidency, and we're not talking about a sitting president here."

"But," Beecker responded, "there are international laws to which the U.S. is a signer that grant immunity to heads of state for any act they perform while in office."

"Those laws are to protect the sovereignty of nations, and even then, all nations that signed on to the UN Convention Against Torture have waived immunity in the case of the crime of torture, and the U.S. is a signer on that one, too." Timothy said. "There is no protection in international law for a torturer. It's been shown over and over again."

"Well, well. You have done some of your homework. Here's your assignment for tomorrow. I want a complete history of cases involving presidential immunity, a list of all heads of state who have been prosecuted for torture, a summary of all national and international laws addressing the issue of torture, analysis of any U.S. prosecutions of U.S. citizens for acts of torture, and your short list of potential co-conspirators. The library closes at midnight; you have ten minutes to collect this paper mess and get out of here. Do not cause a disturbance. I will see you back here at nine a.m. tomorrow. Don't be late."

Beecker left the room, and the obedient foursome followed his instructions.

Chapter 10

No man is above the law and no man is below it:
nor do we ask any man's permission when we ask him to obey it.
—Theodore Roosevelt

They booked a room at the Charles Hotel. Four laptops connected to the Wi-Fi, and each took-on one of Beecker's assignments. The arrival of room service with black coffee and sandwiches caused a short interruption in the clicking keys and flashing computer screens. At five in the morning, the caffeine wore off, and they agreed to break until seven.

When the wake-up call came, the team went back to work after quick showers. They huddled over their results at eight and agreed they were prepared to meet Beecker at nine.

Otto Beecker arrived at the library at nine-thirty and found the team gathered around the study table drinking strong coffee and trying to hide their anger at his lack of punctuality. Beecker held a printout in his hand, took his seat, and set it on the table in front of him. He looked around the table, smiled at the group, pulled out a pen, and began drawing lines across the page.

Timothy said, "Professor Beecker, we have—"

"Hold it Madegen," Beecker said without looking up. He set his left elbow on the corner of the page to steady it and held up his left hand, palm out toward Timothy. He kept scratching lines across the page with his right. When he got to the bottom of the page, he handed it to Timothy.

"You're going to need one of these attorneys, Madegen. That's a list of my students who graduated twenty years ago. They're all seasoned. I crossed off the ones you shouldn't bother with. They're either not good

enough or don't have the balls. The three men left on there are the best
of the bunch. They're experienced and smart. If you can get them to do
it, any one of them would do a good job of prosecuting the case. They're
practicing attorneys, and they'll be easy to contact. Do not use my name."
Beecker got up from the table, walked to the door, and started to leave.

"Aren't you going to look at the research we did last night?" John
asked. "We have it here." And he waved a sheaf of papers.

Beecker re-closed the door but kept his hand on the knob.

"What for? I told you, once you leave here, I'm done with this. I'm
sure you did what I told you, and now you have the basic research done
to prepare your case. I want you to get out of Cambridge this morning.
Don't tell anyone you were here, and above all, do not mention my name
in connection with anything. Goodbye and good luck."

He went through the door and started to close it but re-opened it.

"And, Annie, you better start spinning things real fast, because the
morning papers are already questioning Madegen's where-a-bouts and
speculating on whether Bush is immune from prosecution because of his
position and the MCA."

Beecker closed the door and was gone.

John broke the stunned silence in the room, "I think that went well."

"OK, we shouldn't have expected much more from Beecker, but he
did force us to lay some ground work," Timothy said. "And the work we
did last night has given me a whole new perspective on our approach. He's
right about the video. It's not enough, and we need to get some experience
on the team. I'll start making the calls right away.

"Annie, get to work on a press release. We'll need to get something
out tonight for tomorrow's news cycle. We're going to have to use the
press to educate the public on the issue of immunity. You can use
the Marcos example.[35] Give the article one of those side boxes with

---

35   Beginning in March 1986, civil lawsuits were filed in US courts alleging that
      Philippino opposition activists were the victims of water torture by the Marcos
      Dictatorship. In 1996 the US Court of Appeals for the Ninth Circuit found the
      Marcos Estate guilty of human rights violations, including the use of the "water
      cure." United States Court of Appeals Ninth Circuit. Maximo HILAO, Class
      Plaintiffs, Plaintiff-Appellee, v. ESTATE OF Ferdinand MARCOS, Defendant,
      Imelda R. Marcos; Ferdinand R. Marcos, Representatives of the Estate of Ferdinand
      Marcos, Defendants-Appellants. Nos. 95-16487, 95-16145. Decided: December
      17, 1996
      http://caselaw.findlaw.com/us-9th-circuit/1279729.html#sthash.Cn4lJfCJ.dpuf

definitions for jus cogens and non-derogable.[36,37] Make it clear, simple, and understandable to any reader with a high school education. We have to get the public on our side. You'll be writing a series. Write it so they'll want to follow you. We'll proof the legal stuff before it goes. You can't get any credit for this, Annie; you're on the team. Give it to your contact and let him have the byline. See if he can get it syndicated. We want it in every newspaper in the country.

"John and Clarissa, go down the list of co-conspirators and make a suggestion on charges for each one. Then start working on the presentations for the grand jury. Let's pack up and get back to Washington before they notice we've been gone," Timothy said.

---

36 Jus cogens is Latin for "compelling law"; a fundamental principle of international law that is accepted by the international community of states as a norm from which no derogation is permitted.

37 Non-derogable: Certain human rights have been considered so important that they cannot be limited or suspended under any circumstance. The right to be free from torture is non-derogable in international law.

CHAPTER 11

Timothy gave Annie the job of finding four thousand square feet of furnished office space for the prosecution team. She located a suite of offices in a building on K Street that had been vacant since the demise of John Kerry's political action committee in 2008. Timothy met her at the street entrance, and they took an elevator up. When the doors slid open on the sixth floor, Annie couldn't contain her excitement. She grabbed his hand and pulled a surprised Timothy to the end of the corridor, where she swung open the door to a large corner office with a wall of windows.

"This will be yours, Tim," she announced as she danced and spun across the empty room. "And I'll have the connecting office right through there."

Timothy stood still at the door, reflecting on the statement the office made about his position. The formality of the space made him realize the enormity of the task he'd taken on. For the first time, he felt the full weight of his burden, and it sobered him. Annie tugged at his sleeve, dragging him over to the floor-to-ceiling windows, where they stood next to each other, looking down at the square below. Annie seemed to sense his mood and tried to lighten the moment. She put her hand on his arm and pointed out the horse-mounted statue of a Union soldier on its granite pedestal in the center of the square below.

"I looked him up. It's Major General James B. McPherson, a civil war soldier. He was a great strategist. He'll be an inspiration to you," Annie said.

Timothy thought of his soldier father. So dedicated. So courageous. "Thank you, Annie." He looked around the room and smiled at her. "It's perfect." Then he turned back to the window. "And the General will remind me of all the men and women who have gone before, fighting for human rights. That man fought for an end to slavery, others for the dignity of all human beings. Now it's our turn."

He put his arm around Annie and pulled her to him, before he realized what he was doing, then backed away.

"So sorry, Annie."

She saw the glint in his eye. She brushed his arm and took a step back.

"So, General Madegen, do you have any orders for the day?" she asked, standing at attention, shoulders back.

Her presence fortified him, and he responded, "Yes, Lieutenant, order the troops to assemble and report for duty."

* * *

Timothy went straight to the task of recruiting an experienced prosecutor from Beecker's short list. He had no doubt he needed experienced help. His first call went to the office of Robert Carpenter. He listened politely to excuses ranging from an exorbitant mortgage, to the high cost of malpractice insurance, and a high-maintenance wife. Robert wished him well, but the risk of alienating important clients was too high.

Brian Duran's wife answered his home phone and informed Timothy that Brian had passed away over a year ago. She kept him on the phone in tears over her loss and the irony of his heart rupture during the early morning workout he hadn't missed in twenty years.

The last candidate was Jacob Radovich. Timothy called his Baltimore office. A secretary put him right through.

"Yeah, who's callin'?"

"Mr. Radovich, I'm Timothy Madegen. I'm—"

"Yeah, I know who you are; you're all over the papers. What d'ya want?"

"I'm calling to see if you might be willing to work with me on the prosecution team."

"Lookin' for somebody who knows what they're doin', eh, kid?"

"I am hoping to find an experienced prosecutor to—"

"Who else you askin'?"

"Well, Robert Carpenter was too busy, and I was going to ask Brian Duran but—"

"Did Beecker put you up to this? How's Ol' Otto doin'?"

"Could we talk about the case, sir?"

"Sure. You got a tiger by the tail there, son. I'll talk to you, but it's got to be face-to-face. You willin' to come up to Baltimore?"

"Yes, sir, as soon as possible."

"Meet me tomorrow at the Patterson Park Boat Lake. There's a bench at the north end of the lake. Make it around eight in the morning."

Two hours on the bus from D.C. to Baltimore gave Timothy time to wonder about Jacob Radovich. His brusque tone on the phone surfaced some of Timothy's suppressed insecurities. What if everyone was right about the futility of fighting the Washington establishment? Could he be fooling himself, ignoring the obvious? Was Radovich going to wring him out with a hard logic twist and hang him up like a limp rag? The phone introduction had been terse, but he *had* agreed to meet, and Otto Beecker *had* recommended him.

He watched out the window at the start-stop rhythm of a long column of cars and trucks creeping along on their morning commute as his bus glided past them in its privileged lane. A poorly-tuned diesel truck ahead of them belched thick, black smoke that leaked an oily odor into the bus. The fumes, combined with the gentle rock of the coach, gave him a mild case of motion sickness. He was relieved to get off when the bus arrived in Baltimore. He took a cab from the bus station.

Timothy found Radovich sitting on a wooden bench as promised. He leaned forward with his elbows on his knees, holding the morning tabloid open in front of him. His black wingtips needed a shine, and he wore a wrinkled flannel suit. A stained fedora shaded his face. He looked way out of place among the carriage-pushing mothers and morning joggers. When Timothy stopped in front of him, he looked up without surprise and offered his hand.

"Right on time, Madegen."

Radovich gave Timothy a genuine smile that deepened the wrinkles in his cheeks.

"Thanks for meeting me so early," Radovich said as he brought his heavy six-foot frame to a standing position. He folded the newspaper and tucked it under his arm.

"It's a beautiful day, let's take a walk."

Timothy felt a reassuring presence in the man. He fell in alongside Radovich on the sidewalk.

"Thank you for seeing me on such short notice, Mr. Radovich."

"You can call me, Jacob."

"And I'm, Timothy."

"Alright, Madegen, so tell me. What d'ya got planned, son? I have ta admit, I'm intrigued, or I wouldn't be wasting my time with you."

Timothy told Radovich about the case he was preparing, including the background research Beecker had forced on them and the list of potential co-conspirators. They walked side-by-side on the path around the lake, past children feeding bread to the ducks under the watchful eyes of their mothers. Radovich listened intently, neither asking questions nor reacting in any way until Timothy finished.

"So we all know the saying about grand juries," Radovich said. "And I think you got more'n a ham sandwich here. I followed the shenanigans that Bush's legal team ran back then—damn embarrassing for the legal profession, damn embarrassing. I knew somebody with balls would come along to challenge them sooner or later, and I commend you for makin' the effort. But are you sure you're up to it?"

Radovich stopped walking and turned to Timothy. He stepped back to let a cyclist pass between them on the sidewalk. "Are you in this for the long haul, kid?" He gave Timothy a hard look. "I mean, are you ready to take the heat when the torches come out? They will, you know. You got a real ally there in Henry Jarvis, and he can take it, but you, and the rest of your team, are gonna have to stand tall when the dirt flies. Do you know what I mean? They'll hit you from all sides at once. You'll think the whole world is out to get you, and it'll be close to the damn truth. You'll be vilified and threatened from every legal angle they can drum up. Maybe even violence. It's gonna be hard, Timothy, real hard."

"It can't be any worse for me than it was for the people they tortured."

Thoughts of Axel Johnson's story about his father came back to him. He remembered the broken man on the basement floor, who couldn't stand to live any longer with his demons. He recalled the words from his dad's letter. He was going all in. He owed him. "I won't let those people down; I can take it; I swear I won't let them down, Jacob."

Radovich considered Timothy, looking in his eyes for evidence of his will. Timothy didn't blink.

Radovich turned away and began walking again. "I might work with you on this, Madegen, but you're gonna need to know some things about me—if I decide to do it. There are some prosecutors who want to win at any cost. That's not me, pal. I won't prosecute a man I know is innocent. You got a list of potential co-conspirators. The important thing there is *potential*. I will not ruin anybody's good name just because I can. There's gotta be some real evidence before I'll be party to an indictment. Do you get me?"

"Yes, sir."

"I want some solid proof that President Bush really did order that torture. See what I mean? It's not so simple."

"I agree, sir. It's my full intention to work within the law on everything we do. You have my word on that."

"That's nice, Madegen, but there's lots of unscrupulous prosecutors who 'work within the law,' but don't mete out justice. They try'n get a conviction anyway they can to build their fancy careers. They exclude evidence, mess with the jury pools, horse-trade with the defense—the list goes on. And I will not be involved in any political vendettas. Now I know you will be accused of that, and as long as it's not true, I'm OK with it. It's got to be about the law, but if it's really about politics, count me out."

"I have no trouble with your moral convictions."

"It's more than that Madegen. If I find anything like that goin' on, I'll turn into a whistleblower. I'll be your worst enemy. Are you getting me?"

Timothy stuck out his hand to Radovich. "I want you on board, Jacob."

"Any money in it?" Radovich asked.

"Not much."

"I figured."

Jacob Radovich took Timothy's hand.

"OK, you're on, boss," he said and flashed a broad grin.

* * *

The offices filled up with assistants, paralegals, phone lines, and computer equipment. John, Clarissa, and Jacob took spaces next to the conference room at the other end of the hall, down from Timothy and Annie. The once quiet offices came to life. The K Street address became a target for the news media, and a security firm was employed to limit access. Timothy bristled at the need to walk through a metal detector at the entrance to the building, but the head of security convinced him it was necessary, and he acquiesced. Humorless plain-clothed agents in black suits, wired with ear pieces, checked people in at the door, and walked the perimeter of the building.

Annie worked on a series of background articles describing the operation of a generic grand jury and explaining legal constructs that the team felt the public needed to understand if they were to gain their support. Her reporter contact got the series syndicated, and a web-tech put the documents up on a website.

John walked into Timothy's office and closed the door.

"Hey, Timothy, you gotta listen to this; you're a big topic on talk radio."

He switched on a portable radio, and the talk show host ranted, "—here's how you got to look at this stuff. What if a terrorist had a member of your family, your mother or sister or brother, and they were going to chop off their head? Now if you had a prisoner who knew where this guy was, wouldn't you want the government to use any and all techniques they could to make him talk? Those enhanced interrogation techniques worked. You can read about it in the *Washington Post*. That's why Abu Zubaydah started squealing like a stuck pig when they waterboarded him. Timothy Madegen is on a rant to pacify a bunch of misinformed, oversensitive, crybaby, bleeding heart liberals who can't stand the thought of anyone having to endure a little 'dunk in the water and—'"

"Turn that thing off, John." He sat back in his chair with a smile on his face. "Guess there are some minds we can't change and shouldn't try to."

"Just so you know," John said as he left the office.

Annie waged the battle for public opinion on radio, TV, and in print. She complained to one TV network that showed continuous reruns of a popular thriller series that portrayed torture as normal, effective, and glamorous. She gave moral support to an independent group who organized an Internet campaign to petition sponsors to withdraw their support from the show. Newspaper opinion pieces disparaged Annie's series of articles as an elite liberal attempt to show off using Latin language and arcane legal concepts that nobody cared about. Talk radio hosts couldn't stop themselves from running the ticking time-bomb scenario over and over.

The ultimate justification for torture was given as "the proof is in the pudding"—no more airplanes flying into New York skyscrapers.

All of the television networks and cable media outlets made requests for Timothy to appear, but no matter how hard she tried, Annie could not get Timothy to go.

"It's not the right time, Annie. I'll do it, but not until it's the right time." Timothy didn't feel shy about it. That wasn't it. He felt that as the leader of the prosecution effort, it was best for him to hold his cards close until the exact right time when he could get maximum benefit from playing his trump.

When pressure from the media grew too great to ignore, Timothy decided that Radovich should do it. Jacob didn't relish the notoriety of the task, but he did enjoy banter with the press and the media. One of his appearances on a Sunday morning talk show gave the press lots of material for the following Monday's editions.

"Jacob Radovich, you have accepted the assignment of principal prosecutor for the grand jury investigating alleged torture. Can you give us a basic understanding of the government's inquiry?" moderator William Davis asked.

"No. You guys know that all grand jury proceedings are secret. The only reason you know the subject is 'cause somebody leaked it, which we are investigating."

"Can you tell us who's being investigated?"

"No. That's secret too."

"OK, well let's talk about the special prosecutor, Timothy Madegen. This is an attorney just one year out of Harvard Law School. Some say he's much too inexperienced to be taking on such a controversial issue involving high-level elected officials."

"You said that about high-level officials, not me. Look, Bill, it's been years since the Abu Ghraib pictures came out, and the secret CIA sites were exposed to the citizens of this country. Out of a population of three hundred million, there's only one guy in the whole country with the guts to stand up and say this is wrong. That's Timothy Madegen. You want to question his experience? Why don't you question the experience of all the federal prosecutors who hid their collective heads in the sand for ten years and pretended it didn't happen? Pretended nobody is to blame. Why don't you ask the members of the Senate subcommittee on human rights about their qualifications for the job they're supposed to be doing? Interview the Attorney General and ask him if he's qualified to prosecute the crime of torture. Let's ask the House majority leader why he hasn't tasked the House subcommittee on crime to investigate who's to blame? And when ya ask 'em, and they give you their usual evasive non-answers, or bullshit committee reports, or self-serving excuses, remember it's Timothy Madegen who has the education, the will, and the character to face up to a tough question that nobody else wants to touch. You people need to stop picking at trifles and start looking at the whole picture. Timothy Madegen is the right man for the job, the only man willing to take it on. Stop all the second-guessing and get ready to support the man."

"So you think he can do it? Does he really have the courage?" Davis asked.

The red began to rise in Radovich's face. "What? OK, let's talk about courage. Where was your courage, William Davis, when the Bush administration was lying to the American people about weapons of mass destruction and Saddam Hussein's non-existent links to Al Qaeda? Where were you when President Bush sent the U.S. Army and Air Force to destroy Iraq for having WMDs, but no WMDs were found and he went around joking about it and got re-elected? What have you done about the dozens of innocent people sitting in limbo for years in Guantanamo Bay? You question Madegen's courage and ability? You, sir, are not qualified to ask that question."

"Uh…thank you, Jacob. We'll be right back with more from Jacob Radovich," William Davis said.

The papers had a hey-day over Bill Davis's predicament, but requests for interviews with Radovich came to an abrupt end.

CHAPTER 12

The team held seven a.m. status meetings, six days a week. The office was closed, locked, and secured on Sunday.

Timothy was enjoying coffee on a quiet Sunday morning with the *Times* open on the kitchen table in John's apartment when William Mayfield rang the bell. Timothy buzzed him up. Mayfield started as soon as Timothy opened the door.

"Where's Johnny? What are you doing here? I knew it! I knew he was involved with you," Mayfield said and rushed into the living room scanning for his son.

John appeared from the hall, "Hi Dad, what a surprise!" His smile was hopeful.

"What the hell do you think you're doing, John? Why don't you answer my calls? Senator Brandt told me you quit on him. He probably would have fired you anyway, when he found out you're involved in this bullshit. Do you know how many favors I called in to get you that job?"

John's smile was gone. "I know, Dad, but—"

"No, you don't know," Mayfield said. "You don't know jack. I want you out of this. Madegen's crazy, and you're going to forget it and go back to Brandt and beg for your—"

"Wait a minute, Dad, you don't understand—"

"Oh, no! I understand completely." Mayfield's baritone grew in volume. "I understand that the pressure I'm getting from congressmen, bankers, and the god damn Governor is all because my son, and his friends, are creating a national crisis, and I want it to stop."

Timothy backed away from the father and his son without any attempt to referee the confrontation. He sensed his participation would add fuel to a well-lit conflagration.

John came close to his father and spoke to him face-to-face. "I'm sorry, Dad, we can't stop. The torture has to stop. This is not about the usual Washington influence peddling or dirty campaign tricks—it's not about money or power. This is about torture, a crime against humanity. This is the most important work I can do. I won't stop because it makes you and your friends uncomfortable. I won't stop until this is finished, and we can be sure it never happens again."

"I don't give a damn about a bunch of terrorists getting the treatment. This is America; we don't go after our ex-presidents like this. You're making a mess of this country, and I want it stopped."

"Forget it, Dad. This is important—somebody's got to do it. I'm sorry it's causing you trouble, but we're going ahead with it. You know torture is wrong, and nobody else is willing to make the call. It's been ten years. The justice system we studied in school is broken. We want it fixed, and it won't be fixed until this torture issue is resolved, and the guilty are punished. Putting a few scapegoats in jail is not enough.[38] Prosecuting the people who blew the whistle is a cover up and a scare tactic.[39] You can't come in here and tell me to stop what we're doing because you don't like it."

"Johnny, you have to understand the spot I'm in. I didn't rise to the top on my exceptional brain. Nobody does. I owe a lot of people, a lot of favors, and they're calling them in. I can't ignore these people, John. They expect me to have some influence over my own son. I'm in the game, whether I like it or not, and I'm going to have to play."

---

38   Wikipedia "Abu Ghraib torture and prisoner abuse" subparagraph "Repercussions." https://en.wikipedia.org/wiki/Abu_Ghraib_torture_and_prisoner_abuse#Repercussions

39   Former Central Intelligence Agency officer John Kiriakou sentenced to 30 years for revealing CIA torture program. http://www.democracynow.org/2013/1/30/ex_cia_agent_whistleblower_john_kiriakou

"You can join our team, Dad, but there is no way I'm joining yours."

"Then I'll fight you anyway I can. And I have a lot of powerful people who'll help me. You're sticking your nose where it doesn't belong, Son. This isn't over. Don't say I didn't warn you."

"Thanks for the heads-up, Dad. I've seen you in action. I know what to expect."

Mayfield turned from his son, glared at Madegen, and pointed his finger at him. He turned back to John. "He's in for it too, all of you are. Henry and Isabel too." He turned and left. The slam of the door echoed for a moment in an otherwise silent room.

"Guess you knew that was coming," Timothy said.

"Yeah, I've been putting it off. Glad it's over." John's shoulders slumped, and he fell into the couch.

"What do you think he'll do?" Timothy asked.

"There's not much he can do. You're too well-known for him to get physical with you. He'll probably get pushy with Uncle Henry and Aunt Isabel, but that won't get him too far either. I kinda feel sorry for him, because this really will hurt him—I mean status and influence-wise—but there's nothing I can do about that. I had an unrealistic hope he might understand. It was a small hope."

"Thanks for standing up for me, John."

"And you're a big pain in the ass, Tim." John gave Timothy a wry smile. "Hey, it's Sunday. Let's get some beers and watch the game. Tomorrow's gonna be real interesting."

CHAPTER 13

Torture usually gets you whatever you want to hear. And people are usually much more forgiving of this method. Mostly because they're never quite sure any of it really happened.
—Robert Jackson Bennett, *City of Stairs*

Timothy assigned a jury selection specialist to summon two hundred District of Columbia citizens to report for their civic duty. After wading through stacks of juror questionnaires and holding one-on-one interviews, the specialist submitted the names of twenty-three qualified grand jurors and six alternates. Timothy approved them without comment, recalling Jacob's admonition about jury manipulation. He didn't want to be accused of stacking the deck. Timothy signed the summonses and had them issued.

Two weeks later, the chosen jurors assembled in a small oak-paneled courtroom at the Moultrie Courthouse. Timothy, Clarissa, John, and Jacob sat at the prosecutor's table in front of the jury box. The jurors were arrayed in four rows behind a low railing. Timothy looked them over, curious about their motivations. Some looked anxious. Others seemed shy in their unusual surroundings. He thought to himself how important these people were to his pursuit of justice. Would they be open to the evidence he presented or work against him? His critics were right in one respect—he wished he had more experience. He realized how lucky he was to have Jacob on the team.

When black-robed Judge Jarvis entered the room, the clerk

announced him. "All rise, the Special Grand Jury for the U.S. District Court, District of Columbia is now in session, Judge Henry A. Jarvis, presiding."

The judge took his place on the bench. The seal of the U.S. District Court filled the wall behind him. The Stars and Stripes, and the District of Columbia flag flanked the seal on either side.

"Good morning, ladies and gentlemen," Jarvis said. "Please be seated. We are calling to order the Special Grand Jury. Are the attorneys ready?"

"Ready, Your Honor," Madegen said a little too loudly, revealing how he felt about the start of proceedings.

"The clerk will swear in the jury," Jarvis said.

"The jurors will please stand and raise their right hand," the clerk instructed. "Do each of you swear that you will fairly consider the evidence before this court and that you will return a fair decision according to the evidence and the instructions of the court, so help you, God? Please say I do."

The jurors responded in unison, "I do."

"You may be seated."

When the jurors were settled, the judge began his instruction. "The Court has selected you to perform this important duty and essential public service. A grand jury is selected and organized to inquire into the commission of crimes within its jurisdiction, determine the likelihood of guilt, and find indictments against supposed offenders. The grand jury is also a way to protect citizens against unfounded prosecution."

Jarvis smiled and spoke in a slow and easy rhythm to release some of the tension he saw in the anxious eyes of the inexperienced jurors.

"As members of the grand jury, you have a duty to bring attention to violations of law you may know of or discover. Grand juries have broad investigative powers, use them."

Jarvis asked for a volunteer juror to act as foreperson. A middle-aged man with a full salt-and-pepper beard offered his service, and a petite gray-haired woman stood up.

"What is your background, sir?"

"Retired Navy, Your Honor. Twenty years of service on land and sea. Chief Petty Officer for the last three years."

"Do you think you can handle twenty-two undisciplined civilians, Chief?" the judge asked with a smile.

"I'm a civilian now, sir. No problem."

"What's your name, Chief?"

"Robert Levy, Your Honor, but they call me Scooter."

"Thank you, Scooter."

Jarvis turned to the woman.

"Good morning to you, mam. May I ask your name?"

"You may, Judge. I'm Louise Allen. I haven't commanded any sailors or ships, but I raised six children and managed to stay married to the same man for thirty-five years. I know a thing or two about working with people and negotiating tough issues."

"You may be more qualified than Scooter, Mrs. Allen. Do any of the other jurors want to offer their service or have an objection to either of these candidates?"

No one spoke up.

"In that case, I appoint Robert Levy as foreman and Louise Allen as deputy foreperson. You will be given instruction about your duties by the prosecuting attorney, Timothy Madegen, and his staff."

Then the judge began his charge to the jurors. "Ladies and gentlemen: You are now a sworn grand jury with all of the duties and privileges given you by law. I want to take a few minutes to give you specific instruction which you must follow in your deliberations.

"You are being asked to consider the facts as they pertain to two questions and only these two questions. First, does the act of waterboarding a human being constitute the crime of torture under United States Code, Title 18, Crimes and Criminal Procedure? Second, if you find that waterboarding is torture, is there probable cause to indict former President George W. Bush for committing that crime by authorizing or directing agents under his control to waterboard certain individuals?"

Robert Levy jumped up from his seat. "Your Honor, I didn't sign up for this. You want us to investigate a President of the United States. I can't do that."

"You are sworn in, Scooter, and you will be held in contempt of this court if you fail to do your duty."

"But who are we to second-guess a president?" Robert turned to the jury, looking for support. "He served this country for eight years; he deserves our respect. He doesn't deserve to be attacked for making tough decisions."

"He's a man, just like you and me, Scooter," Jarvis said. "We are all subject to the same laws no matter who we are. The prosecutor will present you with the evidence he has assembled. It will be your job to determine if a crime has been committed and if there is probable cause to accuse the subject of committing it. Do your duty, sir."

"I'm a patriotic American. President Bush was my Commander-in-Chief. There is no way he should be charged with a crime. He was a good President, and he should be respected."

"No one is above the law, Scooter. Do your duty, or I will hold you in contempt."

Levy considered the judge, then pointed toward the attorneys at their table on the side of the room. "Those guys are going to have a tough time convincing me to hand you an indictment," he said glaring at the judge.

"That's their job. You'll be an excellent counterpoint to the prosecutors."

The judge returned to his instructions. "You should all be skeptical like Robert. Listen to the evidence, decide on the facts, then look carefully at the law, and make your decision on that basis. We will not meet again until you have completed your work."

The judge left the bench, and the jurors filed out. They were bused a few blocks away to the location of the grand jury room in the United States Attorney Office building on 4th Street.

Louise Allen took a stream of questions from the other jurors. She handled the inquiries with an authoritative demeanor that irked Robert Levy, who seemed less accessible to the other jurors, especially the women. It was an all-ages array of people; most of them were well dressed and business-like, showing a visible concern for their unfamiliar surroundings.

The jurors were directed to a private stairwell which took them to a third-floor meeting room that would be the home of the grand jury for the tenure of their duty. The windowless room was spare. Painted cinderblock walls gave the room a prison-like feel. Bare-bulb fluorescent fixtures in the ceiling didn't soften the atmosphere. The room was cold, but it warmed slowly as it filled up. Jurors took places in pew-like rows facing the prosecutor's table. Robert Levy and Louise Allen sat side-by-side at a small table at the front of the room facing the jurors.

Clarissa welcomed them with administrative instructions and an outline of the process for the rest of the week. She handed out a twenty-page document of instruction.[40]

---

40   Handbook for Federal Grand Jurors. Published by the Administrative Office of the United States Courts, Washington, D.C.
http://www.ndd.uscourts.gov/jury/jury_handbook_grand_jurors.pdf

After answering some housekeeping questions, she told the jurors to study the written material and dismissed them until 8:00 a.m. the next day, when the prosecutors would begin presenting evidence.

* * *

"Ladies and gentlemen, this is attorney, Jacob Radovich," Madegen said the next morning. He stood before the jury with Jacob at his side. "He will be presenting evidence that we believe will convince you that the interrogation technique known as waterboarding, used by the CIA during the years 2001 to 2005, is torture, without a doubt."

Madegen took his seat as Jacob began.

Radovich presented himself in the same wrinkled suit he wore the day Timothy met him in the park. "You can stop me anytime you want to ask a question. I want us to be informal, and I want all of you to understand the information I'm giving you. So if you don't get it—ask. I like questions. I'm gonna give you details on the waterboarding used by the CIA. The descriptions come from government documents which are now public. None of this stuff is classified. The documents I refer to are available to all of you in a packet we have prepared.

"First, what is waterboarding? It's not a pretty picture. Think of it like this. The prisoner is naked, strapped to a plank, and immobilized. He's completely under the control of his captors. Put yourself there if you can. Three or four big guys have you tied down naked on a plank. The description I'm going to give you is gleaned from hundreds of pages of CIA documents, Department of Justice memos, and a report by the International Red Cross."[41]

Radovich opened a file folder, looked at the jury to assure himself he had their attention. "I'm going to read you some excerpts from a memo by a senior Justice Department attorney to a CIA attorney. It describes the basic waterboarding technique."

He began to read. "'In this technique, the detainee is lying on a gurney that is inclined at an angle of 10 to 15 degrees to the horizontal, with detainee on his back and his head toward the lower end of the gurney. A cloth is placed over the detainee's face, and cold water is poured on the cloth from a height of approximately 6 to 18 inches. The wet cloth creates

---

41   Mark Benjamin, Water boarding for Dummies, Salon, March 9, 2010, http://www.salon.com/2010/03/09/waterboarding_for_dummies/

a barrier through which it is difficult—or in some cases not possible—to breathe."[42]

Radovich looked up from his reading. "It's getting' hot in here," he said, then took off his jacket, and hung it on the back of a chair. "I'll continue reading from the same memo.

"'…We understand that if the detainee makes an effort to defeat the technique (e.g. by twisting his head to the side and breathing out of the comer of his mouth); the interrogator may cup his hands around the detainee's nose and mouth to dam the runoff, in which case, it would not be possible for the detainee to breathe during the application of the water. In addition, you have informed us that the technique may be applied in a manner to defeat efforts by the detainee to hold his breath by, for example, beginning an application of water as the detainee is exhaling.

"'During the use of the waterboard, a physician and a psychologist are present at all times. The detainee is monitored to ensure that he does not develop respiratory distress. If the detainee is not breathing freely after the cloth is removed from his face, he is immediately moved to a vertical position in order to clear the water from his mouth, nose, and nasopharynx.'"[43]

Jacob glanced up at the jury. "I had to look it up. The nasopharynx connects the back of your nose to the back of your mouth," he said and went on reading.

"'The gurney used for administering this technique is specially designed so that it can be accomplished very quickly if necessary. Your medical personnel have explained that the use of the waterboard does pose a small risk of certain potentially significant medical problems and that certain measures are taken to avoid or address such problems. First, a detainee might vomit and then aspirate the emesis.'"[44]

Radovich wrinkled his nose when he said, "That's breathe in his puke in case you were wondering." Then he continued reading. "'To reduce this risk, any detainee on whom this technique will be used is first placed on a liquid diet. Second, the detainee might aspirate some of the water, and the resulting water in the lungs might lead to pneumonia. To

---

42   Steven G. Bradley, Principal Deputy Assistant Attorney General, Memorandum for
     John Rizzo, Senior Deputy General Counsel, Central Intelligence Agency, May 10,
     2005. Item 13, page 15.
     http://www1.umn.edu/humanrts/OathBetrayed/olc_Bradbury051005.pdf
43   Ibid
44   Ibid

mitigate this risk, a potable saline solution is used in the procedure. Third, it is conceivable (though, we understand from OMS [Office of Medical Services], highly unlikely) that a detainee could suffer spasm of the larynx that would prevent him from breathing even when the application of water is stopped and the detainee is returned to an upright position. In the event of such spasms, a qualified physician would immediately intervene to address the problem, and, if necessary, the intervening physician would perform a tracheotomy.'"[45]

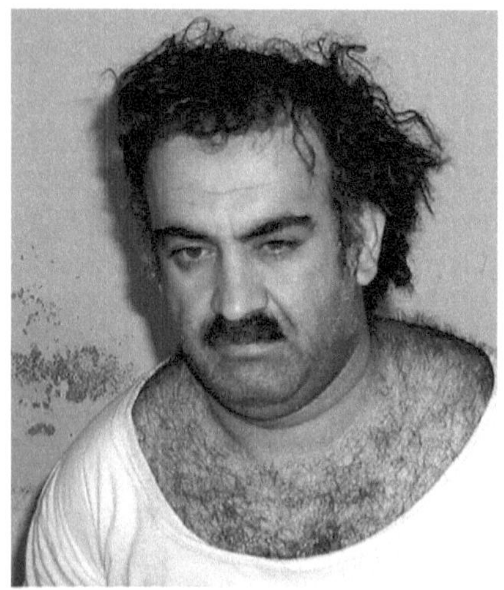

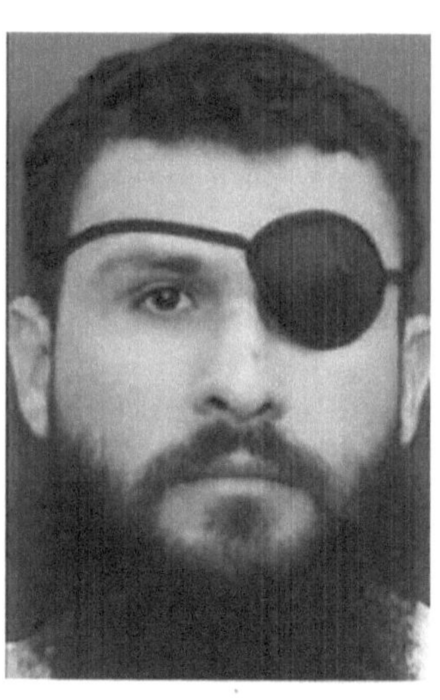

Khalid Sheikh Mohammed

Abu Zubaydah

"Oh, my God!" a woman uttered, then looked down, embarrassed by her outburst. Jacob looked up from his reading at the sound. All of the jurors appeared stunned. It was easy to see they didn't want to hear any more, but there was more. Jacob read from a CIA Office of Medical Services report.[46]

"'An "application" during a waterboard session is the time period in which water is poured on the cloth being held on the subject's face. Under

---

45   Ibid

46   OMS, Guidelines On Medical And Psychological Support To Detainee Rendition, Interrogation And Detention. CIA Office of Medical Services, December 2004. Page 19.
https://www.thetorturedatabase.org/document/cia-memo-oms-guidelines-medical-and-psychological-support-detainee-rendition-interrogation?search_url=search/apachesolr_search/rendition then download pdf

the D.C.I. [Director of Central Intelligence] interrogation guidelines, the time of total contact of water with the face will not exceed 40 seconds. The vast majority of applications are less than 40 seconds, many fewer than 10 seconds. Individual applications lasting 10 seconds or longer will be limited to no more than six applications during any one waterboard session. The Agency will limit the aggregate of applications to no more than 12 minutes in any one 24-hour period.[47]

"'In our limited experience, extensive sustained use of the waterboard can introduce new risks. Most seriously, for reasons of physical fatigue or psychological resignation, the subject may simply give up, allowing excessive filling of the airways and unconsciousness. An unresponsive subject should be righted immediately, and the interrogator should deliver a sub-xyphoid thrust to expel the water. If this fails to restore normal breathing, aggressive medical intervention is required.'"[48]

Jacob looked over the jury for an indication that they understood. He turned to the foreman.

"Robert, does your wristwatch have a second hand?"

"Yes, sir."

"Let's try a little experiment. I'd like everyone on the jury to take three deep breaths and then expel that last one completely and hold that. Robert will count off forty seconds to see how that feels."

The jury members did as directed. The first juror gasped for a breath after twenty seconds; by the thirty-second mark, they were all breathing heavily.

"Now think of what it might be like if you went to take that first breath but got a nose full of water instead of air, and after that, you tried to draw breath through a wet rag. The water pour might be only for forty seconds, but that wet cloth could be on the prisoner's face for minutes," Jacob told them.

"But they deserved it, they're terrorists," a woman in the second row shouted, still out of breath.

"Are they?" Jacob asked. "We'll talk about that later."

"How do we know what you're telling us is true?" asked a man in the front row.

"I'll give you the government's documents I read from. Every fact I read is drawn directly from those reports. Why would they want to put

---

47   Ibid

48   Ibid page 18

this stuff in writing, if they weren't doin' it?" Jacob asked.

"Is that all, Mr. Radovich?" asked Louise Allen. It was clear she wanted him to finish.

"Not quite," said Jacob. "There are other Enhanced Interrogation Techniques that were authorized to be used on the detainee before, after, and between waterboard sessions including keeping them awake for seven days straight by shackling them in a standing position with their hands tied to a bolt in the ceiling, slamming them into a wall using a collar around their neck, cramming the detainee into a small box, dousing them with cold water, slapping their face and body." [49,50]

Radovich paused to let the gasps and groans from the jury subside.

"So ladies and gentlemen, that completes my tutorial on what the Bush administration called enhanced interrogation techniques which they authorized the CIA to use on suspected terrorist subjects. Next, we will take a look at U.S. laws and accepted legal definitions of torture. If you're not sure the waterboarding that President Bush authorized is torture, you'll have a chance to consider it, in more legal detail, in our next session. Any questions?"

The jurors sat perfectly still, staring at Radovich. There wasn't a sound in the room except for his voice.

"Oh, by the way, that waterboarding technique I described—it was applied 183 times to prisoner Khalid Sheikh Mohammed and 83 times to detainee Abu Zubaydah." [51]

---

49   Memorandum for John A. Rizzo, Senior Deputy General Counsel, Central Intelligence Agency, from Steven G. Bradbury, Principal Deputy Assistant Attorney General, Office of Legal Counsel, Re: Application of 18 U.S.C. §§ 2340–2340A to the Combined Use of Certain Techniques in the Interrogation of High Value al Qaeda Detainees (May 10, 2005)
http://www.derechos.org/nizkor/excep/combined.pdf

50   Memorandum for John A. Rizzo, Senior Deputy General Counsel, Central Intelligence Agency from Steven G. Bradbury, Principal Deputy Assistant Attorney General, Department of Justice, Office of Legal Counsel Re: Application of United States Obligations Under Article 16 of the Convention Against Torture to Certain Techniques that May Be Used in the Interrogation of High Value al Qaeda Detainees (May 30, 20005)
http://www.justice.gov/sites/default/files/olc/legacy/2013/10/21/memo-bradbury2005.pdf

51   Central Intelligence Agency, Inspector General, SPECIAL REVIEW. COUNTERTERRORISM DETENTION AND INTERROGATION ACTIVITIES (SEPTEMBER 2001- OCTOBER2003) (2003-7123-1G)
https://www.thetorturedatabase.org/files/foia_subsite/pdfs/CIA000349.pdf

Radovich looked at each of the jurors. He made eye contact where he could, bouncing from one person to another as he spoke the words.

"One—hundred—eighty—three—times."

The room was quiet.

"Think about it."

CHAPTER 14

*Is it only in the army in the Philippines that Americans sometimes
commit deeds that cause all other Americans to regret?*
—Theodore Roosevelt, 1901, Relating reports of water torture in the
Philippines to lynching in the south.

Julie Branson was the only passenger on a Learjet that climbed out from Dulles for the short hop to LaGuardia. A uniformed limo driver greeted her on the ramp and took her bags. He delivered her to a luxurious Manhattan hotel. An hour later, the limo reappeared to take her to meet her dinner companion. When the maître d' escorted her to William Mayfield's table at the Russian Tea Room, his dazzled dinner guest was pleased to meet him.

"Thank you, Julie, for making the trip on such short notice," Mayfield waved off the waiter and rose from his chair to seat her at his table. He sized her up: middle age, trim, dark hair, too much make-up, an insincere smile. He was confident he could work with this woman.

"Not at all, Mr. Mayfield. I understand your concern for your son, John. I hope I can help you." There was no mistaking the look in her eye; she was fascinated by the gilded arches, the impressionist oils on the wall behind him, and his fashionable business attire.

"Yes, I am concerned about my son—and my brother—who you work for."

"Judge Jarvis is your brother?"

"Step brother, same mother."

A white coated waiter brought menus and recited the day's entrées.

"Let's order, and we'll talk about my son after dinner," Mayfield said.

He ordered dinner for both of them with Julie's approval. Mayfield made small talk and listened politely to her life story, while black-tie waiters brought dinner in courses. He gave Julie a conspiratorial wink, when their conversation lagged, and they realized they were voyeurs, listening to the young lovers who flirted at the next table. When Mayfield was satisfied that the martinis, food, and elegant wine had prepared the groundwork, he ordered a slice of double chocolate cake. He got to the point, while they shared the dessert.

"Julie, I'm terribly worried about my son, John. He's gotten mixed up in this grand jury thing with that media ham, Timothy Madegen. I'm afraid he's gonna get hurt. Madegen has hypnotized Judge Jarvis too. It's like some kind of con game. They're all taken in."

"I know what you mean, Mr. Mayfield," she paused to take a bite of chocolate and looked up at Mayfield. "I didn't like that Madegen from the first day, when he came to see the judge. I saw through him the minute he walked in the door."

"What happened in that first meeting with Henry?"

"I don't know, but the judge wasn't going to see him, until his wife forced it."

"You see, Julie, Isabel's been taken in too. There's something odd about this guy, and I need to protect my son and my brother. Can you tell me what's going on in that grand jury room?"

"It's secret, Mr. Mayfield. All grand jury proceedings are secret. No one is supposed to know, until there's a decision to indict or not."

"But you know, don't you?"

"I file a copy of the daily transcripts for the judge."

"Do you read them?"

"It's hard not to know some of it, since I have to make sure the copies are full and complete."

"I don't want you to break any trusts, Julie, but can you give me an overall idea of what's happening? How the jury is taking the evidence?" Mayfield refilled her wine glass.

"I guess I won't be breaking any laws, if I tell you that one of the jurors is already firmly against the whole thing."

"Can you get me his name, Julie?"

"All the jurors' names are secret."

"Just between us, Julie. I won't share the information with anyone."

"There's this one guy, he's the foreman, Robert Levy. He told the judge he didn't think they should even be having the grand jury. He says President Bush should be respected for making tough decisions. He's pretty outspoken."

Mayfield dropped his fork. "Anybody else?"

"Louise Allen is the deputy foreperson. I don't know anything about her."

William Mayfield emptied the last drop from the wine bottle into Julie's glass.

"I'm going to need the whole list, Julie. I promise, it's only to protect my son and brother."

"Well, I guess I could—"

"Meet me next week in D.C. I'll call you later with a meeting place. We'll have lunch."

"Try to make it close to the office. I only have an hour."

"That's fine, Julie. Please enjoy the rest of your weekend in New York. Ask Mannie, the concierge at the hotel, to get you good seats at a Broadway show. It's all on me. I'll have my plane and pilot ready to take you back to D.C. whenever you're ready. And Julie, we never met, OK?"

* * *

William Mayfield stopped his sedan in a no-parking space in front of a brick office building at the corner of 4th Street and Atlantic. He waited in the car for three men to pass by on the sidewalk before hurrying into the building where the Smithson Detective Agency had its office. Paul Smithson lifted his three hundred pounds off his chair and came around the desk to meet Mayfield.

"Thank you for coming, Mr. Mayfield," Smithson said and offered his hand.

Mayfield gave him a peremptory handshake. "I have a sensitive job for you, Smithson. I need total privacy on this."

"We are very discrete, sir."

"I want your best people on this." Mayfield looked around the small, shabby office. "You do have other resources, don't you? I need you to investigate the whole team. Starting with Timothy Madegen and going right down the line: Clarissa Morrison, Annie Young, Jacob Radovich, Henry Jarvis, all of them, even Henry's wife Isabel. I want anything you can give me that's in the least bit controversial from their past or present activities."

Mayfield sat in a chair in front of Smithson's desk. Smithson listened to every detail and wrote notes on a yellow legal pad.

"Do you want them followed? We can shadow them for a couple of days and get a pretty good idea of their routines."

"Yes, put an agent on each one of them. I want everything." Mayfield said. "I want their entire histories; make this your company's priority. I need you to put me ahead of all your other clients, and I'll pay for it."

"Yes, sir, Mr. Mayfield."

"Then I want vitae on every one of the twenty-three grand jurors. I'm getting a list for you. Go deep on Robert Levy and Louise Allen. You might have to get your hands dirty, Paul. Do you know what I mean?"

Smithson gave Mayfield a knowing smile. "Yes, we'll need a retainer. We can get started right away."

Mayfield pulled out a checkbook. He looked around the drab office, then at the wear-shiny jacket on Smithson. He scribbled an amount on the check, signed it, and handed it to the detective. Smithson's eyes widened when he read the number.

"We'll be on this immediately, sir. I'll give you a report in twenty-four hours."

"No. This is strictly confidential, Paul. I don't want you to contact me in any way. I'll call you. Understand?"

Smithson looked up from his legal pad and nodded.

"Yes, sir. I get it."

The two men stood up and shook hands across Smithson's desk. William Mayfield moved toward the office door.

"I'll call you in a couple of days," he said, turned, and left.

Chapter 15

Anybody with real combat experience understands
that torture is counterproductive.
—Andy Messing, Retired Major,
U.S. Special Forces and Director of the National Defense Council

Timothy Madegen called the grand jury to order. "The prosecution is responsible for presenting the jury with both evidence and applicable law. Today we'll look at the law governing torture, including national laws of the United States and International Laws the U.S. has committed to upholding. We'll offer legal definitions of torture for you to compare with what you heard last time about the technique of waterboarding."

He turned to Clarissa Morrison and indicated her with his outstretched hand.

"Clarissa is an expert on these laws, and she will be making the presentation to you today."

"Thank you, Mr. Madegen," she said. Timothy returned to a seat at the prosecutor's table, and Clarissa approached the jury. Her navy pants suit and man's tie were a severe statement on the seriousness of the subject she was about to tackle. Shiny, blonde hair falling over her shoulders made a striking contrast.

"Why don't we vote now and get it over with?" a man said, standing in front of his seat in the last row at the back of the jury. "We heard plenty about waterboarding last time. I'm ready to vote."

"What is your name, sir?" Clarissa asked.

"Mairston, Bob Mairston. I'm an Iraq war vet, and I know more about what you people are talking about than anybody in this room." Mairston was a little over five feet tall. His gray hair was buzz-cut, and his body was stocky. He wasn't a midget, but his stature made his head look a little too big for his body. His Lilliputian appearance contrasted with his demanding disposition.

"Mr. Mairston, we haven't presented all the evidence yet. The judge asked the jurors to consider *all* of the evidence before making a decision. We ask you to keep an open mind and not jump to a conclusion without some deliberation with your fellow jurors."

"Well, I don't want to offend anybody, but this waterboarding thing is a war subject, and who else you got here that knows anything about war? Your foreman's a swabbie, and your vice-foreperson is a housewife. Let me tell you—"

"Mr. Mairston, I'm going to have to stop you right there. Please refrain from personal attacks. You will be free to express your opinion on the evidence during deliberations, but until all of the evidence is presented, you are charged with keeping an open mind and holding back your opinions."

"Ahhh—this is a waste of time." He looked around for support but found none. "OK, blondie." He waived a hand as if giving her permission. "Go ahead."

Timothy jumped to his feet, but Clarissa's reply resettled him.

"Clarissa—Mister Mairston—my name is Clarissa Morrison," she said with professional control that didn't hide the rise of her color, nor limit the clear understanding of her meaning by Mairston and the others. Her eyes never left him as he sat back down. It took her a second to regain her composure.

"Thank you," she said as she returned to her presentation. "Now let me outline the laws that apply. If you take some notes on this, it will help later, when we talk about the details.

"The Code of Laws of the United States of America is the official compilation of all the federal laws of our nation. It is often referred to as the U.S. Code or 'USC'.

"USC Title 18—Crimes and Criminal procedure, Chapter 113c— Torture, is the first law you should consider. It is the guiding principal on torture for our nation.

"This code defines torture: '…torture means an act committed by a person acting under the color of law specifically intended to inflict severe physical or mental pain or suffering…'

"It is up to you jurors to decide if you agree with the prosecuting attorney that waterboarding, as described and directed in Bush administration memos, is torture. It is clear that the waterboarding was done by a person acting under the color of law. The memos are enough evidence for that. If you agree that giving a person the feeling they are drowning is an infliction of severe physical and mental pain, then you have to agree that waterboarding is torture.

"If you don't think waterboarding a person 183 times, interspersed with slamming them against a wall, cramming them into a small box, forcing them into stress positions and dousing them with cold water, meets the definition of torture under the USC, you're probably not going to vote for an indictment.

"But let's reserve our judgment for a moment. There are other laws that apply. After the end of World War II, 196 countries signed the Fourth Geneva Convention. Because it was ratified by the U.S. Senate in 1955, it is now part of U.S. federal law. Here is the repudiation of torture per the Fourth Geneva Convention.

"'…Persons taking no active part in the hostilities…shall in all circumstances be treated humanely…the following acts are and shall remain prohibited at any time and in any place whatsoever with respect to the above-mentioned persons…a) violence to life and person, in particular murder of all kinds, mutilation, cruel treatment and torture'[52]

"The Bush administration tried to argue that the Geneva Conventions didn't apply.[53] The Supreme Court rejected that opinion and confirmed that Article 3 of the Fourth Geneva Convention does apply to all detainees.[54]

---

52   Article 3 of the Geneva Convention (III) Relative to the Treatment of Prisoners of War, August 12, 1949, [1955] 6 U.S.T. 3316, 3318, T.I.A.S. No. 3364.
http://www.loc.gov/rr/frd/Military_Law/pdf/GC_1949-III.pdf

53   Alberto R. Gonzales, Memorandum for the President, Decision Re Application of the Geneva Convention on Prisoners of War in the Conflict with Al Qaeda and the Taliban, January 25, 2002.
http://nsarchive.gwu.edu/torturingdemocracy/documents/20020125.pdf

54   Supreme Court Of The United States, Syllabus, Hamdan V. Rumsfeld, Secretary Of Defense, Et Al. Certiorari To The United States Court Of Appeals For The District Of Columbia Circuit, No. 05–184. Argued March 28, 2006—Decided June 29, 2006
http://caselaw.findlaw.com/us-supreme-court/548/557.html

"There are other treaties to which the United States is a signatory which prohibit U.S. officials from mistreating prisoners. Primary among those treaties is the United Nations Convention Against Torture and Other Cruel, Inhuman or Degrading Treatment or Punishment, (CAT).[55]

"CAT declares in part: '… torture means any act by which severe pain or suffering, whether physical or mental, is intentionally inflicted on a person for such purposes as obtaining from him or a third person information…when such pain or suffering is inflicted by or at the instigation of or with the consent or acquiescence of a public official or other person acting in an official capacity.'[56]

"Pay special attention to that last part about public officials instigating, consenting, or acquiescing to the conduct of others performing the prohibited acts," Clarissa said. "We are going to talk about that particular issue later on."

She stood at the low rail that separated the jury from the tables at the front of the room. Some jurors looked away, uncomfortable with her look, others returned eye contact, confirming they'd heard the full import of what she'd said.

"Ms. Morrison," Robert Levy called from the foreman's table.

Clarissa turned to him.

"How are we supposed to figure all this legal stuff? We aren't attorneys. We don't know what the law means by severe pain or suffering or any of that. You guys have studied law and know what all those terms mean, but we don't. Seems like, we have an impossible job to do here. Louise and I have been talking about this, and she agrees with me."

"Yes, I do," Louise said. "Why can't we get some legal expert to tell us if waterboarding is torture? Why do *we* have to decide?"

"Thank you for considering that, Robert and Louise," Clarissa said. "We can give you the opinions of some legally trained experts if you like."

"We *would* like," Robert said, and several heads in the jury pool nodded their concurrence.

"OK, can you help us with this, Mr. Madegen?" she asked.

Timothy rose from the prosecutor table and approached the jury. "Several legal opinions have been given on this subject, and they are all

---

55   Convention Against Torture and Other Cruel, Inhuman or Degrading Treatment or Punishment.
       http://www.unhcr.org/49e479d10.html

56   Ibid.

in the public domain. You might consider the opinions of active duty and retired Judge Advocates General, known as JAGs, who are military attorneys. Four active duty, Army, Navy, Air force and Marine Corp JAGS and four retired JAGS declared that waterboarding is torture.[57]

"Three respected U.S. Senators stated in a letter that waterboarding is illegal.[58] One of those senators is an ex-JAG. One of them, Senator McCain, was the victim of torture during his capture during the Vietnam War.

"You should consider the opinion of the current president on this matter. President Obama has stated that waterboarding is torture.[59] The chief law enforcement officer of the United States, Attorney General Eric Holder, stated publicly that waterboarding is torture."[60]

Robert Levy spoke up. "So the United States Attorney General has said waterboarding is torture, and the law says torture is a crime. Why are we fooling around with this? Do you have any more evidence we need to hear?"

Timothy wanted to be cautious about assuming he had made his case on this subject, but it appeared it was time to move on to the next issue.

"There is more evidence," Timothy said, "a lot more, but we don't have to consider all of it the way a trial would. We'll leave this now, but we can come back to it later, if the prosecution determines the jury needs more. Unless any of the jurors have questions on the subject of waterboarding, we will consider whether there is sufficient evidence to determine that President George W. Bush committed a crime by authorizing torture."

"Aren't we going to hear from somebody who disagrees with your conclusion on waterboarding?" a juror in the front row asked. "This whole thing seems a little one-sided to me."

Timothy walked up to the jury box and spoke directly to the questioner.

---

57   Think Progress, "Retired Judge Advocates General Write To Leahy Condemning Water boarding, by Amanda Terkel Posted on November 3, 2007 .
http://thinkprogress.org/jag-letter-waterboarding/

58   Letter to Michael Mukasey from Senators McCain, Graham and Warner, Oct 31, 2007 http://www.mccain.senate.gov/public/_cache/files/2ff245f8-ec97-466e-a24e-144415abc000/103107-mccaingrahamwarnerresponsetomukasey.pdf

59   CSPAN video of Obama news conference. April 29, 2009.
http://www.c-span.org/video/?285574-3/presidential-news-conference

60   *New York Times*, January 16, 2009, Transcript of confirmation hearing of Attorney General Eric Holder http://www.nytimes.com/2009/01/16/us/politics/16text-holder.html?pagewanted=all&_r=0

"I understand your concern, sir, but this is not a trial. Remember, we're only trying to decide if there is good reason to suspect a crime has been committed, and that we have probable cause to indict someone we think is the perpetrator. It will be up to a defense team to present the other side, if we do have an indictment."

Bob Mairston said, "Then let's vote on the waterboarding thing and get on to whatever is next."

"No, Bob, that's not what the judge instructed. He wants you to hear all the evidence the prosecution is prepared to present on all issues. Then all of the jurors will deliberate in private to decide what they want to do. You have to listen to the rest of it before you can vote," Timothy said. "So if there are no more questions for Clarissa, I'm going to introduce attorney John Mayfield to present evidence that President Bush is guilty of directing torture."

"We're ready to go ahead with the next subject," Robert Levy said.

"OK, we'll pick this up tomorrow. This grand jury is in recess for the day," Timothy said.

CHAPTER 16

Seems to me you have to say, as unlikely as that is, it would be absurd to say that you can't stick something under the fingernails, smack them in the face. It would be absurd to say that.
—Justice Antonin Scalia
BBC Radio's Law in Action Interview February 12, 2008

John Mayfield announced, "It's out!" as he passed through Timothy's office door followed by Clarissa, Radovich, and Annie. "The Senate Intelligence Committee torture report is on the printer. A five-hundred-page executive summary is packed with info, and it's brutal."[61]

Madegen looked up from his desk at the four excited people converging on him. It was typical John: sleeves rolled up, tie loose at the neck, totally absorbed. Timothy tilted back in his chair, relieved to hear that Senator Feinstein had succeeded in overcoming pressures to run out the clock until reactionaries could get control of the intel committee and bury the report.

"There's a lot of gruesome detail in there," Radovich said standing in front of Timothy's desk. His face reflected his disgust at what he'd read. Usually, Radovich moderated the group. He was the sage in the stew whose wisdom kept things from boiling over when his younger

---

61   Senate Select Committee on Intelligence, Committee Study of the Central Intelligence Agency's Detention and Interrogation Program. Forward;, Findings and Conclusions; Executive Summary. December 3, 2014.
http://www.amnestyusa.org/pdfs/sscistudy1.pdf

associates got heated up. "Chaining naked people in freezing rooms, and rectal feeding is only part of it. De Sade would have loved this. Even so, the 'Findings and Conclusions' seem to give President Bush a pass."

When Timothy's phone started ringing, he hit a button to silence it.

Clarissa stood next to Radovich. "Nobody can read that report and still question, whether waterboarding is torture," she said. "But, they do try to put all the blame on the CIA, saying they misled the White House and Congress about the brutality of what they were doing. It's like they're trying to suggest there's bad waterboarding, and OK waterboarding— and the CIA lied to them about which one it was doing."

"It's spin, typical political maneuvering—confuse the issue," Clarissa said, her excitement fit with John's hyperbole. "We can't stop the grand jury from hearing this stuff. We'll have to walk them past the misinformation, or they could fall for it."

Annie pushed through from behind Radovich. "There *is* one sweet spot in there," she said, pointing her finger at the papers Radovich held. "The report makes a solid case that torture didn't work, but that won't stop them from continuing to slant it the other way. Cheney and Bush are already out there with statements about how they had to do it to protect the American people."[62,63] She looked up from her notebook. "A couple of papers are running a crony puff piece on Bush. They claim his decision to use waterboarding is the reason we found Osama Bin Laden."[64]

"We've gotta worry about the public believing the far rights's factoids, Tim," Annie said.

"You know how people hear what they wanna hear. A lotta people have seen *Zero Dark Thirty.*[65] It gives the impression that torture played a key role in finding Bin Laden, but few know the Acting Director of the

---

62   Dismissing Senate Report, Cheney Defends C.I.A. Interrogations, New York Times, By Peter Baker Dec. 8, 2014
       http://www.nytimes.com/2014/12/09/world/dismissing-senate-report-cheney-defends-cia-interrogations.html

63   CNN video, President Bush,
       https://www.youtube.com/watch?v=mlr0pjNLIDI

64   CIA chief: Waterboarding aided bin Laden raid. May 3, 2011
       https://www.vosizneias.com/82956/2011/05/03/washington-cia-chief-waterboarding-aided-bin-laden-raid/

65   Zero Dark Thirty, Sony movie released January 11, 2013.

CIA said that's not true.[66] We need to launch a campaign to get people to understand that torture didn't work. I'll try to get Jeff to print a few grafs of hard news on the intel report."

John handed her a few pages. "Here's the forward from Feinstein. She makes the point that President Obama stopped the torture with an executive order, but a future president could re-instate it with the stroke of a pen. Make sure you get that in your story, Annie."

Phones began ringing all over the offices. John closed the door to shut out the noise.

Timothy smiled at the enthusiasm of his team. "We all know the senate report won't convince the Justice Department to prosecute anyone." He stood up to get their attention. "They've already declared that anyone who acted under the cover of the Office of Legal Counsel memos will not be prosecuted.[67] They claim there isn't enough evidence to get a conviction. It's up to us now; an indictment by our grand jury is the only way to stop our government from torturing again."

They decided to split up the report into one hundred page pieces and have the entire document read by morning. When his secretary broke in to announce a call from Isabel Jarvis, Timothy broke up the meeting and took the call.

"It's something personal, Timothy. I want to meet with you, but not in D.C. Meet me for lunch over in Annandale. There's a sandwich restaurant close to the highway."

"Of course, Isabel," Timothy said, surprised by the request.

"And Timothy, bring somebody with you just in case we're seen. I don't want to be talked about in the D.C. gossip columns."

* * *

Annie agreed to drive Timothy to the meeting with Isabel.

"I hope I don't get us lost, Tim. Once I leave the Capitol area, I'm in

---

66   Acting C.I.A. Chief Critical of Film 'Zero Dark Thirty',By Scott Shane. New York Times, December 22, 2012 http://www.nytimes.com/2012/12/23/us/politics/acting-cia-director-michael-j-morell-criticizes-zero-dark-thirty.html?_r=1&.

67   Statement Of Attorney General Eric Holder On Closure Of Investigation Into The Interrogation Of Certain Detainees, August 30, 2012. http://www.justice.gov/opa/pr/statement-attorney-general-eric-holder-closure-investigation-interrogation-certain-detainees

unfamiliar territory," Annie said.

"You're not a local?"

"I don't know where you got that impression; I'm a Montana ranch girl. I'm still terrified driving on these expressways in all this traffic."

"You have family back in Montana?"

"My adoptive parents. They're really sweet. They raised me from birth, and I love them. They're always trying to get me to come home, especially my dad. To be truthful, I feel more comfortable riding horses and ropin' calves, than dealing with D.C. drama."

"What brought you here?"

Annie smiled at Timothy's inquisition.

"It was Jeff, the reporter Jeff Blake. We met in college, and when we graduated, we got married. He wanted to come to Washington, and I was OK with it. The marriage lasted six months after we got here. He's really a great guy, but we don't fit together. I couldn't tell you what it was; it just didn't work. When we separated, I stayed on—lack of imagination, I guess.

"What are you going to do when this is over, Tim?"

She turned south, crossed the Potomac, and took the first exit off the busy Memorial Highway. Her aggressive merge between two semi's had Timothy white-knuckled for a moment, but he didn't complain.

"That's a good question. I haven't given it any thought. I know I'll never get another job at Justice. Are you sure this is the way?"

"Don't worry. I'll turn on the GPS as soon as we're out of this traffic."

"Maybe I'll get started with a private law firm. I might have to leave Washington behind for a less intense legal scene."

"Could be boring after this."

"I wouldn't mind a little boring right now. What about you, Annie?"

"I'm thinking that being part of your team could be the highpoint of my career. I'll be marked like you for having gone all out against the establishment and broken all the accepted conventions. Maybe I'll go back to Montana and try the domestic thing; you know, find a guy and raise a bunch of kids. There are worse ways to live, and I miss my family back there. My brother's married with a three-year-old. Sometimes it makes me jealous."

The authoritative female voice from the GPS interrupted. "In one quarter mile, turn right."

"Do we really need that thing?" Timothy asked.

"Yes, we'd be lost in a minute without her. We're going to have to ride along with Samantha 'til we get there. What do you think Isabel Jarvis wants to meet about? Am I gonna get a scoop out of this? How is she involved in all this?"

A semi-truck with two trailers roared past them. Annie slowed and made an unnecessary veer to the right as the behemoth passed by. Timothy rocked from side to side at the maneuver.

"Sorry," Annie said, looking over at her passenger. "So, what about Isabel?"

"She's my influence on Judge Jarvis. And no, you're not getting a scoop. This is private. The judge is a courageous man, but he wouldn't be working with us, if it wasn't for Isabel. She and I both have family members who were tortured. She was actually closer to it than me. She was a young girl in Chile, when Pinochet terrorized the country. Her brothers and uncles disappeared, and their mutilated dead bodies were delivered back to her family. They were afraid her father would be next, so they escaped the country."

"How horrible for her!" Annie said.

"She hasn't forgotten it. She can't forget it. She told me once about when she was ten-years-old, she opened the front door of her house one morning to find her dead uncle on the door step. I learned about my father's torture long after it was over, but she had to live it, as it happened in Chile. I know she'll have some strong opinions about the senate report."

They found Dice Burgers right off the Columbia Pike. It was too early for the lunch crowd, but a few patrons sat at tables over coffee. Timothy and Annie took a booth and waited for Isabel. Kitchen sounds competed with Vivaldi's impression of summer, playing in the background.

Isabel spotted them the moment she entered. "Many thanks for meeting me, Timothy. Who is your pretty companion?" she asked offering her hand to Annie.

"Isabel Javis, meet Annie Young, our political advisor and media expert."

"My pleasure, Annie," Isabel said, and seated herself at the table opposite them.

"So far to come for a meeting, Timothy, but it was necessary. They're following me. You are probably being followed and don't know it. This senate report is making them nervous. They're starting to turn on each other. Did you see the interview today on FOX, where Cheney put

Mr. Bush in middle of it?[68] Cheney says Bush knew everything. All the techniques. So much for that—what do you call it— plausible…?"

"Plausible deniability. No, we haven't seen that yet," Annie said. "Thanks for bringing it to our attention. How do you know somebody is following you?" Annie made an involuntary glance out the window.

"I'm not a secret agent, but these people are so stupid. It's obvious to me."

"Are you sure, Isabel?" Timothy said. "Seems a bit melodramatic, doesn't it?"

"When you see the same person every day, wherever you go, it speaks for itself. Pay attention, my friends, you'll see. But this is not what I want to talk to you about. It's Henry. He's not taking the pressure well. The telephone at our house is ringing all the time, and I can't imagine what it is like for him to go through a crowd of so many reporters every day at his court. Sometimes there are protesters, and some of them are not nice people."

"We're getting that, too," Timothy said.

"This is very hard on him. He's not used to being a rebel. He likes to get along." Isabel's look was sincere. "For his mind, this is exhilarating, but for his body, exhausting. This is why I asked to speak with you."

"What can we do to help him?" Timothy asked.

"There's not much I can ask of you but to get done quickly. Don't let it drag on. For Henry's sake, we must get through this as soon as possible."

"Do you think we'll lose his support, Isabel? Do you think they'll get to him?"

"Don't worry, Timothy, he won't give in. He's committed, but he can only give so much. If you get an indictment, it's going to be worse; so for God's sake, make it very quick, please."

"We'll finish the grand jury as soon as we can, we're almost there," Timothy said, his grave look reflected his concern for Henry and Isabel. "The senate report is going to make it a lot easier."

Isabel left them at the table as quickly as she had come.

"That's an extraordinary woman," Annie said, as they watched her through the window returning to her car.

"We're lucky to have her support," Timothy mused. "If it wasn't

---

68   Fox news interview with Dick Cheney by Bret Baier,. December 11, 2014
      http://www.foxnews.com/politics/2014/12/11/cheney-defends-cia-interrogation-
      techniques-calls-senate-report-flawed/

for her, we'd never have gotten this far. We're going to take her concerns seriously, Annie. We're going to fast- track the grand jury."

"Can we take five right now and have a burger to fortify ourselves for the battle to come?" Annie said with an alluring smile.

Timothy was caught off guard but quickly recovered. "You got it." He signaled for the waitress. "Two burgers with everything."

"And fries?" Annie asked.

"And fries," Timothy told the waitress.

"I'll have onions, if you do," she said.

"Now you're talkin'."

* * *

Annie punched in "home" on the GPS. Timothy turned on the radio for a news update but clicked it off again, when his cell phone rang. It was John Mayfield.

"Tim, you aren't going to believe this. Scalia just came out for torture!"

"What? I'm going to put you on the speaker, so Annie can hear this."

"It's getting worse every day," John said. "Judge Scalia, Supreme Court Justice Scalia, has stated that it's OK to torture people under certain circumstances. He buys into the ticking time-bomb scenario. It's on the AP about an interview he did for Swiss TV."[69]

Annie and Timothy shared incredulous glances.

"Keep your eyes on the road, Annie," Timothy said. "John, we have to speed up the grand jury process. The atmosphere around us is getting more toxic every day. All this talk about whether it works or not is fogging the issue."

"I get it, Tim. I'm ready to present the case for Bush's accountability to the grand jury."

"We just heard that Cheney has stopped protecting Bush. It's a big breakthrough. Make sure you include that in your presentation."

"Perfect. Sounds like the united front is crumbling—and it's every

---

69　Mark Sherman, Scalia: Hard to rule out 'extreme measures', Associated Press, December 13, 2014
http://www.dailymail.co.uk/wires/ap/article-2872466/Scalia-Hard-rule-extreme-measures.html

man for himself."

"This Scalia thing isn't going to help our case, John. This guy is one of the most conservative justices on the court. He's an originalist, and the conservatives love him. How can he ignore the law like that? He must know we're bound by the Convention Against Torture. It clearly states there are no exceptional circumstances that permit torture."[70]

"Timothy, this is no foolin'. Radio Television Suisse interviewed Scalia when the senate report came out. He doesn't think adding a new technique would be against the law. Scalia said in response to a hypothetical ticking time-bomb scenario—'You think it's clear that you cannot use extreme measures to get that information out of that person?'"[71]

"If we end up at the Supreme Court with this, it's going to be interesting to hear Scalia defending that position next to eight other justices," John said.

"Let's hope it never goes that far."

"Get real, Tim, that's where we're headed, if we get an indictment out of the grand jury."

Timothy looked out the car window at the lush green countryside streaming by. A herd of cows grazing with their calves reminded him of Annie's story. He worried about what was happening to his country. He hated the way laws were being twisted by dishonorable men in power.

"Are you still there?" John asked.

"Yes, John. You're right. We're going all the way with this. Meet me in my office when I get back to D.C. See you in about an hour."

They hung up the phone.

"Hey, Annie, speed it up a little. We've got lots to do."

They didn't notice the late model sedan with heavily tinted windows that followed them out of the parking lot or the powerful motorcycle with Land of Lincoln plates that slid in line three hundred yards behind the sedan.

* * *

William Mayfield idled his Cadillac in the cell phone waiting area on

---

70   Supra 55.

71   Amanda Terkel, *Scalia Defends Torture: It's 'Absurd' To Say The Gov't Can't 'Smack' A Suspect 'In The Face'*, Thinkprogress.
     http://thinkprogress.org/politics/2008/02/12/19522/scalia-torture/

Rudder Road at Dulles airport. Private investigator Paul Smithson got out of the car parked behind Mayfield, walked up to the driver side window, and knocked a signal for Mayfield to roll down. As he started to speak, the reverse-thrust-roar of a landing jet forced him to wait, and he coughed at the fumes of spent jet fuel. He tried to hand an envelope in through the half-open window.

"What's this?" Mayfield asked, refusing to take it.

"It's a package of photos and activity logs on the subjects."

"I don't want anything from you but a verbal report. What have you got on Madegen? I need something I can use to stop this guy."

"There isn't much. His background is as clean as Mother Theresa's. We did follow him to a meeting with Isabel Jarvis, but we couldn't get close enough to find out what they talked about."

"Any hanky-panky going on there?"

"No, they met out of town at a burger joint. Came separately and left separately. That woman Annie Young was with Madegen. There are a couple of things about her. She was married to the reporter Jeff Blake, who's been doing all the stories about the grand jury in the *Times*, but I don't know what you can do with that."

"And?"

"She put herself through school working as an exotic dancer."

"That's good, Smithson. The boy prosecutor has a stripper on his staff. I want pictures of that."

"I tried, there aren't any. The place closed down a couple of years ago. She wasn't a stripper; she was an exotic dancer."

"We're going with stripper. Get one of the tabloids to publish it. It'll be red meat for the conservative talks. Keep working on that. What about the others?"

"There isn't much of anything on them either. We looked at everything and came up dry."

"Dammit, Smithson! I'm paying you a lot of money. I want something I can use. They're all over me about this. Get me something. My dick is on the table here. Get me something on Madegen that will put a stop to this whole grand jury thing and do it quick."

"I don't know what you want. I can't just make stuff up."

"Sure you can. This is Washington. D.C. Remember death panels and weapons of mass destruction? They make shit up here all the time. Do whatever you need to do. Do you get me? There's one of the grand jurors you need to work on. Bob Mairston. Get him to tell you what's going on in that jury room. Something that will discredit the grand jury, get it squashed. I want to read about it in the papers."

Mayfield handed Smithson a thick envelope through the window.

"There's enough cash there to do it. There'll be plenty more when it's done. Don't call me. I'll call you."

Smithson jammed the envelope into his inside jacket pocket.

Mayfield left him standing in the road and sped away.

* * *

Annie smiled when Timothy appeared at her door. He stepped into Annie's office wearing a worried look and carrying a copy of the D.C. tabloid, *Express*. "Jacob brought me this. He thought it would be better if I told you." He handed the paper to Annie.

"What!" she said when she read the bold headline: **SPECIAL PROSECUTOR EMPLOYS STRIPPER**. She looked over at Timothy in astonishment. "What have you been up to, Tim?"

Timothy smiled at her assumption. "Read the article, Annie."

Annie read out loud, "'District of Columbia society is agog over the rumored affair between Special Prosecutor, Timothy Madegen, and his political advisor, Annie Young, an erstwhile stripper from Montana. Young is reported to have worked her way through college—'"

"This is absurd, Tim. I wasn't a stripper. I danced in a club, but it was a kind of burlesque show. This is a lie. They have no right to make up stories about me—and you!"

"I'm sorry Annie. Jacob and Henry warned me this kind of thing would happen. I thought they would attack me and Henry, but it didn't occur to me they would involve you too."

"I'll make them print a retraction." Her nostrils flared, and her face flushed. "They can't get away with this. We need a retraction right now!" She paused to read more of the article.

"I'm afraid it's a little late for that." Timothy tried to hide his amusement. "Jacob told me the conservative talk radio hosts have glommed on to the story, and it's all over the AM stations. If your dad listens to those guys, you better call him right away."

"Oh! I hadn't even thought of that. I have to call him," she said and started to pace. "I have to call Jeff. I have to call the *Express* and give them a piece of my mind. I have to—"

Timothy took Annie's hands and stopped her. "It's OK, Annie.

We'll get through this."

She looked up at him, her face taut. "I know, Tim, but you shouldn't have to put up with it. It's an obvious attempt to turn public opinion against you. It's more about you than me, but it still makes me mad."

"You go ahead and call your dad. Then I'm taking you to dinner, and we'll start off with a nerve-numbing martini."

"Aren't you worried about what D.C. society will say, if they see you having dinner with me?"

"Screw 'em."

"This is a side of Timothy Madegen I haven't seen before," Annie replied with a broad grin. "I'll be ready in ten minutes."

CHAPTER 17

Timothy carried a twelve-inch stack of reports into the jury room. He piled them on the desk in front of Robert Levy and handed him a list off the top.

"This is an inventory of the documents your jurors requested. They're available to you for as long as you need them, but they must not leave the jury room. We'll lock them up every night."

"Is the senate report in there?" Louise Allen asked as she leaned over for a look at the list.

"Yes, and if you want any of the documents referenced in the report, just let us know," Timothy said. "Today, I'm going to present evidence that President George W. Bush authorized torture. Please call the grand jury to order."

Levy pounded his gavel.

When the last of the jurors finished their conversation, Timothy began. "Ladies and Gentlemen, in the past few days, we have presented evidence that should have convinced you that waterboarding is torture, and therefore, a crime under U.S. statutes and international law. Our nation has successfully prosecuted numerous individuals for waterboarding. There's a legal concept called judicial estoppel that states that a party to a legal action—in this case, the federal government—can't take a position in one pleading and claim the opposite position in another instance of the same act.

"The Convention Against Torture, which is part of U.S. law, states there is no acceptable excuse for torture. Every human being, no matter who they are or what they've done, has the right to be free from torture.

"Today we will present evidence that President George W. Bush ordered waterboarding—ordered torture. According to our laws, a person who orders the commission of a crime, commits the crime. In other words, if you order torture, the law will consider you a torturer."[72]

Bob Mairston stood up. "How much more of this are we going to have to listen to before we can vote?" The red anger in his voice was clear.

"We should be able to wrap this up today, Bob," Timothy said, ignoring the blatant aggression in Mairston's challenge. "We're planning to release the grand jury for deliberations starting tomorrow. When everyone has had a chance to discuss the evidence, your foreman will call for a vote."

"Let's all listen carefully to Mr. Madegen and be prepared to discuss the case tomorrow," Levy said.

Timothy began by showing the video of George Bush admitting to authorizing the waterboarding of three people.[73] The darkened room was silent as the jury watched the confession.

When the lights came back up, he read from pages of Bush's memoir where he admitted to authorizing the waterboarding of Abu Zubaydah.[74]

"Abu Zubaydah was waterboarded eighty-three times," Timothy said.

"The book also recounts his permission to waterboard Khalid Sheikh Mohammed. It reads—'George Tenet asked if he had permission to use enhanced interrogation techniques, including waterboarding, on Khalid Sheikh Mohammed…"Damn right," I said.'[75]

"A third detainee, Abd al-Rahim al-Nashiri, was waterboarded at

---

72 USC Title 18 - CRIMES AND CRIMINAL PROCEDURE §2. Principals.
(a) Whoever commits an offense against the United States or aids, abets, counsels, commands, induces or procures its commission, is punishable as a principal.
(b) Whoever willfully causes an act to be done which if directly performed by him or another would be an offense against the United States, is punishable as a principal.
http://www.gpo.gov/fdsys/pkg/USCODE-2009-title18/html/USCODE-2009-title18.htm
73 Supra 3. Approximately thirty minutes into video.
74 Supra 2. Pages 168-169
75 Ibid. Page 170

least three times."[76]

Mairston stood up again. "So what?" He was almost shouting. "You people need to put your big-boy pants on. Sometimes you need to do things you don't like to protect yourself. The other guys wouldn't bat an eye at waterboarding. This country would be overrun by terrorists if it wasn't for George Bush. I've heard enough—"

"—I'm not going to debate you, Mairston." Timothy's face tightened, and his hands fell to his side in balled fists. "But I will ask you for the courtesy to listen to my presentation of facts before this jury." The other jurors seemed embarrassed by the confrontation. Timothy waved an arm to indicate the others. "These folks deserve your respect, and that means giving them an opportunity to decide for themselves."

"This is nonsense, all this legal angling and twisting." Mairston sat down, then got to his feet again to make another statement. "It's all a bunch of legal mumbo jumbo as far as I'm concerned."

"Do you want to be excused from the jury, Bob? We can proceed without you if you can't honestly agree with the process. We don't want to coerce you into going against your principles."

"You'd really like that, wouldn't you? Oh no, I'm not going anywhere. You can't get rid of me like that."

"Then please take your seat, Bob. I promise you I don't have much more to cover, and you will soon be able, even encouraged, to express your personal opinion."

"This is nuts! Go ahead," Mairston said and sat down. "I'll have plenty to say when you're done."

Timothy nodded and picked up where he'd left off. "President Bush opened the door to waterboarding and other forms of torture when he declared Article 3 of the Geneva Conventions did not apply to al Qaeda or Taliban detainees.[77] A few years later, when the U.S. Congress passed a law that would have specifically outlawed waterboarding, President Bush killed it, saying, 'Unfortunately, Congress recently sent me an intelligence authorization bill that would diminish these vital tools. So today, I vetoed it. And here is why: The bill Congress sent me would take away one of the most valuable tools in the war on terror—the CIA program to detain and

---

76   Senate Select Committee Intelligence Committee Study of the CIA's Detention and Interrogation Program Executive Summary, December 3, 2014. Page 67. http://www.amnestyusa.org/pdfs/sscistudy1.pdf

77   Bush memo, "Humane Treatment of Taliban and al Qaeda Detainees." February 7, 2002. http://www.pegc.us/archive/White_House/bush_memo_20020207_ed.pdf

question key terrorist leaders and operatives.'[78] When Bush says 'tools,' that's a euphemism for enhanced interrogation techniques that we've already seen amount to torture.

"Even though he admitted to authorizing waterboarding in the video you just saw, and in his memoir, the Senate Intelligence Committee report seems to say that President Bush was not aware of the techniques the CIA was using.[79] We have included in the documents supplied to your jury foreman, a recent interview with Vice-President Dick Cheney in which he stated that President Bush was fully briefed on the techniques and approved of them, and in fact, discussed the program with him in daily meetings.[80] Consider President Bush's own words in the video you just watched—'And finally, just so you know, in the book, I walk you through, getting this uh, this capability, this tool, passed by the United States Congress so it is now available to any president to use, should he or she choose to do so.'[81] That was a reference to the Military Commissions Act of 2006 which was passed by bipartisan majority in the U.S. Congress."[82]

Timothy walked back around the prosecutors' table and stood in front of his chair. He began putting materials in his briefcase. It was a minute before he closed the case and carried it with him back to the jury benches to deliver a final thought.

"So I leave you to your deliberations. We believe we have proved to you that waterboarding is torture, that it was directed by President George W. Bush, and it is a crime under USC Title 18. If you agree that there is probable cause to put President Bush on trial for torture, you should return a decision of a true bill.

"At this time, the prosecuting attorneys will leave you to your deliberations under the guidance of your foreman. We are available to

---

78   Text of President Bush's radio address to the nation, March 8, 2008, as released by the White House.
     http://www.nytimes.com/2008/03/08/washington/08cnd-ptext.html?ref=washington
79   Supra 61. Findings and Conclusions #7. Page 6.
80   Dick Cheney, Meet the Press, December 14, 2014.
     https://www.nbcnews.com/meet-the-press/meet-press-transcript-december-14-2014-n268181
81   Supra 3
82   Senate bill S. 3930. The Military Commissions Act of 2006. An act to authorize trial by military commission for violations of the law of war, and for other purposes. Section 8.
     https://www.congress.gov/bill/109th-congress/senate-bill/3930

answer any questions about the proceedings," Timothy said.

"We'll need several more copies of the senate report, Mr. Madegen," Louise Allen said.

"Yes, Louise. Mr. Radovich will take care of that immediately."

He eyed every juror, then spoke to the foreman.

"Mr. Levy, I turn the grand jury over to you."

Timothy motioned for the other prosecutors to follow him out of the room.

CHAPTER 18

"Yeah, all right, but everyone knows they torture people," mumbled
Sam.
"Do they?" said Vimes. "Then why doesn't anyone do anything about it?"
"'cos they torture people."
Terry Pratchett, *Night Watch*

Judge Jarvis spent two days answering aggressive questions before the Senate Judiciary Committee, where he was asked to defend his decision to call the Special Grand Jury. They spent hours probing the validity of his authority to assign a special prosecutor. Eighteen committee members glared down at the judge from their elevated dais. The judge sat alone at a conference table, his notes before him with a microphone on a desktop stand. The gallery was packed with dozens of reporters.

Timothy watched the proceedings on a screen in his office. He worried that he was responsible for putting the judge in such a tough spot.

Senators hit Jarvis with a continuous barrage of questions about the constitutionality of the Judicial Branch investigating the Executive Branch. Jarvis made it clear he had that responsibility, just as the Legislative Branch had the responsibility to investigate the other branches of government when necessary. He fended off insinuations about the quality of decisions he'd made in prior cases which had no bearing on the current issues.

"And why did you sponsor Timothy Madegen to the Harvard Law School?" the committee chairman asked.

"Because he had demonstrated by his academic and personal accomplishments that he deserved the chance to succeed. We need to recognize in this country that there are students who are capable, even though they don't come from certain privileged family backgrounds. What does that have to do with my authority to call the grand jury?"

"Wasn't it because your nephew, John Mayfield, asked you to sponsor Madegen?"

"Yes, Johnny asked me to help him, but that doesn't mean he didn't deserve the support."

"And isn't your nephew on the grand jury prosecution team?"

"Yes, and he's fully qualified."

"What part is your wife, Isabel, playing?"

"That, Senator, is out of order," the judge said.

Then came this statement from the ranking member.

"Judge Jarvis, to put it to you in plain English, I think you have over-stepped your authority. There is suspicion of impropriety, and you should be removed from the bench by impeachment. I will do everything in my power to make that happen. Do you have a response to that?"

Jarvis stared at his accuser for a long moment, then scanned the row of senators who looked down on him, waiting. He took the microphone off its stand and leaned forward over the table in front of him. The dam broke.

"Senators—and I'm speaking to all of you—you think you can bully me into going along with your petty partisan bickering and sniveling obfuscation of the truth. The leadership of this country is suspected of directing or allowing our government to torture people. Some of those people were guilty, some of them innocent, but none of them deserved to be treated as less than human beings. That's not an opinion; we all saw the pictures. It has been years since this came out, and this body, the United States Senate, can't even get a summary of the Intel Committee Report issued without the CIA blacking out so much of it that it's unreadable.[83] We have the executive branch spying on the legislative branch, and there are no consequences.[84] CIA operatives destroyed video tapes of torture sessions—with impunity.

"The Justice Department is so frightened by the full 6,900-page

---

83   Senate, CIA clash over redactions in interrogation report, *The Washington Post*, August 5, 2014. http://www.washingtonpost.com/world/national-security/senate-cia-clash-over-redactions-in-interrogation-report/2014/08/05/2f904f04-1ce0-11e4-ab7b-696c295ddfd1_story.html

84   Dianne Feinstein: CIA interfered with Senate Intelligence Committee, March 11, 2014 http://www.politico.com/multimedia/video/2014/03/dianne-feinstein-cia-interfered-with-senate-intelligence-committee.html

report that they locked it up and haven't even read it. The legislative branch is ignoring the failure of an executive to do its duty to follow a clear trail of evidence.

"Clueless pundits banter about whether torture worked or not, and ignore professional interrogators who say unequivocally that it does not. But you know what—it worked on you—it terrorized you and the entire US government. You're all intimidated and paralyzed by fear of the facts.

"You want to threaten me with impeachment? Go ahead. But you better watch out for what the American people will do to you at the polls, because I will not go quietly. You want to speak in plain English? OK, here—Timothy Madegen has more honest sagacity than all of you put together, and he has my full support. Nothing you can say will change that. Do your damnedest, but there are millions of people on the side of justice—and we will overwhelm the power of one hundred pompous senators."

Jarvis rose from his seat, laid the microphone down on the table with an amplified thud, and said, "I have nothing more to offer. Goodbye." He turned and left the room.

The gallery of reporters stood up in unison, throwing questions at him, and following him out, while the chairman of the committee gaveled for order.

Chapter 19

Winston Churchill said, "In wartime, truth is so precious that she should always be attended by a bodyguard of lies." The truth of our country's descent into torture is not precious, it is noxious.
But it has also been attended by a bodyguard of lies.
Opening Statement of Sheldon Whitehouse in Judiciary Subcommittee Hearing on Torture, Wednesday, May 13, 2009

Robert Levy straightened up in his seat at the foreman's table and watched the last of the twenty- three jurors take their seats. He tapped the sound block three times, but the jurors' babble went on unabated. Louise Allen looked at Levy with a frown, took the gavel from his hand, lifted it head-high, and brought it down hard on the wood round. The room quieted on the fourth blow. The fifth strike echoed off concrete block walls in the otherwise silent jury room. Louise handed the gavel back to Levy with a satisfied smile and nodded for him to begin. He stood to speak and read from his notes.

"Fellow jurors, the prosecutors have completed their presentation of evidence. Now it's up to us to make a decision about these matters. I remind you that the judge has instructed us to consider the evidence carefully. We are to determine if there is probable cause to believe that a crime has been committed, and if there's probable cause to believe it was committed by the person being investigated." He scanned the room to satisfy himself, that he had the jurors' attention.

"We are *not* tasked with determining guilt or innocence, only whether there is sufficient cause to issue an indictment that will bring the case to trial. Now is the time to express your opinions to each other, and if necessary, ask questions of the prosecutor."

When Levy finished his statement, he looked down at Louise for support.

"There are twenty-three of us," she said. "We'll give each of you a chance to speak. Our discussions will not be recorded. No electronic recordings, no court reporter. Our deliberations are private. Please feel free to speak your mind."

"We've all heard the same stuff," Bob Mairston said. "Why can't we just vote and get the hell out of here?"

"We'll vote after everyone has been heard, Bob, not before," Levy said.

One of the jurors raised a tentative hand. Levy looked at his name badge. "Go ahead, Michael."

"I pay attention to the news every day. What I'm hearing is that the CIA got lots of good information from waterboarding these terrorists, and that saved many innocent lives. Why should we prosecute Bush for doing what he had to do to protect us?"

Another juror, Ellen, a gray-haired woman with a soft voice, spoke up, "We aren't tasked with deciding if waterboarding worked or not, Michael. Our job is to decide if it's torture. I think it's torture, and that's a crime."

"She's right about our charge," Levy said. "Our job is to determine if a crime was committed, the question of whether waterboarding worked or not isn't relevant."

"But what if they didn't waterboard Khalid Sheik Mohammed, Robert? What if they didn't get the information they needed to find Osama Bin Laden? He'd still be out there terrorizing us," Michael's voice pitched up in concern.

There was a strain in Ellen's voice when she replied. "Let's not believe the BS, OK? KSM was waterboarded in 2003. The information they claimed came from him was so hot, they found Osama Bin Laden eight years later. Are you kidding me?"

Louise pounded the gavel. "Can we let that go for now and get back on topic here? We should all set aside the question of whether waterboarding worked or not. The question is—is it a crime? Let's stay with that."

Levy recognized another juror. "Go ahead, Harry."

"It seems clear to me that waterboarding is a crime," Harry said.

"President Obama and his Attorney General have called it torture. We prosecuted the Nazis, the Japanese, Ferdinand Marcos, our own soldiers, and even a Texas sheriff for waterboarding to get confessions. We don't need to decide this; our courts have done it. Why are we even discussing it? Waterboarding is torture, it's a crime."

A juror in the back of the room spoke up. "What about all the legal counselors that disagreed with that? They wrote memos that defined torture and said waterboarding doesn't meet the definition."

Ellen answered him. "All those opinions were withdrawn because they were considered poor judgment and sloppy lawyering."[85] She shook her head at the speaker, her gray hair fell in her eyes and she brushed it back. "Those attorneys claimed the Geneva Conventions didn't apply either, but the Supreme Court ruled them wrong on that too.[86] I'm with Harry." Ellen turned to meet the eyes of the jurors behind her. "Look at it this way. Even if waterboarding someone one time isn't torture, and I'm not saying it isn't, any reasonable person would have to agree that doing it to someone 183 times is torture. Come on!"

Bob Mairston joined in, "So you're going to take the legal opinion of—what's your occupation, Harry?"

"Mechanic."

"You're going to take the legal opinion of a mechanic over that of licensed attorneys? That's silly," Mairston said as he threw up his hands.

"It doesn't take a law degree to know when torture is torture, sir," Ellen's clipped speech gave away her suppressed frustration.

Levy turned to another juror who had his hand up. "Yes, James."

"If you remember from our first day, when I introduced myself, I am a second-year law student. You all might not be familiar with—"

"Oh great," a boiling Mairston interrupted. "Now we have a wanna-be-attorney instructing us."

"I have as much right to speak as anyone in this room, sir."

Louise took the gavel from Levy and gave it a good rap. "Let's not attack each other, folks. We all have the same rights in here. We're equals. Bob, I want you to stop the personal attacks and let people speak their minds, whether you agree with them or not. Got it?"

Mairston stood still glaring at her. The room waited in silence.

"Got it?" she asked again louder, staring back, waiting.

---

85   Supra 23.
86   Supra 54.

Seconds passed before he responded.

"OK, OK, have your little speeches," Mairston said and released his stare, rolling his eyes up at the ceiling.

There was a tense quiet until Levy addressed James, "Please continue James, what were you saying?"

"I haven't said anything until now, but I've been bothered from the very beginning about why we are *only* considering probable cause that this one person committed a crime." He fumbled through the pages of a stapled document, then looked up at Levy.

"I don't think it's fair to target one man as being responsible for the waterboarding, when the evidence shows he followed the advice of government attorneys telling him it was legal."

"What is that document you're reading from?" Louise asked James. "Is it one of the official grand jury documents?"

"Yes, it's one I requested.[87] It tells how the so called *War Council*, consisting of John Yoo and Alberto Gonzales in the Justice Department, William Haynes, DOD General Counsel, and David Addington, Dick Cheney's counsel, excluded opinions of other government attorneys and told Bush what he wanted to hear."[88]

"How do *you* know what the president wanted to hear?" Mairston said louder than necessary.

"All right, I don't know that, but why would his attorneys be giving these legal opinions if their boss wasn't asking for them?"

Levy weighed in. "James, are you suggesting we expand this grand jury investigation to include other potential perpetrators? That's not what the judge instructed us to do."

"It's our investigation, sir." James spoke with an authority that got the respectful attention of the others. "A grand jury is an independent body.[89] We can investigate any crime or any person we want to."

"If James is right," Ellen said, looking around the room, "it *is* our duty to follow the trail wherever, and to whomever, it leads."

---

87 Michael P. Scharf, The Torture Lawyers, 20 Duke Journal of Comparative & International Law 389-412 (2010)
    http://scholarship.law.duke.edu/djcil/vol20/iss3/4

88 Jack Goldsmith, *The Terror Presidency: Law And Judgment Inside The Bush Administration.* W.W. Norton & Company, New York (2007). Pages 22-23.

89 Judicial Conference of the United States, March 2005, Model Grand Jury Charge section, item 3.
    http://cldc.org/wp-content/uploads/2012/10/model-gj-charge.pdf

Several jurors murmured their agreement.

"Are you people nuts?" Mairston stood up and spun around to address each of the jurors face-to-face. "We'll be here forever. Let's keep to our knitting and be done with this. Why do you want to listen to this college kid? We do what the judge asked for and nothing more. This is stupid."

Levy gaveled for attention. "Sit down, Bob. I'll take this up with Mr. Madegen. He'll be able to tell us for certain what we can and can't do. This session of the grand jury is hereby concluded."

* * *

Paul Smithson had little trouble tracking down Bob Mairston. He waited at the far end of the bar in Mairston's favorite neighborhood watering hole, sipped a bourbon-rocks and listened to the cheerless opinions of two regulars watching a ball game on an overhead screen and second-guessing the team's coach on every play.

Smithson avoided eye contact with the others, keeping his gaze down on the bar top. He ran his fingers over the raised grain of time-worn oak and admired the dark patina that years of human touch and distilled spirits had wrought.

All heads turned to Mairston, when he stepped through the door. Smithson got up from his stool and hailed him like a long lost friend. He recognized Mairston from the stack of photos he'd studied of jurors coming and going at the courthouse.

"Bob? Bob Mairston? Hey, remember me? Ron Smith," he said and stuck out his hand to Mairston, who took it with a confused smile.

"Oh, come on, Bob—high school—remember? You were on that conference-winning football team, and I was in the glee club. I'll never forget that fifty-yard run you made in the game against Central." Smithson played his con with a steady confidence that was hard for his target to question.

Mairston pretended to recall the game and accepted the drink Smithson offered. They stood at the bar.

"Hey, we didn't exactly run around in the same circles, but those were some good days back then, eh?" Smithson patted Mairston on the back like an old pal. "What are you up to now, buddy?"

"Retired Army. Did four tours in Iraq. I'm a civilian now."

"Wow, did you see any action over there?"

"Don't remind me!" Mairston turned to the bartender. "Can we get some whiskey over here." The bartender slid two generous glasses down the bar top to the two men.

"Pretty tough duty, eh? Let me buy you one, you guys never get enough credit." Smithson dropped a fifty-dollar bill on the bar. His compliment fell on fertile ground.

"You don't know the half of it. I had just made warrant officer when the fucking JAGs had a problem with the way I pushed my guys on a night raid. I didn't mean for the kids to get it, but how the hell you gonna know when you break down a door and find a bunch of rag heads makin' plans around a table?" The thought of it seemed to make Mairston thirsty; he swallowed a double. "One of my guys saw an AK-47 move, and he got trigger happy, and the spray finished everybody in the room. I told the JAGs he was just scared, but that didn't carry any water." Mairston drank the second glass and called for more.

"You mean you got a court-martial for what one of your guys did?"

"No, they nailed him, not me, but they wouldn't let me re-up after that. Twenty years of watchin' my ass, and they don't want to know me after one little screw up that wasn't even my fault."

"What a shame," Smithson said. "Four tours, wow!"

"Yeah, that was good clean war fighting. Now I'm involved in this stupid grand jury thing with a bunch of liberal assholes. I'm not supposed to talk about it." Mairston looked around the room, then motioned Smithson to take a seat in a booth at the back. They carried fresh drinks with them and sat across the table from each other.

"Since I know you, I guess I can tell you a little." Mairston leaned in and kept his voice low. "There's nobody in that damn jury room that has a bit of sense. It's FUBAR all the way."

"What? Fubar?"

"Fucked up beyond all recognition."

"Can't be all that big a deal," Smithson said.

"Oh yes it can." Mairston leaned across the table and lowered his voice to a whisper.

"They want to indict the President—Bush—I mean. It's crazy. The man gives eight years of his life to this country and what does he get for it? Are you with me?"

"Seriously? What's the charge?" Smithson gave Mairston his full attention.

"They say he ordered torture."

"Un…believable!"

"I know. He protected all three-hundred million of us from the goddamn terrorists, and now they want to crucify him for doin' what he had to do. But it gets worse." Mairston made a nervous scan of the room. "Hey, you won't tell anybody that I talked to you, will you?"

Smithson looked wounded. "Of course not, Bob. You can trust me. Sounds like you need to kick this around with somebody that's got your back. I'm totally discreet." And he ran his thumb and forefinger together across his lips like he was closing a zipper.

"OK, I could get in real trouble if they found out I was talking to you. Anyway, some kid on the jury wants to go after everybody. It's like he wants us to charge everyone from the President on down to the guy that swept the cells at Guantanamo."

"You're kidding? Can they do that?"

"I don't know, but I don't trust the prosecutors or the judge to stop 'em." Mairston emptied his whiskey glass and pounded it hard on the table. The bartender looked over at the noise, and Mairston cued him for a refill.

"What are you gonna do, Bob?" Smithson asked with a serious look of concern. "Can you quit the jury?"

"No, they won't let you quit without a good excuse, and I never run from trouble anyway."

The bartender came over with two fresh glasses and tipped a bottle to top them up.

"Hold it, Angelo," Mairston said and took the whiskey down in one swallow.

"One more, Angelo."

The bartender refilled his glass and left them.

Smithson lifted his glass, "Here's to keeping the damn liberals from taking over this country."

They both drank.

"What can you do?" Smithson tried a second time.

"That's my problem. I don't know how to fight these people," Mairston said, his tongue thick from the alcohol.

"Hey, I don't know much about grand juries except they're supposed to be secret," Smithson said, intrigue evident in his voice. "Maybe you should make an anonymous call to the papers and blow the whistle on them. That might kill it, if the public knows what's going on and people start making a fuss."

"Kinda like *Deep Throat*?"

"Yeah, like that, only this time it's to protect a President, not to get him. You'd be a hero for acting on your principles and not letting them run over you."

Mairston brightened at the thought. "That's what I'm gonna do, Ron. Angelo!" he called to the bartender. "Bring me and my friend Ron another round. Make them doubles."

When the drinks arrived, they clinked their glasses in a toast with broad smiles. "Here's to doing our duty," Mairston said.

"Bob, I know a reporter at the *Times*, and I have his private number. You can trust him to keep his sources confidential. Set up a meeting with him, and he'll know how to take it from there. It'll be completely anonymous."

Smithson pulled out his cell phone for the number and wrote it on a napkin for Mairston. He looked at his watch, jumped up, and told Mairston he was late for dinner with his wife and ran out.

* * *

Jeff Blake phoned Annie from his desk at the *Times* at five minutes after midnight and woke her from a deep REM dream.

"Who is it?" she mumbled, leaning up on one elbow to flip on the lamp and get a look at the bedside alarm clock.

"It's Jeff, Annie. You better get up. Somebody's got a mole on Madegen's grand jury, and he's talkin' a blue streak."

"What is it?" she asked trying to shake off her drowsiness. "Can't it wait for morning?"

"No, you need to get to Madegen and Jarvis right away. They're printing the morning headline right now, and you're not going to like it. It's three inches high in bold Garamond—**RUNAWAY GRAND JURY ON WITCH HUNT**. I haven't seen the copy, but it can't be good. I got a peek over the editor's shoulder before he ran me off. The article says the jury is looking at indicting everyone who's had anything to do with the enhanced techniques. Your judge is gonna freak!"

Annie sat up, wide awake, and reached for her robe.

"Can you meet us, Jeff? I know it's a gamble for you, *please*."

"Where and when?"

"Hold tight, I have to get Tim. I'll call you back."

Annie dialed her cell phone for Timothy and dropped it on the bed in speaker mode while she dressed. When Timothy heard the news, he knew they had to brief the judge before the paper came out. After several calls, all agreed to meet with Jarvis at his home within the hour. Timothy included Jacob Radovich in the meeting.

* * *

Isabel Jarvis brought the team together in her formal living room as they arrived one-by-one in the early morning dark. She was perfectly groomed in the middle of the night, only her night clothes seemed out of place. When they had all been settled, the judge joined them, disheveled but alert.

Jarvis surveyed the small crowd. "Isabel tells me we're having a crisis meeting about the grand jury." He settled into the chair Isabel had set out for him.

"Yes, sir," Timothy said, moving to the edge of his seat on a small sofa. "We think it's important for you to know before the rest of the world. The *Washington Times* is printing a morning headline and story that's going to cause some major fall-out."

"Go ahead, Madegen," Judge Jarvis accepted the news with a calm bearing.

"The headline is **RUNAWAY GRAND JURY ON WITCH HUNT**, and the story is based on a reporter's interview with one of our jurors. We don't know who. The gist of the story is that the grand jury is going beyond investigating President Bush and including everyone who had any involvement in the enhanced techniques—and not only waterboarding."

"Is this the first you heard of this, Madegen?"

"No, sir. The jury foreman came to me yesterday asking for my opinion on whether the grand jury could do this. I gave him a promise to look into it. It's a gray area; I wanted to be able to give him a definitive answer. It's the news story making it urgent."

"What are your jurors saying?" Jarvis asked.

"Their position is that President Bush did not act alone and should not be used as a scapegoat to allow other perpetrators to avoid prosecution. The discussion hasn't gone very far at this point, but the lawyers of the so-called 'war council' were brought up as having some culpability. We have a law student on the jury who started this."

"I see. Good for him. Another Timothy Madegen in the making, maybe," the judge said, smiling his approval. "It's a good legal question. There have been decisions on both sides of this issue because the law is so vague, and the Supreme Court has been silent on it. I lean toward your jury's position, but you are correct about needing a definitive answer. What are our options for rebutting the story?"

"This is Jeff Blake, sir." Timothy indicated Blake. "He's a reporter with the *Times* and has been working with Annie on articles about the grand jury. Is there any opportunity here, Jeff?"

"Well, I don't want to be a traitor to my employer, but we could get some attention at the *Post*." The discomfort on Blake's face was evident.

Annie encouraged him. "We have to counter the witch hunt theme with something and do it fast, Jeff."

"Look, I can't be directly involved, but maybe you can beat the *Post's* afternoon edition. They're going to feel pretty left out this morning. They'll be anxious to use whatever you give them."

"Then do it," the judge said. "I don't want to bias your work on this, but it is true that the Justice Department determined that Bybee and Yoo failed to provide competent legal representation, failed to exercise independent legal judgment, and committed professional misconduct.[90] And we do have an ex-Vice President saying he would have the CIA do it again and bragging he was a 'big supporter of waterboarding.'[91] So I'm not surprised at the direction the grand jury is taking. I'm willing to support it, but you'll have to show me it's within the legal processes of the law."

The judge turned his attention to the other side of the room where Jacob Radovich sat listening.

"Jacob, I'm glad to see you on this team."

"Thank you, sir."

"I want you to seek the advice of Otto Beecker on this, Jacob. He's a smart man who can get to the point faster than anyone I know."

"I'll contact him immediately, sir."

"I think you'll have better luck with Otto if you wait until the sun comes up." Jarvis said with a smile and stood up. "Thank you all for keeping me informed. You've got a lot to do, so I won't keep you. Timothy, I'm with you, son. Good night." The judge left the room, and the team broke up.

---

90   Supra 23. Conclusion. Page 201

91   *This Week* Transcript: Former Vice President Dick Cheney February 14, 2010.
     http://abcnews.go.com/ThisWeek/week-transcript-vice-president-dick-cheney/story?id=9818034

Timothy was the last to leave. Isabel held him back at the door.

"This is not your fault, but it isn't helping Henry's stress."

"I know, Isabel. I'm sorry. I'll do my best to handle it without drawing him in."

"Oh no, he wants to be involved, and he's not complaining. It's me, looking out for him. Do your best, my dear," she said, and she gave Timothy a hug before he left the house.

CHAPTER 20

The highest levels of the U.S. military, the Defense Department, and the White House must be held accountable for putting our troops at greater risk and diminishing America's moral authority across the globe.
— Lawrence Korb, former Naval Intelligence Officer and John Halpin, Senior Fellow, Center for American Progress.

Jacob Radovich led John Mayfield into a Pound Hall lecture room and down a steep side aisle past rows of students in tiered theater seats. Professor Otto Beecker was in the process of delivering a screed on the constitutional foundations of corporate personhood.

Beecker saw them enter but continued lecturing until they reached the front of the room, where they stood waiting for his recognition. Forty law students, thankful for the diversion, turned to examine the intruders. Beecker stopped speaking and considered them for a moment, then turned back to his students.

"Since I've lost the attention of this entire class, we'll pick up our examination of the fourteenth amendment next Thursday." He opened a drawer in his lectern, threw in his whiteboard markers, and slammed the drawer shut with a bang that echoed across the lecture hall. "Be ready to answer questions on the cases assigned in the syllabus. Class dismissed."

There was a rustle of paper and the sound of laptops clicking shut as the class made for the exits.

Beecker addressed the two intruders. "You people just cheated a whole class out of a one-hour lecture that their parents paid good money for. I hope this isn't a waste of everybody's time, Jacob." Beecker aimed the challenge right at Radovich's nose, then addressed John. "I never expected to see you again."

"Pleasure to see you, professor," Radovich said. "You know why we're here." Radovich had long ago lost the subservient posture that Beecker demanded from his students and graduates.

Beecker remained at his place behind the lectern. He shouted to a student lingering at the back of the room. "Get out of here, Hunter. This is a private meeting. And close the doors behind you." The reluctant student got up and left.

"Runaway grand jury. Bah!" Beecker turned back to his visitors who moved in closer to the front of the lectern. "There's no such thing, and that editor should be disciplined for his ignorant headline. Runaway from what?[92] Once Jarvis impaneled those twenty-three people, his job was done. From then on, the jurors are in charge. Not the judge, not the prosecutors—the jurors. That jury has to operate in accordance with the law, but they are not limited in their investigations by anything else. They're a self-directed body. They can look at what the judge assigns, or what the prosecutor gives them, or any individual on the jury can suggest accusatory choices. Madegen has created a monster; now he's going to have to deal with it."

"We get that, sir," John Mayfield said, "but we're concerned about how to handle the jury once they've done their investigations. It would be very unusual for the grand jury to prepare an indictment—if that's what they decide to do—instead of the prosecutor. The jury foreman asked Timothy for a reading on all this, and we're not sure what to tell him."

"Twenty years ago, was it, Jacob? You must have slept through my lecture on grand juries. Either you slept, or your mind was on that redhead that sat in front of you with the big—"

"Careful, Otto. I married the girl."

"Sooo, I underestimated you, Jacob. Well done! But that doesn't change the fact that you missed my lecture, or you probably wouldn't be here right now."

---

92   Roger Roots, *If It's Not A Runaway, It's Not A Real Grand Jury*, Creighton Law Review, Vol. 33, No. 4 1999-2000, 821.
      https://www.nationallibertyalliance.org/files/juristdocs/Runaway%20Grand%20Jury.pdf

PRESENTMENT

The federal grand jury is an independent body with the power to bring criminal charges by approving a prosecutor's indictment or by making a presentment on its own initiative. A presentment is a grand jury statement that the jury has reason to believe a person has committed a crime and should be tried in a court of law.

The grand jury's authority is derived from The Constitution of the United States of America, Amendment V which states: *No person shall be held to answer for a capital, or otherwise infamous crime, unless on a presentment or indictment of a Grand Jury …*

The Supreme Court of the United States confirmed the authority of the grand jury in 1973 in United States v. Calandra,[1] where Justice Powell stated in his published opinion: *…the Founders thought the grand jury so essential to basic liberties that they provided in the Fifth Amendment that federal prosecution for serious crimes can only be instituted by "a presentment or indictment of a Grand Jury"…*

In another ruling of the Supreme Court, in United States v. Williams,[2] Justice Antonin Scalia delivered the opinion of the court in 1992: "… *the grand jury is mentioned in the Bill of Rights, but not in the body of the Constitution. It has not been textually assigned, therefore, to any of the branches described in the first three Articles. It "is a constitutional fixture in its own right…In fact, the whole theory of its function is that it belongs to no branch of the institutional Government…"*[3]

The basis for reality in this story relies on the independent power granted to the grand jury by our constitution to bring a presentment; and the authority in the Federal Rules of Criminal Procedure given to an attorney for the government to sign an indictment.[4] In our story, Timothy Madegen is the prototype of that government attorney.

1.   United States v. Calandra (No. 72-734), 414 U.S. 338, Argued: October 11, 1973, Decided: January 8, 1974. http://www.law.cornell.edu/supremecourt/text/414/338#writing-USSC_CR_0414_0338_ZO

2.   U.S. Supreme Court, United States V. Williams, 504 U.S. 36 (1992) 504 U.S. 36 United States, Petitioner V. John H. Williams, Jr. Certiorari To The United States Court Of Appeals For The Tenth Circuit, No. 90-1972, Argued January 22, 1992, Decided May 4, 1992.
http://www.law.cornell.edu/supct/html/90-1972.ZO.html

3.   Federal Rules of Criminal Procedure, Rule 7(c)(1). Page 42
http://www.gpo.gov/fdsys/pkg/USCODE-2011-title18/pdf/USCODE-2011-title18-app-federalru-dup1.pdf

4.   Federal Rules of Criminal Procedure Title I. APPLICABILITY. Rule 1. Scope; (b) Definitions. The following definitions apply to these rules (1) "Attorney for the government" means: (D) **any other attorney authorized by law to conduct proceedings under these rules as a prosecutor.** Page 15.
http://www.gpo.gov/fdsys/pkg/USCODE-2011-title18/pdf/USCODE-2011-title18-app-federalru-dup1.pdf

"What does that mean?" Radovich asked.

"We've been worried from the beginning about getting the Attorney General to sign the indictment we're pushing for," John said. "Now, with the jury wanting to expand their investigation, it's going to be even tougher to get the AG to sign."

"You better go back and read the rule about indictments again, Jacob. It doesn't say the Attorney General or an Assistant Attorney General has to sign it. It says 'an attorney for the government.' The District Court for the District of Columbia is part of the government, and Timothy Madegen is an attorney for the court. He's qualified to sign an indictment. But there's more to consider."

Beecker opened the lectern drawer, took out a red marker, and turned to the white board at the front of the room. He wrote: *Amendment V.*

"You know it; it's the criminal rights clause. *'No person shall be held to answer for a capital or otherwise infamous crime, unless on a presentment or indictment of a Grand Jury...'*" Then he wrote *Presentment.* "That's what you're missing. A presentment doesn't have to be signed by the AG; the jury can make a presentment on their own. Then it will be up to Jarvis as to whether he takes the accusations in the presentment to trial. You've got a good guy there in Henry. If you give him a serious presentment, he'll go all the way for you."

"They claim it's obsolete—*presentment*," Jacob said.

Beecker leaned forward with both elbows on the lectern, jutted out his chin, and spoke directly to Radovich.

"Don't believe the legal obfuscation, Jacob. The executive and legislative branches are scared to death of grand juries because they can't control them. They tried to neuter them in 1946 with their *New Rules of Criminal Procedure,* but they blew it.[93] Instead of eliminating the process of *presentment*—which was their goal—they ignored it. In my opinion, they couldn't eliminate it, because *presentment* is plainly authorized by

---

93 Federal Rules of Criminal Procedures, TITLE 18, APPENDIX—RULES OF CRIMINAL PROCEDURE , NOTES OF ADVISORY COMMITTEE ON RULES—1944. Rule 7. The Indictment and the Information.
Note 4. explaining Subdivision (a) of the same Rule (stating that grand jury "presentments," or non-government-approved accusations, "are obsolete, at least as concerns the Federal courts"). Page 42
http://www.gpo.gov/fdsys/pkg/USCODE-2011-title18/pdf/USCODE-2011-title18-app-federalru-dup1.pdf

the U.S. Constitution, and they didn't want to tackle a constitutional amendment. Instead, they decided to pretend it wasn't there. It's still a legal construct, and you can still use it. You don't need the Justice Department to sign off on it. It's a prerogative of the grand jury, and you have a special prosecutor that can sign it and turn it into an indictment. There's a lot of respectable legal opinion that thinks the *presentment* is still a viable approach and should be used more often by grand juries."[94] Beecker gave both attorneys a searching look, then he focused on Radovich again.

"You better face up to the fact you're playing a game of hardball, mister. If you people aren't ready to take some risks to challenge the establishment, you might as well quit right now. Do you know what I'm saying here?"

"I know what you mean, Otto," Jacob said.

"So stop asking if you can do this or that. Do it! When you get a fastball like this, swing at the son-of-a-bitch."

Jacob Radovich felt a smile creep over his face at the professor's blunt advice. It brought back memories of twenty years ago. Radovich stuck out his hand to Beecker, who looked at it for a moment, then took it.

"Tell Madegen I'm proud of him," Beecker said. "And I'll be prepared to submit an amicus brief when this goes to SCOTUS. It's important, what you're doing. There are going to be a lot of legal professionals who will pitch in when the time comes. In the meantime, *illegitimi non carborundum!*"

* * *

Annie took a call from the security guard at the front door. A man with legal credentials from a Texas law firm in Beaumont, carrying a letter from the Texas Attorney General, was asking to speak with Mr. Madegen. Timothy agreed to meet him in his office.

The sharp heel-click of the man's lizard skin cowboy boots preceded him down the hall. His appearance at Timothy's office gave a new meaning to the concept of darkening one's door. His head barely cleared the top of the doorway. He had the neck of a brahma bull, and his shoulders almost touched both sides of the door frame. He wore a formal western business suit with silver tipped bolo necktie and held a dark blue Stetson in one

---

94   Renne B. Lettow, *Reviving Federal Grand Jury Presentments, The Yale Law Journal,* [Vol. 103: 1333 Only available by subscription.

hand with a briefcase in the other.

"Frank Bean, Mr. Madegen, a pleasure to meet you," he said with a warm smile.

Timothy came around his desk to meet him and shake hands. He offered Bean a chair, and they took seats: Timothy in his desk chair and Frank Bean in front of the desk.

"Nice to be up here in D.C. We've been havin' some weather down in the Lone Star State."

"What can I do for you, Mr. Bean?"

Bean pulled a copy of the *Washington Times* out of his briefcase, held it up to his chest, brought a hand around in front of it, and pointed an index finger at the headline above the fold.

"What are you going to do about this here witch hunt, Mr. Madegen. This is *your* grand jury, isn't it?"

Timothy watched Bean position the newspaper face-up on the desk and push it toward him.

"I'm the Special Prosecutor, Mr. Bean, but it isn't *my* grand jury. It's an independent body, and I don't think it's right to disparage a grand jury investigation as a witch hunt. Don't believe everything you read in the papers." Timothy was getting an intuition about where the interview was heading.

Bean was not deterred. "I represent some folks who have concerns about the whole idea of this grand jury investigation. There are some individuals that don't think it's right for people to be lookin' at stuff that happened over ten years ago, and some of these folks can get real hard to control, if you know what I mean."

"No, I don't know what you mean, Mr. Bean."

"Please call me Frank. I came here because I'm concerned about your safety, Timothy. I know you got fired from Justice, and that means you can't get the security you used to have and we—"

"So what do you think I should be concerned about, Frank?"

"Well, I don't know exactly, but with the grand jury going off on its own the way it is. You know what they're saying, *runaway jury on a witch hunt,* and all that. You've got a leaker on that jury for one thing. These people are thinking it might be better to kinda let this group of jurors go and start over with another, more responsible group that's all. You can do that, can't you?"

Bean leaned forward and gave Timothy a conspiratorial smile.

"And where would we get that *more responsible* group of jurors,

Frank?"

"That's where we could come in and provide you with jury selection help that would make sure you don't have all the trouble you have now. There's people that will pick up the tab for it. Might even be somethin' in it for you, too. We can make life a lot easier for you, see?"

Timothy could see clearly. He watched Bean twist a heavy gold ring on his finger. The design was in the shape of the state of Texas with a small diamond positioned right about where Austin would be.

"Yes, Frank, I see. But you need to understand that this grand jury is doing exactly what it's supposed to do. These jurors are following the trail where it leads, and it's a big job because there are a lot of issues with many people involved. The newspapers call it a runaway jury and use charged words like 'witch hunt' but that doesn't change the fact that these jurors are doing their job, and it's a job that needs to be done."

Frank Bean lost his friendly smile. He stood up and leaned forward with both hands on the desk towering over Timothy. "I'm concerned about you, Madegen. I hope I don't read the papers one day and find that a certain special prosecutor got in his car, switched on the ignition, and got blown sky high. You know what I mean?"

"Don't worry, that won't happen," Timothy said with a roguish gleam in his eye.

"How can you be so sure?"

"I don't own a car, Frank."

It was Timothy's turn to smile, and he stood up as a signal to Frank Bean that the interview was over. He picked up the newspaper and handed it back to Bean.

"Let me walk you out, Frank. I don't think you'll need to come back here again."

CHAPTER 21

*I have been hard pressed to find a situation where anybody can tell me
that they've ever encountered the ticking-bomb scenario…a show like
24…makes all of us believe that this is real–it's not.
Throw that stuff out, it doesn't happen.*
—Jack Cloonan, FBI special agent

Timothy called his team together in the main conference room at the K Street offices for a reassessment after the grand jury leak to the *Washington Times*. John Mayfield and Clarissa Morrison sat on one side of the table with Annie Young and Jacob Radovich across from them. Timothy took the chair at the head of the table.

"We've got to get control of this jury." John made a sour face. "We can't have them going off willy-nilly and spilling the beans to the press."

"Control of the jury is exactly what we don't want, John," Timothy spoke in a soft voice that projected a comfort the others lacked. "What do you think, Jacob?"

"The boss is right. If it looks like we put the jury up to this, it'll be harder for the public to accept. The last thing we want is an accusation of prosecution jury tampering. There's no problem with the grand jury doing their thing. It's as it should be." He looked from John to the others to emphasize his point. "We should try to plug the leak but letting the jury do their investigation as they see fit is the best thing that could happen."

Annie Young started to speak, then stopped, then started again. "I know this is going to sound contrary, but I'm not so sure the leak is a bad thing." She directed her comments at Timothy. "We need the public on our side; you said that from the very beginning. How we gonna get them to go with us if they're in the dark? The more they know, the better, Tim."

"But the leaker is spinning everything against us," Clarissa said. "We could lose control of the dialogue. That's what worries me."

"Maybe, Clarissa," Annie answered. "But we have the law on our side. The leaker is a lawbreaker, and we can paint him as a renegade and make him and his position appear anti—well—anti whatever we want it to be. Don't you see? Our story is that the jury is trying to do the right thing, and the leaker is a bad guy trying to stop the good guys from doing their job."

Timothy leaned back in his chair. He raised his arms and settled his hands behind his head with inter-twined fingers. After taking a deep breath, he grew a smile that spread from his lips to his eyes. There was a quality to his confidence that burned through the gloom and brightened the room.

"Our political advisor is absolutely right. We need to play the hand we're dealt and play it to our best advantage. We have right on our side; that's our trump. How can we lose?"

"I agree," Radovich said. "Even Otto's with us now. That wouldn't have happened without the publicity. He offered to go to the Supreme Court with us. He gave us an answer for the jury foreman, an alternative to the indictment. There's a constitutional way to go, and he thinks it'll work."

"*Presentment*," John said.

"You guys are going to have to fill me in on that one," Annie said, looking around the table for an explanation.

"I'll explain it to you after the meeting, Annie," Radovich said. "Right now, we need to focus on the game plan."

"If we want to look *laissez-faire*, we should stay away from the jury," Clarissa said. "We don't want to give the leaker any ammunition he can use to say we're influencing them. We don't need to. All the information they want is in the public sphere. Let them find it. There are a lot of smart people on that jury. We can work with the foreman and leave it at that."

"Let the jury run its course and help them with legal documents when they're ready," John said.

"We can't ignore the leak, though," Timothy said. "I'll get the FBI to look into it."

"Have them check out Mr. Bean, too," Annie said. Her concern was obvious to Timothy.

"It's nothing." But he could see Annie wasn't convinced. "OK, I'll have them look into Frank Bean, too," he said with a tinge of annoyance.

"And find out who's following Isabel," she added.

CHAPTER 22

*There was no actionable intelligence gained from using enhanced
interrogation techniques on Abu Zubaydah that wasn't,
or couldn't have been, gained from regular tactics.*
— Ali Soufan, FBI supervisory special agent, 1997–2005

The grand jury room buzzed. Robert Levy had requested a network of laptops. Jurors worked in teams searching for information about the detention and treatment of prisoners by the U.S. government since the September 11th attacks. There was a lot of it. A network printer hummed with printouts, and a library of documents in loose-leaf binders grew on the table vacated by the prosecuting attorneys.

The law student, James, organized a group of jurors to study U.S. Code and treaties. Under his guidance, they assembled a hierarchy of applicable statutes. James and four others gathered around a table where he fielded legal questions.

"How we goin' to know if treaties against torture have any meanin' in U.S. courts?" The question came from a black man in his fifties with short-cut, curly gray hair.

"There are U.S. laws and also international treaties that the U.S. has signed-on to, Jackson," James said. "The U.S. laws are covered under US Code Title 18, Crimes and Criminal Procedure. If congress has ratified a treaty, then it applies too."

James looked at four blank faces.

"A treaty is ratified when the U.S. Senate votes to agree to its terms, then its provisions apply just like our other federal laws.[95,96] Sometimes there are arguments about how the treaty applies. Attorneys are still arguing about whether all of the provisions of the Geneva Conventions ratified by the United States in 1955 apply to us.[97] *We* aren't going to worry that. We'll leave that to the judges."

A female member of the group looked doubtful. "How are we supposed to decide which laws and treaties apply to this crime? We aren't lawyers or judges."

James had a ready answer. "Remember, we only have to show probable cause to believe the law has been violated. We don't have to prove it. That's the job of the trial attorneys, and they'll have a lot more resources and experience than us. Let's go through the legal statutes and treaties and figure out what *probably* applies. That's the best we're gonna be able to do."

A young girl raised a tentative hand.

"Go ahead, Marla," James said with an encouraging smile.

"I'm not sure if this is important, but I found this report by the United States to the UN Committee Against Torture in 1999, where our country made a commitment to ban all kinds of inhumane stuff. Listen to this," she began reading: "'...*Every act of torture within the meaning of the [Convention Against Torture] is illegal under existing federal and state law, and any individual who commits such an act is subject to penal sanctions as specified in criminal statutes.*'"[98]

"That, my friend, was before George W. Bush was sworn in," James said. "We had a stated policy against torture, but Mr. Bush changed all that less than a year after he became President. That's when our country broke its promises and ignored our laws and treaties."

The team went to work on a summary of applicable law with an

---

95   Michael John Garcia, International Law and Agreements:Their Effect upon U.S. Law. Congressional Research Service, January 23, 2014.
     https://www.fas.org/sgp/crs/misc/RL32528.pdf

96   U.S. Constitution, Article VI, clause 2.

97   Meera Rajnikant Shah, Unnecessary Complications For Basic Obligations: Medellín V. Texas And Common Article 3. 2010. Columbia Human Rights Law Review.

98   Consideration Of Reports Submitted By States Parties Under Article 19 Of The Convention Initial reports of States parties due in 1995 Addendum United States Of America*[15 October 1999] Report to United Nations Convention against Torture and Other Cruel, Inhuman or Degrading Treatment or Punishment, Subcommittee Against Torture. Page 26, Section B, Paragraph 100.

excerpt of text from each one.

USC Title 18, CRIMES AND CRIMINAL PROCEDURE. Chapter 7, Assault. *Whoever, within the special maritime and territorial jurisdiction of the United States, and with intent to torture (as defined in section 2340), ... Shall be fined under this title or imprisoned not more than twenty years, or both.*[99]

USC Title 18, CRIMES AND CRIMINAL PROCEDURE. Chapter 113C, Torture, Section 2340. Torture. (definition)... *"torture" means an act committed by a person acting under the color of law specifically intended to inflict severe physical or mental pain or suffering upon another person within his custody or physical control...*[100]

Geneva Conventions Common Article 3. *...the following acts are and shall remain prohibited at any time and in any place whatsoever... violence to life and person, in particular murder of all kinds, mutilation, cruel treatment and torture; ...outrages upon personal dignity, in particular humiliating and degrading treatment;...*[101]

Universal Declaration of Human Rights. Article 5. *No one shall be subjected to torture or cruel, inhuman or degrading treatment or punishment.*[102]

Convention against Torture and Other Cruel, Inhuman or Degrading Treatment or Punishment. Article 2. Paragraph *2. No exceptional circumstances whatsoever, whether a state of war or a threat of war, internal political instability or any other public emergency, may be invoked as a justification of torture. 3. An order from a superior officer or a public authority may not be invoked as a justification of*

---

99   USC Title 18, Part I, Chapter 7, Assault. §114

   http://www.gpo.gov/fdsys/pkg/USCODE-2011-title18/pdf/USCODE-2011-title18-partI-chap7-sec114.pdf

100 USC Title 18, Part I Chapter 113C, Section 2340.   http://psm.du.edu/media/documents/us_regulations/federal_law/us_law_federal%20torture_statute.pdf

101 International Committee of the Red Cross (ICRC), Geneva Convention Relative to the Treatment of Prisoners of War (Third Geneva Convention), 12 August 1949, 75 UNTS 135, available at: http://www.refworld.org/docid/3ae6b36c8.html

102 Universal Declaration of Human Rights, adopted by the UN General Assembly on 10 December 1948. http://www.un.org/en/documents/udhr/index.shtml#a5

torture.[103]

International Covenant on Civil and Political Rights (ICCPR) Article 7… *No one shall be subjected to torture or to cruel, inhuman or degrading treatment or punishment.*[104]

European Convention for the Protection of Human Rights and Fundamental Freedoms, Article 3, Prohibition of torture. *No one shall be subjected to torture or to inhuman or degrading treatment or punishment.*[105]

American Convention on Human Rights. Article 5. Right to Humane Treatment. *2. No one shall be subjected to torture or to cruel, inhuman, or degrading punishment or treatment. All persons deprived of their liberty shall be treated with respect for the inherent dignity of the human person.*[106]

The team worked for hours developing their list of applicable laws. It was Jackson that sat back in his chair and let out a slow whistle that seemed to summarize the feelings of the entire team.

"Looks to me like anybody and everybody worldwide has declared torture to be a crime," Marla said and looked around at the others. "There can't be anybody arguing with that."

James nodded. "It's called *jus cogens*—a legal term for a concept that has universal acceptance. It means it has the highest possible standing in common law. This assembly of laws proves that point. Nobody condones torture, or inhumane or degrading treatment. Look at the Convention

---

103 Convention against Torture and Other Cruel, Inhuman or Degrading Treatment or Punishment. December 10, 1984.
   http://www.un.org/ga/search/view_doc.asp?symbol=a/res/39/46
104 International Covenant on Civil and Political Rights.Adopted by the General Assembly of the United Nations on 19 December 1966. Article 7.
   https://treaties.un.org/doc/Publication/UNTS/Volume%20999/volume-999-I-14668-English.pdf
105 European Convention for the Protection of Human Rights and Fundamental Freedoms , Section I, Article 3.
   http://www.echr.coe.int/Documents/Convention_ENG.pdf
106 American Convention On Human Rights "Pact Of San Jose, Costa Rica". Article 5.
   https://www.oas.org/dil/access_to_information_American_Convention_on_Human_Rights.pdf

Against Torture, which was ratified by 136 countries. The International Covenant on Civil and Political Rights (ICCPR) was ratified by 153 countries, including the United States in 1992. And there are U.S. constitutional protections against interrogations under torture in the Fourth, Fifth and Eighth Amendments."

"I think we've taken care of our job to identify the laws violated," Marla said.

James leaned forward in his seat and looked around at the satisfied faces of the others.

"I'm afraid we're not done," he said. "If we're going to be true to this investigation, we have to look at the whole picture. Remember—there were a lot of people involved in promoting the enhanced interrogations. There was legal advice used to rationalize torture that the majority of attorneys in this country think is bogus. There were people kept in the dark about what was going on. Does anybody else think we have probable cause to believe that there was a conspiracy to commit the crime of torture?"

A woman who had been passive until then spoke up. "Oh my God! You're making my head hurt, Son. What else are we going to have to look at?"

"It's not all that complicated, Theresa. There is a law that states that if two or more people work together to commit a crime or engage someone else to commit a crime, those people are guilty of the crime just like the perpetrator."[107] James continued, "There's a long list of people in the Bush administration, and maybe even in Congress, who have broken that law."

"OK, are you through now?"

"Not quite." James' face was stern, not happy, when he spoke. "There are a lot of people who know about the crimes that have been committed. If they know about the crime but don't report it to an authority who can prosecute the perpetrator, then they have committed a crime. It's called misprision."[108] If an official does not perform their duty and prosecute a

---

107 USC. CONSPIRACY. Title 18– Part I, Chapter 19, section 373 - Solicitation to commit a crime of violence.
http://www.gpo.gov/fdsys/pkg/USCODE-2011-title18/pdf/USCODE-2011-title18-partI-chap19-sec373.pdf

108 USC MISPRISION Title 18 - CRIMES AND CRIMINAL PROCEDURE, PART I – CRIMES, CHAPTER 1 - GENERAL PROVISIONS, Sec. 4 - Misprision of felony.
http://www.gpo.gov/fdsys/pkg/USCODE-2011-title18/pdf/USCODE-2011-title18-partI-chap1-sec4.pdf

known offender, they commit a crime of accessory after the fact."[109]

"That could be everybody in this country. Everybody knows about the torture, and nobody is doing anything to get the torturers prosecuted," Jackson said.

"That, sir, is exactly why we're here."

---

109 Ibid Section 3 - Accessory after the fact.
    http://www.gpo.gov/fdsys/pkg/USCODE-2011-title18/pdf/USCODE-2011-
    title18-partI-chap1-sec3.pdf

CHAPTER 23

Annie teased, "Don't you have a home?" She held the door open and leaned in with one hand on the knob and the other on the jamb.

Timothy looked up from his paperwork. His eyes re-focused, as if he were returning to the room from some far off place.

"Not really," he said with a sigh, grinning at Annie. "But John hasn't kicked me out yet, so I don't actually qualify as homeless right now."

Annie dropped into the chair in front of Timothy's desk. "What are you doing here? It's almost ten o'clock."

"I'm reading the foreman's report on jury deliberations. It looks like they're goin' for it. They've been asking Jacob lots of questions about the law."

Annie stifled a yawn. "Can't you leave it 'til tomorrow?"

Timothy closed the folder and pushed it into a slot in the wire frame on his desk. "I should ask you the same question. Why so late?"

"I've been putting together a brief for Jeff. He's writing another article to counter the witch hunt spin, and he had to have it tonight for tomorrow's edition of *The Times*. I just emailed it off."

Timothy got up and pulled on his jacket. "Good, let's get out of here."

They said goodnight to a bored security guard and passed from the well-lit lobby onto a gloomy street.

"Which way you goin'?" he asked, securing the top button of his coat against the night chill.

"Metro at I street. Will you walk me across the square past the old soldier?"

They were a mile from Foggy Bottom, but the mist was thick. The gray bulk of government buildings loomed all around them, and fuzzy light spheres marked the fog-dimmed lamp posts that lined the empty street. Annie wrapped a scarf tight around her neck against the cold damp seeping in at her collar. They pushed their hands deep in their pockets and walked toward the soft outline of General McPherson in the center of the square.

"How do you think it's going, Timothy? It's a way bigger job than any of us ever imagined."

"Nothing is going as planned, and everything is going right. That report I was reading shows we have some competent jurors working on this, and there are men and women on that jury who appreciate the importance of what they're doing."

A man came toward them out of the fog. Annie took Timothy's arm and pulled in next to him. The walker's image blossomed from gray to soft colors and back to gray again as he passed them.

"You never doubt yourself, do you?" Annie said. It was a comment more than a question.

"I've got to do this for my dad, Annie. He would feel betrayed and angry, if he knew what his country has done."

"Only for him? You must have some personal stake in this."

"He suffered torture at the hands of the North Vietnamese. Some of the same tortures you read about in the Senate report. Now his country has forgotten his sacrifice and the sacrifice of all the other men and women who have fought to protect our ideals. From the President on down, they approved torture. They became the enemy we fought."

"Where's your dad now?"

"He's gone. He couldn't stand living with the memory of the torture. I miss him. I miss his strength, but I'm thankful he never knew our shame."

"I'm sorry."

As they reached the general's statue, Timothy heard footsteps, but the sound was hard to locate in the fog. Several paths radiated from the monument, and they couldn't decide which one to take. When Timothy finally realized they'd passed the right walkway, they laughed and retraced their steps.

"Why didn't you stay at Justice, Timothy? You could have worked it from the inside?"

"No, Annie. I tried that. No one at Justice would deal with it. My boss refused to discuss it. We're not going around the system because we want to—we're doing it because the system isn't working. There are letters in my files to prove it, if they didn't delete them when they fired me."

"What kind of letters?"

"A letter to the Attorney General with a transcript of George Bush's video confession. That one got a half-page response written by a staff member saying to take it up with the FBI.[110,111] The same letter went to Senator Sheldon Whitehouse and Senator Lindsey Graham who serve on the Senate Crime and Terrorism subcommittee. No response at all from them.[112] Representative John Boehner got a letter too—no response.[113]

"Guess that was the end of it then?" Annie asked.

Timothy took his hands out of his pockets and blew some warm breath on them.

"No. A letter went out to FBI Director, James Comey, with copies to Graham and Whitehouse.[114] Again, no response."

"Are you sure they got the letters?"

"Oh yeah—they got 'em. They were sent certified, and there's a record of receipt."

"There was a letter sent to the new AG, Loretta Lynch, too. No response from her either."[115]

"Why do you think they're ignoring this?"

"You tell me, Annie—you're the political scientist."

"I can only guess that they're scared to death. They don't want to

---

110 Author letter to Eric H, Holder Jr. Attorney General of the United States, May 30, 2014.

111 Letter from U.S Department of Justice, Criminal Division, by Correspondence Management Staff, August 11, 2014 to Author.

112 Author letter to Senator Lindsey Graham and Senator Sheldon Whitehouse, May 30, 2014.

113 Author letter to Representative John Boehner, June 26, 2014.

114 Author letter to FBI Director James Comey, with cc Senators Lindsay and Whitehouse, January 27, 2015

115 Author letter to Attorney General Loretta Lynch. May 21, 2015. Copies to Senator Lindsey Graham, Senator Sheldon Whitehouse, FBI Director James B. Comey.

acknowledge those letters, because if they do, they'd have to do something about them." Annie scrunched her shoulders to raise her collar against the cold at the back of her neck. "They want to pretend they never got them. They probably don't know what to do. They're political animals and prosecuting a president for torture has zero political upside."

"Maybe I am naïve," Timothy said. "But I always thought we elected men and women because we trusted them to promote our national values and national interests. When they misuse their power, and we let them get away with it, I worry about our democracy. It's disheartening. Many people want to pretend the torture didn't happen or have convinced themselves that it's OK. Prosecuting a President and his administration is completely out of their comfort zone.

"Some would protect the perpetrators at any cost. They only want to protect their image and their power. If they can bring down the grand jury and put a stop to the investigation, it'll bury the issue for a long time.

"The Bush administration has a legacy. Because no one has been prosecuted for their flaunting of the law, others are emboldened to follow them. The most recent UN report on detention in Afghanistan details continuing torture at U.S. military facilities that were turned over to the Afghan government.[116] It's still going on, Annie. And today, right now, the Chicago police department operates a CIA-like black site for their own purposes in plain view near downtown Chicago."[117]

Timothy looked over his shoulder, trying to locate the sound of footsteps.

"Are you sure this is the best way?" Annie asked. "That Senate report is a real chance for the American people to know what happened."

"Ah, the report," Timothy took Annie by the shoulders and stopped her on the walkway.

They stood facing each other; the thickening fog obscured everything beyond a few feet. His stern expression startled her.

"Do you mean the executive summary of the Senate report that has

---

116 Update on the Treatment of Conflict-Related Detainees in Afghan Custody: Accountability and Implementation of Presidential Decree 129, United Nations Assistance Mission in Afghanistan Office of the United Nations High Commissioner for Human Rights, February 2015, Kabul, Afghanistan. Pages 70 and 71. http://docslide.us/documents/unama-detention-report-2015.html

117 The disappeared: Chicago police detain Americans at abuse-laden 'black site, The Guardian, February 24, 2015. https://www.theguardian.com/us-news/2015/feb/24/chicago-police-detain-americans-black-site

been so heavily redacted that half the information in it will never see the light of day—is that the report you're talking about?"

"Yes, but—"

"The report that goes on and on about whether torture is effective and never addresses the legality of torture?"

"Well, I—"

"Or do you mean the full six-thousand-page report that took three years to assemble and is still not issued three years after it was completed?"[118]

"OK, OK, I'm sorry I mentioned it!"

"The one Senator Burr has demanded the Obama administration return so he can suppress it?[119] That report?"

Annie put a hand on Timothy's arm, and he got control of his irritation.

"I'm sorry." His speech came softer. "It's frustrating, Annie."

"OK, I get it," she said.

"No. This grand jury is the only way."

While Timothy spoke, Annie watched the silhouette of a man emerge from the mist. She lifted her arm to point over Timothy's shoulder and leaned in closer to him. Timothy turned to follow her signal.

"Axel Johnson," the man said as he emerged from the fog. He extended a hand as he approached. "It's been a few years, Timothy, but you should remember me from your dad's funeral."

Timothy recognized the man who'd told him about his father's ordeal. Fifteen years had added wrinkles, and his cheeks were sagged, but he had clear brown eyes and looked fit for a man in his sixties. He took the man's hand with a feeling of comfort he didn't quite understand.

"What are you doing in Washington?" Timothy asked.

"I need to talk to you," Johnson said.

"This is Annie Young, Mr. Johnson. We're on our way to the Metro. Come with us, and we'll get out of the cold."

They boarded the underground at the McPherson Square station

---

118 Kara Brandeisky and Sisi Wei ,Timeline: *The Tortured History of the Senate's Torture Report.* Pro Publica, April 8, 2014.
     http://projects.propublica.org/graphics/torture-report

119 Mark Mazzettijan, C.I.A. Report Found Value of Brutal Interrogation Was Inflated. New York Times, January 20, 2015.
     http://www.nytimes.com/2015/01/21/world/cia-report-found-value-of-brutal-interrogation-was-inflated.html?_r=1

and sat across from each other in the train car: Annie and Timothy on one side, and Axel Johnson on the other. The train jerked to a start and rocked gently as it accelerated away from the station. Rail noise and rushing air made a background to their conversation.

"I've been keeping track of you since I saw your picture in the papers, Timothy. I had a feeling things might get rough for you, so I've been following you around for the last few weeks. Actually, I've been following the people who've been following you."

"Why? Who's been following me?" Timothy asked.

"I feel I owe it to your dad to keep tabs on you since he's not around. You're going to be surprised to know who's been stalking you."

Annie took the cue and turned to Timothy.

"See Timothy, I told you we needed to be worried about that Bean guy. Now you'll have to take him seriously."

"Frank Bean?" Johnson shook his head. "He's all hat and no action. He's not somebody you need to worry about. There are far more dangerous people who'd like to stop your investigations. You really do need a bodyguard, Timothy."

"Come on. This is getting way too dramatic. This is the United States of America. We have laws," Timothy said.

"And we don't torture people, right?" Johnson asked.

Timothy looked at him without responding.

Johnson went on. "There've been at least eight government officials assassinated in the last fifteen years in this country. Two of them were district attorneys, and one of them was a judge.[120] I'm worried about Isabel and Henry Jarvis too."

When the train reached the end of the Orange Line track at Vienna/Fairfax, they disembarked and took a waiting taxi.

"I have some rooms in Cleveland Park down by the zoo," Johnson said. "We'd better go there, and I'll fill you in on what I know."

---

120 List of assassinated American politicians, Wikipedia.
      http://en.wikipedia.org/wiki/List_of_assassinated_American_politicians

CHAPTER 24

*Obama had the audacity to say, "I have unequivocally prohibited the
use of torture by the United States." Ladies and gentlemen,
torture in the United States has always been illegal.*
—Rush Limbaugh

Jacob Radovich pulled back a chair and dropped a thick file on the
foreman's table. His six-foot linebacker frame overshadowed the
seated Robert Levy and Louise Allen. He settled into a chair across
the table from them to deliver his findings on the subject of presentment.
They leaned in to hear him over the hum of juror conversations echoing
off the cinder block walls of the jury room.

"So we can look at any crime and anybody we want to with this
presentment thing?" Levy asked Radovich.

"You have that authority, and it's a powerful thing. You better be
careful you don't abuse it. You can hurt some innocent people if you're
careless."

Louise was quiet. Radovich watched her make nervous doodles on a
pad in front of her. She looked down at the desk.

"What are you thinking, Louise?"

She gave Radovich a troubled look. "This is too big, Jacob. We can't
do this. It's too much. We aren't smart enough. There's legal issues we
have no right to tackle. Why us? Why should we be saddled with all these
decisions? What right to do we have to decide? Bob Mairston has a point.
We aren't prepared to make decisions that could destroy an ex-president

of the United States. And how can we even process five hundred pages in the Senate CIA report, two hundred fifty pages in the Senate Armed Services Committee report, and all those footnotes? We're only twenty-three people. It's overwhelming!"

Radovich reached across the table and touched her hand. "You have just stated the reason nobody else is willing to tackle this, from Obama on down. It seems too hard. But we can do it, Louise. We're here to help you. Me and Timothy and John and Clarissa. We want you to succeed, and we won't abandon you."

"I'm having some doubts too," Levy said. "Where do we stop with charging people? There's half the Bush cabinet, military people from Rumsfeld to soldiers in the field, CIA directors and operatives, government attorneys, medical people. There must be hundreds of people involved in this. What are we gonna do, Jacob, charge all of them?"

"You're right. You can't identify everyone involved in the torture. You're going to have to limit yourself to those that authorized or supported it. When you look at individuals who may be responsible, ask yourself, 'If this person hadn't participated or given their support, would the torture have happened? Could this person have prevented it?' I think you'll find you'll have only ten or fifteen people who had the position and the power to authorize the actions of many more."

Then he turned to Louise. "You need to step back from it and take a top level view. You are not amassing evidence; you are only to determine if there is probable cause to suspect someone of committing a crime. Your most important tool is common sense, and I know you have it. Stay with that concept, and I think you'll find the job more manageable."

"So we don't have to use all the evidence, only what we need to decide?" Louise relaxed against the back of her chair.

"Right, leave the details to the prosecutors, who will present all the evidence at trial," Radovich said. "All you're doing is giving them the opportunity to do that."

"And we aren't going any further than the top level people who set the stage for the torture?" Robert asked.

"Keep it to those who ordered it or supported those who ordered it."

"Does that mean we're going to let the actual torturers off the hook?"

"No, there are going to be a lot more people exposed when this goes to trial. Right now they're all being protected by false immunity ginned up at the top level. Once that's removed, the whole Potemkin Village is coming down."

Levy and Allen called the jury together and told them they had decided to satisfy their duties by preparing a presentment to the court.

Bob Mairston stood up, speaking through tight lips, "What does that mean?"

"It's our prerogative and our duty," Levy said. "We are an independent body, Bob. If we learn of a crime that has been committed and—"

"More legal mumbo jumbo to ramrod silly accusations against the President?"

"…it's our duty to bring it to the attention of the court."

"We're supposed to decide on an indictment," Mairston turned to the other jurors. "The judge said so, not something these guys dreamed up." Then he spun back to Levy. "Do the prosecutors know about this?"

Louise Allen came around the table and stepped into the space between Mairston and Levy. "We don't have to take direction from the prosecutors. An indictment would be brought by the prosecutor and approved or disapproved by us, but a presentment is something we can make on our own initiative—and that's what we've decided to do."

"Well, I'm going to see the judge about this," Mairston said holding his arms straight down at his sides, fists clenching and releasing. "There's nothing in the Grand Jury Handbook about this presentment stuff.[121] We'll see about this!"

Mairston signaled to the jurors that supported him, Jill Aceers and Ed Pemler, who followed him out. They left the jury room slamming the door behind them.

Robert Levy gave the jury five days to read the 525-page Senate Intelligence Committee Executive summary and the Senate Armed Services Committee report on DOD treatment of detainees.[122] Their assignment was to identify interrogation techniques that amounted to torture, or degrading or inhumane treatment, and to identify individuals who they considered responsible for allowing it to happen.

During those five days, the ambiance in the jury room was library-like, with only the sound of shuffling paper and note taking, and the occasional cough or sneeze. But when the jury broke for coffee, the room filled with loud discussion.

"Did you see that note in the Senate CIA report about this Khan

---

121 Supra 40.

122 Inquiry Into The Treatment Of Detainees In *U.S. Custody Report Of The Committee On Armed Services, United States Senate*, November 20, 2008.
https://www.gpo.gov/fdsys/pkg/CPRT-110SPRT48761/pdf/CPRT-110SPRT48761.pdf

guy they tortured, then found out they had the wrong man?"[123] Ellen asked a small group at the coffee table.

"That's nothin'," Harry told them. "They shackled this guy, Gul Rahman, partially naked so he had to sit on a bare concrete floor, and he died of hypothermia.[124] There wasn't even disciplinary action against the CIA officer involved.[125] One agent reported they chained a guy to a wall in a standing position for seventeen days and never even looked in on him. He said some of the detainees cowered like a kenneled dog when they opened the door to their cell."[126]

"The Army people were just as bad as the CIA," Michael said. "We all saw the Abu Ghraib pictures, but when you read the Senate Armed Services report, it's worse than the pictures. Do we really have to read all this stuff?"

"They're terrorists!" Bob Mairston stepped in. "Who cares what the CIA did to them? They wanted to kill us! I didn't go to Iraq to kiss terrorist asses. I went there to kill 'em. Who cares how they were treated when they got captured?"

"Three thousand dead on September 11th," Jill Aceers said. "That's what gives us the right to interrogate these people any way we want to."

"And it worked," Ed said. "We got Osama Bin Laden."

The others groaned and took their coffee to their seats. When everyone finished reading the documents, Levy called the full jury to order.

"Louise had discussions with each of you about what we learned from the reports. Now we are going to make a working summary of the offenses and categorize them. We'll do this by voice vote."

He began the process by asking for discussion on solitary confinement, the first item on Louise's prepared list.

Harry pulled out documents on solitary. "I did a lot of research on this one. There are several discussions in the Senate CIA Report and the Armed Services report that disclose solitary confinement as a basic part of the detainee regimen. I also note that there are 80,000 prisoners in solitary confinement in U.S. prisons right now.[127] They're confined in

---

123 Supra 76. Page 16, note 33.

124 Ibid. Page 54.

125 Ibid Page 55. Note 277

126 Ibid Page 49-50. Note 240

127 Jacob Alderdice, Recap of *PLAP Solitary Confinement Panel, Harvard Civil Rights –Civil Liberties Law Review.*

    http://harvardcrcl.org/recap-of-plap-solitary-confinement-panel/

windowless rooms for 22-24 hours a day, for weeks, months, sometimes for years.[128] It destroys them mentally. Listen to this report on the impacts of solitary confinement." He read from a printed page "'…paranoid and hallucinatory features and also by intense agitation and random, impulsive, often self-directed violence'."[129]

Bob Mairston laughed and threw his arms wide in the air. "This is rich." He looked at Jill and Ed. "Now they want to follow bleeding heart Harry-the-Mechanic into prosecuting every warden of every prison in the country."

"That's not what I was going to say, Bob," Harry replied. "My point is that solitary confinement is torture, and there's plenty of medical evidence to support that claim. The fact that it's common practice in U.S. jails doesn't make it any less abhorrent. It's still torture."

It took a little more discussion for a consensus to congeal that solitary confinement is torture.

Waterboarding had already been discussed in detail and found to be torture by everyone but Mairston, Jill, and Ed.

Ellen brushed back her gray hair and stood up to make her case. "Some of these techniques aren't torture, but they're still against the law. Use of nudity to make a prisoner feel vulnerable is degrading. Does anybody disagree with that?"

"I'm with you, Ellen," Louise said. "Combine nudity with cold temperatures and splashes of cold water, and you have torture, but by itself, nudity is degrading and violates all the laws on detainee treatment."

James brought up the technique of confining a prisoner to a box measuring 21 inches by 2.5 feet by 2.5 feet for 29 hours.[130] "Another obvious torture technique. Can we all agree on that one?"

"Where's the evidence that Bush or Cheney or any of them authorized that?" Mairston asked. "You don't have any evidence they did, son."

"They set the stage for it, Bob. It wouldn't have happened if they hadn't torn up Geneva and the Convention Against Torture. Maybe they didn't design the exact torture, but they're responsible."

---

128 Center for Constitutional Rights, *TORTURE: The Use Of Solitary Confinement In US Prisons.* http://harvardcrcl.org/recap-of-plap-solitary-confinement-panel/

129 Herman Reyes, *The Worst Scars Are In The Mind: Psychological Torture.* International Review of the Red Cross. Volume 89 Number 867 September 2007. page 607. https://www.icrc.org/eng/assets/files/other/irrc-867-reyes.pdf

130 Supra 76. Page 42.

"Another ridiculous charge!" Mairston said. "It was rogue CIA agents that did it, not them."

The jury agreed that holding a subject nude, depriving them of sleep for two-and-a-half days with arms shackled over head for as long as sixteen hours qualifies as torture.

Another technique they considered torture was known as "hanging," involving handcuffing one or both wrists to an overhead horizontal bar for 22 hours each day for two consecutive days.[131]

Bob Mairston, Jill Aceers, and Ed Pemler made objections to accusations or excuses for the use of every technique, but after a few of their disruptions, they were politely listened to by the other jurors and dismissed without comment.

The jury found it to be inhumane to threaten to harm a detainee's family—including threats to harm the children of a detainee, threats to sexually abuse the mother of a detainee, and a threat to "cut [a detainee's] mother's throat."[132]

Sleep deprivation, where the detainee was forced to be awake, standing, for 180 hours (more than 7 days) was considered a clear instance of torture.[133]

Threatening detainees that they would be killed was considered inhumane by the jury.[134]

Louise Allen assembled a committee to identify individuals who were part of the leadership group that promoted torture.

They looked at the involvement of George W. Bush first. The video confession of him stating that he approved waterboarding was important, but there were other considerations. It was President Bush who issued a memorandum granting the CIA authority to establish secret prisons.[135] In doing so, he authorized a violation of The Convention Against Torture which requires that a detainee be given immediate assistance to contact his home state.[136]

The President issued another memorandum that stated his administration would not honor the Geneva Convention requirement for

---

131 Ibid, page 498
132 Supra 61, #3. Page 4.
133 Ibid. #3. Page 3.
134 Ibid #3. Page 4.
135 Supra 76, Page 11
136 Supra 55. Article 6.

humane treatment of Al Qaeda or Taliban prisoners;[137] thereby relieving the CIA of responsibility for treating detainees humanely.

Under his unilateral authority, President Bush approved a list of enhanced techniques in the interrogation of Abu Zubaydah, when George Tenet, then director of the CIA, requested them.[138,139] These included cramped confinement, facial slaps, sleep deprivation, stress positions, slamming a detainee into a wall, prolonged standing, and waterboarding. All were considered inhumane and degrading. Some qualified as torture standing alone. Taken together, over long periods of time, the committee agreed they amounted to torture.

Later, when the Congress tried to pass a law limiting CIA interrogation techniques to those in the Army Field Manual, George Bush vetoed the legislation, allowing the CIA to continue their torture program.[140]

When the jurors finished their look at George Bush's involvement, the committee members discussed other potential perpetrators.

"I think we should examine Dick Cheney's part," James said.

Ellen wanted to look into the government attorneys and their torture memos.

Harry thought it would be important to investigate the psychologists who were the architects of the CIA torture program.

A young woman, Jennifer, with a stack of paper in front of her and a pencil behind her ear, had concerns about the involvement of medical people.

Louise Allen realized the extent of the task. She looked for a way to spread out the work and force the information into a consumable form.

"OK, we spent all day on the President. We worked well together as a team, but we're going to have to divide up the work. Each of us will take one or two subjects to work on. We'll start again tomorrow morning.

---

137 George W. Bush, Memorandum for the Vice President, the Secretary of State, the Secretary of Defense, the Attorney General, chief of staff to the President, Director of Central Intelligence, Assistant to the President for National Security Affairs, and Chairman of the Joint Chiefs of Staff, re: Humane Treatment of al Qaeda and Taliban Detainees. February 7, 2002,
http://www.pegc.us/archive/White_House/bush_memo_20020207_ed.pdf
138 Supra 2. Pages 168,169
139 Tenent, George, *At the Center of the Storm*, Harper Collins Publishers, 2007. Pages 366, 367.
140 Supra 61, #6. Page 6.

Before we go tonight, we need to make a list of potential perpetrators and assign investigators. Tomorrow, we'll work independently. A short brief—that's all we want on each person: one, tight, concise page that summarizes that person's involvement and culpability. You might have to consult with James for questions on the law."

* * *

Julie Branson called William Mayfield that night.

"Thought you might want to know they're going after Dick Cheney next."

"What have you got, Julie?" Mayfield asked.

"They're working on a list of perpetrators and Dick Cheney's name came up; that's really all I know."

"I want you to give me anything you can get on this—potential charges against Cheney, which juror is proposing them, anything else that relates to Dick Cheney. What about Mairston? Anything new there?"

"I think he has a couple of conservative jurors on his side now. It's like the three of them against the other twenty," she told him.

"Call me anytime you get anything on this. I want to know everything as soon as it happens."

"I'll put you on my speed dial."

"No, Julie! Don't do that. We have to be discreet. Memorize my number, destroy any paper you have it written on. There *will* be a reward, Julie. Stay with me on this, OK?"

"More than a trip to New York?"

"Much more, Julie, much more."

William Mayfield hung up the phone with Julie Branson and dialed for Paul Smithson.

"Don't screw this up, Smithson. We need to put an end to this thing and fast."

"What's happening?"

"They're taking on Cheney. I was afraid of this. I want you to get Mairston to kill this grand jury. No more of your goons following Madegen around and making threats."

"Those weren't my guys, Mr. Mayfield. I don't know who that was. Somebody else is working this."

"Well they're idiots. We have to make this go away even if it means creating a goddamn headline incident. I want this to be stopped from the inside. Do you get me, Smithson?"

"How am I supposed to do that?"

"Get Mairston to leak some more grand jury information. Get him to make some accusations about jury tampering. Find out who the other two jurors are that support him and get to them, too. Do I have to spell it out for you?"

"No, sir. I know what to do."

CHAPTER 25

Torture does not work.
—Porter Goss, former director of the CIA

I sabel Jarvis entered her bright morning-room carrying the *Washington Times*. She held the paper in front of her chest for her husband to see the two-inch-high headline from his place at the breakfast table.

"GRAND JURY COMPROMISED—JURY TAMPERING CITED."

Henry looked up from his coffee and eyed Isabel with obvious disdain for the message on the page. "Are you still OK, Isabel? I'm sure you didn't expect this stuff—but I did."

She frowned at him over the top of the paper, then set it on the table in front of her. She spun it around so she could read the lead paragraph.

"Judge Henry Jarvis is under pressure from the White House, the Attorney General's office, and the Chief Justice to terminate proceedings of the Bush grand jury due to violations of secrecy laws and alleged jury tampering by un-named operatives. Some say that Special Prosecutor Timothy Madegen has lost control of the jurors, and the integrity of the grand jury has been compromised. Unidentified sources have revealed the grand jury has assembled a list of over fifteen people who might be charged, including ex-President Bush and ex-Vice-President Cheney, in addition to their advisors and legal counsel..."

She stopped reading and looked over at the judge.

"Henry, I've always been proud of you, but now I can't tell you how much I appreciate what you're going through. No, I didn't think it was going to be this hard. The hate calls, the protesters, the press—I should have known. I'm sure I don't feel half of the burden you carry. I'm still with you all the way, Henry."

"Good," he said and smiled at the earnest look on his wife's face, "because I'm going to see this thing through to the end. If this jury isn't allowed the freedom to do its duty, if the bastards can kill this one, there will never be another chance."

"What about the leaks, and the jury tampering?"

"Both illegal. They're being investigated. Timothy called on the FBI to look into it. It's not a good enough reason to terminate this grand jury. It's my call, and that's the way I see it. That headline is an editorial masquerading as news."

"Your brother, William, called yesterday. He wants to talk to you about Madegen and Johnny's involvement."

"Oh boy! I'm sure William is getting an earful from those politicians he hangs around with. They'll be calling in all their favors. I think I'll have to avoid William until this is over. I don't want tomorrow's *Post* doing an expose on a feud between me and my brother."

"Did Timothy tell you about his guardian angel that appeared out of the fog the other day?"

"No," the judge said. "But he sure needs one. We all do."

* * *

When Jacob Radovich found out about Axel Johnson, he made no comment, but he insisted on debriefing the man. Nobody wanted more complications than they already had, but Jacob was all about "knowledge is power." Besides wanting to vet Axel, Jacob wanted to get whatever information he had.

Annie set-up a closed-door meeting in Timothy's office that included herself, Axel, Radovich, and John Mayfield.

Timothy sensed the distance in Axel's greeting when he introduced him to John.

"Are we all cleared for top secret here?" He asked Timothy with a look that implied he wasn't so sure.

"No problem, Axel, you can be frank and honest," Timothy said.

"All-righty-then. Mr. Mayfield, we are going to be saying some things about your dad that might surprise you," he said looking John in the eye.

John's smile told him a lot. "You won't surprise me no matter what you tell us about Dad. And I assure you that everyone in this room is confident that I am not my dad's mole. He's my dad, and I love him as a father, but we have different politics and values, so please don't pull any punches."

"William Mayfield is not on your side, Timothy."

"I know," Timothy replied. "We all know. Go ahead, Axel."

Axel Johnson briefed the room on his activities for the last few months. Finding Timothy's photo on the front page of the papers, moving into an apartment in D.C., using his army intel training to shadow each of them.

He told them there were so many investigators involved it was hard to keep track of all of them. Everybody had at least one tail on them. He'd identified CIA, FBI, a firm out of Chicago, and one out of Houston. There were so many of them, he was afraid they were going to smash into each other. The night Annie and Timothy met him in the Square, he had been routinely following a black sedan he'd seen surveying them.

"Mr. Mayfield is the most active player. He works through manipulation," Axel said. "He's got a private investigator working three of your jurors and a reporter that prints whatever he wants him to."

"Who's the reporter?" Annie asked.

"Which jurors?" Radovich asked.

"Your friend Jeff will know the reporter; he sits on the other side of a divider in the cubicle next to him."

"Charlie? He's got Charlie? I can't believe he's got Charlie," she said as she squeezed her hands and paced the room behind Timothy's desk.

"They've got a juror by the name of Mairston filling them in on the grand jury. I don't have names of the other jurors working with Mairston. We could have the FBI arrest Mairston and the private investigator Smithson right now, or wait for a little more information and get the whole gang of them. Here's where it gets tough, John. Smithson will probably give up your dad if he's arrested."

John dropped into a chair, his shoulders dropped, and he examined his shoe laces. "It's his game. I can't play it for him. Oh well."

"We could hand that to the FBI to decide," Timothy said then looked over at John. "Or we might want to do nothing right now. This could be a big distraction, and the jury is close to making their decision."

"What else?" Radovich asked.

"Somebody's following Isabel, but I don't know who that is. It's like there's a circus in town, and everybody in the country has sent somebody to watch the action."

"What about Frank Bean? Is he still here?" Anne asked.

Axel smiled when he heard the name. "I told you before, don't worry about Frank, Annie. He came to town, met with Timothy, had a fabulous French meal at his client's expense, and went home to collect his check. He's a big over-dressed dud."

Jacob Radovich had been sitting back, taking it all in. He got up from his seat and stepped in front of Axel Johnson.

"This is only the beginning, isn't it?"

Axel looked up at the man in front of him. The two sexagenarians studied each other.

"Yes," Axel said.

"Who do we need to worry about?"

"Timothy and Annie," Axel said. "They think if they got Timothy, everything would fall apart. They think if they got Annie, Timothy would give it up."

"Why would they think that?" Annie asked.

"It's what they think, I've heard talk."

"What do you mean by *get?*" Timothy asked.

Axel turned to Timothy. "They'd like to frighten you off, like Bean tried, but if that doesn't work, it could get physical."

The room digested Axel's analysis.

"Do you have anybody that can help you bodyguard them?" Radovich asked.

"No, it's just me. I can cover both of them, but they have to stay together."

"What about Isabel?" Jacob asked.

"Make it the FBI's problem," Axel said.

Timothy and Annie moved into Axel's rooms, and Axel joined the team.

CHAPTER 26

Once you have been tortured, you can never belong in this world.
There is no place that [will] ever be your home.
—Roma Tearne, Mosquito

Robert Levy requested an experienced paralegal for preparation of formal charges. Radovich arranged for Sandra, a focused thirty-year-old, who arrived with her own laptop, ergonomic keyboard, and lightning-fast typing ability to put the jury's decisions on paper in two concentrated six-hour sessions.

Levy gave the jurors three full days to review and comment on the presentment document that Sandra prepared. Some minor changes were agreed upon, and Sandra printed final copies for the jurors and the prosecutors.

The next day, Robert called the grand jury to order, and Louise called the roll. All twenty-three jurors were present.

"Is there anyone in this room who has not been given the opportunity to freely state their opinion or concerns regarding the content of the final presentment?"

"I object to the whole document," Bob Mairston snapped. "We were instructed to prepare an indictment, and that's what we should have done. This whole grand jury is out of order."

"Noted, Bob. Do you feel you've been heard?"

"You heard me."

"Anyone else?"

"My name is Jill Aceers, and I want everyone to know I agree with Bob."

"Me too," Ed Pemler said.

"Also noted. Anyone else?" Levy scanned the jurors. "With no further discussion, we are prepared to vote on the presentment as written. We will vote by secret ballot. Please indicate your decision by writing *approve* or *disapprove* on your ballot. Harry will distribute the ballots. Louise will collect them. James and Michael will count them and report."

The jury room was quiet except for the sound of pens scratching and paper being folded. The atmosphere in the room was somber. Jurors respected the privacy of their fellows and displayed a seriousness that affirmed the gravity of the declaration they were making. No one spoke except for some low grumbling among the Mairston troika.

James and Michael tallied the votes, and James announced the results.

"There were seventeen ballots cast," James reported. "Three jurors did not cast a ballot. Three blank ballots were returned. Of the seventeen completed ballots cast, sixteen approved and one disapproved. The presentment is passed as written."

Robert Levy stood up. "I will sign the presentment as your foreman and declare the decision of this grand jury to the court. We will deliver the presentment to the judge in his courtroom at nine tomorrow morning. It is your duty to attend. You are dismissed for the rest of the day."

The jurors rose from their seats with heavy sighs. They began congratulating each other. Some couldn't wait to get out of the room; others lingered and promised to stay in touch with new-found friends.

As conversations lifted, and they moved toward the door, Robert Levy had one last word for them. "Remember, you are still a grand jury until you are dismissed by the judge. All the rules still apply. No documents are to leave this jury room, and our proceedings are still secret. Have a nice evening. Bob Mairston, please stay behind for just a minute."

Levy signaled Mairston to come with him to a private corner at the back of the room, opposite the exit door.

"I'll have to ask you to give me the copy of the presentment you have in your jacket pocket, Bob."

"What are you talking about? Are you accusing me—"

"Let me have it, Bob. We can either take care of this right here between you and me, or I can call for a bailiff to intervene. Let's not do that."

Mairston bristled. "I'm leaving; I'm done with all of you. Get out of my way." He pushed past Levy and raced for the door.

"Don't Bob—you won't make it to the street. This won't go well for you. You'll be committing a serious crime if you walk through that door."

Mairston's steps slowed, then stopped. He turned back to Levy, his breathing was heavy, and his head jerked from side to side. "Fuck you," he said, his voice shaking. He took a few menacing steps toward Levy, then pulled the document out of his inside coat pocket, and threw it in the air at Levy. "Fuck all of you!"

The unbound pages fluttered to the floor behind him as he turned and left.

* * *

Twenty jurors filed into the jury box and waited for the judge to take the bench. Their whispered conversations created an unintelligible babble in the courtroom. The jury foreman sat in the front row next to the aisle. He flipped through pages of a document, moving his lips in silent preparation. Robert disliked public speaking but refused to let Louise stand-in for him. Chief Robert Levy does not shirk his duty. Louise sat behind him and leaned forward to put a hand on his shoulder.

"We're all with you, Robert," she said, and he turned to give her a nervous smile.

Timothy, Jacob, Clarissa, and John waited. The light of Clarissa's ginger blonde hair shone like a beacon in the huddle of black and gray suits in the courtroom.

Timothy spoke on his phone to Annie, who was busy making arrangements for his public announcement of the grand jury decision. His thoughts raced ahead to how he would handle it. His hand touched the worn white envelope in his coat pocket. Lines from his father's favorite poem came to him. The time had come when he needed to keep his head and trust himself. He'd have to make allowance for the doubters, too.

He glanced across the table at John and Clarissa. Their support and faith in him had been essential over the last few weeks. He looked over at Radovich, whose face wore a stern expression that reflected his concern for the ramifications of what they were about to do. Madegen recalled Jacob's admonition that first day in the park. "…are you ready to take the heat when the torches come out?" It was easy to be brave back then, but this was the now.

John broke Timothy's reverie with a whispered sing-song declaration,

"Here come da judge."

The court clerk announced Jarvis as he entered the room. "All rise for the Honorable Henry Jarvis."

There was a low rumble as the jurors and prosecutors stood, while the judge took his chair.

"Please be seated, ladies and gentlemen."

There were no spectators or reporters in the courtroom. A court recorder at a stenotype machine and two bailiffs were the only other people in the room.

"We are here to receive the decision of the special grand jury tasked with investigation of alleged torture ordered by ex-President George W. Bush," Jarvis' voice was flat. His eyes focused on the jury box, then on the prosecution table. "Special Prosecutor Madegen, please report whether the grand jury has delivered an indictment in the form of a true bill or has brought no bill as a result of their deliberations."

Timothy rose from his seat. He approached the podium in front of the bench and glanced at Levy, who nodded an affirmation that he was ready.

"Your Honor, I want to take this opportunity to congratulate the members of the special grand jury on the successful completion of their work. The grand jury is not submitting an indictment but has determined that justice can only be served by making a presentment to the court in lieu."

The jurors watched the face of the judge, several still nervous about how their decision to discount his explicit instructions would be received, but Jarvis gave no clue to his thoughts.

Madegen went on. "They are exercising their authority in accordance with the right granted to them by Amendment Five of the United States Constitution. In my opinion, they have made the right decision considering the breadth of the investigation. With your permission, I will ask jury foreman Robert Levy to read the presentment."

"Before we hear the details of the grand jury presentment, can you confirm that all members of the grand jury are in attendance, Mr. Madegen?"

"All members were asked to attend, Your Honor. Three jurors have chosen not to."

Jarvis turned to the clerk seated below him on his right. "The clerk will call the role of grand jurors and note presence or absence for the record."

The clerk read the role and noted the absence of Mairston, Aceers and Pemler.

"You may go ahead, Scooter, please read your presentment," the judge said with an encouraging smile for the ex-Navy Chief.

Levy joined Madegen at the lectern. Timothy shook his hand, spoke softly in his ear, then returned to his seat.

"Thank you, Your Honor," Levy said in a voice that was barely audible.

"Please move closer to the microphone, Robert," Jarvis said.

Levy adjusted the mike on its stand, shuffled from one leg to the other, and reset his reading glasses. He looked up at the judge, then down at his documents.

"Thank you, Your Honor. We have prepared this presentment, and the grand jury has voted to endorse it with a total of sixteen jurors in agreement. I will now read the presentment."

Levy paused to watch Clarissa deliver a copy of the document to the court recorder and the judge, then began.[141]

"In the United States District Court for the District of Columbia. The United States of America versus George W. Bush, Richard B. Cheney, Condoleezza Rice…" Levy stopped and looked up at the judge. "Do you want me to read them all, Your Honor? There are seventeen defendants."

"Yes, Scooter, take your time. It will be necessary for you to read the entire presentment."

"**GEORGE W. BUSH**, President of the United States, 2001-2009.

RICHARD B. CHENEY, Vice-President of the United States, 2001-2009.

CONDOLEEZZA RICE, National Security Advisor, 2001-2005; Secretary of State, 2005-2009.

DONALD H. RUMSFELD, United States Secretary of Defense, 2001-2006.

JOHN D. ASHCROFT, Attorney General of the United States, 2001-2005.

---

141 Note to reader. A complete copy of the grand jury presentment can be found in the appendix of this book.

GEORGE J. TENET, Director of Central Intelligence, 1996-2004.

JOSE RODRIGUEZ, CIA Counterterrorism Center, 2001-2007.

ALBERTO R. GONZALES, White House Counsel, 2001-2005; Attorney General 2005-2007.

DAVID S. ADDINGTON, Counsel to the Vice-President, 2001-2005.

JOHN C. YOO, Deputy Assistant Attorney General, 2001-2003.

JAY S. BYBEE, Assistant Attorney General, 2001-2003.

STEVEN G. BRADBURY, Assistant Attorney General, 2004-2009.

WILLIAM J. HAYNES, Department of Defense General Counsel, 2001-2008.

GEOFFREY D. MILLER, Commander Detention and Interrogation, Guantanamo Bay, 2002-2004; Commander Abu Ghraib, 2004-2006.

JOHN A. RIZZO, CIA Legal Counsel, 1995-2009.

JAMES E. MITCHELL, Contract Psychologist with CIA 2002-?

JOHN B. JESSEN, Contract Psychologist with CIA 2002-?

Count 1:	Commanding, aiding, abetting, the torture of individuals in control of the United States Government.
Count 2:	Conspiring to enable torture by authorizing secret detention and constructing and promulgating false legal analysis.
Count 3:	Committing acts of torture.
Count 4:	Commission of war crimes—grave breaches of the Geneva Convention 12 August 1949 Common Article 3. Count 4 is related to counts 1, 2 and 3.

Count 5: Destruction, alteration, or falsification of records in Federal investigations.

General Allegations: The defendants were agents of the United States Government in positions of trust by election, appointment or contract...”

Levy read from the presentment for forty-five minutes, pausing only for the occasional sip of water. Jarvis sat back in his chair, his attention vacillating between the document in his hands and Robert at the lectern, but making no comment. When Levy finished, he closed with a statement of approval.

“The presentment is signed by myself as Grand Jury Foreman and Deputy Foreperson, Louise Allen. This is the complete presentment, Your Honor.”

Levy looked over at Madegen who nodded for him to proceed. “The grand jury has completed its duty, and the jurors ask that you dismiss us.”

The judge didn’t respond to the request.

“Thank you, Scooter. Well read. Please be seated.”

Jarvis watched Levy walk back to the jury box. When he was seated, the judge looked down at the document on his desk and began paging through it in a slow deliberate examination. He stopped to read some sections, then turned more pages. The courtroom waited in silence. When he finished, he leaned forward from the bench.

“Mr. Madegen, do you concur with the findings of the grand jury as presented by Mr. Levy?”

“I do, Your Honor, and I am prepared to sign the presentment as the attorney of record for the government.”

“Then I accept the presentment and will proceed to trial. Ladies and gentlemen of the jury, we thank you for your service. The grand jury is hereby dismissed.”

Jarvis rose to leave.

“All rise,” the court clerk announced.

The judge left the bench, and the court room quickly emptied out.

The prosecution team followed the departing jurors into the foyer where they were confronted with microphones and cameras. Timothy was grateful Annie had prepared him for the encounter.

“Special Prosecutor Madegen, what was the decision of the grand jury?”

“The grand jury made a presentment which was accepted by the court. I will have detailed comment for you at a press conference within a few hours."

Timothy spoke into microphones held by out stretched arms and metal booms. "As expected, there will be an arraignment on all counts. A trial will be scheduled in the near future."

"Was there any discussion about the fact that you are charging an ex-president and ex-vice president? Did the judge have any concern about this establishing a precedent?"

"President Bush and Vice President Cheney held the highest offices in our government, but in the end, they are just citizens like you and me. If they and the others have committed the crimes as charged, they will be brought to justice the same as any one of us would be, but that will be up to the jury."

"Do you believe it is possible to find twelve unbiased people to fill a jury in Washington, D.C.?"

"It's done every day. I'm confident there are qualified citizens for the jury."

"Is it true that the Chief Justice of the Supreme Court has asked Judge Jarvis to resign?"

"I don't know; you'll have to ask them. Thank you for your time. We won't be answering any more questions right now."

The reporters kept the questions coming, but Timothy ignored them. Axel led him through a detail of state troopers who made way for the prosecution team to get out of the building and into waiting vehicles.

CHAPTER 27

Annie flew into Timothy's office with a cell phone at her ear. He looked up from the open briefing book on his desk.

"Yes. Yes sir, we can be there on time," Annie was breathless. "I know, I know. Yes, it has to be right at six. Just a minute." She held the phone to her chest and pointed at it with the index finger of her free hand. "CBS!"

She vibrated with excitement, nodding to the caller, and finished the call. "No sir. No question, he'll be at the podium right at six-o-four."

Annie punched the hang-up button on her cell phone. "This is it!" Her faced was flushed. "They're going to give you live coverage on the 6:00 p.m. news. It's prime-time coast to coast. Two networks will be broadcasting it!"

"Good job, Annie," Timothy said.

"I'll run over to the press club with Clarissa and prep the reporters," she said.

"No, stay with me. Let John and Clarissa do it. I want you here right now."

The burden of shaping public opinion rested squarely on Timothy's shoulders. He'd been preparing for this press conference, aware of his grave responsibility. Thoughts of his father's sacrifice and despair lingered. A sense of duty to victims of torture motivated him.

"How do you feel about addressing the whole country on your television debut, Tim?" Annie asked.

"Nervous—scared—ready."

It had come down to this; he was relying on the conscience of the American people. The unwelcome scenes from Abu Ghraib flashed through his mind in horrific succession like an obscene slide show. The awful descriptions of torture in the Senate report wouldn't leave him. Glib rationalizations by those who condoned torture, and their cavalier unconcern for innocent people damaged by it, surfaced an anger he knew he had to hold in check.

The time had come for the American people to face the reality of what their country had done and show the world that U.S. claims of justice and human rights are not just rhetoric. The political system had sidetracked the justice system. The courage to face facts and their consequences had been absent. National leaders had tried to ignore the problem, but until they faced it, it would only linger—a moral transgression—a smoldering coal in the national conscience.

"Should I call for a car now?" Annie's excitement calmed when she sensed the tension in Timothy, but she remained sanguine in an effort to lift his mood.

"No, Annie. Let's walk. I could use some fresh air. It's the same walk Archibald Cox took before he stood up to a president. Ask Axel to come with us; we'll go through the square."

Radovich joined them. They crossed the square at a diagonal for the twenty-minute walk to the National Press Club.

Timothy organized his thoughts, with Annie at his side and the others following behind them. He prepared himself to announce the trial of a former president of the United States. A trial on felony charges would require the defendant to be present at the opening of the trial. He knew he was setting the stage for a contest of wills. No one on his team could sense his anxiety. They were buoyed by his outward calm. He pushed doubts aside and decided to take it minute by minute.

An alert press club staffer caught them at the entrance to the building and led them to a lobby elevator. They followed their guide through bleak hallways leading to the back entrance of the theater. In a holding room, off to the side of the stage, John picked up a call on his cell phone. He stepped quickly to Timothy and handed him the phone. "Henry Jarvis for you."

"Timothy, I want you to know I'm with you today," Jarvis' voice was clear and firm. "You've convinced me we're doing the right thing."

"Thank you, Your Honor."

"Keep your wits about you. It's your show. Stand tall and take charge. You can count on me all the way."

"Yes, sir. Your confidence means a lot. And please let Isabel know I'm speaking for her tonight."

"We'll be watching. When the phone starts ringing, we're going to take all the calls, so don't feel you're out there all alone," the judge said. "We'll be standing with you in spirit."

* * *

Henry set the handset back in the charger and smiled at Isabel.

"How'd I do?"

"Thank you," Isabel said. "That was perfect."

"I meant it, Isabel. Madegen's passion is contagious, and it's a little embarrassing that I had to be pushed so hard to take this on." He paced the room between a seated Isabel and a small television.

An announcer spoke into the TV camera. "We are expecting Special Prosecutor Timothy Madegen to announce the decision of a grand jury that investigated controversial detainee treatment during the years after the September 11, 2001, attack on the World Trade Center." The image switched to a second announcer. "This may be an historic event; it is rumored that Madegen will announce charges against former President George W. Bush."

The TV image switched occasionally to an empty stage with a bank of microphones in front of a podium flanked by a single American flag. Television pundits seated behind a semi-circular table traded opinions and commentary.

Isabel leaned into sofa pillows at her back and patted a spot at her side, calling Henry to join her. She took his hand as he sat down. "Timothy deserved the respect you gave him, and the support."

Their moment was interrupted by insistent pounding on the Jarvis front door. Henry stepped out of the study, leaving Isabel to wait for the news conference. He stiffened when he opened the door to his half-brother, William Mayfield.

"Henry, I've been trying to contact you for days." Mayfield's gaze darted about before settling on his brother. He smelled of alcohol and sweat. "You have to pull the plug on this thing, or they're going to ruin me."

"Calm down, Bill. What's going on?"

Mayfield pushed into the hall, and Henry closed the door.

"You can't go ahead with this trial. You have to stop it, right now, today."

"Come in. Sit down with me and Isabel. We're watching the Madegen news conference."

"Madegen! That guy's the problem. He has to be stopped. Why have you let that madman con you? I don't want to talk to Isabel; I need to speak to you in private."

"OK, let's go down to the billiard room, and we'll have a drink."

Henry poured two fingers of whiskey and handed Mayfield a glass. He took the drink down.

"That's better," he said, looking a little steadier than when he'd come in.

"Why is this indictment so important to you, Bill?" Henry looked over his glass, watching his brother pour himself a second drink. "You act as if you were a named defendant."

"It might as well be me." He gave Henry a doleful stare. "There are powerful people in this country who support each other. Madegen's going to name some defendants who belong to those groups. They're—"

"How do you know who he's going to name, Bill. The grand jury proceedings are secret. Why don't you relax a little and wait until Madegen gives his press briefing, then you'll know—?"

"Oh come on, Henry, this is Washington. Everybody knows what that kid is going to say. I've been getting calls from people who know, and they know things about my financial dealings that can take me down. They want the trial killed, or they'll ruin me. They're not joking."

Henry listened to William with a frown that cut creases in his cheeks and forehead. "You know I can't help you, don't you, Bill?"

"Can't or won't? You have total control over this. There won't be a trial without you. There's plenty of reasons to stop the trial. They'll be making all kinds of pre-trial motions to kill it. All you have to do is accept one."

"But I won't."

"What's the matter with you, Henry? We're brothers. I would do it for you."

"You're asking me to break the law with a prejudicial ruling that has nothing to do with the case. No, Bill. You're going to have to face the consequences of whatever it is you've done. I'm not going to bail you out by abandoning our country's system of justice—no!"

"Look, Henry, I won't say anything to anyone about this. Those people really know how to keep things quiet. No one will ever know we even—"

"No, Bill."

A red flush colored Mayfield's face and his shoulders dropped. "Well fuck you, you pompous son-of-a-bitch." He threw his half-full glass at the wall, and the pool table was showered with glass and bourbon. "I don't know why I even came here in the first place. I'll show myself out." He turned to leave.

Henry's speech was slow and calm. "If I were you, Bill, I'd go to a federal prosecutor and make a plea before your friends spill the beans. It will go easier."

Mayfield turned back to glare at Henry. "Don't give me advice about something you don't know nothin' about. Leave me the hell alone, and you better watch your back."

"Are you threatening me, Bill?"

"It's not me, Henry. Just watch out," Mayfield said and left the room.

Henry refilled his glass and took a sip. The room seemed eerily quiet after Mayfield left. He set the full whiskey glass on the bar and returned to Isabel.

"Who was it, Henry?" Isabel muted the television when he came back into the study.

"It was my brother, William."

"Why didn't you invite him in? I haven't seen William in ages."

"He's got a problem. I don't know exactly what it is, but some of his associates are putting a lot of pressure on him to get me to stop the trial. They're threatening him, and he's asking me to help him, but there's nothing I can do. He thinks I'm a pompous ass."

"Sometimes you are," Isabel said tongue in cheek.

"He thinks I should skirt the law for him because he's my brother."

"He should know you would never do that."

"No, I won't. I'm the Chief Judge of the United States District Court for the District of Columbia. It does sound pretty pompous, doesn't it?

Like a ceremonial office with few day-to-day responsibilities. It's so far from that. I occupy the same chair that Judge John Sirica did in 1974 when he prevailed in a test of wills with President Richard Nixon.

"In a lot of ways, Sirica had an easier job. Back then the legal battle was waged by the Justice Department with the support of the Senate and the Judiciary. We have a different situation here, Isabel. The Executive is absent, famously 'looking forward, not backward.' The Senate issues a report that completely ignores involvement of the White House. Even the Judicial arm is unable to mount the courage to support me, when there is obvious evidence of wrongdoing. I've got my neck stuck way out there with Madegen." The judge sat down next to Isabel.

"I know I've asked a lot of you, Henry," she said.

"It's OK, Isabel. You've been right about everything, and it's you who gives me the courage to face it."

* * *

Timothy handed the phone back to John. A staffer wearing a headset and boom-mike motioned to Annie.

"It's time," she said.

He turned to her and accepted the briefing book. They stood facing each other in an awkward silence, until she slipped in close and threw her arms around him. She held him tight for a moment, then kissed his cheek. A flush rose on Timothy's neck and face. He stepped back, gave her a smile and a shy wink, then turned and walked out on the stage to the lectern. His face bore the remnants of a subtle grin.

The tension of anticipation fell away even as he stood alone looking out at a room full of staring faces. The lone American flag at his side was little company. A respectful quiet settled on the room. Annie and the others filed in after him to take seats reserved in the front row.

"Good evening," he said into a bank of microphones. The sound of his amplified voice startled him. "My name is Timothy Madegen, and I'm Special Counsel appointed to grand jury proceedings initiated by the Honorable Henry A. Jarvis. A few hours ago, the grand jury made a presentment to Judge Jarvis charging seventeen defendants with five counts including authorizing torture, conspiring to enable torture, war crimes, committing torture and destruction of evidence of torture. As attorney for the government, I have approved the grand jury's presentment."

This was the statement the crowd of reporters had been waiting for.

There was a rustle of notebooks. Cell phone screens lit up as text messages went out.

"I will list the defendants, and detail the charges and alleged crimes, but first I will give you some background into the investigation and proceedings so far."

The heat of the stage lights made his face damp, and he fished a handkerchief out of his pants pocket to wipe his forehead. Timothy looked nervous before the packed crowd. He took a sip of water and continued.

"The court impaneled a special grand jury to look into potential crimes authorized by Presidential Memorandum of Notification, September 17, 2001. When the current administration refused a subpoena to produce the document, the judge made a charge of criminal contempt and exercised his prerogative to appoint a special prosecutor to investigate the charge. I am that Special Prosecutor.

"At first, the grand jury investigation focused on presidential authorizations given to the CIA to create secret detention centers worldwide. When the grand jury found out about the torture perpetrated in those prisons, their inquiry expanded. The grand jury followed linkages that led to members of the President's cabinet, CIA officials, and Justice Department attorneys who authorized and rationalized the torture of detainees. The grand jury studied the report of the Department of Defense on detainee treatment, the Senate Intelligence Committee Executive Summary, and interviews with officials and detainees. They simply followed the facts. All twenty-three jurors were present for all of the deliberations and participated freely."

Timothy looked out at the reporters and closed his briefing book.

"A critical decision was whether waterboarding is torture. Once the jury decided there is probable cause to believe it is torture, the investigation picked up steam and examined responsibility for it. The grand jury sought answers to the questions: who, what, where, when and why. With that knowledge, they found probable cause to believe crimes had been committed and identified those believed to be the perpetrators.

"Remember, the defendants charged here must be presumed innocent until they are tried by a jury of twelve of their peers. The crimes alleged are very serious; if what is alleged is true, a trial will bring justice to those responsible; however, no amount of legal procedure can mend the damage done to those who were tortured."

A few minutes into his presentation, Timothy felt his adrenaline kick in. He leaned into the bank of microphones, and his voice was loud and confident. He returned to the briefing book to read off the list of defendants, then explained the five charges. When he finished and opened the floor to questions, a flurry of hands went up.

Timothy pointed to a man in the audience. "The man in the blue jacket in the second row. Can we get a mike over to him?"

"Thank you, Mr. Madegen. The sensational nature of your charges against President Bush and members of his former cabinet has drawn world-wide attention. Do you expect President Bush to appear in court to answer these charges? There have already been issues of immunity raised."

Timothy turned from the questioner to address his answer to the entire room.

"Great question. Yes, I expect all of the defendants to appear. Appearance in court is required for anyone charged with a felony. It is important that the defendant hear and understand the charges against him. As to the second part of your question, there is no immunity from criminal prosecution for any government official. Immunity is not an issue here. The lady in red—way in the back."

It took a moment for an aide to bring her a microphone. Timothy waited.

"Thank you for taking my question, sir. Your list of defendants includes several who were in President Bush's cabinet. Why have you not included front-line soldiers, who may have actually performed the enhanced interrogation techniques?"

"The grand jury studied this issue and chose to charge those who were responsible for the *policy* of torture. There may be others who should be charged, but the jury determined that its duty to the American people was to bring the instigators to justice. They have probable cause to believe that without authorization from the White House, most of the torture would never have happened. There are two defendants charged who designed the torture regimen, also known by the euphemism 'Enhanced Interrogation Techniques'. Those defendants have admitted to actually waterboarding detainees. Others may come to light during the trial."

"I'm looking for a friendly face out there," Timothy said as he scanned the room.

The audience laughed at Madegen's mild sarcasm.

"Jeff Blake, what's your question?"

"Mr. Madegen, you said in your prepared statement that there has been damage done to our nation, to all of us. Can you elaborate on that statement?"

"Your question addresses the root of the matter, Jeff. First of all, the United States and its citizens have always tried to be a model for the rest of the world in honoring human rights. Sanctioning torture is a betrayal of that promise. If we as a nation allow it to go unpunished, we are complicit in torture—every man and woman in this country. Second, we have individuals who have confessed to authorizing the torture and even performing the torture. It is impossible for us to claim to be a nation of laws if these people are not brought to justice under our system. If we continue to ignore these transgressions because of the power and positions of the perpetrators, we make a mockery of our justice system."

A bald man in a t-shirt and jeans, who seemed out of place in the sea of coats and ties, caught Timothy's attention. "Mr. Madegen, how do you respond to some who say the grand jury has been on a partisan witch hunt? This is Washington, D.C., after all."

"I object to your use of an emotionally charged term to describe the work of the grand jury. The grand jury consisted of twenty-three citizens who should be thanked for doing a difficult job. You will find as the trial progresses, the grand jury based their decisions on facts. Not rumor, not hearsay, not guesswork, not politics, but on the facts. To address your second, 'some people say,' insinuation. I am not partisan. I am not registered with either of the major parties or any other party for that matter. I am doing my duty under the law. That's it."

Madegen turned away from the man. "The lady with the carnation in her lapel."

"Mr. Madegen, some of the alleged crimes in these charges were committed over fourteen years ago. Why has it taken so long for the government to bring charges, and aren't you well past the time allowed by the statute of limitations?"

"I cannot answer why it took so long for there to be charges for these crimes. I suggest you ask that question of your legislators, Attorneys General, and other political leaders. I can tell you that there is no statute of limitations when it comes to the crime of torture. That is true of U.S. law and International law. I might also point out that torture is a crime for which there is no excuse, no extenuating circumstances, no ticking-time-bomb scenario that makes it acceptable. All human beings have an absolute right to be free from torture and other cruel, degrading, and inhumane treatment. That right is non-derogable, it cannot be suspended for any reason—ever."

"This gentleman in the front row."

"Mr. Madegen, some say—"

"There you go again with that 'some say' business. Who says? Name the people that are saying whatever you want to talk about."

"Well, I don't know exactly who—"

"Next question." He pointed at a woman in the third row.

"Mr. Madegen, can you tell us the key evidence that led the grand jury to this indictment?"

"First of all, it's not an indictment. The grand jury made a presentment to the judge which is the jury's prerogative under its authority per the U.S. Constitution. Look it up. Secondly, the grand jury proceedings are secret. I have given you their decision; it will be up to the prosecution trial lawyers to develop the detailed case of evidence.

"Thank you, ladies and gentlemen, for your kind attention." Timothy smiled at his audience, picked up his briefing papers, and started for the stage exit.

Several reporters stopped him to shake his hand and express their gratitude for his perseverance and courage. Axel and Radovich broke up the group, ushered Timothy off the stage, and held back reporters at the stage door.

Annie squeezed past them and hurried to catch up with Timothy. "You knocked 'em out," she said, flashing a proud smile. "It couldn't have gone better. Tomorrow we'll see what the American people think."

He took her hands in his and looked at her. "You know we're sunk if they don't join us, don't you?"

"You did a good job," Annie assured him. "Don't worry. They'll be with us. I'm sure of it."

Timothy's body sagged with the physical let down that comes after a challenging performance. He accepted Annie's invitation for a car to take them back to K Street.

Chapter 28

...the United States and its people have always tried to be a model for the rest of the world in honoring human rights. Sanctioning torture is a betrayal of that promise. If we as a nation allow it to go unpunished, we are complicit in torture—every man and woman in this country.
—Timothy Madegen

The death threats came soon after the press conference. White powder spilled from a letter addressed to Timothy, and a biological detection system was installed in the mail room. The suspicious substance was found to be confectioner's sugar, but all of the incoming mail was scanned from that day on.

The message machine attached to John Mayfield's unlisted phone line recorded messages intended for Timothy from several different callers—they were far from polite.

Isabel had the house land-line disconnected, but calls kept coming on her cell.

When Julie Branson answered the judge's office phones, the look on her face made it easy to guess the content of the calls. She begged the judge to get a male staffer to replace her on the phones, and he did.

One night, walking to the Metro at the end of the day, Timothy and Annie were accosted by two men, who were abruptly taken into custody by several FBI agents who seemed to appear out of nowhere.

Clarissa complained to Radovich about the men she saw watching her come-and-go for two days in a row. Jacob called the D.C. police about them and was told not to worry; they were watching the watchers.

None of these attempts to intimidate Madegen had any lingering effect. He did, however, pay attention to the Senate Select Committee on Judicial Overreach, which was launched a week after the news conference to determine if there was sufficient cause to bring charges against him and Henry Jarvis. Madegen worried about possible committee interference with trial witnesses, and the potential that senators could grant immunity to any of the accused in return for their testimony. When Timothy and Jacob met with senate committee lawyers to ask that the hearings not be televised, they got a cold reception from senate attorney Bobby Archeletto.

"These are public senate committee hearings, Madegen, and you have no standing to interfere with them," Archeletto said.

They sat at a conference table in the Hart Senate Office Building where Timothy perceived himself to be on enemy territory.

"We're conducting a criminal trial, Bobby," Timothy said. "Your committee is interfering with the legitimacy of the proceedings. We're not asking you to fold the hearings, just get rid of the TV cameras and promise your senators won't issue any offers of immunity to defendants or potential witnesses." Timothy asked it as a favor; he thought it was a reasonable request considering the aggressive personal attacks he was getting from the committee.

Archeletto knew Madegen couldn't force the issue. "We believe the American People have the right to see their senate at work."

"We could take this to the courts," Radovich said. "You're attacking the Judiciary in those hearings. The judges won't go easy on you."

"Go ahead. You know as well as I that judges have a tradition of avoiding interference with the Congress. You guys are already out on a constitutional limb; I wouldn't try it if I were you. There's no reason the committee would, could, or should turn off the cameras. We're done here gentlemen." Acheletto got up from the table. Before he reached the door, he turned to face Timothy and Jacob. "We think you're arrogant for even asking the question," he told them, then turned and left them sitting alone, stunned at their reception.

When the committee chairman released a letter from Madegen that put his request in writing, Timothy learned a lesson in public relations. Editorials accused him of trying to hold back important information from the public. One questioned whether the special prosecutor was working against the prosecution team by keeping secrets. "When are the American People going to get to know about the proceedings of the secret grand jury?" began an editorial tirade in the *Times*. "What is Timothy Madegen trying to hide from us?"

Madegen's press conference had been viewed by sixty percent of the U.S. adult population and parts of it were re-broadcast worldwide. The networks and blogs replayed his statement of responsibility. *"If we as a nation allow it [torture] to go unpunished, we are complicit—every man and woman in this country."*

It was that statement—that every citizen could be blamed for torture—that got everyone's attention. Some took it as an insult; many more realized it was a wake-up call.

* * *

Jeff Blake's editor offered him a man-on-the-street interview assignment, and Jeff jumped at it. It was a perfect follow-up to the *Times* front page banner headline—**NOT IN OUR NAME**—printed above a color photo of thousands filling the mall and surrounding the monuments. Jeff ventured out into the D.C. streets among organized groups and individuals carrying home-made signs declaring opinions on the state of the American justice system and torture.

Jeff's first interview was with a tiny Asian-American woman who wore a faded Chicago Cubs baseball cap and rushed to comment as soon as she saw his recorder and microphone.

"I have something to say," she said.

"Why are you out in the streets today?" Jeff asked her.

"I want to be here with everybody who's horrified about the things our government has done." She pulled at his arm to bring the microphone down to her. "I don't want anyone to think my silence is approval. We are not the kind of people who excuse torture."

"What do you think of the trial?" Jeff asked.

"It is right. There are people all over the country, all over the world, who think it is time for our citizens to wake up to what happened and punish those responsible."

People began crowding in, to hear the comments and have their say. A bearded man in a business suit forced his way through the crowd to get to Jeff's microphone.

"Why has it taken so long to bring these people to trial in this country? It's embarrassing." Jeff held the microphone up to the man. "The Canadians tried to do it back in 2011.[142] When Obama became president, he squashed an investigation by the Spanish courts."[143]

A small crowd gathered around Blake. A middle-aged woman carrying a sign, NO MORE SECRET ARRESTS, shouted. "The Bush people even pressured the Germans to drop legal action against CIA agents that tortured a German citizen. It was a case of mistaken identity!"[144]

Jeff tried to take control of the conversation, "What party do you guys belong to?"

There were Republicans, Democrats, Greens, independents. A teenage girl holding a sign—NO MORE TORTURE—told him, "Torture isn't a political question, mister. It's a moral issue."

"What about those who say President Bush shouldn't be prosecuted for something that was out of his control?" Jeff asked.

Three women who each carried the same sign—RESPECT THE PRESIDENCY—pushed through to Jeff. "President Bush didn't torture anybody." One of the women dropped her sign down and edged into the microphone. "It was a few bad apples that did it."

"This trial is a disgrace for this nation," another said. "We were attacked! He saved us!"

"Command responsibility," the bearded man countered. "Bush was commander-in-chief. We prosecuted Japanese political and military leaders for torture done by their subordinates. Check out Nuremberg. And they hung Yamashita for it."[145]

The women turned on the businessman, "He got Saddam Hussein, didn't he? He needed intelligence to get him."

---

142 Francis Boyle, Lawyers Against the War, Letter to Canadian Prime Minister Stephen Harper, August 25, 2011. http://www.nightslantern.ca/law/LAW.George.W.Bush. Visit.ltr.Aug.24.2011.pdf

143 David Corn, *Obama and GOPers Worked Together to Kill Bush Torture Probe, Mother Jones*, December 1, 2010.
http://www.motherjones.com/politics/2010/12/wikileaks-cable-obama-quashed-torture-investigation

144 Andy Worthington, Wikileaks: *Bush and Obama Pressured Spain, Germany, not to Investigate U.S. Torture, The World Can't Wait.*
http://www.andyworthington.co.uk/2010/12/08/wikileaks-revelations-that-bush-and-obama-put-pressure-on-germany-and-spain-not-to-investigate-us-torture/

145 Frank A. Hart. Yamashita, Nuremberg And Vietnam: Command Responsibility Reappraised .International Law Studies, volume 62.

"Saddam Hussein had nothing to do with the attack on the Trade Center," the man replied.

"Oh yes he did. Why do you think we invaded Iraq?" the woman asked.

A boy in a high school letter jacket said, "We invaded Iraq for the oil. Where do you get your misinformation, lady?"

"We're getting off the subject, folks," Jeff said. "Why are you here? What's bringing you out into the streets?"

"I'm here to support Timothy Madegen," said a woman with a child in a pouch on her back. "He's taken on a difficult job, and he needs us to back him up."

A tall, blonde-headed boy squeezed up to the mike. "I'm a law student, and I think this is a watershed case for our justice system. If we can't try a confessed torturer, I'm going to quit law school."

The crowd around Blake continue to grow. A tattooed biker in a denim jacket with a *Pagan's* slogan on the back got into it with a soldier in uniform. The crowd opened up to avoid swinging fists.

A policeman separated the two and tried to disperse the crowd. "Put that microphone away, you're causing trouble with that thing," he told Jeff.

"Are you trying to suppress the free expression of these people, officer?"

"No. I'm just trying to keep the peace. Shut that thing off."

"Free speech, free speech…" The crowd began to chant.

The officer looked around at the crowd, backed away, and left through an aisle the crowd opened up while their shouts followed him out, "Free speech, free speech…"

Blake was surprised by how much the people on the street wanted to talk. They spoke freely to his microphone. They seemed to be getting a confessional relief from their shame and frustration—an absolution.

Annie read Jeff's interview piece to Clarissa the next day.

"Still fighting the great information divide," Clarissa said. "You would think all these modern communication systems would help people learn the truth, but instead it makes it easier for propagandists to peddle their own version of the facts."

"We can only hope that the majority get the truth, Clar. We can only hope."

* * *

The trial dominated discussion on the right and the left.

Right-leaning talk radio celebrated soaring listener ratings.

"They're martyring President Bush. The lefties always hated the man with their trumped up voting conspiracies and unsubstantiated links to the Saudis. The man had the balls to break a few rules to protect you and me, and this is what he gets for it. It's un-American. Madegen and his crowd are a bunch of whining crybabies!"

The left didn't shout so loud, but they didn't have to. They were proud to talk about trial evidence and show the Bush confession video, over and over.

"Timothy Madegen has forced our leaders to face the truth about torture," one announcer said. "We are finally catching up to the Canadians. They've already called for legal action against Bush. And a court in Kuala Lumpur has tried and convicted Bush, Cheney, Rumsfeld and their attorneys in absentia."[146,147]

146 Katherine Gallagher, Matt Eisenbrandt. Center for Constitutional Rights and Canadian Centre for International Justice, Letter to United Nations Committee against Torture, July 17, 2014. http://ccrjustice.org/sites/default/files/assets/17%20July%202014%20Final%20Reply%20UN%20CAT%20CCR%20CCIJ.pdf

147 Yvonne Ridley, Foreign Policy Journal, Bush Convicted of War Crimes in Absentia, May 12, 2012. http://www.foreignpolicyjournal.com/2012/05/12/bush-convicted-of-war-crimes-in-absentia/

CHAPTER 29

*...[t]his is not CIA's program. This is not the President's program.
This is America's program.*
—Michael Hayden, CIA Director 2006-2009,
referring to the CIA's detention and interrogation program.[148]

Attorney Reginald B. Konen certainly qualified as famous. In his twenty-three-year career, he had defended some of the most psychopathic criminals humankind has ever produced. He relished the idea of defending George W. Bush and the others. Julie Branson announced Konen over the intercom to Henry Jarvis, who waited in his chambers with Timothy and Radovich.

"Already colluding with the prosecutors, I see," Konen said as he walked in followed by an assistant. "Did I miss any conspiratorial conversation?"

"One more word like that, and I'll have you barred from the case, Konen." Jarvis lowered his chin and glared across the room. "This is not a game, and you will conduct yourself in a respectful manner, or the defendants are going to have to do without your services."

"Just a little joking arou—"

"There'll be no joking around, sir. I've seen you in action before, and I won't have it in my presence or in my courtroom. Sit down."

"But I—"

"Sit down, counselor!"

---

148   Supra 61. #6. Page 6.

Everyone took seats in front of Jarvis' desk. Konen tried to overcome his admonishment with a nervous smile for Timothy and Jacob.

"You're twelve minutes late Mr. Konen. We are all busy people. I expect you to be on time in the future."

"Sorry, judge. Had a TV interview that went a little long." He still wore the powder and eye highlighter, an affectation that was meant to be noticed. He settled into his chair, unbuttoned his suit jacket, and straightened the creases in his trouser legs. Satisfied with his grooming, he looked up to see Jarvis still staring at him.

"I won't be concerned about your self-promotion, but I'm sure I don't have to tell you that you will not be allowed to make public comments about this case until it is over. Do you understand?"

Konen straightened from a slouch to a ramrod posture with his feet flat on the floor and made a sidelong glance at the other attorneys. It was clear he got the message. It wasn't going to be business as usual, and maybe he'd gotten off on the wrong foot with the judge.

"I apologize for keeping you waiting, Your Honor. Can I proceed with my motion to dismiss now?"

"Are you familiar with the prosecuting attorneys, Timothy Madegen and Jacob Radovich?"

Timothy and Jacob nodded at Konen. "We've met," he said with a sniff and a grimace that implied a bad odor.

"And who is your associate?" Jarvis asked.

"Mr. Willis is an assistant attorney with my firm. He's here as a witness to the proceedings," Konen said.

The judge acknowledged Willis with a nod. "Just a moment, gentlemen." He punched the intercom button and told Julie Branson to come in to record the meeting. Julie entered immediately with a steno pad and took a seat next to the judge, facing the attorneys. "Go ahead then, Mr. Konen, I'm ready to hear your motion."

"Your Honor, I represent all of the defendants charged in the presentment." Konen stood up and approached the judge at his desk. "We motion for dismissal of all charges on the basis of necessity to maintain an orderly detention environment at all sites including those in Europe, Iraq, Afghanistan, and Guantanamo Bay, during the first intense years of the War on Terror. The conduct of the CIA and the U.S. military was foreseeable in the need to maintain peace, security, and safety in stern and difficult environments and to obtain the intelligence needed to protect our country from further attacks after the catastrophe on September 11,

2001." He waved his hands as if shooing a fly. "The charges are naïve and hurtful to dedicated public officials who bore a heavy responsibility to protect us from serious threats to our country."

Henry listened to the motion, then turned to Madegen. "Does the prosecution have any comment on the motion to dismiss?"

Madegen came forward to stand beside Konen. "Your Honor, the grand jury has stated in the presentment that the defendants are charged with conduct that is unlawful under multiple U.S. and international laws. Our nation has extensive experience with incarceration of law-breakers and prisoners of war, which has not required a need for secret detention or subjecting detainees to cruel, inhumane, or degrading treatment to maintain order." He turned to look directly at Konen. "Professional interrogators with years of experience have testified that the so-called enhanced interrogation techniques promoted by the defendants often yield false information which is counterproductive to the mission to protect us. We suggest that the defense prepare themselves to face the facts of their client's conduct and not attempt to make weak excuses for it."

Jarvis' response came immediately. "Mr. Konen, your motion to dismiss is denied."

Konen was undeterred. "Your Honor, I make a motion for dismissal on the basis that the grand jury's decision to make a presentment instead of an indictment is a flawed process and is not permitted by the Federal Rules of Criminal Procedure."

"Federal rules do not disallow presentment," Timothy said. "There is a note in that procedure which comments that presentment is obsolete.[149] I submit that a Model-T Ford is obsolete, but it can still get you across town."

Konen opened his mouth to respond but said nothing.

Radovich joined the two attorneys in front of the judge. "Does the defense claim that the authority given a grand jury by the Fifth Amendment of the U.S. Constitution does not apply? We are not aware of any change to Amendment Five that modifies its clear wording, 'unless on a presentment or indictment of a grand jury'."

A heavy sigh issued from Konen at the involvement of Radovich, whose argument finished the discussion.

"Motion denied," Jarvis said. "Anything else, Mr. Konen?"

---

149 Supra 93.

"Your Honor, all of the defendants, at the time of the actions indicated in the charges, were government employees, and they were acting in good faith. They should not be punished for doing their job in keeping our country safe. I make a motion to dismiss all charges."

Radovich stepped in between Timothy and Reginald Konen. "Your Honor, the defendants are mature individuals who held responsible positions of power at the highest levels in the United States Government."

"That's right," Konen said. He spoke at Radovich with a false grin that bared his teeth. "They made tough decisions that had to be made quickly. Sometimes they made a mistake."

"These are not naïve persons," Radovich said as he stepped in closer to Konen and spoke to him with a cold stare. "Many of them have legal credentials. Anyone doing a cursory search of the internet would find that the U.S. government has prosecuted others for waterboarding, and that it is considered torture."

"Is that where Mr. Radovich learns the law, on internet blogs?" Konen asked.

Radovich turned away from Konen and spoke to the judge. "If Mr. Konen would take the time to review prior case law, he would realize that for anyone to claim they did not know their acts were illegal, or that they were unaware of the impact of their rulings and direction, over a period of more than five years, is asking one to suspend belief."

Konen countered, "And Mr. Radovich is—

"Enough gentlemen!" The judge's shout put an end to the sparring.

"Motion to dismiss is denied," the judge said. "Take your seats gentlemen. Mr. Konen, if you can come up with a reasonable motion to be considered by this court, I will entertain it."

Konen didn't sit, instead he said, "The statute of limitations has run out, Judge. It's well past the eight-year limit on prosecution. It's unfair to the defendants that these charges weren't brought earlier so they could have had the benefit of a speedy trial. To try them now is unconstitutional."[150]

Timothy had been waiting for this one. "Mr. Konen is far behind the times with this argument, Judge. The Patriot Act signed into law by President Bush in October of 2001 removed the limitations on prosecution for torture.[151] There is no limitation if the crime involves an offense which resulted in, or created a foreseeable risk of death or serious bodily

---

150   US Constitution, Amendment VI, Rights to Fair Trial

151   18 USC 3286 (b) No Limitation. https://www.law.cornell.edu/uscode/text/18/3286

injury to another person. There is no doubt that controlled drowning, waterboarding, creates a foreseeable risk of death."

"Mr. Konen, if you can bring me legal evidence that the statute of limitations has run out on these charges, I will dismiss them. But until you do, your motion is denied. Please do not waste our time with posturing and floating trial balloons in the future." He turned to Julie Branson. "Julie, do we have a schedule for the arraignment?"

"Yes, sir, two weeks from today."

Jarvis sat back in his chair and folded his hands in his lap. "We will conduct the arraignment on that schedule. Don't be late, Konen. I expect all of the defendants to be in attendance."

"But, Your Honor, they are all going to plead not guilty and plead the Fifth Amendment privilege to not testify. Why do they need to attend?"

"Listen carefully, Mr. Konen," the judge said. The muscles in his jaw bulged his cheeks. "This is a criminal trial; your clients are charged with serious crimes. If they do not show up at the arraignment, they will be rounded up by federal marshals. Do you hear me? Rounded up! None of us want that to happen sir, so bring them with you."

Reginald Konen tried to make the best of it with a smile for Timothy, a snarl for Jacob, and a nod to the judge. He signaled for Willis to join him as he moved toward the door. Timothy and Jacob followed him out.

The judge watched them go.

"Type those notes up for me, Julie. I want to review them before they're filed."

* * *

Julie couldn't get the notes typed fast enough. As soon as she delivered the copy to Jarvis, she returned to her desk and dialed William Mayfield.

"Mr. Mayfield, I have news for you," she spoke in a low voice into the phone.

There was a loud background hum on the other end of the line.

"Julie, it doesn't matter anymore. I'm in the air over Puerto Rico right now, and I'm going to be south of the border for a while. Don't call me anymore. I'll catch up with you when I get back. Might be a long time, dear. Bye."

"But Mister Mayfield, you promised—"

The click and silence on the other end of the call was definite. She slammed the phone down, then reconsidered, picked it back up, and dialed her connection at the *Post*.

* * *

Jeff Blake parked his car at the back of the *Washington Times* lot on New York Avenue and called Annie on his cell.

"They're gonna try'n make Madegen look like a psycho. They know about his dad and how he found him after the suicide. They're trying to link his dad's torture to the torture trial and make it look like some kind of personal obsession."

"Personal? Damn it, Jeff, it *is* personal," she said a little too loud, then softer as she rose from her desk chair with the remote handset, crossed the room, and closed the door connecting her office to Madegen's. "It's personal for all the people who were tortured. There were scores of people detained and lots of them abused. That Senate report got all the attention, but it's not only what the CIA did, the U.S. Army did it too. We need to remind people of what happened back then. That's the story that will balance the spinmeisters."

"Well, you're gonna have to get me some specifics." Jeff gave a restless sigh. "They won't be any help here at the paper. They've got the whole research department diving into Madegen's past. I'll need some powerful stuff to get them to run anything counter to their preconceived one-track line." Jeff watched an associate walking past his car. He waved and smiled at her. "I'm gonna have to get back to my desk before I attract too much attention."

"Has your paper gotten anything from the defendants yet?" Annie asked.

"None of them will talk to us," Jeff said with a forced laugh. "The celebrity reporters over at the *Post* have the inside scoop on those people. Woodward's been one-on-one with most of them at one time or another. All I can tell you is every famous lawyer in the country is volunteering to represent them. They have their pick. I have to go, Annie."

"Wait. I know. Can you do a survey story? The country's lost track of what happened over ten years ago. Torture and abuse was going on all over the world—Europe, Guantanamo, the Middle East. That Senate report gave all the attention to CIA detainees, but there were more, lots more."

"OK, yeah. I think I can get something like that past the weekend editor, and your guys can spin off it on the Sunday talk shows. That'll work. Get me the facts, and I'll put it together. We've got about twenty-four hours if you want it in Sunday's paper."

"We're on it, Jeff."

"If I get your stuff tonight, I'll have the article for your review in the morning. Is Mr. Madegen still looking at this stuff before we print?"

"Yes. I'll go over it with him as soon as you fax in the copy."

"So, what's with you and Madegen, Annie?"

"What do you mean?" Annie said, although she knew exactly what Jeff meant.

"Well? Are you guys—"

She smiled, considering what to reveal to her best friend. "He's an enigma, Jeff. I work with him every day, but he's distant and hard to read. It's like he's completely involved in this process, and there's nothing else in his life. Sometimes I see a small glimmer of emotion in him, but then it's gone, and we're back to business."

"So what keeps you going, Annie? Why are *you* so committed to this?"

"Part of it's the cause, and part of it is Tim's honest desire to make things right. He makes me feel like we can win. I'm hooked, Jeff."

"Don't let it consume you, Annie. I know how you can get."

"They say to never take advice from your ex."

"Just be careful about investing too much in this guy."

"We'll see," she said. "We'll see." Annie's voice softened. "You're my best friend, Jeff. Thank you, thank you, thank you."

There was a brief silence. "We do make a good team," Jeff said. "Gotta go! Bye!"

* * *

Annie called on Clarissa for help, and the two of them went to work in Annie's office. They sat in front of computer screens at opposite ends of a work table that became covered with files, coffee cups, and a half empty box of cold pizza.

"We want to give people a perspective on the trial. Remind them of what was going on over ten years ago," Annie said. "Some people never knew the whole story of U.S. detentions. Most people have heard about Guantanamo Bay and Abu Ghraib, but there were a lot more detention sites."

"What I'm seeing is the U.S. led the development of a world-wide network of detention centers with the cooperation of lots of countries," Clarissa said. "It's a little unnerving that it was done so quickly, and so many countries were willing to support it."

"The Senate report identified eight color-coded CIA black sites,"[152] Annie said. "Some enterprising journalists broke the code. Four were in Afghanistan, and the others were in Poland, Lithuania, Romania, and Thailand."[153]

John Mayfield came into the office from the hall. "What are you two doing here so late? It's after seven. Aren't you ready to call it a day?" He came up behind Clarissa and looked at her screen.

She twisted around to look up over her shoulder at him. "We're working to a deadline, John. Jeff Blake has to have our research by tomorrow morning if he's going to make the Sunday paper."

"Looks like you're researching CIA black sites, but by the look of it, you haven't found all of them," he said, then pulled a chair over next to Clarissa. "Try Googling-up 'CIA proxy sites.' They're prisons in countries that cooperated with the CIA where secret detention and interrogation took place."

Clarissa punched in the search term. "We've got nine more black sites, Annie.[154] That makes thirteen countries that collaborated secretly to host CIA interrogations."

"You're not done, ladies," John said. "What about the countries that enabled the so-called 'renditions.' There were more than fifty that allowed secret flights in and out of their airports.[155] And some of those countries did the CIA's dirty work for them. They might have been worse than the CIA."

Annie looked up from her screen with a gasp. "Oh my god!" Her

---

152   Adam Goldman and Julie Tate, *Decoding The Secret Black Sites On The Senate's report On The CIA Interrogation Program*, *Washington Post*, December 9, 2014. http://www.washingtonpost.com/blogs/worldviews/wp/2014/12/09/decoding-the-secret-black-sites-on-the-senates-report-on-the-cia-interrogation-program/?postsha re=3411418143614830

153   *Globalizing Torture CIA Secret Detention And Extraordinary Rendition*, Open Society Justice Initiative, 2013. http://www.opensocietyfoundations.org/sites/default/files/globalizing-torture-20120205.pdf

154   Huffington Post. *More Than A Quarter Of The World's Countries Helped The CIA Run Its Torture Program* Posted: 12/09/2014 8:34 pm EST Updated: 12/11/2014 11:59 am EST
http://www.huffingtonpost.com/2014/12/09/cia-torture-countries_n_6297832.html

155   Ibid.

chin dropped. "Listen to this quote from an ex-CIA agent. 'If you want a serious interrogation, you send a prisoner to Jordan. If you want them to be tortured, you send them to Syria. If you want someone to disappear— never to see them again—you send them to Egypt'."[156]

Clarissa got up and came over to look at the quotation on Annie's computer screen.

"Who said that?" she asked. "A lot of those detainees were innocent. Do you know about the CIA bounty program?[157] They paid up to $5,000 a head for people accused of being a terrorist. That's a big temptation in Afghanistan or Pakistan where workers average $200 a month."

"I'm not surprised innocent people were accused," Annie said.

"So we've identified over sixty-three countries that participated in one way or another in the U.S. detention, rendition, and torture program. That's more than twenty-five percent of all countries on the planet! No one should question Bush's international leadership. When it comes to secret arrest, he'd be hard to beat."

John took over the keyboard at Clarissa's station. "There were a lot of black sites and lots of countries involved, but do you have any idea how many people were detained at those places?" he asked Annie and Clarissa.

"The Senate report has reams on the CIA," Clarissa said. "There were at least a hundred nineteen detainees in the record at clandestine sites world-wide, and thirty-nine of those are known to have been subjected to the enhanced interrogation techniques."[158] Two of them died.

Annie found the numbers on Guantanamo. There were 780 detainees between 2002 and 2009.[159] Nine detainees died in custody.

Clarissa drew on her photographic memory. "In his State of the Union address in January of 2003, President Bush said we had detained over 3,000 suspected terrorists.[160] That's three months before the Iraq war started, and the U.S. took over Saddam Hussein's prison at Abu Ghraib."

---

156 Stephen Grey, *America's gulag*. New Statesman, 17 May, 2004. http://www.newstatesman.com/node/159775

157 Michael Di Paolo, *The Lucrative Bounty Program*, New York Law School, February 5, 2014. http://www.detainedbyus.org/the-lucrative-bounty-program/

158 Supra 61. Findings and Conclusions. #15. Page 12.

159 *New York Times, The Guantanamo Docket.* http://projects.nytimes.com/guantanamo/detainees

160 Text of President Bush's 2003 State of the Union Address Jan. 28, 2003 Courtesy eMediaMillWorks, The Washington Post. http://www.washingtonpost.com/wp-srv/onpolitics/transcripts/bushtext_012803.html

John's fingers clicked the keyboard. "There were up to 3,800 detainees in Abu Ghraib at one point in time. The International Committee of the Red Cross reported that military intelligence officers told them seventy to ninety percent of those detained were arrested by mistake.[161] There's no data on the total number who were processed through there over the next four years. We have pictures of some of them being tortured, but we don't know how many were abused." More keyboard clicking. "Nobody knows exactly how many detainees were held by U.S. forces at the Bagram Air Base in Afghanistan, but a Freedom of Information Act resulted in finding that at least 645 were held there, and some of them were beaten to death."[162]

Annie looked over the top of her screen at John. "Thanks for pitching in John. That should be enough for Jeff's article. I'll put it all together for him with the references and email it over. You two can take off if you want."

Clarissa and John left Annie to her work, which she was just wrapping up when Timothy opened the connecting door and came in.

"What now, Annie?" he asked.

"We're helping Jeff Blake out with some research. How are things going with the trial prep?"

Timothy's face broke into a mischievous grin. He cleared a space and sat on the table next to Annie's computer dangling his legs. "I wish you could have been there, Annie. The defense made several motions to the judge which were shredded like a low flying duck at an NRA rally." They laughed together as they imagined Timothy's cartoon.

---

161 Report of the International Committee of the Red Cross (ICRC) On The Treatment by Coalition Forces of Prisoners of War and Other Protected Persons by The Geneva Conventions in Iraq During Arrest, Internment and Interrogation. February 2004. Page 8.
http://www.derechos.org/nizkor/us/doc/icrc-prisoner-report-feb-2004.pdf
162 Timothy Golden, *New York Times, In U.S. Report, Brutal Details Of 2 Afghan Inmates' Deaths, Top of Form Bottom of Form* May 20, 2005
http://www.nytimes.com/2005/05/20/world/asia/in-us-report-brutal-details-of-2-afghan-inmates-deaths.html

CHAPTER 30

*Justice will not be served until those who are unaffected are
as outraged as those who are.*
—Benjamin Franklin

S lender white booms, topped with dish antennas and wrapped with spiraling feeder cables, telescoped into the air like a forest of robotic trees growing out of the tops of white boxes painted with network logos. A line of vans stretched in both directions along the curb in front of the E. Barrett Prettyman Federal Courthouse on Constitution Avenue where the United States District Court for the District of Columbia did its business.

Washington, D.C. knows how to prepare for an important event. A security perimeter of barricades and squads of policemen held back a growing crowd at the building entrance, admitting those with credentials, and directing activists, protesters, and curious tourists to the demonstration area set up in neighboring John Marshall Park. Street vendors had prepared carts and awnings in the early morning hours across the lawn from a twenty-yard-long row of green port-a-potties.

Hopeful reporters gossiped and waited in line outside the front entrance of the courthouse for their turn at the metal detectors. They were intently aware of the uniqueness of an arraignment of seventeen high-level federal officials and the spectacle of an ex-president and ex-vice-president being charged with crimes. Self-important federal agents processed them with stern instructions and practiced impatience.

In the hallway outside the courtroom, camera crews in blue jeans and t-shirts shouldered video equipment to capture every word of makeup-heavy commentators, who sparred for the attention of an attorney or a defendant. Reginald B. Konen dallied in the hall, generous with his time for on-camera interviews, which he could stretch to fill a full five minutes.

Attorneys in look-alike dark suits and blue-white shirts carrying fat leather briefcases jammed the floor in front of the bar. Long-faced lawyers consulted with their clients, confirming the seriousness of their concern and trying to instill confidence in their firm's ability to develop a winning defense. Some defense attorneys had the difficult job of satisfying clients who were themselves attorneys, loaded with questions and full of suggestions on how to handle the case.

Jarvis had made it a condition of the arraignment that there would be no cameras or general public in the courtroom. Ten lucky reporters were chosen by lottery from a pool of one hundred. One sketch artist was allowed in.

Federal officers filled every open space around the courtroom walls, vigilant for any sign of disruption. The room hummed with energy until a side door opened. The crowd went slowly silent when President Bush stepped through the door and stopped. He gave a half smile and looked over the courtroom as if expecting to find familiar faces to chat with. A marshal directed him to the defendants' seating area. Vice-President Cheney followed, staring at the furniture with a scowl that kept everyone including his attending attorney at bay. Conversations restarted as the rest of the defendants filed in.

Henry Jarvis showed them respect by entering as soon as they were seated.

The squeak of the judge's chamber door preceded the clerk's announcement. "All rise for the Honorable Henry Jarvis."

A chaotic rumble filled the air as almost one hundred people rose from their seats. Vice-President Cheney made a statement by being the last person to stand.

Jarvis took his place at the bench. "Let's be seated." He put on his reading glasses, opened the briefing book in front of him, then took the glasses off, and peered down over the edge of the bench to examine the courtroom before him.

The mahogany-paneled room waited; all eyes on the judge. In front of him, to his left, was the prosecutor's table where a nervous Timothy

Madegen and confident Jacob Radovich sat with John Mayfield.

Before the bar to his right was the defending attorneys' table at which Reginald Konen sat with Jake Willis. Behind them in two rows of chairs setup for the occasion sat the seventeen defendants and their personal attorneys. Beyond the bar, in church-like pews, the assigned reporters and defendant support teams filled every available seat. The jury box was empty. A clerk and court recorder took their places on the semi-raised dais to the judge's right. The recorder looked with awed expression at President Bush and Vice-President Cheney.

"Mr. Konen, can you confirm that all of the defendants are present?"

The seventeen defendants whispered to each other, sometimes jotting notes and passing them back and forth.

Konen rose to respond. "Yes, Your Honor. Your brief contains a list of defendants with the names of each of their personal attorneys."

The judge found the list and read down the page. "Looks like an attorney jobs program, seventeen defendants and seventeen law firms representing them." He looked around the courtroom until his eyes focused on Reginald Konen. "You are representing President Bush, Mr. Konen?"

"Yes, sir. President Bush has agreed to engage me. And in the interest of efficiency, all of the defense attorneys have asked me to present motions for all defendants for the purpose of this hearing."

"Do you have any objection to that, Mr. Madegen?" Jarvis asked.

Timothy leaned over to Radovich for a quiet discussion, then turned back to the judge. "We have no argument with Mr. Konen representing all defendants for common motions, Your Honor."

Radovich caught Konen's eye, raised an eyebrow, and grinned at him. Konen ignored him.

"Have each of the defendants been given the opportunity to review the text of the presentment, the charges against them, and the applicable laws?"

"They have, Your Honor," Timothy said.

"Do any of the defense attorneys disagree?" the judge asked and looked down the row of defendants and attorneys. There was no objection.

"Does the defense wish to make any motion prior to entering a plea?"

When Konen approached the bench, Jacob Radovich got up from his seat.

"We wish to have each defendant tried separately, Your Honor, due to the fact that testimony from one of the defendants might reflect on another and thereby prejudice the jury." Konen's head jerked around when he noticed Radovich approach behind him, then he turned back to the bench. "It is common practice to request individual trials for each defendant, and we believe this is a fair petition considering these charges."

Radovich took a position next to Konen, almost touching him, shoulder to shoulder. Konen moved away.

"What does the prosecution say with regard to the defense motion?"

"Thank you, Your Honor," Radovich said. "I would like to bring to the attention of the court that there is a common thread that touches all of the defendants. They are all charged with violations under either count one or two. Fourteen of the defendants are charged with conspiracy. It is logical that they be tried together; it's that kind of offense. Eleven of the defendants are charged with authorizing torture, which is also related to the conspiracy charge. Again, it makes sense to include them in one trial. In the interest of judicial efficiency, we disagree with the defense motion for separate trials."

Jarvis thought for a moment. "I am concerned with the jury's ability to consider evidence for or against so many defendants," Jarvis said. "Our jurors are not trained in the law, and we must keep it manageable for them. They could easily become confused over what testimony and evidence applies to which defendant." His look of concern became more brooding. "I am inclined to sever individual defendants for trial."

Konen stepped forward to address the judge. "We renew our motion for separate trials for each of the defendants, Your Honor. Please consider that fairness favors this approach."

Jarvis turned to Timothy. "What does the Special Prosecutor say?"

Timothy came to stand beside Radovich. "Seventeen separate trials puts the prosecution at a disadvantage. The defendants have identified and briefed their counsel, but the prosecution will have to assemble and inform a team of prosecuting attorneys, at least one for each trial."

"I'll give you enough time to prepare for the other trials, Madegen. We'll set the trial for President Bush to begin in four weeks. The other sixteen trials will be held under assignment to other district court judges and begin in forty-five days."

"Is there anything else, Mr. Konen?"

Konen looked at the array of defendants and attorneys. He smiled at Jacob Radovich, then turned back to the judge. "No, sir."

"Madegen?"

"No, sir."

"Will the defendants please rise?" the judge asked. "We will ask each of you in turn to state your plea. You may plead not guilty, guilty, or nolo contendere. We'll start with you, sir." He pointed to one of the defendants at the end of the row. "State your name, your plea, and go right down the line."

All of the defendants pled not guilty in terse statements that implied a common desire to complete the hearing as quickly as possible. Only a few made comment with their pleading.

President Bush said, "Our government does not torture."

Vice President Cheney said, "We were very careful to stop short of torture."

When all the pleadings were complete, Jarvis asked, "Is there anything else from the defense or the prosecution before we close this hearing?"

Konen spoke again, "Your Honor, the defendants are all well-known citizens and busy with important responsibilities. We request that they be allowed to sign a waiver of presence, here in open court, so that they will not be required to attend all of the proceedings including the final jury decision, if they do not wish to attend."

"Does the prosecution object, Mr. Radovich?"

"No objection, Your Honor. We expected this request."

"I will allow it, Mr. Konen," the judge said. "The defendants are waiving their right to be present at all proceedings, but the court is not waiving its right to require their attendance if found to be necessary for the process of the trial. Do you understand and agree?"

"Agreed," Konen and Radovich voiced together.

Willis passed around waivers and collected the signed copies.

"The trial of President Bush is set for four weeks from today," Jarvis said. "Do not bring me any motions for extension—they will not be approved. We are going to get this over with in a dignified and professional manner. This arraignment is adjourned." The judge left the bench and the courtroom.

Marshals kept reporters at bay as the defendants filed out the way they came in.

Reginald Konen approached Jacob Radovich with a cocky grin. "Hey, Jacob. How does it feel to be in the spotlight after twenty years of babying destitute clients in trivial cases? This will put you on the map, man!"

"It's not about me, Konen; it's about justice for people who haven't been getting any." Jacob stood with his shoulders back and his chin out. His eyes drilled through Konen. "A little friendly advice for you, Reggie. You'd better keep your clients off the talk shows. Every time they open their mouths, we get more evidence to work with."

"My clients won't need to talk. They have lots of people who will be defending them every day before and during this trial. Money is no object. We'll take the media away from you and Madegen. See you in thirty days, pal."

Konen spun on his heel and headed back to the cameras in the hall. Radovich watched him go with an amused expression that morphed into a confident smile.

* * *

The jury selection process started a week later. One hundred potential jurors answered their summons to appear in the Jarvis courtroom for Q&A by prosecutors and defense attorneys.

Jake Willis represented the defense firm, challenging for cause any juror who admitted following media coverage of the Abu Ghraib scandal and the Senate report on the CIA. He made peremptory challenges of anyone who seemed to have a liberal or humanitarian leaning.

John Mayfield and Clarissa Morrison made decisions for the prosecution. They tried to eliminate flag-waving reactionaries and favored jurors in their twenties who would not have been paying attention to news reports and political spin about the war on terror over ten years prior.

It took three weeks to select eighteen potential jurors from which lots were drawn to arrive at a twelve-person jury; the other six attending the trial as back-ups. It was a diverse group of young and old, white and ethnic, male and female.

When jury selection was complete, the judge made a surprise announcement. "Ladies and gentlemen, because of the notoriety of the defendant and the publicity this trial has already provoked even before it has begun, I must require, with much reluctance, that all eighteen jurors be sequestered for the length of the trial."

There was a collective groan from the jury box. Juror number eleven spoke immediately. "I can't, Your Honor. I'm responsible for the care of my invalid brother."

The judge held up a hand. "There may be some jurors who have valid reasons for being excused from a sequestered jury. I will speak with anyone who has such a request in my chambers after we recess." Jarvis looked each juror in the eye, one at a time as he spoke. "Sequestration begins today. The clerk will provide written instruction to each of you. In the meantime, you will avoid discussion of this trial with anyone, including each other, your spouse, and other family members. Under no circumstance should you speak to the press. Court is recessed."

When the door closed behind the judge, the jurors broke their silence. Some spoke with loud anger to their neighbor in the jury box, others looked uncertain about what had just happened to them. There was a general unease about what to expect next. The clerk called for order and took the names of those requesting to see the judge.

CHAPTER 31

The United States is a nation of laws:
badly written and randomly enforced.
— Frank Zappa, musician, singer, & songwriter (1940–1993)

Paul Smithson exhausted every avenue in his attempt to contact William Mayfield over a period of several days. At first the phone didn't answer, then it reported "out-of-service-area." He tracked down Mayfield's office. The door was locked, and no one responded to his knock.

With his main source of income gone, Smithson started prospecting. He left a message for Reginald Konen saying he had information relating to the case, and that he had been working with William Mayfield, stepbrother of Judge Henry Jarvis. It got no reply.

Smithson was lunching at a deli counter on Connecticut Avenue when a dark-haired woman in a tailored suit took the seat next to him.

"Hello, Paul. We want to talk to you." She removed a cell phone from her purse and offered it to Smithson. "Take it to your office and call the number in the address book. There's only one. Leave your name on the voice mail and wait for us to call you back."

"Who are you?"

"You can call me 'Sheila.' If you use that phone for any other purpose, it will go dead. Bye, Paul."

He admired her walk as she left; the staccato rhythm of her stiletto heels clicked across the tile floor. In a moment she was gone.

Smithson went directly to his office where he followed the woman's instructions and waited. An hour later, he received a call from a male voice.

"I have a job for you, Paul. I want you to coordinate demonstrations at the U.S. District Courthouse on Constitution Ave."

"Who is this?"

"You won't need to know who I am, only that you will be well paid if you do as you're told. Open your top desk drawer. You will find an envelope with your name on it."

Smithson opened the drawer and withdrew a large manila envelope. He tore it open and found several large bills and a typed list of names and numbers.

"There's five thousand dollars there. Do as we say, and we'll make regular payments. The people on that list are all supporters of George Bush. I want at least one hundred of them demonstrating in front of the courthouse every day of the trial. The more people you can get out there, the more you will be paid. Can you do that?"

"Yeah, I can do that," he said without hesitation. "What do you want the demonstrators to do or say?"

"Don't worry about that. They'll know what to do. All you have to do is get them out there. Remember, the more people, the more you'll get paid. There's several thousand on that list, get a team together to make the calls. I want them out there the day the trial starts and every day until it ends."

"How will I get paid?"

"It'll happen."

The phone went dead. Smithson tried to dial it again, but the phone didn't work.

CHAPTER 32

*Military necessity does not admit of cruelty—that is, the infliction of
suffering for the sake of suffering or for revenge, nor of maiming or
wounding except in fight, nor of torture to extort confessions.*
—Proclamation by Abraham Lincoln, April 24, 1863.

The torture trial of President George W. Bush began on schedule at 9:00 a.m. five days after final jury selection.

Jarvis opened the trial with a gavel blow that echoed about the mahogany paneled walls of the courtroom. Twelve jurors and five alternates sat in padded chairs in the jury box on his left, one alternate juror had been excused. Spectators and journalists packed elbow to elbow on hard wooden benches behind the bar. Isabel Jarvis sat in the front row behind the prosecutors. She was dressed in a somber tailored suit. The dark blue jacket opened at the neck displaying a whiter-than-white pearl necklace that Henry had given her years before on their tenth anniversary. The radiance of the necklace matched the glow of pride she felt for her courageous husband. No one in the crowd knew her for the judge's wife, but her natural presence caused them to give her space in the pews.

At the prosecutor's table, Timothy Madegen, Jacob Radovich, and Annie Young huddled over Timothy's opening statement, penciling in last-minute changes.

The defense table was occupied by Reginald Konen and Jake Willis. The defendant, George W. Bush, was not in attendance.

"Members of the Jury, I thank you for your service to this court." Jarvis began. "Please pay close attention to the instructions I am about to give you."

When Jarvis looked up from his reading, he was startled to notice Isabel in the gallery and gave her a small smile, which she proudly returned.

"President George W. Bush is accused of authorizing torture, conspiring to enable torture, and committing war crimes. The defendant has entered a plea of not guilty. You must presume he is innocent. The Government has the burden of proving the charges.

"It is to the evidence introduced in this trial, and to that alone, that you are to look for proof. If you have a reasonable doubt, you should find President Bush not guilty.

"We will now hear opening statements from Special Prosecutor, Timothy Madegen, followed by defense attorney, Reginald Konen. Mr. Madegen, proceed."

Timothy rose from his seat, had a brief word with Annie, then took a position in front of the jury.

"Ladies and Gentlemen of the jury, as prosecutor, I will endeavor to prove that President George W. Bush, during his time in office, authorized, enabled, and conspired to cause members of the CIA and Department of Defense to torture detainees in their custody—a war crime."

Timothy leaned forward, his hands gripping the front rail of the jury box, the focus of his eyes moving from juror to juror as he spoke.

"We will present documents and witnesses showing that President Bush authorized secret detention in locations around the world for the purpose of concealing the torture, that he authorized specific torture techniques to be used on detainees, and that he was aware of their continued use between the years 2001 through 2006.

"We will show that he conspired with members of his cabinet and Justice Department attorneys to pervert and distort our legal system by developing false legal cover for himself and the torturers. We will present witnesses with firsthand knowledge of his public confession of guilt.

"We will settle the question about waterboarding and show that it is torture. You will learn that many who have used it before have been prosecute in U.S. criminal and military courts. We will show that today, there are abundant mature and responsible leaders who acknowledge that waterboarding is torture. We will show that President Bush knew or should have known that he was ordering torture.

"President Bush committed these crimes while in his position as head of the United States government. It was his leadership that caused detainees to be tortured, many of them innocent people.

"He did these things in the name of the American people, in *your* name. He must be found guilty and held to account for these crimes, or you can be sure another president in the future will repeat these atrocities. If you do not find him guilty, you will be sending the message that you approve of what he has done. The world is watching us. You carry a heavy burden. I trust in your judgment. Thank you."

Timothy made a slight bow to the jury and turned to the judge. "Your Honor, the prosecution has completed its opening statement."

Konen gave the opening argument for the defense.

"My name is Reginald B. Konen, and I am proud to appear before you to defend one of the most selfless and courageous men our country has ever known."

Konen paced back and forth in front of the jury box as he spoke.

"President George W. Bush responded to the unprecedented attack on our nation on September 11, 2001, just months after he was sworn into office. Faced with a new enemy, who had no respect for innocent human life, President Bush had the courage to take extraordinary measures to keep us safe—to keep *you* safe. His leadership in forging our military and intelligence responses insured that we suffered no subsequent attack. Instead, he took the fight to the enemy all over the world.

"It would be beyond belief to sanction or punish this man who did everything he could to save our country from a second attack."

Konen spoke about careful legal analysis, the urgency of ticking time-bombs, an enemy that operated outside the accepted laws of war. At the forty-five-minute mark, some eyelids in the jury box began to droop. George Bush's life story, carefully edited, took him another half hour to deliver. He was coming up on the two-hour mark when Jarvis interrupted him.

"Mr. Konen, if you have much more to go, we might have to give the jury a five-minute courtesy break."

"No, Your Honor. I want to finish up by reminding this jury of the sacrifices President Bush has made during eight years of public service. Ladies and Gentlemen, please give the defense a fair hearing and set aside any biases. If you do that, we will prove that President Bush is innocent of all charges. Thank you."

There was an audible sigh from the jury box.

"Thank you, Mr. Madegen and Mr. Konen," the judge said. "We will recess until one o'clock, at which time the prosecution should be prepared to present their first witness."

* * *

Timothy opened in the afternoon. "The prosecution will present evidence that the accused is guilty of the charges listed in Count 1: Commanding, authorizing, aiding, abetting the torture of individuals in control of the United States Government. A violation of USC Title 18, Part I, Chapter 1, § 2–Principals. Mr. Radovich, please proceed."

Timothy returned to the prosecutor table, and Radovich stood to replace him. "The prosecution calls Ms. Shirley Parsens."

A U.S. marshal opened a door at the side of the courtroom and escorted a small, gray-haired woman from the waiting room to the witness box. The clerk swore in the witness.

Radovich began the questioning. "Ms. Parsens, what is your occupation?"

"I am the Executive Director for the Jackson County Library."

"Do you recall where you were on November 14th, 2010?"

"Yes, I was at Miami Dade College on that day."

"And what were you doing there?"

"I was attending the Annual Miami Book Fair International."

"Did you attend any notable discussion sessions during the book fair?"

"Yes, sir. I attended a discussion by President George W. Bush on his memoir, *Decision Points*."

"Ms. Parsens, we are going to play a video of that event and ask if you are familiar with it. Please direct your attention to the video monitor. Annie, please show the video."

Everyone in the courtroom turned to the monitor to watch a video of President Bush speaking at the Miami Book Fair. On the video, President Bush said, *"I approved techniques, including waterboarding, on three people."*[163] The video stopped leaving a still image of the president on the screen.

"Ms. Parsens, is this video a fair and accurate representation of the event you attended on November 14th, 2010?"

"Yes, sir. It is."

"Do you recall President Bush speaking the words you just heard

---

163   Supra 3.

him speak in the video?"

"Yes, sir. I do."

"Do you agree that President Bush spoke those words of his own free will without anyone's coercion or influence?"

"I do."

"Objection!" Konen said. "The witness cannot know if President Bush was speaking without anyone's influence."

"Sustained," Jarvis said.

Radovich withdrew the question. "Thank you, Ms. Parsens, no more questions."

The judge asked Konen. "Does the defense want to cross examine?"

"Yes, Your Honor." Konen took his time rising from his chair. "We are familiar with this video. Ms. Parsens, did the president say why he approved those techniques?"

"I think it was to save lives," she said.

"If you would please run another minute of the video," he said to Annie. "Starting right where you left off."

The screen lit up and Bush carried on. *In my book, I make two points clear. One, the information we received from those on whom we used enhanced interrogation techniques, saved, American lives. And secondly, I could not have lived with myself had I not, under the law, used the techniques, to get the information, so that our folks could react and prevent attack.*

"Do you recall that speech?"

"I was there, and it looks like a true video of what he said. I do know he said he authorized water—"

"No more questions, Your Honor," Konen said on top of her last words.

"Does the prosecution have any more questions for this witness?"

"No, Your Honor," Radovich said.

"You may step down, Ms. Parsens. Thank you for your testimony," Jarvis said.

Radovich called the next witness, a man who was also present at the Miami Book Fair event, and who also validated the accuracy of Bush's statements in the video. When he called the third witness for the same purpose, the judge reacted.

"Mr. Radovich, how many witnesses do you plan to call to prove the accuracy of the video statement?"

"Your Honor, there were over one hundred people in attendance at that speech. We were able to identify almost fifty. Every one of those can validate the video. If the defense is willing to stipulate that they accept the video confession as true and factual, we can skip the remaining witnesses on this issue."

"Well, Mr. Konen?"

"We will stipulate it is true that President Bush ordered waterboarding, but we do not agree that waterboarding is torture."

"Is that acceptable to you, Mr. Radovich?"

"Yes, sir," Jacob said and shot a wry glance at Konen. "We'll work on the torture issue next."

Konen glared at Radovich and took his seat.

Radovich stood in front of the jury box. "The prosecution calls Professor Isaac Frank."

The room watched in silence as the professor entered and took the witness chair. The clerk swore him in.

Radovich gave him a smile "Thank you for testifying today, Professor. Please state your current employment for the court."

"Professor of Law, Yale Law School."

He was a thin man, over six feet tall. His jacket seemed shabby in comparison to the attorneys'. Under the jacket he wore a collarless shirt. His hair was crew-cut, and thick, owlish glasses distorted the appearance of his eyes. His lips slanted to one side and moved like a rubbery mask when he spoke.

"What is your experience in practicing law, professor?"

"I was in private practice for several years after law school, spent one year as attorney-advisor in a corporate office, then became a professor of law at Yale, where I am now teaching."

"Do you have a specialty in the law, Professor?"

"I specialize in legal history."

"Have you ever provided legal history research as a service to trial proceedings?"

"I am often called upon to provide background research in support of attorneys at trial."

"Were you asked to prepare historical research for this trial?"

"Yes, sir. Mr. Madegen asked me to research convictions for the crime of waterboarding."

"Konen shot up from his seat, "Objection, Your Honor!"

"Don't shout at me, Mr. Konen." The judge removed his reading glasses and peered over the top of his bench at Konen. "What is your objection?"

"There has been no evidence submitted in this trial that proves waterboarding is a crime."

"Sustained. The witness is asked to refrain from calling waterboarding a crime."

Frank looked at the judge and nodded, then Radovich continued. "And what did your research on convictions for waterboarding show?"

"There have been several convictions for waterboarding under U.S. and International law."

"Please give us an example."

"There was a decision in the case of the United States of America v. Hideji Nakamura, Yukio Asano, Seitara Hata, and Takeo Kita in which a U.S. Military Commission convicted the defendants of torture for waterboarding U.S. troops during World War II."[164]

Konen objected, "The case prosecution offers as evidence is a military commission decision, not a criminal trial decision, and it has no bearing on this case. Military commissions are a substandard system of justice, with rules and charges not contemplated by a U.S. court. These commissions don't protect attorney-client communications; they use coerced evidence and work under rules that block the defense from access to information essential to the case."

Radovich responded. "The decision cited was subject to appeal by U.S. courts, but no appeal was made because of the preponderance of evidence against the accused. It is a well-known and important decision, Your Honor. If Mr. Konen wants to appeal the decision, he is free to do so; otherwise, it stands as valid legal precedent."

"You are overruled, Mr. Konen," the judge said. "Please proceed, Mr. Radovich."

Radovich handed a document to Professor Frank. "Is this a true copy of that decision, Professor?"

---

164 HEADQUARTERS EIGHTH ARMY, United States Army, Office of Staff Judge Advocate, Yokohama, Japan
15 October 1948, UNITED STATES OF AMERICA VS SEITARO HATA, YUKIO ASANO, TAKEO KITA, HIDEJI NAKAMURA.
https://www.google.com/
url?sa=t&rct=j&q=&esrc=s&source=web&cd=1&ved=0CB4QFjAAahUKEwj_t9O61-rGAhXMpYgKHQaAAIY&url=http%3A%2F%2Fwww.
mansell.com%2Fpow_resources%2Fcamplists%2Ffukuoka%2Ffuku_3_tobata%2FIMTFE_Case53_HATA_ASANO_KITA_%2520NAKAMURA_FUK-03.docx&ei=I2ytVb-aL8zLogSGgIKwCA&usg=AFQjCNFz0Z_acJQnGnpwGYb0TBx42jwrXA&bvm=bv.98197061,d.cGU&cad=rja

"Yes, that is the copy I provided Mr. Madegen."

He showed the cover of the document to Konen, who turned away. Radovich then walked over to the jury box and let each juror read the title. Finally, Radovich showed the document to the judge and asked that it be entered into evidence. Then he took a position close to the jury box, forcing the professor to speak in the direction of the jury when he answered the next question.

"Did you find any other legal history that referenced waterboarding, professor?"

"Yes, sir. During the Vietnam action, a U.S. soldier was convicted by court-martial of torture for waterboarding a Vietnamese soldier. A photograph of the waterboarding was published on the front page of the *Washington Post*."[165]

"Objection! A court-martial is conducted under the Uniform Code of Military Justice, not the U.S. code of laws. They aren't the same system of laws, and this case should not be accepted into evidence," Konen yelled.

Jarvis slammed his gavel and leaned forward on his elbows to peer down at the attorney. "Mr. Konen, if you shout at me one more time, I will hold you in contempt. Get a hold of yourself, sir."

Radovich answered Konen. "Courts-martial are authorized under U.S. law, USC 10, § 818.[166] Mr. Konen may not be familiar with this part of the code."

"Objection overruled. Continue Mr. Radovich. Your exhibit is accepted into evidence."

"Thank you, Your Honor."

Annie handed a copy of the front page article and picture to Jacob, who held up the page for the witness to see. Professor Frank confirmed that it was the article he referred to, and Radovich showed it to Konen, and the jury.

"Professor Frank, did you find any history related to waterboarding in the U.S. criminal courts?"

The professor looked over at Konen before he spoke. "There was a case right here in the United States. In 1983, Texas Sheriff James Parker and three of his deputies were charged by the Department of Justice with

---

165 "Interrogation", Washington Post, front page, January 21, 1968.
    http://www.washingtonpost.com/wp-dyn/content/article/2006/10/04/
    AR2006100402005.html

166 10 U.S. Code § 818 - Art. 18. Jurisdiction of general courts-martial

committing a crime by their use of water torture on prisoners. They were each sentenced to ten years in prison."[167]

The case documentation was entered into evidence without comment from the defense.

"Any other U.S. court cases, professor?"

"In 1996, the U.S. Court of Appeals for the Ninth Circuit found the estate of Philippine dictator, Ferdinand Marcos, liable for instances of torture including waterboarding, committed by the Marcos Government."[168]

"Was there a monetary award to the victims, professor?"

"Yes, nearly 10,000 victims were awarded $766 million in compensatory damages and $1.2 billion in exemplary damages."

Radovich looked over the jury and said, "We will remind the jury of this verdict when the time comes."

Konen started to rise, then thought better of it, and remained in his chair.

"Professor, do you know of any prominent people in history that have given an opinion about waterboarding?"

"In recent history," the professor said, "several of our current leaders at the highest levels in our government have declared waterboarding to be torture including President Obama, Attorney General Eric Holder, and Attorney General Loretta Lynch."

"One more question, professor. How difficult was it for you to find the information you presented to the court today?"

The professor looked a little uncomfortable with this question.

"We are not going to re-negotiate your compensation," Radovich said with a smile. "We are only asking if the information is readily available. Did you require access to private legal data bases? Were there any special skills required?"

Isaac Frank shifted in his chair and looked up at the judge but found no support there. "The information I provided to this court can be

---

167	United States of America, Plaintiff-appellee, v. Carl Lee, Defendant-appellant, 744 F.2d 1124 (5th Cir. 1984),
http://law.justia.com/cases/federal/appellate-courts/F2/744/1124/459598/

168	United States Court of Appeals, Ninth Circuit. Maximo HILAO, Class Plaintiffs, Plaintiff-Appellee, v. ESTATE OF Ferdinand MARCOS, Defendant, Imelda R. Marcos; Ferdinand R. Marcos, Representatives of the Estate of Ferdinand Marcos, Defendants-Appellants.Nos. 95-16487, 95-16145, Decided: December 17, 1996
http://caselaw.findlaw.com/us-9th-circuit/1279729.html#sthash.iLkssmk9.dpuf

easily found within a few minutes by anyone capable of using an Internet search engine."

"We have no more questions, thank you, Professor," Radovich said and returned to his seat.

"Mr. Konen, do you want to cross-examine this witness?" Jarvis asked.

"Yes, Your Honor." He walked slowly to the witness box. When he spoke, it was a shot aimed directly at the witness. "Professor Frank, how much were you paid for your testimony?"

"Objection!" Radovich said. "Counsel is insulting the witness. The question implies the professor has broken the law. The witness is not on trial."

"Sustained."

Konen tried again. "Professor, were you contracted to produce the legal history you just presented in this trial?"

"Yes."

"Who contracted you?"

"The Special Prosecutor, Mr. Madegen."

"And did he pay you for the research?"

"Yes."

"If he had not paid you, would you have researched this topic?"

"No."

"So if you had not done this research, would you have come to Washington to testify in this trial?"

"No, I came at Mr. Madegen's request."

"So if he paid you to do the research, and you wouldn't have presented it in this trial without getting paid. Wouldn't you say he paid for your testimony?"

"Objection!" It was Radovich's turn to shout. "Counsel is twisting the normal relationship between an expert witness and a trial attorney. His claim is outlandish!"

"Sustained," Jarvis said. "The last exchange will be deleted from the record. Mr. Konen, I'll have no more of your wild accusations. Professor Frank, please accept the apology of this court for Mr. Konen's behavior."

Konen turned and smiled at Radovich. "I have no more questions," he said. "The witness may be excused."

Jarvis watched Reginald Konen return to the defense table. When Konen was seated, he said. "Mr. Konen, Mr. Madegen, and Mr. Radovich, if you are agreeable to a recess at this time, we will pick this up again tomorrow morning at 9:00 a.m."

Konen spoke softly for the first time that afternoon, "Yes, Your Honor, the defense agrees."

Madegen nodded his assent.

Jarvis' gavel tapped the block. "This court is recessed until 9:00 a.m. tomorrow morning."

Federal marshals escorted the seventeen jurors out of the courtroom.

Outside the courthouse, the park and streets teemed with people waving signs. The jurors watched from their bus windows as the driver made slow progress through the crowds on the way to the Eisenhower Expressway.

Paul Smithson walked the perimeter, observing his handiwork. Many of demonstrators were there because of him. He was about to leave, when Sheila appeared out of the crowd. She wore a manly-looking business suit and a narrow-brimmed Sinatra-style hat tipped so low in front it met the top of her dark sunglasses.

"Good turnout, Paul," she said.

"Nice to see you, Sheila."

"I'm not your friend, Paul. This is business. You'll find five thousand dollars in your desk drawer. The phone is active again. We'll call you with instructions tonight at ten o'clock. Don't miss the call." She turned and melted into the masses.

* * *

Timothy, Annie, Jacob, John, and Clarissa met in Timothy's office.

"You did well today, Jacob," Timothy said.

"Too well," Radovich paced the room, restless. "All Konen's objections fell flat. There was nothing of substance he could object to. He's feeling pretty desperate right now, and his client is going to be putting all kinds of pressure on him. When he crossed Shirley Parsens, I actually felt sorry for him." He stopped pacing and looked at Timothy. "The morning papers can't do anything but report the facts we presented. Konen's gonna feel cornered. He'll do something to distract the media from coverage of the evidence. Whatever it is, it won't be good."

"Do you think any of us are in danger?" Clarissa asked.

John put an arm around her. "No, Clar. He knows better than that. If we were attacked, it would generate sympathy for the prosecution."

"If he wants to create a diversion the press has to cover, it will be something big, outside the courthouse," Annie said.

"They never seem to tire of his press conferences," Clarissa added.

"Hey, we have a big day tomorrow," Timothy stood up from his chair. "Let's forget about Konen and get ready for tomorrow morning."

* * *

Paul Smithson had just finished counting the fifty one-hundred-dollar bills he found in his desk drawer when Sheila's cell phone rang.

"Hello?"

A sullen male voice said, "There's a leather briefcase under your desk. Don't open it. Carry it to the park next to the courthouse tomorrow morning and drop it in a trash can near the center of the park before nine. Don't hang around and don't get caught."

The phone went dead.

* * *

"I saw you in the gallery today," Henry Jarvis said to his wife across the dinner table.

"I had to come," Isabel replied. "All these years I've avoided being involved in your job, but I had to be there today. Julie arranged it for me. You were very impressive up there on that paneled throne, my dear."

Henry smiled and refreshed his wine glass. "And that is why we have paneled thrones, Isabel." He lifted his glass in a little salute. "It gives us judges an edge over everyone else in the room. Do you think it unfair to make them look up at us?"

"A little."

"A bit of formal intimidation does help keep things in order."

"I thought Timothy and Jacob did a good job today, but that Konen fellow is so annoying," Isabel said. "I was disappointed that Jacob didn't bring up Augusto Pinochet as an example of a head of state indicted for torture."

"Rules of evidence, my dear. The Pinochet case is too weak to use since Pinochet died before he could be tried. Even without him, the evidence Jacob presented was solid." He laughed at a thought. "Guess we'll never know how many more Miami Book Fair attendees Madegen had lined up in the witness room."

"How's it going with the Chief Justice, the White House, and the

Congress? Are they still pressuring you?"

"There are a few in the House talking impeachment, but they don't have much support. The Chief Justice could probably find a way to can me, but I get the feeling he doesn't want to get his hands dirty. I let him know I won't go quietly. There's not much they can do now but try to cause a mistrial. I won't let that happen. We have a good jury, and we're going to complete this thing."

Isabel stopped eating and leaned in toward Henry. "I got another one of those phone calls today."

Jarvis looked at her, held his fork in the air for a moment, then went back to his plate. "Isabel, you should stop answering the phone. Let your FBI guard screen your calls."

"I'm OK, Henry, but I'll be glad when this is over."

CHAPTER 33

If the ruling class can make its own laws to suit their purpose,
then the American Revolution has been betrayed.
—Source Unknown

Paul Smithson shifted the brown leather case from side-to-side every few hundred feet to compensate for the weight of it. Even in the cool morning air, sweat glistened on his forehead. The exertion of a four-block walk from the car garage to John Marshal Park would have exhausted his ample body even without the added baggage.

When he finally reached a park bench, he sat for a break and set the case down between his feet. He pulled a handkerchief from his pocket, wiped his forehead, turned away from the NO SMOKING sign posted on the other side of the walk, and lit up a cigarette.

At eight in the morning, there were only a few demonstrators organizing for the day. Several street vendors were erecting pop-up shelters. Groundskeepers swept away debris from the day before. He watched as the trash barrels were emptied and identified one in the center of the park that was being serviced as he sat. He decided that was his target.

He smoked half the cigarette, then snuffed it out under foot. He lifted the briefcase with a groan and started walking for the trash bin. When he got within a few feet of the barrel, he looked around to see if anyone was watching him and realized a man approached from behind.

"Wha'cha got in the case there, Paul?"

Smithson stopped and twisted around to look at the speaker. "Who are you?"

"I asked first," Axel Johnson said.

Smithson looked the black man over, and beads of sweat reappeared on his brow.

"What do you want?" Smithson asked.

"I want to know what's in the briefcase, man. That's all."

"Leave me alone, or I'll call the police."

"OK," Axel said and pulled out his cell phone. "Let me do it."

"Wait! Who are you?"

"That doesn't really matter now, does it? Let's you and I take a seat on that park bench over there and take a look in your briefcase."

"Are you a cop?"

"No, just a concerned citizen."

Smithson took another look at Axel. The blood left his face as he sized up the six-foot black man. He took a step back, and Axel took one forward. Smithson's cheek began to twitch. "How do you know my name?"

"I know a lot about you Paul and that client of yours, William Mayfield. You know—the one who skipped the states for South America. And I know you've been meeting with your paramour too. I just don't know what's in the briefcase."

"What time is it? Is it close to nine?"

Axel looked at his cell phone. "Almost nine, trial's about to start again over in the courthouse."

"What time is it exactly?" Smithson asked. He looked down at the briefcase. The beads were coalescing and running down into his eyes. He wiped at them.

"What's time, Paul? It's unimportant really. It's what we do with it that counts."

"Dammit!" Smithson was shouting now. "What's the fucking time?"

Axel looked at the phone again. "Ten to nine. Kinda jumpy, aren't we? Let's just take a look in the briefcase, and you can get right back on schedule."

"Here, you can have the damn briefcase. I'm leaving," Smithson said dropping the case on the ground and turning to go. Axel grabbed him with one of his huge hands right above the elbow. The five-pronged clamp locked on Smithson's arm like the jaws of pit bull.

"Oh no, you're staying. Open it."

Smithson started to shake. His hands fumbled with the catch and found it was locked. Axel pulled a knife from his pocket and cut the leather strap loose. He pulled the over-flap and the two men looked inside. A loaf of gray putty filled the bottom of the case. A digital clock perched on top with a package of batteries wired to an igniter protruding from the putty.

Axel looked up at Smithson, "This looks like a bomb. What you doin' with a bomb, Paul?"

"Never mind, let's get out of here."

Axel reached into the case to tilt the clock to see the time.

Smithson put his hands up as if to fend off a blow. When nothing happened, his legs gave way, and he sat down hard on the bench. He put his head down between his knees like he might be getting sick.

"I didn't know it was a bomb," Smithson said without looking up.

"Right," Axel said. He pulled out a hand cuff and fixed Smithson to the bench. "Wait right here, I'll call the bomb squad." He set the briefcase next to Smithson and looked around. "Looks like the crowd is getting ready for trial day number two. This will be a good spot to people watch, Paul."

Axel dialed 911 and walked toward the park entrance on Constitution Avenue.

"For God's sake, don't leave me here!" Smithson shouted.

It was eight-thirty-three.

* * *

Judge Jarvis opened the second day of the trial on schedule at 9:00 a.m. with a statement of concern for the accommodations of the sequestered jury. He asked if any juror had been contacted inappropriately. There being no complaints or concerns, he instructed the prosecution to continue.

Radovich was taking the floor when a U.S. Marshal with a phone at his ear ran across the room without ceremony, scaled the dais, and spoke rapidly to Jarvis. The other marshals in the room sprang to attention and a tense interest overcame the courtroom.

"Excuse me, Jacob," the judge said with an even, unaffected voice. "Something's come up, and we are going to evacuate the building. Everyone please follow the instructions of the federal marshals. We'll do this in an orderly fashion just like a grade school fire drill."

Radovich gave Timothy an 'I told you so' grimace and fell in with the others. Jarvis scanned the crowd for Isabel. When he didn't find her, he threw off his robe and followed the direction of the officer assigned to him. The marshals took charge and shouted instructions that emptied the courtroom in minutes.

Outside the building, the street roiled in chaos. People streamed from the exits and joined others exiting the park. Officers instructed them to walk east down Constitution Avenue. Sirens blared from emergency vehicles flashing red and blue lights as they sped through the streets. Policemen manned roadblocks, and a helicopter circled.

The prosecution team walked away from the milling crowds. Timothy got through to Annie after several tries on one of the few open cell phone channels.

"There's a bomb in the park," she said. "Where's John, Clarissa, and Jacob?"

"No worries, they're here with me on the street."

Annie regained her poise. "Axel called me twenty minutes ago. I've been trying to reach you."

"Can you send someone to get us? What happened?"

"It's all over the news. Axel said there was a bomb set to go off at nine, right when the trial started. He was the one who called 911. I'm coming to get you."

"Good." Timothy looked back at the turmoil around the courthouse. "I'm sure we're through here for the day."

* * *

Evening papers ran the story on the front page. **"BOMB SCARE AT BUSH TRIAL."** They reported a suspect in custody but didn't name Paul Smithson. The event diverted coverage from the trial to speculation about responsibility for the thwarted bomb attack.

Pundits delivered scripted talking points. A round-table on one conservative cable network spent hours debating the point. A pretty blonde moderator asked her panel with a straight face, "Could this bomb plot have been discovered earlier by the use of enhanced interrogation techniques?"

Former CIA agent Max Xavier answered, "There's no question we are less secure without the authority to properly interrogate terror suspects. That bomb was seconds away from detonating when the bomb squad defused it. My gratitude goes out to those guys who risk their lives every time we have one of these incidents." His clenched fist fell on the table with a soft thud. "It's unconscionable that we put these men in danger, when it doesn't have to go this far." He spoke in earnest to the moderator, his jaws tight. "With proper interrogations, we can disrupt these terror attacks well before they become dangerous. Think about how many people might have been killed or injured if that bomb had gone off in the crowded park."

"Do you see any connection between the trial and this incident, Max?" the moderator offered.

"Absolutely! My sources tell me the attack was meant to deliver a message to the jury. The terrorists want them to believe our use of enhanced interrogation is making us less safe, when we know—the American people know—that's a bunch of baloney."

"Is there anyone who really believes what the liberal media is pitching in their attempt to convict President Bush?" she asked.

"No. Nobody wants to punish this great man for defending our country. It's crazy that there's a trial at all, and I'm certain he will be exonerated," Xavier said.

* * *

The next morning, Jarvis opened the trial with an admonishment to the jury to ignore the events of the previous day and consider only the evidence presented at trial.

Jacob Radovich stood once more to make the prosecution's presentation.

"In our first session, we heard testimony that George Bush confessed to authorizing waterboarding. We viewed his video confession and reviewed evidence that waterboarding is torture under U.S. and International law. Today we will look at a written confession by the accused."

Radovich picked up a book from the prosecution table and showed the cover to the jury. "This book is titled *Decision Points*. The author is George W. Bush. It is a memoir of his time as President of the United States." He paced back and forth in front of the jury box making certain that every juror had a chance to see the book cover.

"On pages 168 and 169, George Bush confesses in writing that he asked government attorneys to review a list of techniques to be used in the interrogation of detainee, Abu Zubaydah, and personally approved some of those techniques.[169] He wrote that he approved waterboarding.

---

169   Supra 2. Pages 168 and 169.

Attorney Clarissa Morrison will now read those pages into the record."

Clarissa stood at the podium, adjusted the microphone down to her height, and read George Bush's first person account of getting legal opinions from Justice Department and CIA lawyers, then authorizing the enhanced interrogation program. When she finished, she handed the hard-cover book to the evidence clerk.

"Thank you, Clarissa," Radovich said. "President Bush's approval of these torture techniques—"[170]

"Objection." Konen rose from his seat. "President Bush did not approve 'torture techniques.' He approved 'enhanced interrogation techniques.' Counsel is biasing the jury with a false label."

"Sustained," Jarvis agreed.

"Yes, Your Honor." Jacob feigned contrition and started over. "President Bush approved enhanced interrogation techniques to be used on Abu Zubaydah." He spoke in a carefully controlled tone and looked at Konen when he said: "We'll let the jury decide if that is the right name for them."

Radovich, Clarissa, and Timothy huddled for a couple of minutes at the prosecution table.

"Is the prosecution ready to proceed?" Jarvis asked.

Radovich returned to the podium with a page of notes and said, "The prosecution calls Ms. Silvia Townsden."

Clarissa opened the door to the witness room and escorted Ms. Townsden to the witness box for swearing in. She was a small woman. Her body and stature was childlike, but her bearing was serious and sober. Her cropped auburn hair and simple business dress gave her a polished professional appearance.

Radovich addressed the woman, "Ms. Townsend, please tell the court your current occupation."

"I am an attorney in private practice."

"And where were you employed during the period October, 2001 to November, 2008?"

"During that time, I was an investigator with the International Committee of the Red Cross, in Washington D.C."

Clarissa brought Radovich a file folder, which he held up and stated, "I have in my hand the International Red Cross Report on their interview

---

170 Ibid.

of detainees who were subjected to enhanced interrogation techniques."[171]

"Ms. Townsend, are you familiar with this report?"

"Yes, I was one of the principal investigators who contributed to that report."

"Did you interview Mr. Abu Zubaydah about his experience in detention and interrogation by the CIA?"

"Yes, I did."

Radovich turned to the jury. "We are going to read quotations of Abu Zubaydah about his experience under enhanced interrogation. Ms. Townsend, please read what he told you about the waterboarding technique that George Bush approved."

"Objection!" Konen said. "Prosecution is presenting hearsay. This is not direct testimony but is only attributed to the speaker."

"Ms. Townsend, can you confirm for the court that the words attributed to Mr. Zubaydah, were actually spoken by him?" Radovich asked.

"Yes, I can. Mr. Zubaydah's interview with me was recorded, and the report presents an accurate transcript."

Jarvis looked down from the bench at the animated defense attorney. "Are you questioning the veracity of an official International Red Cross Report, Mr. Konen?"

"It's third party testimony, Your Honor. It's hearsay."

"Overruled. Go ahead, Mr. Mayfield."

Konen dropped into his chair.

"Thank you, Judge," Radovich said. "Please read the passage Ms. Townsend."

"'I was put on what looked like a hospital bed and strapped down very tightly with belts. A black cloth was then placed over my face, and the interrogators used a mineral water bottle to pour water on the cloth so that I could not breathe. After a few minutes, the cloth was removed, and the bed was rotated into an upright position. The pressure of the straps on my wounds caused severe pain. I vomited. The bed was then again lowered to a horizontal position and the same torture…'"[172]

Konen sat up and slapped the table in front of him with the palm of

---

171 ICRC REPORT ON THE TREATMENT OF FOURTEEN "HIGH VALUE DETAINEES" IN CIA CUSTODY, February 2007
https://www.nybooks.com/media/doc/2010/04/22/icrc-report.pdf

172 Ibid.

his right hand. "Objection!"

The clap resounded off the mahogany-paneled walls and startled everyone in the court room, including an obviously irritated Jarvis.

Radovich, looked up at the judge, "These are Abu Zubaydah's words, not Ms. Townsends."

"Mr. Konen, there will be no more of your outbursts, or you will be censured. Objection overruled. You may continue Ms. Townsend."

"'...*and the same torture carried out with the black cloth over my face and water poured from a bottle. On this occasion, my head was in a more backward, downwards position, and the water was poured for a longer time. I struggled without success to breathe. I thought I was going to die. I lost control of my urine. Since then, I still lose control of my urine when under stress.*'"[173]

Radovich let the words sink in, then said. "But we don't have to rely on Mr. Zubaydah's description. Here's the description of his reaction to waterboarding as described by the CIA in the Senate report. '*The waterboarding technique was physically harmful, inducing convulsions and vomiting. Abu Zubaydahh, for example, became "completely unresponsive, with bubbles rising through his open, full mouth".*'"[174]

Radovich lifted his gaze and spoke to solemn faces in the jury box. "Abu Zubaydah was waterboarded eighty-three times according to the Senate intelligence report.[175] Detainee Khalid Sheik Mohammed suffered the same treatment 183 times."[176] Radovich's voice became stern when he said, "This is what George Bush admitted to approving. Without his approval, this would not have happened."

"Objection!" Reginald Konen stood up at the defense table. "There is no evidence to show that the enhanced interrogation techniques would not have been used without President Bush's approval. Counsel is speculating."

"Sustained. The jury should ignore Mr. Radovich's last remark," the judge said. "Mr. Radovich, you will refrain from any personal conclusions in the future. The jury should be presented with only verifiable facts."

"Understood, Your Honor. May I proceed?"

"Go ahead."

"Ms. Townsend, please read from your transcript of Abu Zubaydah's

---

173 Ibid. Page 10
174 Supra 61. #3. Page 3.
175 Supra 76. Page 118. Note 698.
176 Ibid

description of being held in a box."

"As it was not high enough even to sit upright, I had to crouch down. It was very difficult because of my wounds. The stress on my legs held in this position meant that my wounds both in the leg and stomach became very painful. I think this occurred about three months after my last operation."[177]

Radovich brought Ms. Townsend another page. "Some enhanced interrogation techniques were used in combination on Abu Zubaydah. Here is his description of stress positions and sleep deprivation. Please continue reading Ms. Townsend.

"I was kept sitting on a chair, shackled by hands and feet for two or three weeks. During this time, I developed blisters on the underside of my legs due to the constant sitting. I was only allowed to get up from the chair to go to the toilet, which consisted of a bucket…if I started to fall asleep a guard would come and spray water in my face."[178]

"Ms. Townsend, remember that you are under oath. Do you confirm for this court that the words you read from the transcript, were spoken in your presence by Abu Zubaydah?"

"Yes, sir. I do."

Radovich added, "There are reports that some detainees were deprived of sleep for as long as 138 hours. That's almost six days without sleep.[179] Abu Zubaydah also reported beatings, use of a collar to slam him against a wall, deprivation of solid food, forced nudity for months, and subjection to cold temperatures," he said and handed the Red Cross report to the evidence clerk.[180]

"We have no more questions for the witness."

"Does the defense want to cross-examine?" Jarvis asked Konen.

Konen didn't look up but shook his head.

"The witness is excused."

Radovich spoke directly to the jury. "We have some of the details of the treatment of Abu Zubaydah, but much of the information is still classified and video tapes of his interrogation were destroyed. Mr. Bush does tell us in his memoir that '…*about a hundred were placed into the CIA program. About a third of those were questioned using enhanced techniques. Three were waterboarded.'"*[181]

---

177 Supra 171. Page 13.

178 Ibid

179 Supra 76. Page 166

180 Supra 171, Pages 14 and 15.

181 Supra 2, page 171

Radovich gathered up his file and returned to the prosecution table. He stood behind the table and spoke to the jury. "Remember the written words that Clarissa Morrison read to you from President George Bush's memoir. He approved the interrogation techniques used on Abu Zubaydah. He authorized the CIA to do these things to Abu Zubaydah." Jacob Radovich stuck his hands in his pockets and stood looking at the jury for a long minute, then he approached the bench and spoke to the judge.

"The prosecution rests its case on the charges against the defendant as specified in Count 1," he said. He turned away and took his seat.

John Mayfield and Timothy Madegen held a whispered conversation. The judge looked at the prosecution with his hands clasped in front of him, a scowl emerging as he spoke. "What are we waiting for Mr. Madegen?"

"Sorry, Your Honor. Go ahead John."

John Mayfield stood to address the court. "The prosecution will now submit evidence that the defendant committed the crime of conspiracy as charged in Count 2: Conspiring to enable torture by secret detention and constructing and promulgating false legal analysis in violation of USC Title 18, Part I, Chapter 113C, §2340A Torture. (c) Conspiracy. We will present evidence that President Bush conspired with the CIA to capture and detain persons in secret prisons for the purpose of interrogation; that he conspired with CIA and Justice Department lawyers to develop false legal cover for torture; and he conspired with the U.S. Congress to change laws for the purpose of immunizing himself and the torturers against prosecution.

"The leader of the conspiracy was President Bush. He conspired with his legal team who worked with the legal counsels of the vice-president, the CIA, the Department of Justice, and the Department of Defense to develop opinions supporting the use of waterboarding and other enhanced interrogation techniques. It was under this false legal framework that enhanced interrogation techniques were implemented by CIA Director George Tenet, CIA Chief of Operations for the Counter Terrorism Center Jose Rodriguez, Vice President Dick Cheney, Secretary of Defense Donald Rumsfeld, and approved by National Security Advisor Condoleezza Rice."

Mayfield walked to the podium in front of the jury. "A simple chronology will show the process of the conspiracy. The following facts are substantiated in U.S. government documents which we now present as exhibits to the court."

Clarissa presented several files to the clerk.

"On September 17, 2001, President Bush initiated the conspiracy by issuing a secret *Memorandum of Notification*. Through Freedom of Information Act requests, it has been determined that the memorandum gave the CIA the authority to 'covertly capture and detain individuals… '[182] This court has subpoenaed the memorandum but the administrations of George W. Bush and President Barack Obama have refused to deliver it to the court. President Bush also authorized use of foreign country detentions to allow the CIA to hold Abu Zubaydah without having to declare his detention to the International Committee of the Red Cross. Secret detention is prohibited by common Article 3 of the Geneva Conventions.

"On February 7, 2002, President Bush issued a memorandum to key members of his cabinet and staff stating that the Geneva Conventions do not apply to Taliban or al Qaeda prisoners.[183]

"On March 28, 2002, Abu Zubaydah was captured. According to President Bush's memoir, he was moved 'to a secure location in another country where the Agency could have total control over his environment.' The CIA asked the president for the authority to use a list of interrogation techniques on Zubaydah as we have shown. Bush requested his attorneys at the Office of Legal Counsel and CIA attorneys to review and approve the list of the interrogation techniques which they did—their part in the conspiracy.

"On August 1, 2002, the Office of Legal Counsel issued a memo which has become known as the torture memo, because it outlines ten interrogation techniques including waterboarding in great detail and approves them for use.[184] These are the techniques President Bush approved to be used on Abu Zubaydah. Later, a review by the Justice Department Office of Professional Responsibility found major flaws in the analysis of the legal conspirators and determined that attorneys John Yoo and Jay Bybee were guilty of incompetence and professional misconduct for failure of judgment.[185]

"During the month of August 2002, Abu Zubaydah was subjected

---

182 Supra 61, #11, Page 9

183 Supra 77.

184 Jay S. Bybee, Memorandum for John Rizzo, Acting General Counsel of the Central Intelligence Agency, Interrogation of al Qaeda Operative, August 1, 2002.
http://www.justice.gov/sites/default/files/olc/legacy/2010/08/05/memo-bybee2002.pdf

185 Supra 23. Page 201

to several of the techniques George Bush authorized as discussed earlier, including being waterboarded 83 times.

"In summary, President Bush conspired with the CIA to set up secret prisons, conspired with his legal counsel to declare the Geneva Conventions inapplicable, conspired with his attorneys to develop legal cover for enhanced interrogation techniques, and authorized their use. The conspiracy included the Director of the CIA, the Secretary of Defense and others.

"But it doesn't end there. President Bush put his legal team to work on writing law to try to make it difficult to prosecute the conspirators for their actions. The president and members of his cabinet conspired with Congress to change the law to immunize themselves from prosecution. The Military Commission Act of 2006 included an amendment to the Detainee Treatment Act of 2005 that gave cover to those who were responsible for authorizing and performing the so-called enhanced interrogations, even for actions done years earlier between September 11, 2001, and December 30, 2005.[186,187] This is 'ex post facto' lawmaking, which is not permitted by our Constitution."[188]

Mayfield looked at Konen when he said, "Which leads us to Count 3. The actual commission of torture. Under USC Title 18, Part I, Chapter 113C,§2340A Torture, subparagraph (c) states that—*'A person who conspires to commit an offense under this section shall be subject to the same penalties (other than the penalty of death) as the penalties prescribed for the offense, the commission of which was the object of the conspiracy'*.

"In other words, anyone who conspires to have someone tortured, is culpable for the act as if they performed the torture themselves. Ladies and gentlemen of the jury, you must consider the fact that President Bush authorized the CIA to use EITs, and they were used on at least twenty-three detainees."

Mayfield came around the podium and looked the jurors in the eye, one at a time, as he said: "The Senate Intelligence Report states that the CIA tortured one of the detainees, Gul Rahman, to death. Tortured—him—to—death."[189]

---

186 Supra 16. Military Commissions Act Of 2006,Public Law 109–366—Oct. 17, 2006

187 Supra 16. Detainee Treatment Act of 2005, as included in the Department of Defense Appropriations Act, 2006

188 US Constitution, Article I, Section 9.

189 Supra 76. Page 54.

John Mayfield returned to stand behind the podium and addressed the whole courtroom. His eyes conveyed a confidence in the veracity of his next words, and the sound of his voice filled the room. "President George W. Bush led a conspiracy at the highest levels in our government to secretly torture detainees under the control of the United States. He is therefore just as guilty of the crime of torture as if he personally did the torturing."

Mayfield looked down at the floor, deep in thought as he walked to the front of the jury box. He put his hands on the railing in front of the jury and lifted his head to scan the three rows of jurors.

"If you agree that we have proven that President George W. Bush authorized torture—Count 1, conspired to develop and promulgate false legal analysis to empower and protect the torturers—Count 2, and therefore committed the crime of torture—Count 3, then he has committed a grave breach of the Geneva Conventions which is a war crime and he is guilty of Count 4."

He then turned around and spoke to the judge.

"The prosecution has made the case that President George W. Bush should be convicted on all four counts. The prosecution rests."

The judge nodded at John Mayfield, then spoke to the defense attorneys. "Mr. Konen, will you be prepared to present the defense tomorrow morning at 9:00 a.m.?"

"Yes, Your Honor."

"Court is recessed," Jarvis said, dropped his gavel and left the bench.

CHAPTER 34

Our national honor is stained by the indignity and inhumane treatment these men received from their captors…After years of disclosures by government investigations, media accounts, and reports from human rights organizations, there is no longer any doubt as to whether the current administration [George W. Bush administration] has committed war crimes. The only question that remains to be answered is whether those who ordered the use of torture will be held to account.
—Major General Antonio M. Taguba (US Army-Retired.)

The trial team gathered at John Mayfield's apartment to decompress following the completion of the prosecution's argument. They sat on stools around John's kitchen counter. Clarissa, protected by a bib apron, warmed hors d'oeuvres in the oven. John, with tie askew and his sleeves rolled to the elbows, tended bar.

Annie handed Timothy a glass of red wine. "So this is what a relaxed Timothy Madegen looks like. I wasn't sure there was such a thing." Her smile rose from her lips into her eyes as she took the seat next to him and held out her wine glass for a clink.

"I'm feelin' pretty good right now, Annie." Timothy touched the rim of his glass to the stem of hers. "It's been a long time coming. Hey, I even got a call from Otto Beecker after the session today. First time he ever complimented me—us—on anything." Timothy looked around at the others and grinned. "He asked about you, Annie."

"That old goat! There's something about him that's endearing, but I couldn't tell you what."

"I'm tempted to call him, now that we've made our case," Jacob said, "but I really don't want to listen to how it would have been so much more effective if only I'd done this or that."

The others laughed.

At that instant, the doorbell rang. John let Axel in.

"Good evening everybody. Sorry I'm late. Had a little trouble getting past the doorman. The usual." Axel looked out of place in jeans, western boots, and leather jacket, carrying a motorcycle helmet.

"Axel!" Clarissa stopped what she was doing and went to him for a hug. "We owe you for stopping that bomb attack."

The delighted look on Axel's face showed how much he appreciated the attention.

"Come and sit down," Timothy gave up his seat for him. "John, if my memory serves me, Mr. Axel Johnson drinks whiskey."

"On the rocks, please," Axel said as he joined the others.

When John handed Axel a glass, Axel took his arm. "I traced your dad, John."

John was startled, and worry showed in his face.

"It's OK, man. He's got a sweet crib in Argentina, and there's nothin' they can do to him, now that he's out of the country. You might have a new vacation destination for a while, buddy," Axel said with a smirk.

John let out a lung full of air. "Thank you! I've been feeling pretty guilty about his troubles."

"You know it's not your fault, don't you?" Clarissa said, putting a hand on his shoulder.

"Yeah, I know, but I worry about him."

"There's somebody else that's taking a hit," Annie said with a soft sadness in her voice. "They fired Jeffery at the paper. They said it was a reduction in force, but everybody knows he's been too supportive of our position and too liberal for the *Times*."

"What's he gonna do?" Axel asked.

"He's feeling a little relieved, now that they made his decision for him. Jeff's kinda excited about getting on with one of the progressive papers or maybe writing for some blogs."

"I'll give him a recommendation, if it'll do any good," Timothy said.

"That would mean a lot to him, Tim," Annie said.

"Hey, do you people talk business every minute of the day?" Axel asked. "Let me tell you some juicy stuff I found out about Konen, and that woman who worked Paul Smithson. She's a real piece of work…"

Axel's gossip entertained Clarissa, John, and Jacob in the kitchen, while Annie drew Timothy out on the balcony where they watched the setting sun paint the tip of the Washington Monument gold, then orange. A few lights popped on in the shadowed western part of the city.

They stood side-by-side at the railing. Timothy took Annie's hand and felt the soft compliance in her touch. "We're making a difference in this town, Annie," he said looking out over the landscape. "We're making them face the truth."

"Thank you for including me, Tim. You and John and the others have changed an ordinary girl into—into someone else. I don't know. I felt it the day you said you wanted me on the team and—"

When she turned to him, he saw the glow in her eyes, the city disappeared, and he kissed her.

CHAPTER 35

Clouds of black smoke already billowed from jagged holes in a glass-and-steel tower when the dark silhouette of an airplane flew into the middle floors of the second building—and an orange fire ball erupted. White and black smoke rose from the wounds in the twin towers, and huge chunks of debris fell toward the street below. The camera lingered on the scene of the burning buildings for several seconds, then the video continued with amateur clips showing people on the street fleeing in panic and terror, pursued by a dark wall of smoke and ash that chased them down city canyons, until the threat engulfed them, and the video went black.

"Never forget that we are considering the courageous response of the President of the United States in reaction to this horrendous attack on the people, land, and institutions of our country," Reginald B. Konen declared.

The video stopped but left a still image of the devastated World Trade Center capped by a cloud of gray smoke. This was Konen's stage setting.

He stood with his back to the scene, letting it add visual drama to the words he spoke. "Terrorists destroyed the World Trade Center Towers, five other trade center buildings, a nearby church, and damaged the Pentagon. Almost 3,000 men, women, and children died. They might have destroyed the U.S. Capitol Building too, except for the bold and selfless actions of citizens onboard a fourth airplane."

The pathos in Konen's voice was a perfect match for the picture of the broken buildings, and the jury listened in rapt attention. "This is the threat that faced President George W. Bush only nine months after taking office. Everything rested on his shoulders. He was the commander-in-chief. The whole country waited for his orders. Nine days later, our government was attacked with anthrax, a deadly biological agent that killed five people and sickened seventeen others. He bore an enormous burden. How could he stop this onslaught?"

Konen lifted the microphone off its stand and took it with him from the podium. "In those tense days, President Bush did not know what other plans the terrorists had, but he was determined to find out and stop them before another attack occurred. It was the quick thinking and bold decisions of your president—President George W. Bush—that saved this country from further disasters.

"You have listened to the prosecution make allegations against this honorable man, who did what he had to do, under the most dangerous conditions this country has faced in decades. He was tested and found able to lead this country, just like another great American president, Franklin Delano Roosevelt, after the surprise attack on Pearl Harbor."

Konen stepped over to the jury box, swung around, and pointed his index finger at the image on the screen. "That was a call to arms, and your commander-in-chief answered the call without a moment's hesitation. We will show you, that he did the right things, acted within the law and saved American lives."

He returned to the podium and picked up his notes. When he looked out at the jury, his face was earnest. "President Bush did what was necessary; it was his job; you gave it to him. You made him your commander-in-chief, when you elected him.

"He knew there would be more plots to attack us, and he wanted to get the information he needed to thwart them. He did not want to wait for the next disaster, so he authorized the CIA to use tough interrogation techniques on captured terrorists.

"Those techniques paid off. It was the information gained by those interrogations that prevented al Qaeda from launching other spectacular attacks against us. Abu Zubaydah furnished detailed information about al Qaeda's organizational structure, key operatives, and modus operandi. He identified Khalid Sheikh Mohammed as the master mind of the September 11th attacks."[190]

At a nod from Konen, Jake Willis picked up a remote from the defense table, and the picture on the screen changed. The burning twin towers were replaced with a hellish scene in gray, showing masked firemen walking through smoking rubble with the skeletal remains of the towers in the background. Konen pointed at the image on the screen.

"That could have happened again—but it didn't. It was the use of enhanced interrogation techniques on Khalid Sheikh Mohammed that led to the discovery of his next plot—the 'Second Wave.' A plan to use East Asian operatives to crash a hijacked airliner into a building in Los Angeles.[191] If President Bush had not authorized these interrogation techniques, there would have been a hole in L. A. to match the one in New York City."

"Objection, Your Honor," Timothy Madegen said. "Counsel is giving the jury false information. The Second Wave plot was disrupted in January 2002, before KSM was captured in 2003.[192] The defense is stating conjecture about an event that did not happen and cannot prove that the information could only be obtained by use of EITs."

"Sustained," said Jarvis. "Mr. Konen, you will keep your facts straight and separate from the image in your crystal ball, sir. The jury will ignore the defense's statement about the event that did not happen."

Konen responded without remorse, "Understood, Your Honor." Then he spoke to the jury like a great-uncle, "Let me be clear on this: these were tough techniques, but they were necessary. Abu Zubaydah told his CIA interrogators why they were necessary. I quote Zubaydah, *'brothers who are captured and interrogated are permitted by Allah to provide information when they believe they have reached the limit of their ability to withhold it in the face of psychological and physical hardship.'*[193] In other words, the interrogator had to safely push the detainee to his limit, so he could do his duty to Allah, then he could speak freely. It was necessary in

---

190 Supra 76. Page 247, note 1392.
191 Ibid
192 Supra 76. Page 252
193 Ibid Page 47 and 48.

dealing with these people."

The judge interrupted, "Mr. Konen, we have had enough of your history lesson. Do you have anything to offer as a defense to the charges made against your client?"

"We are making a case of necessity, Your Honor. President Bush had to do what he did to save lives and—"

"Do you have any other defense, sir?"

Konen returned to his notes on the podium. "The defense calls Dr. Martin Vilier."

Jake Willis moved from the defense table to the witness holding room and escorted a trim man dressed in a business suit to the witness chair. The clerk swore him in.

Konen stood in front of the witness. "Dr. Vilier, please state your medical credentials for the jury."

"I am a medical doctor with over twenty years' experience in pain relief."

"Would you consider yourself an expert in the understanding and diagnosis of pain, Doctor?"

"I am. I have published many articles in medical journals on both somatic pain and visceral pain."

"Are you familiar with an enhanced interrogation technique known as waterboarding?"

"Yes."

"What can you tell us about the pain associated with waterboarding, Doctor?"

"When one considers somatic pain—pain associated with skin, muscles, joints, bones, and ligaments—I cannot find any reason to believe waterboarding would cause this type of pain, since none of those areas are being damaged or threatened in any way. It is the same with visceral pain, which is the pain inner organs would feel. Here again, waterboarding would not cause pain in these organs."

"Can you identify any area of the body that would feel pain during waterboarding?"

"No."

"What do you think a person would be feeling when being waterboarded?"

"They would not feel pain, but they might feel fear—fear of drowning."

"Thank you, Doctor Vilier. The defense has no more questions."

Konen gave the jury a meaningful look and glanced at Radovich as he returned to his seat at the prosecution table.

Jarvis addressed Radovich. "Does the prosecution want to cross examine the witness?"

"Yes, sir."

Radovich conferred with Timothy for a moment before approaching the witness box.

"Dr. Vilier, have you ever been waterboarded?" Radovich asked.

"I don't see—"

"Yes or no, sir?"

"No."

"Have you published any research papers on the effects of waterboarding?"

"Well, no but—"

"Have you ever examined a person who has been waterboarded?"

"No."

"Observed a person being waterboarded?"

"No."

"Thank you, Doctor. The prosecution has no more questions for this witness." Jacob said and returned to his seat.

The witness was excused.

"Mr. Konen, do you have any other defense witnesses?" Jarvis asked.

"We were about to address the legality of waterboarding next."

"Then proceed."

"Let's talk about waterboarding. Let's talk about our own military waterboarding hundreds of our own soldiers every year. We have trained thousands of our military men and women in survival techniques to prepare them in case they are captured by an enemy. The very fact that we subject our own troops to waterboarding is proof that it is not illegal. Who would say waterboarding is OK to use on our troops but too harsh to use for interrogation of a terrorist? The defense calls Master Sergeant Charles Jarkens," Konen said.

A middle-aged man in civilian clothes entered the court room and was escorted to the witness chair, where he was sworn in.

"Please tell the court your current military status, Sergeant." Konen said.

"I'm retired from the U.S. Air Force after twenty-five years."

"Thank you for your service, sir. What was your specialty when you were in the Air Force?"

"I was in the Air Force Security Service. My duties were classified."

"Did you undergo SERE training while in the service?"

"Yes, sir."

"And what did SERE training consist of?"

"It was training to avoid capture and resist interrogation by the enemy. SERE stands for survival, evasion, resistance, and escape."

"Please tell the court about the training."

Jarkens sat tall in his chair. "I was hooded, stripped, and bound hand and foot. Interrogators began questioning me. When I wouldn't give more than my name, rank, and serial number, they forced me into a small box. After an hour or so, I was taken to an interrogation room for more questioning. I refused to answer their questions, and they took me to another place where I was waterboarded."

"Do you consider the waterboarding that you experienced to be torture, Sergeant?"

"No, I understood it to be an interrogation technique, and I was being trained to withstand it."

"Do you have any lingering ill effects from that experience?"

"No, sir. Afterward I felt more confident in my ability to resist interrogation."

Konen turned to the bench. "I have no more questions for this witness, Your Honor."

"Does the prosecution wish to cross-examine?"

Radovich approached the witness stand. "Yes, Your Honor."

"Sergeant Jarkens, everyone in this courtroom appreciates your service to our country, thank you. I have only a few questions about your SERE experience. How many days were you in the simulated capture scenario?"

Jarkens thought for a moment, then answered, "I believe it was over a period of two days."

"During that period, did you ever think you were in serious danger?"

"When I was waterboarded; I felt like I might drown."

"Did you ever think they might actually drown you?"

"No. I knew it was training."

"Do you equate drowning with death?"

"Well, yes. If someone drowned, they would be dead."

"How many times were you actually waterboarded?"

"Twice. They did it to me two times."

"Did you then, or do you now feel you were tortured?"

"No, sir. I knew it was training."

"Are you certain that the waterboarding you received was not torture?"

"Yes I am. Any reasonable person can recognize torture, and that was not torture."

"Are you certain you can recognize torture when you see it?"

"I consider myself a reasonable person, and I can recognize torture."

Radovich looked over at the jury before he turned back to Jarkens.

"Sergeant, there has been evidence presented in this trial that Khalid Sheik Mohammed was waterboarded 183 times."

Sergeant Jarkens eyes grew wide at this.

Radovich continued, "You have experienced being waterboarded twice. We heard you say that at times you felt you might drown, might die, even though you knew it was training. Is that correct?"

"Yes, sir."

"You said that your experience was not torture, but that you would know torture when you see it. Is that correct?"

"Yes, I said that."

"Would you feel you were being tortured, if you were waterboarded 183 times, Sergeant?"

Jarkens looked at Konen who rose from his chair. "Objection. The prosecution is asking the witness for an opinion. The witness is not an expert on torture, nor is he familiar with the conditions under which KSM was waterboarded."

Radovich came back at Konen. "This is the only witness testifying in this courtroom who has had firsthand knowledge of waterboarding. His firsthand knowledge is important and useful for the jury to consider. The question is not whether waterboarding KSM 183 times was torture. We are asking if it is torture to waterboard anyone 183 times. The witness has stated he can recognize torture. We ask that he answer the question—yes or no."

The judge turned to Jarkens. "I am going to overrule Mr. Konen's objection. Please answer the question, Sergeant."

Jarkens sat stunned. He traded stares with Konen.

Radovich repeated, "Is it torture to waterboard someone 183 times, Sergeant?"

Jarkens's answer was almost inaudible. "Yes," he said. "That would be torture."

Radovich turned immediately away from the witness stand and

walked toward the prosecution table. "No more questions, Your Honor."

Konen looked up at the ceiling and breathed a heavy sigh.

"The witness is excused," Jarvis said, and Sergeant Jarkens left the stand. "This court will take a fifteen-minute recess."

* * *

When Jarvis called the court to order for the afternoon session, Konen continued his presentation on waterboarding, and the other enhanced interrogation techniques. He declared that they could not be torture, because they did not cause the serious pain that would qualify them under U.S. law.

"President Bush did not authorize the enhanced interrogations lightly," Konen said. His speech was slow and even; his tone conveyed a genuine concern. "He knew that it was important to insure that our country stands up for human rights and does not torture. That is why he asked his attorneys to make a thorough study of the issue and render a definitive decision."

Konen held up a file. "I am offering into evidence, two important memos that substantiate this case."

He read from the title of the first document. *"Decision Re Application of the Geneva Convention on Prisoners of War in the Conflict with Al Qaeda and the Taliban."*[194] This document states that the commander-in-chief has the right to decide when the Geneva Conventions apply to prisoners." Konen handed the documents to the evidence clerk as he read the titles. *'Memorandum for John Rizzo, Acting General Counsel for the CIA.'*[195] This document prepared by the U.S. Justice Department describes and approves each of the enhanced interrogation techniques as being legally justified because they do not cause severe pain.

"We have shown that the enhanced interrogation techniques authorized by President Bush were legal under U.S. and international Law. They were tough on detainees, but the detainees were terrorists trained to resist interrogation, and the techniques were used sparingly and only when necessary. The President sought and obtained approval of the techniques at the highest level by qualified attorneys in the Justice Department. Waterboarding was and is used in training of our own troops and therefore cannot be illegal.

---

194   Supra 53.

195   Supra 184.

"President Bush's approval of the enhanced interrogation techniques was and is legal under U.S. and international law, and he should be found not guilty of all charges."

He turned to speak to the judge. "The defense rests its case."

Jarvis leaned forward in his chair. "Thank you. Mr. Konen. This court will be in recess until tomorrow at 9:00 a.m., when the prosecution and the defense will present their closing arguments." He gaveled the court to end the session.

Chapter 36

*You have enemies? Good. That means you've stood up
for something, sometime in your life.*
—Winston Churchill

The first slug shattered the plate glass window behind Timothy's desk, missing him by inches and lodging in the picture frame on the opposite wall. A whoosh of air sucked loose papers off his desktop and launched them through the shattered window as the sixth floor office equalized pressure with the outside ambient. A building alarm sounded; the pulsing siren-whistle added to the shock of the moment. Timothy grabbed the arm of a stunned Annie and pulled her off her chair. They hit the floor together, a second before the next round smashed into the overhead light, scattering pieces of fluorescent tube over their backs and salting their hair. They huddled on the floor for minutes after the shooting stopped before crawling out of the office over a carpet littered with white glass fragments. When they reached the hall, Timothy stood, took Annie's hand, and pulled her up.

"You OK?" he asked.

"I think so," Annie said, trying to catch her breath. "I can feel my heart racing."

He put his arms around her and held her until she stopped shaking. They entered a windowless inner office, and Timothy called security.

"That was awful." Annie collapsed into an office chair and sat stunned while Timothy spoke on the phone.

He told the building guard what had happened and had him call for federal marshals and the FBI.

"We're not going back in there," Timothy said. "They've called for a car to pick us up. We'll go over to John's."

"OK," Annie said in a small voice.

In the car on the way to John Mayfield's, the color returned to Annie's face. She punched up Jeff Blake on her cell phone. Timothy could hear the anger in her voice as she gave the reporter an exclusive blow by blow of events. Annie was back.

* * *

The morning headline read: **"SHOTS FIRED AT PROSECUTOR— FINAL ARGUMENTS TODAY IN BUSH TORTURE TRIAL."**

The courtroom was jammed, and the hall outside was filled with cameras, microphones, and reporters. Around the building, protesters carried placards, some calling for justice, while others demanded acquittal. The international media had beefed up their D.C. teams. Regular television programming was replaced with trial coverage on ABC, NBC, BBC, and Al Jazeera. The world was watching.

When the jurors filed in, they were silent. Tension was apparent on every face. News of the attack on Madegen had gotten through to them. They were wary. The buzz of spectator and journalist voices didn't stop when the clerk announced the judge, but the hum slowly dwindled after Jarvis gaveled the sound block a third time.

"This court will come to order." He glared at the spectators, and a few whispered conversations died. "Are the prosecution and defense prepared for their final arguments?"

Madegen and Konen answered that they were.

Jarvis spoke to the jury. "The prosecution will proceed, followed by the defense. The prosecution will have an opportunity for rebuttal, if any. Afterward, I will give you instructions, and you will retire to the jury room for deliberations."

Henry Jarvis turned to the prosecutor's table. "Mr. Madegen, you have the floor."

Timothy took his position in front of the rows of jurors. He spoke without notes. "First, I want to thank the members of the jury for their attention to the evidence presented in this trial. I am sure you are aware of the gravity of the decision that faces you.

"We have shown that the defendant, President George W. Bush, has admitted, on video, in front of a room full of witnesses, and in writing in his published memoir, that he personally authorized the use of enhanced interrogation techniques, including waterboarding, on at least three detainees in U.S. government custody. We have shown that at least one of those techniques, waterboarding, has been declared to be torture by our current Attorney General, a former Attorney General, the current President of the United States, and other responsible government officials and legal experts."

The room was still except for his voice. Every member of the jury focused on the special prosecutor. Reporters scribbled in their notebooks, and others in the gallery sat in frozen attention.

"We have shown that our federal judicial system, state judiciaries, military courts, and international tribunals have successfully prosecuted perpetrators of waterboarding many times in the past, all recognizing it as the crime of torture. We have made the case that President Bush conspired with administration officials in the White House and the Justice Department to develop faulty legal justification for the use of these techniques, when he knew, or should have known, the EITs were torture. We have shown that the legal arguments used by Bush administration attorneys to rationalize this torture are seriously flawed, and that the attorneys who proposed them have been reprimanded by their peers for incompetent work. The Supreme Court of the United States has ruled that the Geneva Conventions apply to Taliban and al Qaeda terrorists, in stark contrast to the advice of government attorneys and the proclamation of the accused. We have proved that President Bush has directed the crime of torture, conspired with others to commit the crime, and is guilty of war crimes under U.S. and international law.

"George W. Bush was elected president in November of 2000 on a platform stressing his strength on defense. When the first attack on U.S. soil since Pearl Harbor happened on September 11, 2001—on his watch—the president and his cabinet panicked. They had failed to protect us from the most damaging attack on our nation in sixty years.

"In the ensuing hysteria, the president and his closest advisors lost their way.

"George W. Bush may have been a President of the United States of America, but in the end, he is just a man who commanded torture. He used his position as commander-in-chief to thwart the law, and he should be brought to justice for his depraved conduct. Torture is a crime against humanity. It was illegal when President Bush took office, it was illegal while he served, and it is still illegal. But the law means nothing, if it is not enforced, and it must be enforced equally for all of us. We cannot have one set of laws for the least among us and another set for the powerful elite.

"Abu Zubaydah was waterboarded eighty-three times. Khalid Sheikh Mohammed was waterboarded one hundred and eighty-three times. How could any reasonable person think that is not torture?

"The defense argues that it worked; the senate intelligence committee report says it didn't. It doesn't matter. It's against the law. It's torture.

"The defense claims it was necessary. Professional interrogators tell us it was not, and that humane methods work better and faster. It doesn't matter if it was thought to be necessary. It is against the law! It's torture!

"We have presented the evidence you need to find President George W. Bush guilty on all counts—commanding torture, in effect committing torture, conspiracy to torture, and war crimes. President George W. Bush cannot invoke the Nuremberg Defense—'I was only following orders.' He gave the orders.

"You should find him guilty as charged. If you do not find him guilty, the United States will have lost its claim to be a country of laws and the world leader on human rights. If we cannot prosecute our leaders when they torture, the stain on our soul will never fade. On behalf of the People of the United States of America, I ask you to return a verdict of guilty as charged against President George W. Bush. Thank you."

Jarvis waited for Timothy to settle in his seat. "The court will recess for a twenty-minute break, after which the defense will address the jury."

Reporters rushed to file their stories, while spectators milled around in the courtroom and hallway. Timothy spotted Isabel Jarvis in the gallery and waved her over to the bar.

"Your summation was excellent, Timothy," Isabel glowed. "You did a great job of addressing the law and the evidence."

They spoke across the short fence separating the attorneys from the gallery.

"Thank you, Isabel." Timothy felt pleased with her compliment, although he sensed a "but" coming. "That speech was a team effort. Your nephew, John, made important contributions."

Isabel reached across the railing and took Timothy's hand. "Timothy, you missed one important point." Her look was soft, and her voice was gentle but firm. "You need to speak about the human misery. We've heard about the laws and clinical descriptions of techniques, but you have to get that jury to understand the toll it takes on victims who will never be whole again. Let them know the heartbreak the victims' families suffer along with them."

There was a distinct change in her expression when she spoke her next words. "And—it is very difficult for me to have sympathy for them, but the torturers are victims too. They will suffer for what they've done. How can they forget such horror?" she asked. "Some were following orders, some were instigators, but all of them will carry the burden of what they've done for the rest of their lives."

Timothy listened closely to Isabel; he felt her meaning—the gap in understanding between those who have been changed by torture and those who haven't. He remembered Axel's story about his father, how troubled his father had been, and his own agony at finding his father's body lying on the basement floor. The words in his father's letter remained indelible on his mind.

When he saw her eyes grow shiny, he came around the barrier, through the small gate and hugged her. "Oh, Isabel. You are so right. Thank you. We'll have our chance to speak of the victims, and I won't let them down."

* * *

"Mr. Konen, you may present the closing argument for the defense. The accused has the right to attend this and every session of this court. Does he continue to waive that right?"

"He does, Your Honor." Reginald Konen rose from his chair.

"Then proceed."

Konen walked to the jury box, his voice was loud and strong. "We are considering the actions of a man of courage who led this country through one of the most dangerous times in our recent history. President George W. Bush stopped what could have been a series of disastrous attacks on our nation. He was our President. Almost three thousand people were killed in an unprovoked attack on our country. In the aftermath, a biological attack was launched which is still unresolved. President Bush took control of the situation with dramatic action that prevented more attacks.

"You have heard from experts that there is no physical pain associated with waterboarding. Our military trainers have subjected thousands of our own troops to waterboarding. How can it be OK to use on our men and women, and too tough for use on a terrorist bent on killing our civilians?

"Some of our best and brightest attorneys approved the legal use of several enhanced interrogation techniques. President Bush had the courage to approve their use against a ruthless enemy and kept us safe by doing so. What he did was necessary, legal, and effective.

"The prosecution references the report of the Senate intelligence committee, but a careful reader of the report will find that President Bush was kept in the dark about misuse of his directives. Some of his closest advisors knew about the abuses, but they failed to tell the president. Yes, we agree that the photographs that came out of the Abu Ghraib detention center showed misconduct, but you can't blame the president for the actions of a few bad apples.

"President Bush authorized use of the enhanced interrogation techniques on a limited number of high value detainees only when it was necessary to protect you. The actionable intelligence gained from those interrogations saved thousands of lives right here on American soil. These were hardened terrorists, trained to resist standard interrogation techniques. There was no other way, and the president knew it.

"Now, years later, when the threat of a nuclear bomb or a dirty bomb has been defeated by this heroic man. Now—when we are safe because of his gutsy decisions. Now—when the crisis is past—they want to second-guess his decisions, made in the most dangerous of times, tough decisions that were right at the moment.

"This court has taken the unprecedented step of charging a former President of the United States with commission of a crime. This has never happened before. This jury must be aware that their decision will set an enduring precedent, and it is important for our democracy that you get it right. If you find the defendant guilty, future presidents will be looking over their shoulder every time they make a decision.

"If you find in his favor and determine him to be not guilty, you will restore the confidence of the American people in the wisdom of the authors of our constitution, who granted emergency powers to the person occupying the office of the presidency."

Konen held up a picture of the smoldering Trade Center.

"This is what forced your president to take immediate and courageous action. You must not punish this brave man for doing what he had to do to save lives. You must find him not guilty of all counts. Thank you."

When Konen sat down, Jarvis offered Madegen an opportunity for rebuttal.

Timothy stood at the prosecution table. "Your Honor, in response to the defense's concern about future presidents, I would remind the jury that no president should fear prosecution as long as they obey the law as required of every other citizen of this country."

After this statement, he walked to the podium and spent several seconds gathering his thoughts. He looked up and saw Isabel watching him, then turned to the jury.

"I would also like to respond to the defense's position that if interrogation techniques don't cause physical pain, it isn't torture. We have heard testimony about interrogation techniques such as slaps, slamming detainees against a wall, forced nudity, waterboarding that induces convulsions and vomiting, keeping detainees awake for up to 180 hours in stress positions with their hands shackled above their heads, entrapment in boxes and more. But there is mental pain that lingers long after the physical wounds heal.

"I want to speak now for all of the victims, and families of victims of torture. I can do this with personal knowledge because my father was tortured by the North Vietnamese. The torture never left him. He re-lived the waterboarding, beatings, and humiliation every day. The physical torment had stopped, but the mental anguish never did. After a few years, my father couldn't stand his misery any longer, and he took his own life. Now I live with the memory of my tortured father. It is for the victims and families of victims that I ask you to return with a guilty verdict.

"And what of the torturers? They're victims too. Are we going to require our soldiers and sailors to carry out orders that force them to renounce their humanity, ignore morality, and perform acts that dehumanize them? Is that what we should ask of our brave sons and daughters?

"If we hide from this reality today, it will be only the beginning. If the United States of America accepts torture, there will be no way to stop it. If U.S. presidents condone torture, all world leaders will feel free to use it. There are candidates for the office of president today promising to bring back torture if they are elected. If George W. Bush is not found guilty, they will do it. We will have created a globe of fear, for that is what torture is for, to instill fear. And then...and then...the only ones who do not live in fear will be those who control the torture chambers. And that would be our legacy for the future of mankind. There would never be anyone, ever again, to stop the torture. There would be those who overcome the fear, but they will be few and easily dealt with. It is up to us, right here, right now. It is for us today to stop the creation of a world of fear, or let it happen. We are responsible either way.

"We, as a country, have to be better. We cannot draw fine lines and parse legalism to avoid our responsibility to be humane to each other. That is not the America I want to live in. When we do wrong, we have to admit it. George W. Bush did wrong. It's clear. He did it. He said he did it. He must be found guilty for the sake of the victims, their families, our troops, and for all the citizens of the United States of America. Thank you."

The courtroom was silent as everyone watched Timothy return to his seat. It was a gavel blow by Henry Jarvis that broke the spell. "Court will recess until one o'clock at which time I will give the jury their instructions for deliberation."

CHAPTER 37

I thought Atticus Finch won't win, he can't win, but he's the only man in these parts who can keep a jury out so long in a case like that.
—Miss Maudie, *To Kill a Mockingbird*

Twelve jurors filed into a windowless jury room. A twenty-foot-long conference table set with plush simulated-leather chairs dominated the space. A small buffet at the far end offered coffee and snacks. The jurors looked drawn. Six men and six women watched a U.S. marshal pull the door shut. An emphatic lock-click followed.

"I don't like the sound of that," Damitra said. "Feels like we're the ones in trouble now." She was a tall African-American woman pouring decaf for Star, a middle-aged New Ager dressed in embroidered jeans and a poncho top. When the two met the first day of trial, Damitra's in-the-moment dynamism charmed Star, and Star's blunt appraisal of events attracted Damitra.

Other jurors stirred aimlessly about the room. They had spent the last weeks as passive observers. Now they faced the oppressive burden of deciding the final outcome. Many regretted having accepted their responsibility.

Two Hispanic men stood in a corner sipping coffee from white Styrofoam cups. They spoke in Spanish.

"I've had it with this trial. I want to get back to my family," Raul said. "If we were back in Mexico, this trial would have been over in one day." He brushed a drop of coffee off his trim black mustache.

Armand laughed at his friend. "Hey, if you ever go to court here, you're gonna be happy you're not in Mexico. Remember, guilty until proved innocent?"

"OK, OK, so we do our duty, but I don't see why we can't wrap this up today."

"I'm as tired of this damn sequester as anyone," Armand said. There were creases in his forehead as he spoke. "I hope my son is taking good care of the business."

A gray-haired octogenarian leaned on his cane, taking slow steps from the coffee mess to a chair at the conference table. He held a coffee cup with shaky balance in his free hand. A burly man with a shaved head pulled out a chair for him.

"Let me help you with that, Jimmy," the younger man said. He took the coffee, while Jimmy settled into his seat.

"Thanks, Bill. Do you think we can get this over with today? I'm runnin' out of steam."

"You and me, both. We'll be done in an hour if the rest of these people can be reasonable."

"Did you hear about the shots fired at the prosecutor?" Jimmy asked Bill.

"Is that what the bus driver was talking about? What happened?"

"Somebody tried to do away with Madegen!" Jimmy responded.

Gina overheard them. "I heard what the driver said," her speech was gruff. She was a block of a woman with crew-cut-length brown hair and stout tattooed arms that stuck out of a man-size t-shirt. "Sounds like a terrorist attack to me. There's too much publicity about this trial, and I think we're all in danger. I hope those marshals know what their doin'. First the bomb in the park, now rifle shots through an office window. What's next?"

It was several minutes before all twelve were settled in seats around the table.

Damitra was the first to get the attention of the whole room. "Who we gonna make foreman? Anybody want the job?"

There was silence from the others. Then the man next to her said, "How about you, Damitra?"

"That ain't the reason I asked, Ed. I don't feel educated enough to be the boss of all of you. I just want to get the ball rollin' here. Somebody with leader experience needs to be the foreman."

"I can do it if you want," Armand said. He looked the part, dressed in wool slacks, a white shirt, and tie. "I have employees, and I know how to organize."

"Let's vote," Damitra said. "All in favor of Armand Baron to be foreman raise your hand."

Eleven hands went up.

"OK," Armand said. "We have our instructions from the judge, and he offered to answer any questions about our deliberations. Are there any?"

"I just want to talk about the whole thing in general," Bill said. "There seems to be a disagreement about whether EITs are torture or not. It seems to me, the first thing we need to do is decide on that. If they're not torture, we're done. That would make our decision easy."

"Fair enough. How do you want to go about this?" Armand asked.

Damitra said, "I think we should go around the table and get each person's opinion."

"OK, let's start on my right," Armand said.

Star didn't hesitate. "It's torture, no question. What else would you call it?"

Raul said, "I'm undecided. I want to hear from the rest of you."

Ed declared: "Torture."

The next person was Gina. "But they said it can't be all that bad, if they do it to our own troops in training. It works on the terrorists because they aren't trained, and our guys are. It's like carrying an eighty-pound pack. It's real hard if you aren't trained, but it's nothin' for a trained soldier."

Manny looked at Gina with wide eyes. "You must be kidding, lady. There's no comparison between walking five miles with a heavy pack and being drowned. I don't care how much training you've had."

"Well, I just don't think our government would harm our own soldiers," Gina said.

"Then you probably haven't heard about the mustard gas experiments they did on our troops back in 1944,"[196] he replied.

"OK, can we stay on the subject?" Damitra interjected. "Jimmy, what's your opinion?"

Jimmy looked at Gina for a few seconds and shook his head. The

---

196 A History of US Secret Human Experimentation.
    http://www.rense.com/general36/history.htm

room waited in respectful silence.

"I fought in the Second World War." Jimmy's speech was slow. "I'm eighty-eight years old. I could have gotten out of that war because I was too young and I could have gotten out of this jury duty because I'm too old, but I didn't want to. I've always been proud of my country up until now. We prosecuted the Japanese for waterboarding G.I.'s—hung some of 'em." He looked around the table. "I say it's torture when they do it to our guys, and it's torture when we do it to theirs. Ain't nobody gonna change my mind on that. That's all I have to say right now."

Several jurors voiced their agreement with Jimmy.

Damitra was the last one to speak. "Me, I don't know much history about WWII or any of that mustard gas stuff, but to me, if you tried to drown me one hundred and eighty-three times—to me, that's torture. I mean, I'd tell you anything you want after you drownded me the first time."

"I have a question," Gina said. "What if—this is just a what if—what if we find President Bush guilty? Is he going to jail, then?"

"We're not supposed to consider punishment," Armand said. "The judge was very specific about that. Guilty or not guilty, that's it. Punishment doesn't have anything to do with determining guilt."

"But he was the president. We can't put an ex-president in jail!" Gina said.

"You can't be considerin' that, honey," Damitra said. "Just pretend he's a ordinary man. It ain't who he is that's important. It's what he done we have to look at."

"Well, I don't think that's right, treating an ex-president like that."

"Gina, if you can't follow the judge's instructions, you should let him know," Armand said.

Gina looked around at the others for support before she turned back to Armand. "I don't know, I guess I can do it your way."

Armand summarized. "We have some disagreement on the torture issue so let's come back to that."

Damitra spoke up. "I wanna talk about the Geneva Conventions thing. How that works on what we're talkin' about here."

"We signed a treaty that made it our responsibility to treat prisoners of war humanely," Bill said.

A woman sitting next to Gina reacted. "Those terrorists didn't treat our people humanely, mister. I went to New York and saw that mess where the towers used to be. Almost three thousand killed and thousands more hurt. We all saw the pictures Mr. Konen showed. That's not humane in my book."

"Let's don't be gettin' confused about what they did, and what we did," Damitra said. "We ain't judgin' the terrorists; we judgin' Mr. Bush."

"But what about an eye for an eye," the woman said, and Gina nodded.

"Far as I know, Mr. Bush has both his eyes," Damitra said. "Let's talk some more about those Geneva rules."

Armand read Geneva Article 3 out loud. Then the discussion veered off to the others accused of participating with Bush in authorizing the EITs. Two women disagreed about the meaning of conspiracy.

"It's not a conspiracy if you don't know what you're doing is wrong," Gina shouted.

"That doesn't make sense," Star stood up and leaned across the table at Gina. "It's a conspiracy when two or more people make a secret plan to do something illegal; whether they know the law or not. Ignorance is no excuse."

"Who you callin' ignorant?" Gina yelled.

Armand tried to diffuse the tension. "Ladies, please be respectful. We have to work together on this."

"She's the one yellin'," shouted Star.

"Oh, and what are you doin' little Miss Hippy Dippy?" Gina said.

The personal attacks frustrated Armand's attempt to calm things, and he looked for somebody to help with the situation. When he finally shrugged in a gesture of failure, Damitra called in the guard, whose presence calmed them down. The room settled into an embarrassed silence for ten minutes until Star apologized, and an abashed Gina acknowledged the peace offering with a penitent smile.

Armand refocused the discussion but diversions continued on unrelated tangents. The frustration level rose. By the end of the day, nothing had been resolved. A disgruntled jury returned to their motel.

* * *

After the second day, a vote by the majority forced Armand to send the Judge a note saying they couldn't get to a unanimous agreement.

The jurors talked about packing up as they waited for the judge to release them.

The judge sent a note back asking them to try harder.

The jury room atmosphere sagged into petulance.

Jimmy Greenly asked the court to allow the jury to view the Miami Book Fair video from beginning to end. The judge refused but made arrangements for them to view the portion of the video that was submitted as evidence in the trial.

Gina Long requested a transcript of the testimony by Dr. Vilier and insisted on reading it out loud to the other eleven. They listened patiently, but it was clear they were humoring her.

Damitra asked for a copy of the International Red Cross report on detainee treatment; she was given those pages that prosecution read during the trial.

* * *

Trial news and discussion filled the airwaves. A tabloid reporter, who saw the exchange between Isabel and Timothy in the courtroom, published an exposé purporting to have discovered a romantic link between the judge's wife and the special prosecutor. Isabel found it hilarious. Henry refused to give it any attention. Annie teased Timothy about it until he begged her to let it go, and she did. She even thought it was funny when a talk radio host intimated her involvement in a lovers' triangle. Timothy was chagrined about the embarrassing episode and made an unnecessary apology to Henry and Isabel.

Timothy, Annie, and Jacob lounged in John's living room where they studied the D.C. papers. Editorials probed what-if questions with contrasting opinions on Bush's future. The free paper studied the possibility of a guilty verdict and the ramifications for the future of the presidency. Their assessment was not optimistic. *Politico* filled two full pages with opinions of former U.S. and foreign diplomats about how the U.S. was being viewed on the international stage. *The Hill* expressed concern for the fairness of the trial and the fallout for Vice President Cheney, who had so vociferously defended the EITs. *The Stars and Stripes* published a right leaning, thinly camouflaged defense of the actions of the former commander-in-chief.

The *Post* ran a series. Would President Bush have a chance on appeal? Would he end up at the Supreme Court? The same court that decided his first election? The court headed by a Chief Justice he had appointed? What would that mean for the Supreme Court? Would they be wise to refuse the case?

Timothy took a call from his old boss at Justice.

"You know, Timothy, I didn't have any choice but to fire you."

"I know, if you hadn't done it, somebody else would have."

"You should know you have a lot of unofficial support over here, Madegen. I just wanted to let you know that."

The united front of the other defendants indicted by the grand jury began to weaken. Many arranged for strategic interviews where they recounted clear memories of the actions of their associates but feigned amnesia about their own participation in meetings and decisions. Political action committees spent millions of dollars on ads aimed at widening the political divide and swaying public opinion in favor of President Bush's acquittal.

Pollsters spouted statistics, and pundits made unfounded statements about the sentiment of the country, never opining on actual guilt or innocence. Representatives of civil liberty and humanitarian organizations offered their spokespeople to anyone with a camera or a microphone.

* * *

On the fifth day of deliberations, the judge called the jury back into the courtroom. There were no attorneys present, no spectators. Twelve red-eyed people filed in; their mood could be summed-up as dour. They had little to say to each other. The judge detected their lack of comity.

"Ladies and gentlemen, I know your task is made more difficult by your sequester, and I realize how much you must be missing your families and your daily routines. I understand this, but it can't be helped. If there is anything I can do to improve your creature comforts, please let me know."

Damitra's hand went up, and the judge acknowledged her.

"Your honor, we need some outdoor time. We been cooped up in a jury room and court room and motel rooms for days. Even prisoners in the pen get time in the yard once a day," she said. Several of the other jurors nodded their agreement.

"Thank you, ma'am. We will see to it right away. It's a nice sunny day today, and we'll make sure you get a chance to enjoy it."

"Thank you, Judge," Damitra said.

"You're very welcome. We should have thought of this. I'm sorry you had to ask," Jarvis said in apology. Then his tone turned grave.

"I am not unaware of the difficulty that faces you in deciding the guilt or innocence of the accused in this case. It is a serious responsibility. Maybe the heaviest responsibility you will ever face in your lifetime.

"We have all made a personal investment in this case, you jurors no less than anyone else, but I have to ask you to continue your deliberations to get to a verdict." The judge scanned the jurors. Each face returned a message, some vacant, some dark, others attentive.

"This case is so important. It is difficult to convey the gravity of the decision you are being asked to make. There has been great expense of time, resources, and effort, not to mention the emotional strain on all of us."

Jarvis came down from the bench, walked around the dais, and stood in front of the jury box. His tone became less authoritative and more conversational. "Failure to agree on a verdict will result in this case remaining open. It will continue to be a burden on our nation." The movement from his elevated perch to intimate contact was effective.

Armand felt free to ask, "Your Honor, I am Armand Baron, the foreman of this jury. We would all like to know the consequence of finding that we cannot arrive at a verdict."

"Thank you, Armand. You should all be wondering, and I want you to understand this. There would be another trial, Armand, and that trial wouldn't be any better than the one we have just completed. Any future jury will be asked to come to a verdict on the basis of the same evidence you have already received. There is no reason to think that another twelve people would be any more conscientious, or competent, or wiser than you folks."

Jarvis stepped right up to the railing in front of the box. His eyes confirmed the sincerity in his words. "I will not ask any one of you to give up an honest belief." He paused to let his statement sink in. "But I must ask you to deliberate without bias and make every effort to consider the evidence and the opinions of your associates on the jury."

Jarvis played the courtroom drama hard and knew when it was right to deliver the final instruction. Everyone in the room was in the moment.

"If a majority of your number is considering conviction or acquittal, the other jurors should search their conscience and reconsider whether your doubts are reasonable or if you should join the majority. I am sure by now, after five days of deliberations, you have all turned the question over and over in your minds. Now, with all sides considered, it is your duty to agree upon a verdict if you can do so."

Henry stepped back from the jury box and surveyed the jurors again. He opened his hands to them, palms up as he made his plea.

"If the evidence does not convince you beyond a reasonable doubt that the defendant is guilty, then you must deliver a unanimous verdict of not guilty.

"Please return to the jury room and work toward a verdict to the best of your ability."

The judge returned to the bench but did not sit down.

"I am available to answer any questions. Please do your duty," Jarvis said in a tone that changed from that of an advisor to a demanding boss. He left the courtroom.

* * *

Later that day, twelve U.S. marshals escorted twelve jurors to John Marshall Place Park next to the courthouse. They walked in pairs with Jimmy Greenly setting the pace; nobody was in a rush to return to the jury room. The day was sunny, and they welcomed the touch of a soft breeze. There were smiles on faces that had been glum.

Jimmy Greenly stopped and leaned on his cane at the sight of the wide lawns. He took a long breath. "Ah, the sweet smell of fresh-cut grass."

The talk was about family and plans for after-trial futures. When they settled at picnic tables in a secured area, marshals served box lunches and permitted them to walk about in a hundred-foot radius with their minders at their heels.

Raul walked off to the edge of the group and smoked a cigarette. Gina complained about the smoke that drifted over, and Raul graciously put it out.

When the lunch boxes were cleared, the group broke up. Each person wandered away for a time of solitude.

After two hours, Armand told the marshals they were ready to return to the jury room.

It was late afternoon when the door closed on them.

Armand asked for attention. "We've been at this long enough. Is there anyone with something new to contribute?"

There was silence at the conference table.

He made another try. "Can anyone offer anything that might help us decide this verdict?"

Damitra leaned forward on her forearms and looked up and down the table to see if anyone else was going to speak before she began.

"I guess we're back where we started—down to tryin' to figure if waterboarding and that other stuff is torture. We all know Mr. Bush ordered it. He said he did it in speeches, and he wrote he did it in his book. So we only need to know if it's torture, like Bill said the first day." She folded her hands together in front of her on the table and looked down at her fingers, then she raised her head and stared across the table at Star who nodded encouragement.

Gina stared at the wall across the room with her arms crossed on her chest, unwilling to look at Damitra. Jimmy Greenly sat back in his chair with his eyes closed; the nodding of his head showed he was listening. Raul whispered to Manny but stopped when Damitra started speaking again. "Any you people have pets? A dog or a cat or bird or somethin'?"

Bill asked Damitra, "What's this got to do with anything?"

"You got a pet, Bill?"

"Yeah, I have a dog, a Shepherd."

"Do you know there are laws against chaining up your dog, Bill?"

"Yes."

"Ever put your dog in a pet carrier?"

"Yes."

"Do you use one just big enough to stuff him in there?"

"No, he has to be able to move around."

"What would you think about a woman who tried to drown her dog in an airport toilet because they wouldn't let her get on a plane with it?"

Gina twisted in her seat and glared at Damitra. "I know what you're doing, and it's bullshit. None of this has anything to do with our case."

"OK, Gina, let me talk on a different subject. When we were out in the park today, everybody was talkin' 'bout their families, and how we want to get back to them. I was thinking about my kids and my husband and my mother and all of them. Now we're back in here dealin' with almost drownin' people and chainin' 'em up and stuffin' 'em in tiny boxes and everything different from our families. But is it really different? 'Cuz I don't think anybody in this room would do those things to their kid or cat or their dog. I think we could decide this, if we put the two together. What if each one of us thought about what it would be like to have their wife or husband or brother or sister stuffed in a box, or chained to the ceiling, or strapped down naked on one of those boards and drownded until they thought they were gonna die?"

"Would you call that torture then? That might be a way to think about it. That's all I got ta say."

* * *

Everyone moved to windowless inner offices in the K Street building. Fluorescent tubes lit the rooms night and day, adding an artificial gloom to their restless mood as they waited for the verdict.

Jacob mused about the jury, "You know, Tim, I'm really worried about those jurors. Reggie made an impression with those Trade Center photos and all that talk about presidential duty. I could see some heads nodding in the jury box."

"We're asking those twelve people to be courageous, to face the truth, to stand-up to power, Jacob. I hope they understand there is more on trial here than the guilt or innocence of one man."

"I think you made that clear, Tim. I'm thinking the longer they deliberate, the better our chances for a guilty verdict."

Annie worried about a hung jury. "Doesn't it mean they might deadlock?"

Radovich shook his head. "We're just guessing, Annie. It could go either way. I'm only saying juries find it harder to get to guilty than they do to not guilty. It's easier to let somebody off, but you could be right too."

When the phone rang, everyone jumped. Clarissa picked it up and looked across the room at Timothy as she listened. "Yes, right away," she said and hung up.

"That was the clerk; jury's ready. Henry wants us at the courthouse in half an hour." She grabbed her briefcase and joined the others as they filed out the door.

* * *

Timothy insisted that everyone join him in court for the verdict. John and Clarissa followed him up the stairs to the prosecutor's entrance, speculating on reasons for the jury's timing. Annie and Jacob followed in tense silence behind them. Axel opened the door to the courtroom at the top of the stair, but before Timothy stepped in, he turned to look back into four anxious faces and gave them a hopeful smile.

"I wish all three hundred million citizens of this country were in that jury box today, because this verdict will show the true character of the American people for all the world to see."

AFTERWORD

"Rise like Lions after slumber
In unvanquishable number—
Shake your chains to earth like dew
Which in sleep had fallen on you—
Ye are many—they are few."
—Percy Bysshe Shelley

Our laws forbid torture, but if these laws are not enforced, the use of torture to terrorize, punish and subjugate people will never stop.

We brag of American exceptionalism—the special character of the United States as a uniquely free nation based on democratic ideals and personal liberty. Our influence on world culture is enormous. History teaches that when the United States leads on human rights, from Nuremberg to Kosovo, other countries follow. Other countries will follow our lead on torture, too. If we fail to prosecute, we signal to governments around the world that they are free to use torture with impunity.

We are at a grave point in human history. What we do today, will determine whether laws against torture are genuine, or only a façade.

Don't forget that the president did not act alone. There are others whose actions must be examined by the courts.

It's up to us. We must prosecute the torturers in our midst, or we will be known forever as the Craven Generation—the generation of Americans who could have put an end to torture but didn't have the courage to act.

APPENDIX

IN THE UNITED STATES DISTRICT COURT FOR

THE DISTRICT OF COLUMBIA

UNITED STATES OF AMERICA

UNITED STATES OF AMERICA(<u>Count 1</u>: Commanding, aiding,
(abetting, counseling, inducing or
v. (procuring the torture of individuals
(in control of the United States
GEORGE W. BUSH (Government. USC Title 18, Part I,
(Counts 1, 2, 3, and 4) (Chapter 1, § 2 –Principals. Count
(1 is related to Counts 2 and 3

RICHARD B. CHENEY
(Counts 1, 2, 3, and 4) (<u>Count 2:</u> Conspiring to enable
(torture by authorizing secret
(detention and constructing and
CONDOLEEZZA RICE (promulgating false legal analysis.
(Counts 1, 2, 3, and 4) (USC Title 18, Part I, Chapter
(113C, §2340A Torture.
((c) Conspiracy. Count 2 is related
DONALD H. RUMSFELD (to Count 3.
(Counts 1, 2, 3, and 4)

(<u>Count 3:</u> Committing acts of
JOHN D. ASHCROFT (torture. USC Title 18, Part I,
(Counts 1, 2, 3, and 4) (Chapter 113C,§2340A Torture
((a) Offense. Count 3 is related to
GEORGE J. TENET (Counts 1 and 2.
(Counts 1, 2, 3, and 4)

JOSE RODRIGUEZ
(Counts 1, 2, 3, 4, and 5) (<u>Count 4:</u> Commission of war
(crimes—grave breaches of the
(Geneva Convention 12 August
ALBERTO R. GONZALES (1949 Common Article 3. USC
(Counts 1, 2 3, and 4) (Title 18, Part I, Chapter 118, War
(Crimes. Count 4 is related to
(Counts 1, 2 and 3.

DAVID S. ADDINGTON
(Counts 2, 3, and 4)

JOHN C. YOO
(Counts 2, 3, and 4)

JAY S. BYBEE
(Counts 2, 3, and 4)
STEVEN G. BRADBURY
(Counts 2, 3, and 4)

WILLIAM J. HAYNES
(Counts 2, 3, and 4)

GEOFFREY D. MILLER
(Counts 1, 3, and 4)

JOHN A. RIZZO
(Counts 2, 3, and 4)

JAMES E. MITCHELL
(Counts 1, 3 and 4)

JOHN B. JESSEN
(Counts 1, 3 and 4)

DEFENDANTS

(<u>Count 5:</u> Destruction, alteration,
(or falsification of records in Federal
(investigations. USC Title 18, Part
(I, Chapter 73, §1519.

<u>PRESENTMENT</u>

THE GRAND JURY CHARGES THAT:

<u>General Allegations</u>

The defendants were agents of the United States Government in positions of trust by election, appointment or contract.

1.   Defendant GEORGE W. BUSH was sworn into office as president of the United States on January 20, 2001.

2.   Defendant RICHARD B. CHENEY was sworn into office as Vice-President on January 20, 2001.

3.   Defendant CONDOLEEZZA RICE was appointed National Security Advisor on January 20, 2001 and served as a chief advisor to the President of the United States on national security issues until January 25, 2005 when she was sworn in as Secretary of State. She served as Secretary of State until January 20, 2009.

4.   Defendant DONALD H. RUMSFELD was sworn in as United States Secretary of Defense on January 20, 2001. He resigned his position on December 18, 2006.

5.   Defendant JOHN D. ASHCROFT was sworn in as Attorney General of the United States on February 2, 2001. He resigned his position on February 3, 2005.

6.   Defendant GEORGE J. TENET was Director of Central Intelligence from December 15, 1996 – July 11, 2004.

7.   Defendant JOSE RODRIGUEZ was Chief of Operations, CIA Counterterrorism Center from September 2001 to May 2002. From May 2002 to November 2004, he was the Director of the CIA Counterterrorism Center. From November 2004 to September 2007, he served as Deputy Director of Operations for CIA Counterterrorism Center.

8.   Defendant ALBERTO R. GONZALES was White House Counsel from January 20, 2001 until February 3, 2005. He served as Attorney General from February 3, 2005 until September 17, 2007.

9.   Defendant DAVID S. ADDINGTON was Counsel to the Vice-President from January 20, 2001 to October 30, 2005. From October 31, 2005 until January 20, 2009 he was Chief of Staff to the Vice President.

10. Defendant JOHN C. YOO was a Deputy Assistant Attorney General in the Department of Justice, Office of Legal Counsel from 2001 to 2003.

11. Defendant JAY S. BYBEE was Assistant Attorney General, Department of Justice, Office of Legal Counsel from November 2001 to March 2003.

12. Defendant STEVEN G. BRADBURY was Principal Deputy Assistant Attorney General from April 2004 to June 2005 and Acting Assistant Attorney General from June 2005 to January 20, 2009.

13. Defendant WILLIAM J. HAYNES was Department of Defense General Counsel from May 24, 2001 to February 2008.

14. Defendant GEOFFREY D. MILLER was Commander of Detention and Interrogation Operations at Guantanamo Bay Detention Facility from November 2002 until March 2004. From April 2004 until his retirement on July 31, 2006, he was Commander of Operations at Abu Ghraib prison in Iraq.

15. Defendant JOHN A. RIZZO was CIA Senior Deputy Legal Counsel from March 1995 through November 2001 and from October 2002 until August 2004. He was CIA Acting General Counsel from November 2001 to October 2002 and again from August 2004 to September 2009.

16. Defendant JAMES E. MITCHELL was an officer in the United States Air Force from 1988 until he retired in 2001. He served as Chief of Psychology at the Air Force survival school at Fairchild Air Force Base in Spokane, Washington. In 2002, after his retirement from the military, as part of Mitchell Jessen and Associates, he received a contract from the CIA to develop enhanced interrogation techniques.

17. Defendant JOHN B. JESSEN, a United States Air Force retiree, was hired in 2002 by the Central Intelligence Agency to design an enhanced interrogation techniques program.

<u>COUNT ONE</u>

<u>Commanding, aiding, abetting, counseling, inducing or procuring the commission of the torture of individuals in control of the United States of America</u>

THE GRAND JURY CHARGES THAT:

Between September 17, 2001 and January 20, 2009 in the District of Columbia and elsewhere, defendants GEORGE W. BUSH, RICHARD B. CHENEY, CONDOLEEZZA RICE, DONALD H. RUMSFELD, JOHN D. ASHCROFT, GEORGE J. TENET, JOSE RODRIGUEZ, ALBERTO R. GONZALES, GEOFFREY D. MILLER, JAMES E. MITCHELL, AND JOHN B. JESSEN, commanded, aided, abetted, counseled, induced, or procured the torture of individuals in control of the United States of America at secret sites in Europe and at military facilities in Afghanistan, Iraq and Guantanamo Bay, Cuba, by approving secret detention and methods of torture including waterboarding, contracting with individuals to commit torture and falsely declaring laws against torture and degrading and inhumane treatment not applicable, a violation of Title 18, United States Code, Part I, Chapter 1, § 2 – Principals.

On or about September 17, 2001, Defendant GEORGE W. BUSH signed a secret Presidential Notification Memorandum authorizing the CIA to capture, hold and interrogate individuals at secret sites in foreign countries, an offense against the terms of the Geneva Conventions, a violation of Title 18, United States Code, Part I, Chapter 1, § 2 – Principals.[1]

On or about January 19, 2002, DONALD H. RUMSFELD declared to the Joints Chiefs of Staff that the Geneva Conventions of 1949 do not apply to al Qaeda and Taliban detainees.[2] This memo resulted in cruel,

---

1   Sixth Declaration of Marilyn A. Dorn, Information Review Officer, Central Intelligence Agency, Item 61, page 34. https://www.aclu.org/files/pdfs/natsec/20070105_Dorn_Declaration_8.pdf

2   Memorandum for Chairman of the Joint Chiefs of Staff, from Donald Rumsfeld, Status of Taliban and Al Qaida, January 19, 2002. http://www1.umn.edu/humanrts/OathBetrayed/Rumsfeld%201-19-02.pdf

inhumane treatment and torture of individuals held by the Department of Defense. The U.S. Supreme Court confirmed that the Geneva Conventions do apply to these prisoners, a violation of Title 18, United States Code, Part I, Chapter 1, § 2 – Principals.[3]

On or about February 7, 2002, GEORGE W. BUSH issued a declaration that the Geneva Conventions do not apply to Taliban and al Qaeda prisoners. The memo instructed the Armed Forces to continue to treat detainees humanely with an implied exception for "military necessity." The CIA was not included in this requirement.[4] This memo resulted in cruel, inhumane treatment and torture of individuals held by the CIA and the Department of Defense, a violation of Title 18, United States Code, Part I, Chapter 1, § 2 – Principals. [5] The U.S. Supreme Court later confirmed that the Geneva Conventions do apply to these prisoners.[6]

On or about August 2002, RICHARD B. CHENEY, JOHN D. ASHCROFT, AND CONDOLEEZZA RICE were briefed on the CIA use of enhanced interrogation techniques, including waterboarding, and approved the use of those techniques,[7] a violation of Title 18, United States Code, Part I, Chapter 1, § 2 – Principals.

On or about July 29, 2003, RICHARD B. CHENEY and CONDOLEEZZA RICE met with CIA General Counsel Muller, JOHN D. ASHCROFT, and ALBERTO R. GONZALES, among others, during which CHENEY and RICE agreed that the CIA was

---

3   US Supreme Court, Hamdan v. Rumsfeld, No. 05-184, Decided June 29, 2006. Syllabus page 6.
http://www.supremecourt.gov/opinions/05pdf/05-184.pdf

4   Scott W. Muller. Memorandum for the Record, "Humane" Treatment of CIA Detainees. February 12, 2003.
http://ciasavedlives.com/bdr/humane-treatment-of-cia-detainees.pdf
http://ciasavedlives.com/bdr/humane-treatment-alQaeda-taliban-detainees.pdf

5   USC Title 18 - CRIMES AND CRIMINAL PROCEDURE §2. Principals.

6   Supra 3.

7   George Tenet, Memorandum to National Security Advisor, June 4, 2004.
http://ciasavedlives.com/bdr/memo-for-nsa-review-of-cia-interrogation-program.pdf

executing approved administration policy in performing interrogations using enhanced techniques, including waterboarding,[8] a violation of Title 18, United States Code, Part I, Chapter 1, § 2 – Principals.

On or about January 28, 2003, GEORGE TENET issued a memo authorizing the use of enhanced interrogation techniques, including waterboarding,[9] a violation of Title 18, United States Code, Part I, Chapter 1, § 2 – Principals.

From September 2001 until September 2007, JOSE RODRIGUEZ served in several positions in the CIA Counterterrorism Center. Under his authority, CIA operatives ran secret prisons where detainees were tortured using methods that included waterboarding, a violation of Title 18, United States Code, Part I, Chapter 1, § 2 – Principals.

On or about November 2002 until March 2004, GEOFFREY D. MILLER commanded the detention facility at Guantanamo Bay, Cuba, and commanded the detention facility at Abu Ghraib, Iraq from April 2004 to November 2004. In both facilities, he oversaw the implementation of torture techniques approved by DONALD H. RUMSFELD,[10] a violation of Title 18, United States Code, Part I, Chapter 1, § 2 – Principals.

During the years 2002 to 2009, JOHN B. JESSEN and JAMES E. MITCHELL contracted with the U.S. Government to develop enhanced

---

8   Senate Select Committee Intelligence Committee Study of the CIA's Detention and Interrogation Program Executive Summary, December 3, 2014. Pages 117 and 118.

9   Guidelines on Interrogations Conducted Pursuant to the Presidential Memorandum of Notification of 17 September 2001, signed by George Tenet, Director of Central Intelligence, January 28, 2003.
     http://www.aclu.org/files/torturefoia/released/082409/olcremand/2004olc12.pdf.
     Note that the title of the document is redacted in the reference copy, however the complete title is stated in the Senate Select Committee on Intelligence, Committee Study of the Central Intelligence Agency's Detention and Interrogation Program, Executive Summary, footnote 280, page 57.

10   William J. Haynes II, General Counsel to SECRETARY OF DEFENSE, Counter-Resistance Techniques, November 27, 2002 and approved by Donald Rumsfeld on December 2, 2002. http://nsarchive.gwu.edu/NSAEBB/NSAEBB127/02.12.02.pdf

interrogation techniques including waterboarding. These techniques were used on detainees in U.S. custody, a violation of Title 18, United States Code, Part I, Chapter 1, § 2 – Principals.

COUNT TWO

<u>Conspiring to enable torture by constructing and promulgating false legal analysis.</u>
THE GRAND JURY FURTHER CHARGES THAT:

In September 2001 and for several years thereafter GEORGE W. BUSH, RICHARD B. CHENEY, CONDOLEEZZA RICE, DONALD H. RUMSFELD, JOHN D. ASHCROFT, GEORGE J. TENET, JOSE RODRIGUEZ, ALBERTO R. GONZALES, DAVID S. ADDINGTON, JOHN C. YOO, JAY S. BYBEE, STEVEN G. BRADBURY, WILLIAM J. HAYNES, and JOHN A. RIZZO conspired to generate and promulgate false legal analysis which encouraged others to perform acts of torture, a violation of Title 18, United States Code, Part I, Chapter 113C, §2340A Torture. (c) Conspiracy.

On or about January 9, 2002, JOHN C. YOO issued a letter to WILLIAM J. HAYNES stating that the Geneva Conventions do not apply to members of the al Qaeda organization or the Taliban militia, a violation of Title 18, United States Code, Part I, Chapter 113C, §2340A Torture. (c) Conspiracy.[11]

On or about January 11, 2002, William Taft IV, Legal Advisor to the State Department, issued a memo to JOHN C. YOO, warning that the legal analysis in YOO's January 9, 2002 draft memorandum was "seriously flawed".[12] JOHN C. YOO ignored the advice. The memo was approved

---

11   Memorandum for William J. Haynes II, General Counsel, Department of Defense, from John Yoo, Deputy Assistant Attorney General, Application of Laws and Treaties to al Qaeda and Taliban Detainees, January 9, 2002.
     http://www2.gwu.edu/~nsarchiv/NSAEBB/NSAEBB127/02.01.09.pdf
12   Memorandum for John Yoo from William Taft IV, Your Draft Memorandum of January 9th, January 11, 2002.
     http://nsarchive.gwu.edu/torturingdemocracy/documents/20020111.pdf.

by JAY S. BYBEE and issued on January 22, 2002, a violation of Title 18, United States Code, Part I, Chapter 113C, §2340A Torture. (c) Conspiracy.

On or about January 25, 2002, ALBERTO R. GONZALES issued a memo to GEORGE W. BUSH stating that opting out of the Geneva Conventions would provide a solid defense against violation of the War Crimes Act (Section 2441), a violation of Title 18, United States Code, Part I, Chapter 113C, §2340A Torture. (c) Conspiracy.[13]
DAVID S. ADDINGTON has been identified as the author of the January 25, 2002 Memorandum for the President which was issued by ALBERTO R. GONZALES stating that the Geneva Conventions do not apply to the conflict with al Qaeda and the Taliban, a violation of Title 18, United States Code, Part I, Chapter 113C, §2340A Torture. (c) Conspiracy.[14]

On or about March 13, 2002, JAY S. BYBEE declared in a memo to WILLIAM J. HAYNES that the president has the authority to transfer detainees to countries where they might be tortured, a violation of Title 18, United States Code, Part I, Chapter 113C, §2340A Torture. (c) Conspiracy.[15]

On or about August 1, 2002, JAY S. BYBEE wrote a memo to ALBERTO GONZALEZ that declares that the infliction of severe physical pain for interrogation purposes does not constitute torture if it does not cause organ failure or death, a violation of Title 18, United States Code, Part I, Chapter 113C, §2340A Torture. (c) Conspiracy.[16]

---

13   Memo From Alberto Gonzales To President Bush, "Application of the Geneva Convention on Prisoners of War to the Conflict with al Qaeda and the Taliban", January 25, 2002.
     http://nsarchive.gwu.edu/torturingdemocracy/documents/20020125.pdf
14   Executive Intelligence Review, Cheney's Lawyer Addington Penned Key Torture Memo, July 16, 2004
     http://www.larouchepub.com/other/2004/3128addington_memo.html
15   Memorandum for William J. Haynes, II, General Counsel, Department of Defense by Jay Bybee, March 13, 2002.
     http://www2.gwu.edu/~nsarchiv/torturingdemocracy/documents/20020313.pdf
16   Memo for Alberto R. Gonzales, Counsel to the President, August 1, 2002, by Jay S. Bybee. http://www2.gwu.edu/~nsarchiv/NSAEBB/NSAEBB127/02.08.01.pdf

JOHN C. YOO violated his fiduciary responsibility to give sound legal advice to the President of the United States by issuing several memos redefining torture to give the appearance that certain torture techniques are lawful, a violation of Title 18, United States Code, Part I, Chapter 113C, §2340A Torture. (c) Conspiracy.[17]

STEPHEN G. BRADBURY issued a memorandum to JOHN A. RIZZO stating that certain interrogation techniques including waterboarding do not violate U.S. law, a violation of Title 18, United States Code, Part I, Chapter 113C, §2340A Torture. (c) Conspiracy.[18]

JOHN A. RIZZO sought legal cover for CIA torture as evidenced by a memo from the Justice Department Office of Legal Counsel responding to his question about the elements of the crime of torture,.[19] and a request for Office of Legal Counsel approval of specific torture techniques for use in the interrogation of Abu Zubaydah, a violation of Title 18, United States Code, Part I, Chapter 113C, §2340A Torture. (c) Conspiracy.[20]

STEVEN G. BRADBURY provided false legal cover to the CIA to use techniques individually and in combination, including waterboarding, that are clearly torture, a violation of Title 18, United States Code, Part I, Chapter 113C, §2340A Torture. (c) Conspiracy.[21]

---

17   John Yoo Memo To Alberto Gonzales stating that certain torture techniques are legal. August 1, 2002.
http://nsarchive.gwu.edu/torturingdemocracy/documents/20020801-3.pdf

18   Memorandum for John A. Rizzo, Senior Deputy General Counsel, Central Intelligence Agency, from Steven G. Bradbury, Principal Deputy Assistant Attorney General, Office of Legal Counsel, Re: Application of 18 U.S.C. §§ 2340–2340A to the Combined Use of Certain Techniques in the Interrogation of High Value al Qaeda Detainees (May 10, 2005) http://www.derechos.org/nizkor/excep/combined.pdf.

19   John Yoo letter to John Rizzo, July 13, 2002.
http://www.justice.gov/sites/default/files/olc/legacy/2009/08/24/letter-rizzo2002.pdf

20   Jay Bybee ,Memorandum for John Rizzo Acting General Counsel of the Central Intelligence Agency. August 1, 2002.
http://nsarchive.gwu.edu/torturingdemocracy/documents/20020801-2.pdf

21   Supra 18

DONALD H. RUMSFELD approved interrogation techniques to be used at Guantanamo Bay, Cuba detention facility including waterboarding. RUMSFELD approved the techniques contained in a series of memos by military commanders and military legal counsel who may also be subject to conspiracy charges, a violation of Title 18, United States Code, Part I, Chapter 113C, §2340A Torture. (c) Conspiracy.[22]

On or about December 2002, Alberto Mora, U.S. Navy General Counsel objected to the techniques approved by DONALD H. RUMSFELD. RUMSFELD conspired with WILLIAM J. HAYNES to obtain a memo from JOHN C. YOO falsely stating that the techniques did not violate U.S. or international law, a violation of Title 18, United States Code, Part I, Chapter 113C, §2340A Torture. (c) Conspiracy.[23]

COUNT THREE

Committing an act of torture under the color of law specifically intended to inflict severe physical or mental pain or suffering (other than pain or suffering incidental to lawful sanctions) upon another person within his custody or physical control.

THE GRAND JURY FURTHER CHARGES THAT:

Beginning in September, 2001 and for several years thereafter, GEORGE W. BUSH, RICHARD B. CHENEY, CONDOLEEZZA RICE, DONALD H. RUMSFELD, JOHN D. ASHCROFT, GEORGE J. TENET, JOSE RODRIGUEZ, ALBERTO R. GONZALES, DAVID S. ADDINGTON, JOHN C. YOO, JAY S. BYBEE, STEVEN G. BRADBURY, WILLIAM J. HAYNES, GEOFFREY D. MILLER, and

---

22 Various authors, series of memorandum. October 11, 2002 through December 2, 2002.
    http://www.washingtonpost.com/wp-srv/nation/documents/dodmemos.pdf

23 John Yoo, Memorandum for William J. Haynes II, General Counsel of the Department of Defense Re: Military Interrogation of Alien Unlawful Combatants Held Outside the United State. March 14, 2003.
    https://www.aclu.org/files/pdfs/safefree/yoo_army_torture_memo.pdf

JOHN A. RIZZO violated USC Title 18, Part I, Chapter 113C,§2340A Torture (a) Offense by directing or conspiring to have others perform acts of torture.

On or about August 2002, JAMES E. MITCHELL and JOHN B. JESSEN, water boarded detainee Abu Zubaydah at a CIA black site in Europe.[24]

On or about March 2003, JAMES E. MITCHELL water boarded detainee Khalid Sheikh Mohammed at a CIA black site in Europe.[25]

<u>COUNT FOUR</u>

<u>Commission of war crimes, especially grave breaches of the Geneva Convention, 12 August 1949, Common Article 3, including violence to life and person, in particular murder of all kinds, mutilation, cruel treatment and torture; taking of hostages, outrages upon personal dignity, in particular humiliating and degrading treatment.</u>

THE GRAND JURY FURTHER CHARGES THAT:

By developing false rationale stating that the Geneva Conventions do not apply to al Qaeda and Taliban detainees, with the result that detainees were tortured or treated with violence, cruelty, humiliating and degrading treatment, JOHN D. ASHCROFT, ALBERTO R. GONZALES, DAVID S. ADDINGTON, JOHN C. YOO, JAY BYBEE, STEVEN G. BRADBURY, WILLIAM J. HAYNES AND JOHN A. RIZZO, failed in their fiduciary duty by supporting their principals in the commission of war crimes, a violation of USC Title 18, Part I, Chapter 118,War Crimes Commission of war crimes—especially grave breaches of the Geneva Convention 12 August 1949 Common Article 3.

---

24 Supra 8. Page 40. Code name Swigert is James Mitchell. Code name Dunbar is Dr. Bruce Jessen.

25 Jason Leopold, Psychologist James Mitchell Admits He Waterboarded al Qaeda Suspects. Vice News. December 15, 2014.
https://news.vice.com/article/psychologist-james-mitchell-admits-he-waterboarded-al-qaeda-suspects

By declaring, ordering or approving instruction to members of the U.S. Armed Forces that the Geneva Conventions do not apply to al Qaeda and Taliban detainees, GEORGE BUSH, RICHARD CHENEY, CONDOLEEZZA RICE, DONALD H. RUMSFELD, GEORGE TENET, JOSE RODRIGUEZ, GEOFFREY D. MILLER, JAMES E. MITCHELL, AND JOHN B. JESSEN, facilitated the commission of war crimes by those under their command, a violation of USC Title 18, Part I, Chapter 118, War Crimes, Commission of war crimes—especially grave breaches of the Geneva Convention 12 August 1949 Common Article 3.

COUNT FIVE

Destruction of Federal Property with the intent to avoid criminal prosecution by destroying evidence.

THE GRAND JURY FURTHER CHARGES THAT:

On or about November 9, 2005, JOSE RODRIGUEZ destroyed or ordered destruction of ninety-two video tapes documenting the interrogations of Abu Zubaydah and Abd al-Rahim al-Nashiri, who were interrogated on or about 2002. Some of the tapes included the waterboarding of one or more of the subjects. The tapes were destroyed to avoid their disclosure in potential future investigations of the CIA torture program by the U.S. Senate. Seven days after the media exposed the CIA secret prisons, JOSE RODRIGUEZ destroyed video tapes of the torture of Abu Zubayda. Destruction of Federal records is a crime under USC Title 18, Part I, Chapter 73, § 1519 Destruction, alteration, or falsification of records in Federal investigations and bankruptcy.

Robert Levy, Foreperson

Louise Allen, Deputy Foreperson

Timothy Madegen, Special Prosecutor

Joseph Suste Books

Sharp Obsidian by Joseph Suste

Sharp Obsidian lays bare the inner struggles of a father and his strong-willed teenage daughter when she begins to test life's boundaries. Her father refuses to let destructive influences twist her morals, and dispirited, he commits his daughter to a teen recovery camp. She is indignant but meets the challenge with grit, uncovers her true essence, and matures into a savvy young woman

ISBN: 978-1-941049-83-9
5.25" x 8" 250 Pages • Trade Paper

Weaning: A Natural Step
A Gentle Nudge in Story Form

Dedicated to all of the mothers of the world and their beautiful children.

My daughter went to a bookstore to find a gentle way to nudge her son into thoughts of weaning. When she couldn't find a book on the subject, I offered to write one.

Every child is unique. Some kids wean themselves early, and others need extra time. Some need a suggestion from mom. This book is designed to help parents introduce the idea to their child in a gentle way.

13-Digit ISBN: 978-1-941049-81-5
Specs: 8.5" x 8.5" Four Color 30 Pages

About the Author

Joseph Suste published his first novel, *Sharp Obsidian*, in 2014, about a headstrong teenage girl testing boundaries and her panicked father. Suste's activist attempts to stop abusive interrogation tactics inspired this book. The story is a plea to the American people to remember a dark period in U.S. history and to reclaim national humanitarian values by bringing the guilty to justice. Suste turned to writing in his sixties, taking creative writing classes at Southern Oregon University. He's an engineer, real estate broker, actor, playwright, fiction writer, and poet.

For More Information, visit his website:
JosephSuste.com

Acknowledgments

No one ever does anything alone, and it pleases me to make this small tribute to the members of the HayWire Writers' Workshop who believed in me, kept me going when I felt doubtful and gave me blunt criticism when I needed it. My gratitude goes out to Ruth Wire, Joshua Hendrickson, Hilary Jacobson, Cynthia Rogan, and Madeleine Sklar. The manuscript benefited from the careful edits of my dear sister, Valerie Kavlick, and good friends Joseph Charter and Maria Ciamaichelo.

Finally, it was the professional editing of John Paul Owles that made this author look good.

www.ingramcontent.com/pod-product-compliance
Lightning Source LLC
Chambersburg PA
CBHW032118180726
48284CB00002B/611